The Faber Book of Fevers and Frets

The Faber Book of
FEVERS AND FRETS

Edited by D. J. Enright

faber and faber

LONDON · BOSTON

First published in 1989
by Faber and Faber Limited
3 Queen Square London WC1N 3AU

Photoset by Wilmaset, Birkenhead, Wirral
Printed in Great Britain by
Richard Clay Ltd, Bungay, Suffolk

A CIP record for this book is available from the British Library

ISBN 0-571-15095-0

As far as concerns my own sickness, am I not infinitely more indebted to it than to my health? It is to my sickness that I owe a *higher* health.

Friedrich Nietzsche, 'Nietzsche Contra Wagner', 1888

For all interest in disease and death is only another expression of interest in life, as is proven by the humanistic faculty of medicine, that addresses life and its ails always so politely in Latin, and is only a division of the great and pressing concern which, in all sympathy, I now name by its name: the human being, the delicate child of life, man, his state and standing in the universe.

Hans Castorp, in Thomas Mann's 'The Magic Mountain', 1924

I am sick — if I should die what would become of me? We forget ourselves & our destinies in health, & the chief use of temporary sickness is to remind us of these concerns. I must improve my time better.

Ralph Waldo Emerson, 'Journals', 25 March 1821

I am a living candle. I am consumed that you may learn. New things will be seen in the light of my suffering.

'Leonard L.', a post-encephalitic patient of Oliver Sacks

Contents

Editor's Note

Full names of authors are given on their first appearance. Dates are of composition or first publication when known; otherwise the author's dates are given, as also in the case of posthumous publication. Translators are named on the first occurrence of a particular work (or part of it); when no translator is credited, the editor himself is responsible for the English version.

The editor is obliged to the following for help of various kinds: Jonathan Barker, Toby Buchan, John Charlton, Shirley Chew, Madeleine Enright, Petra Lewis, David Rawlinson, Jacqueline Simms, Piotr Sommer, Will Sulkin, Anthony Weale, and The London Library.

Introduction

In her essay 'On Being Ill' Virginia Woolf professes surprise that illness has failed to find a place among the prime themes of literature. A slight attack of influenza brings wastes and deserts of the soul to view, and when, under gas, we have a tooth removed, we confuse the dentist's 'Rinse the mouth', as we regain consciousness, with 'the greeting of the Deity stooping from the floor of Heaven to welcome us'. But no, writers prefer the feats and the afflictions of the mind, the nobler stuff of love and battle and jealousy.

Proust she admits as a rare exception: scattered through his pages there must be a volume or two about disease. She makes out so strong a case for illness as a worthy subject, albeit insisting that to look it square in the face would require the courage of a lion-tamer, that it seems graceless to suggest that she is mistaken in her assumption, and illness is and always has been the business of writers. We suspect that for the sake of the essay she is exaggerating the premiss and simulating the surprise.

Yet there is some truth in her premiss. It has been said that 'sick people', as we now think of them, hardly existed before the beginning of the nineteenth century. Illness was seen as just one among the expected hardships of everyday life, bestowing no special status and eliciting no special consideration. Advances in medicine and in communications have since turned our attention increasingly towards sickness, aided in this by a growing preoccupation with self and, it may be, a dwindling confidence in an eternal afterlife of perfect health. (Even the inmates of Hell were healthy; they needed to be.) People have become readier to talk about disease; there are more diseases to talk about, and more therapies to hear about.

Of late, public interest in questions of health has equalled interest in political matters, if not become identified with it, and a new sophistication has developed. Passive suffering – which may affect us as a contradiction in terms, but Yeats said it was no theme for poetry – has given way to active exploration. This could be a sign that we are at least physically fitter these days.

In earlier times male authors were obsessed with gout, an excruciating but genteel ailment, socially analogous to the long finger-nails of the mandarin – Sam Weller's father deemed it the consequence of too much ease and comfort and recommended, as a sovereign cure, getting married to 'a widder as has got a good loud woice' – while female authors devoted themselves to the spleen and the vapours and (a topic enthusiastically shared by men) the pangs of love. Death was the really big subject; and what led up to it, unless it occurred on a notable battlefield, was of no great consequence.

Even so, the clash between what Carlyle termed 'the etherial spirit of a man' and 'two or three feet of sorry tripe full of —' did exercise old writers, such philosophers, scholars and historians as Plato, Robert Burton, Montaigne, Sir Thomas Browne, Defoe. Nor did poets and dramatists fail to muse on the disparity between the willing spirit and the weakly flesh, the fiery soul and the pigmy body. The twentieth century has identified and differentiated diseases, but it didn't discover or invent them all.

While it has to be conceded that illness can at times be followed by death, this anthology is chiefly concerned with ailments and anxieties well short of the fatal. A good deal of the material is light-hearted, even comical, for humour has been found a serviceable substitute for the lion-tamer's courage. And much of it, I venture, casts light on our notions of health and our expectations from life, on the diversity (not to mention bizarrerie) of human experience and response to circumstance. Susan Sontag intimates that sickness is one of the two kingdoms between which, citizens of both, we pass with our bags and baggage. And, as the saying goes, 'Sickness is felt, but health not at all', or only when it is lacking.

Whether doctors turn to writing as a blessed relief from their professional labours or as a natural complement to them allows of no simple answer. Quite a few of the writers featured in this book are or were medical men. Dr Edward Lowbury, who lists more in his paper on 'Medical Poets' (*Essays by Divers Hands*, Vol. XLV, 1988) quotes Chekhov as telling a friend, 'Medicine is my lawful wife and literature is my mistress. When I get tired of one I spend the night with the other', and adding that if he didn't have his medical work, he doubted whether he could have given his leisure to literature. In a poem of his own, Lowbury wonders if the doctor-poet might not live twice, by aping Apollo, god of both the arts,

> As healer at whose touch
> Fevers dissolve, while pains beyond the reach
> Of medicine might be cured
> By the music and the compelling word.

Thomas Fuller, the compiler of *Gnomologia: Adagies and Proverbs* (1732), was himself a physician, and 'Study sickness while you are well' is the advice offered by one of his inclusions. To those students of humanity who pick up the present compilation, the editor says 'Good health!'

Generalities

'Great lord of all things, yet a prey to all.' How could man, created in the image of God, be reduced to fevers, frenzies, dropsy, dysentery, convulsions and suchlike unsightly afflictions? Milton, the great authority on effects and causes, reveals how disease and disfigurement came into the world. It was all the patient's fault.

The Archangel Michael, with his mildly soft spot for mankind, holds out no hope of a permanent cure but advances a partial preventive or palliative, one that has been urged on us regularly ever since: moderation in all things, simply and succinctly formulated for Adam's benefit as the rule of *not too much*.

The Lord God of the Old Testament is considerably brisker, and under no obligation to justify his ways. Whatsoever a man soweth, that shall he also reap. Yet, so Robert Burton contends, the illness may be the cure: at least it procures our better spiritual health. But John Donne, a modernly minute observer of himself, complains that although his brows sweat copiously he is unable to eat the bread thus earned, and that, since he was formed to think, it seems hard that melancholy should come as an unsought by-product of thinking. A similar sentiment will be voiced by Baudelaire: 'Funny sort of medicine that stamps out one's principal function!'

Adducing what appears to be the Almighty in another guise and equally unanswerable, philosophers tell us that the diseases which destroy us are just as natural as the instincts which preserve us. These things are sent to try us, the less sophisticated mutter stoically, not always specifying what we are being tried for. To which, grateful to his doctor for allowing him to smoke his cigars, Brecht adds that each of us has his or her cross to bear – inadvertently or perhaps ironically employing a Christian figure of speech.

The effect of bad health, Sydney Smith said, was to make him so confused that he couldn't remember whether there were nine articles and thirty-nine muses or the other way round. And Jane Carlyle once described herself as so ill that she felt like a snake trying to stand upright on its tail. However poor our condition may be in other respects, the poverty of language alleged by Virginia Woolf is clearly a myth. The word came very near the beginning, primed to express our pain and sorrow, and sometimes helping us to bear them.

Prognosis

'Some, as thou saw'st, by violent stroke shall die,
By fire, flood, famine; by intemperance more
In meats and drinks, which on the earth shall bring
Diseases dire, of which a monstrous crew
Before thee shall appear, that thou may'st know
What misery th' inabstinence of Eve
Shall bring on men.' Immediately a place
Before his eyes appeared, sad, noisome, dark,
A lazar-house it seemed, wherein were laid
Numbers of all diseased, all maladies
Of ghastly spasm, or racking torture, qualms
Of heart-sick agony, all feverous kinds,
Convulsions, epilepsies, fierce catarrhs,
Intestine stone and ulcer, colic pangs,
Demoniac frenzy, moping melancholy,
And moon-struck madness, pining atrophy,
Marasmus, and wide-wasting pestilence,
Dropsies and asthmas, and joint-racking rheums.
Dire was the tossing, deep the groans; Despair
Tended the sick, busiest from couch to couch;
And over them triumphant Death his dart
Shook, but delayed to strike, though oft invoked
With vows, as their chief good, and final hope.
Sight so deform what heart of rock could long
Dry-eyed behold? Adam could not, but wept,
Though not of woman born; compassion quelled
His best of man, and gave him up to tears

A space, till firmer thoughts restrained excess,
And scarce recovering words his plaint renewed:
   'O miserable mankind, to what fall
Degraded, to what wretched state reserved!
Better end here unborn. Why is life giv'n
To be thus wrested from us? Rather why
Obtruded on us thus? Who if we knew
What we receive, would either not accept
Life offered, or soon beg to lay it down,
Glad to be so dismissed in peace. Can thus
Th' image of God in man, created once
So goodly and erect, though faulty since,
To such unsightly sufferings be debased
Under inhuman pains?'

Diagnosis

'Their Maker's image,' answered Michael, 'then
Forsook them, when themselves they vilified
To serve ungoverned appetite, and took
His image whom they served, a brutish vice,
Inductive mainly to the sin of Eve.
Therefore so abject is their punishment,
Disfiguring not God's likeness, but their own,
Or if his likeness, by themselves defaced
While they pervert pure Nature's healthful rules
To loathsome sickness; worthily, since they
God's image did not reverence in themselves.'

Prescription

'I yield it just,' said Adam, 'and submit.
But is there yet no other way, besides
These painful passages, how we may come
To death, and mix with our connatural dust?'
   'There is,' said Michael, 'if thou well observe
The rule of *not too much*, by temperance taught

In what thou eat'st and drink'st, seeking from thence
Due nourishment, not gluttonous delight,
Till many years over thy head return.
So may'st thou live, till like ripe fruit thou drop
Into thy mother's lap, or be with ease
Gathered, not harshly plucked, for death mature:
This is old age; but then thou must outlive
Thy youth, thy strength, thy beauty, which will change
To withered weak and grey; thy senses then
Obtuse, all taste of pleasure must forgo,
To what thou hast, and for the air of youth
Hopeful and cheerful, in thy blood will reign
A melancholy damp of cold and dry
To weigh thy spirits down, and last consume
The balm of life.' To whom our ancestor:
     'Henceforth I fly not death, nor would prolong
Life much, bent rather how I may be quit
Fairest and easiest of this cumbrous charge,
Which I must keep till my appointed day
Of rend'ring up, and patiently attend
My dissolution.' Michaël replied:
     'Nor love thy life, nor hate; but what thou liv'st
Live well, how long or short permit to Heav'n.'
            John Milton, *Paradise Lost*, 1667

But it shall come to pass, if thou wilt not hearken unto the voice of the LORD thy God, to observe to do all his commandments and his statutes which I command thee this day; that all these curses shall come upon thee, and overtake thee:

The LORD shall make the pestilence cleave unto thee, until he have consumed thee from off the land, whither thou goest to possess it.

The LORD shall smite thee with a consumption, and with a fever, and with an inflammation, and with an extreme burning, and with the sword, and with blasting, and with mildew; and they shall pursue thee until thou perish.

The LORD will smite thee with the botch of Egypt, and with the

emerods, and with the scab, and with the itch, whereof thou canst
not be healed.

The LORD shall smite thee with madness, and blindness, and
astonishment of heart.

The LORD shall smite thee in the knees, and in the legs, with a
sore botch that cannot be healed, from the sole of thy foot unto the
top of thy head.

And thou shalt become an astonishment, a proverb, and a
byword, among all nations whither the LORD shall lead thee.

Deuteronomy, 28

The study of the bubonic plague in India has thrown light upon a bit
of Biblical history hitherto not understood. When the Philistines
restored the sacred ark to Israel, they sent with it, as an atonement to
JAHVE, 'five golden tumours and five golden mice' (1 Samuel vi. 4,
Revised Version). What the mice had to do with it has been the
mystery. The Montreal *Medical Journal* elucidates it in an article by
Dr J. G. Adami. A peculiar thing about the plague in India is, that it
attacks rats and mice. This was noticed at Hong Kong in 1894.
These vermin, when infected, desert their holes without fear of man,
a phenomenon noticed by an old chronicler in England in the
seventeenth century. What is said in 1 Samuel v. 12, 'the men that
died not were smitten with the tumours', exactly corresponds to the
fact that the swellings characteristic of the disease (called 'bubonic',
from Latin *bubo*, a tumour) are more noticeable in cases that are not
fatal. The breaking out of the disease in one Philistine city after
another, as the ark was carried from place to place, marks the
infectiousness of the plague, and so does the fact that those who
carried the ark back to Israel carried the plague with them. This is
described in 1 Samuel vi. 19 as a Divine judgement: 'Because they
had looked into the ark of the Lord, He smote of the people seventy
men and fifty thousand men.' The Authorized Version in this
passage translates the Hebrew for swelling by 'emerods' (haemorrhoids, or piles), which renders the account of a great mortality
incredible; the Revised Version 'tumours' is correct enough, but
unintelligible. The mouse, which in the fable gnawed the cord that
fastened the lion, has once more done service in freeing this story of

mystery, and given an unmistakable realism to what many have regarded as merely a legend from three thousand years ago.

J. Dyer Ball, *Things Chinese*, 1892

Illness is the night-side of life, a more onerous citizenship. Everyone who is born holds dual citizenship, in the kingdom of the well and in the kingdom of the sick. Although we all prefer to use only the good passport, sooner or later each of us is obliged, at least for a spell, to identify ourselves as citizens of that other place.

Susan Sontag, *Illness as Metaphor*, 1978

In the different ages the following complaints occur: to little children and babies, aphthae, vomiting, coughs, sleeplessness, terrors, inflammation of the navel, watery discharges from the ears.

At the approach of dentition, irritation of the gums, fevers, convulsions, diarrhoea, especially when cutting the canine teeth, and in the case of very fat children, and if the bowels are hard.

Among those who are older occur affections of the tonsils, curvature at the vertebra by the neck, asthma, stone, round worms, ascarides, warts, swellings by the ears [an alternative reading is 'priapism'], scrofula and tumours generally.

Older children and those approaching puberty suffer from most of the preceding maladies, from fevers of the more protracted type and from bleeding at the nose.

Young men [i.e. 'the young'] suffer from spitting of blood, phthisis, acute fevers, epilepsy and the other diseases, especially those mentioned above.

Those who are beyond this age suffer from asthma, pleurisy, pneumonia, lethargus, phrenitis, ardent fevers, chronic diarrhoea, cholera, dysentery, lientery, haemorrhoids.

Old men [i.e. 'the old'] suffer from difficulty of breathing, catarrh accompanied by coughing, strangury, difficult micturition, pains at the joints, kidney disease, apoplexy, cachexia, pruritus of the whole body, sleeplessness, watery discharges from bowels, eyes and nostrils, dullness of sight, cataract, hardness of hearing.

Hippocrates, ?460–?377 BC, *Aphorisms*; tr. W. H. S. Jones

Donne in his Sickness

The first alteration, the first grudging of the sickness
Variable, and therefore miserable condition of man! this minute I
was well, and am ill, this minute. I am surprised with a sudden
change, and alteration to worse, and can impute it to no cause, nor
call it by any name. We study health, and we deliberate upon our
meats, and drink, and air, and exercises, and we hew and we polish
every stone that goes to that building; and so our health is a long and
a regular work: but in a minute a cannon batters all, overthrows all,
demolishes all; a sickness unprevented for all our diligence, unsuspected for all our curiosity; nay, undeserved, if we consider only
disorder, summons us, seizes us, possesses us, destroys us in an
instant. O miserable condition of man! which was not imprinted by
God, who, as he is immortal himself, had put a coal, a beam of
immortality into us, which we might have blown into a flame, but
blew it out by our first sin; we beggared ourselves by hearkening
after false riches, and infatuated ourselves by hearkening after false
knowledge. So that now, we do not only die, but die upon the rack,
die by the torment of sickness; nor that only, but are pre-afflicted,
super-afflicted with these jealousies and suspicions and apprehensions of sickness, before we can call it a sickness: we are not sure we
are ill; one hand asks the other by the pulse, and our eye asks our
own urine how we do.

The strength and the function of the senses, and other faculties,
change and fail
It was part of Adam's punishment, *In the sweat of thy brows thou*
shalt eat thy bread: it is multiplied to me, I have earned bread in the
sweat of my brows, in the labour of my calling, and I have it; and I
sweat again and again, from the brow to the sole of the foot; but I eat
no bread, I taste no sustenance: miserable distribution of mankind,
where one half lacks meat, and the other stomach!

The physician is afraid
I observe the physician with the same diligence as he the disease; I see
he fears, and I fear with him; I overtake him, I overrun him, in his
fear, and I go the faster, because he makes his pace slow; I fear the
more, because he disguises his fear, and I see it with the more

sharpness, because he would not have me see it. He knows that his fear shall not disorder the practice and exercise of his art, but he knows that my fear may disorder the effect and working of his practice. As the ill affections of the spleen complicate and mingle themselves with every infirmity of the body, so doth fear insinuate itself in every action or passion of the mind; and as wind in the body will counterfeit any disease, and seem the stone, and seem the gout, so fear will counterfeit any disease of the mind.

Upon their consultation, they prescribe

Take me, then, O blessed and glorious Trinity, into a reconsultation, and prescribe me any physic. If it be a long and painful holding of this soul in sickness, it is physic if I may discern thy hand to give it; and it is physic if it be a speedy departing of this soul, if I may discern thy hand to receive it.

They apply pigeons, to drive the vapours from the head

Fevers upon wilful distempers of drink and surfeits, consumptions upon intemperances and licentiousness, madness upon misplacing or overbending our natural faculties, proceed from ourselves, and so as that ourselves are in the plot, and we are not only passive, but active too, to our own destruction. But what have I done, either to breed or to breathe these vapours? They tell me it is my melancholy; did I infuse, did I drink in melancholy into myself? It is my thoughtfulness; was I not made to think? It is my study; doth not my calling call for that? I have done nothing wilfully, perversely toward it, yet I must suffer in it, die by it.

I sleep not day nor night

O eternal and most gracious God, who art able to make, and dost make, the sick bed of thy servants chapels of ease to them, and the dreams of thy servants prayers and meditations upon thee, let not this continual watchfulness of mine, this inability to sleep, which thou hast laid upon me, be any disquiet or discomfort to me, but rather an argument, that thou wouldst not have me sleep in thy presence . . . But as I know, O my gracious God, that for all those sins committed since, yet thou wilt consider me, as I was in thy purpose when thou wrotest my name in the book of life in mine election; so into what deviations soever I stray and wander by occasion of this sickness, O God, return thou to that minute wherein thou wast pleased with me and consider me in that condition.

John Donne, from Devotions upon Emergent Occasions and
Several Steps in my Sickness, 1624

Sickness, diseases, trouble many, but without a cause. *It may be 'tis for the good of their souls: pars fati fuit* [it was part of their destiny], the flesh rebels against the spirit; that which hurts the one must needs help the other. Sickness is the mother of modesty, putteth us in mind of our mortality; and, when we are in the full career of worldly pomp and jollity, she pulleth us by the ear, and maketh us know ourselves . . . And were it not for such gentle remembrances, men would have no moderation of themselves; they would be worse than tigers, wolves, and lions: who should keep them in awe? *Princes, Masters, Parents, Magistrates, Judges, friends, enemies, fair or foul means, cannot contain us, but a little sickness* (as *Chrysostom* observes) *will correct and amend us.*

Robert Burton, The Anatomy of Melancholy, 1621

Is not disease the rule of existence? There is not a lily pad floating on the river but has been riddled by insects. Almost every shrub and tree has its gall, oftentimes esteemed its chief ornament and scarcely to be distinguished from the fruit. If misery loves company, misery has company enough.

Henry David Thoreau, Journal, 1851

Some think there were few Consumptions in the Old World, when Men lived much upon Milk; and that the ancient Inhabitants of this Island were less troubled with Coughs when they went naked, and slept in Caves and Woods, than Men now in Chambers and Feather-beds. Plato will tell us, that there was no such Disease as a catarrh in Homer's time, and that it was but new in Greece in his Age. Polydore Virgil delivereth that Pleurisies were rare in England, who lived but in the days of Henry the Eighth. Some will allow no Diseases to be new, others think that many old ones are ceased, and that such which are esteemed new, will have but their time. However, the Mercy of God hath scattered the great heap of Diseases, and not loaded any one Country with all: some may be new in one Country which have been old in another. New discoveries of the Earth discover new Diseases: for besides the common swarm, there are endemial and local Infirmities proper unto certain Regions, which in the whole Earth make no small number: and if Asia, Africa, and America should bring in their List, Pandora's Box would swell, and there must be a strange Pathology.

Sir Thomas Browne (1605–82), *Letter to a Friend upon Occasion*
of the Death of his Intimate Friend

It is, indeed, a tedious and withal a melancholy business to take too much care of ourselves, and of what injures and benefits us; but there is no question but that with the wonderful idiosyncrasy of human nature on the one side, and the infinite variety in the mode of life and pleasure on the other, it is a wonder that the human race has not worn itself out long ago . . . Could we, without being morbidly anxious, keep watch over ourselves as to what operates favourably or unfavourably upon us in our complicated civil and social life, and would we leave off what is actually pleasant to us as an enjoyment, for the sake of the evil consequences, we should thus know how to remove with ease many an inconvenience which, with a constitution otherwise sound, often troubles us more than even a disease. Unfortunately, it is in dietetics as in morals; we cannot see into a fault till we have got rid of it; by which nothing is gained, for the next fault is not like the preceding one, and therefore cannot be recognized under the same form.

Johann Wolfgang von Goethe's autobiography, *Poetry and Truth*,
1809–31; tr. John Oxenford

I have had one of my savage headaches. For a day and a night I was in blind torment. Have at it, now, with the stoic remedy. Sickness of the body is no evil. With a little resolution and considering it as a natural issue of certain natural processes, pain may well be borne. One's solace is, to remember that it cannot affect the soul, which partakes of the eternal nature. This body is but as 'the clothing, or the cottage, of the mind'. Let flesh be racked; I, the very I, will stand apart, lord of myself.

Meanwhile, memory, reason, every faculty of my intellectual part, is being whelmed in muddy oblivion. Is the soul something other than the mind? If so, I have lost all consciousness of its existence. For me, mind and soul are one, and, as I am too feelingly reminded, that element of my being is *here*, where the brain throbs and anguishes. A little more of such suffering, and I were myself no longer; the body representing me would gesticulate and rave, but I should know nothing of its motives, its fantasies. The very I, it is too plain, consists but with a certain balance of my physical elements, which we call health. Even in the light beginnings of my headache, I was already not myself; my thoughts followed no normal course, and I was aware of the abnormality. A few hours later, I was but a walking disease; my mind – if one could use the word – had become a barrel-organ, grinding in endless repetition a bar or two of idle music.

What trust shall I repose in the soul that serves me thus? Just as much, one would say, as in the senses, through which I know all that I can know of the world in which I live, and which, for all that I can tell, may deceive me even more grossly in their common use than they do on certain occasions where I have power to test them; just as much, and no more – if I am right in concluding that mind and soul are merely subtle functions of body. If I chance to become deranged in certain parts of my physical mechanism, I shall straightway be deranged in my wits; and behold that Something in me which 'partakes of the eternal' prompting me to pranks which savour little of the infinite wisdom. Even in its normal condition (if I can determine what that is) my mind is obviously the slave of trivial accidents; I eat something that disagrees with me, and of a sudden the whole aspect of life is changed; this impulse has lost its force, and another, which before I should not for a moment have entertained, is all-powerful over me. In short, I know just as little about myself as I do about the Eternal Essence, and I have a haunting suspicion that I may be a mere automaton, my every thought and act due to some power which uses and deceives me.

Why am I meditating thus, instead of enjoying the life of the natural man, at peace with himself and the world, as I was a day or two ago? Merely, it is evident, because my health has suffered a temporary disorder. It has passed; I have thought enough about the unthinkable; I feel my quiet returning. Is it any merit of mine that I begin to be in health once more? Could I, by any effort of the will, have shunned this pitfall?

> George Gissing, *The Private Papers of Henry Ryecroft*, 1903

Jonathan Swift and Alexander Pope: a Correspondence

I think you ow me a Letter, but whether yo do or not I have not been in a condition to write. Years and Infirmatyes have quite broke me. I mean that odious continual disorder in my Head. I neither reed, nor write; nor remember, nor converse. All I have left is to walk, and ride. The first I can do tolerably; but the latter for want of good weather at this Season is Seldom in my Power; and haveing not an ounce of Flesh about me; my Skin comes off in ten miles riding because my Skin and bone cannot agree together. But I am angry, because you will not Suppose me as Sick as I am, and write to me out of perfect Charity, although I should not be able to answer. I have too many vexations by my Station and the Impertinence of People, to be able to beare the Mortification of not hearing from a very few distant Friends that are left; and, considering how Time and Fortune hath ordered matters, I have hardly one friend left but your Self.

> Swift to Pope, 2 December 1736

Your very kind letter has made me more melancholy, than almost any thing in this world now can do. For I can bear every thing in it, bad as it is, better than the complaints of my friends. Tho' others tell me you are in pretty good health, and in good spirits, I find the contrary when you open your mind to me: And indeed it is but a prudent part, to seem not so concern'd about others, nor so crazy ourselves as we really are: for we shall neither be beloved or esteem'd the more, by our common acquaintance, for any affliction or any infirmity. But to our true friend we may, we must complain, of what ('tis a thousand to one) he complains with us; for if we have known him long, he is old, and if he has known the world long, he is out of humour at it. If you have but as much more health than others at your age, as you have more wit and good temper, you shall not have much of my Pity: But if you ever live to have less, you shall not have less of my Affection.

                              Pope to Swift, 30 December 1736

I cannot properly call you my best friend, because I have not another left who deserves the name, such a havock have Time, Death, Exile and Oblivion made. Perhaps you would have fewer complaints of my ill health and lowness of spirits, if they were not some excuse for my delay of writing even to you. It is perfectly right what you say of the indifference in common friends, whether we are sick or well, happy or miserable. The very maid-servants in a family have the same notion: I have heard them often say, Oh, I'm very sick, if any body cared for it! I am vexed when my visitors come with the compliment usual here, Mr Dean I hope you are very well . . . What hath sunk my spirits more than even years and sickness, is reflecting on the most execrable Corruptions that run through every branch of publick management.

                              Swift to Pope, 9 February 1737

Let this, however, be an opportunity of telling you – What? – what I cannot tell, the kindness I bear you, the affection I feel for you, the hearty wishes I form for you, my prayers for your health of body and mind; or, the best softenings of the want of either, quiet and resignation. You lose little by *not hearing* such things as this idle and base generation has to tell you: you lose not much by *forgetting* most of what *now* passes in it. Perhaps, to have a memory that retains the past scenes of our country and forgets the present, is the means to be happier and better contented. But, if the *evil* of *the day* be not intolerable (though sufficient, God knows, at any period of life) we *may*, at least we *should*, nay we *must* (whether patiently or impatiently) bear it, and make the best of what we cannot make better, but may make worse. To hear that this is your situation and your temper, and that peace attends you at home, and one or two true friends who are tender about you, would be a great ease to me to know, and know from yourself.

                              Pope to Swift, 12 October 1738

Did a man dream he was a sick butterfly,
Or a butterfly dream it was a sick man?
Throughout the body's metamorphoses
All joys are met with, and all miseries.
Now the wings falter, torn by pain –
How will they bear me to a further flower?
Fingers and hands are failing now –
Can they mix ink to stir my feeble brain?
Fly while you are able, butterfly;
Man, try your skills while still you may.
Whoever the dreamer, whatever the dream,
One thing is certain: we suffer as we seem.

Tao Tschung Yu, 'Old Philosopher', ?18th century

1

Smoke your cigars: that was my doctor's comforting answer!
With or without them one day we'll end up with the undertaker.
In the membrane of my eye for example there are signs of cancer
From which I shall die sooner or later.

2

Naturally one need not be discouraged for that reason
For years such a man may carry on.
He can stuff his body with chicken and blackberry in season
Though naturally one day he'll be gone.

3

Against this there's nothing one can contrive either with
        schnapps or sharp practice
Such a cancer grows subtly; one feels nothing inside.
And perhaps you are written off when the fact is
You are just standing at the altar with your bride.

4

My uncle for example wore trousers with knife-edge creases
Though long selected to go elsewhere.
His cheeks were still ruddy but they were churchyard roses
And on him was not one healthy hair.

5
There are families in which it is hereditary
But they never admit it nor condemn.
They can distinguish pineapple from rosemary
But their cancer may be a hernia to them.

6
My grandfather, though, knew what lay ahead and made no query
And was prudent, punctiliously doing what the doctor said.
And he even attained the age of fifty before becoming weary.
One day of such a life is more than a dog would have led.

7
Our sort know: no point being envious.
Each man has his cross to bear, I fear.
Kidney trouble is my particular curse
I've not had a drink in more than a year.
> Bertolt Brecht, 'On his Mortality', 1923; tr. H. B. Mallalieu

Adieu my dear Emerson. *Gehab' Dich wohl*! Many affectionate
regards to the Lady Wife: it is far within verge of Probabilities that I
shall see her face, and eat of her bread, one day. But she must not get
sick! it is a dreadful thing sickness; really a thing which I begin
frequently to think *criminal*, – at least in myself. Nay, in myself it
really *is* criminal; wherefore I determine to be *well*, one day.
> Thomas Carlyle, letter to Ralph Waldo Emerson, 5 November 1836

This is what I gathered. That in that country if a man falls into ill
health, or catches any disorder, or fails bodily in any way before he is
seventy years old, he is tried before a jury of his countrymen, and if
convicted is held up to public scorn and sentenced more or less
severely as the case may be. There are subdivisions of illnesses into
crime and misdemeanours as with offences amongst ourselves – a
man being punished very heavily for serious illness, while failure of
eyes or hearing in one over sixty-five, who has had good health
hitherto, is dealt with by fine only, or imprisonment in default of

payment. But if a man forges a cheque, or sets his house on fire, or robs with violence from the person, or does any other such things as are criminal in our own country, he is either taken to a hospital and most carefully tended at the public expense, or if he is in good circumstances, he lets it be known to all his friends that he is suffering from a severe fit of immorality, just as we do when we are ill, and they come and visit him with great solicitude, and inquire with interest how it all came about, what symptoms first showed themselves, and so forth, — questions which he will answer with perfect unreserve; for bad conduct, though considered no less deplorable than illness with ourselves, and as unquestionably indicating something seriously wrong with the individual who misbehaves, is nevertheless held to be the result of either pre-natal or post-natal misfortune.

The reader will have no difficulty in believing that the laws regarding ill health were frequently evaded by the help of recognized fictions, which everyone understood, but which it would be considered gross ill-breeding to even seem to understand. Thus, a day or two after my arrival at the Nosnibors', one of the many ladies who called on me made excuses for her husband's only sending his card, on the ground that when going through the public market-place that morning he had stolen a pair of socks. I had already been warned that I should never show surprise, so I merely expressed my sympathy, and said that though I had only been in the capital so short a time, I had already had a very narrow escape from stealing a clothes-brush, and that though I had resisted temptation so far, I was sadly afraid that if I saw any object of special interest that was neither too hot nor too heavy, I should have to put myself in the straightener's hands.

Mrs Nosnibor, who had been keeping an ear on all that I had been saying, praised me when the lady had gone. Nothing, she said, could have been more polite according to Erewhonian etiquette. She then explained that to have stolen a pair of socks, or 'to have the socks' (in more colloquial language), was a recognized way of saying that the person in question was slightly indisposed.

. . . if a person ruin his health by excessive indulgence at the table or by drinking, they count it to be almost a part of the mental disease which brought it about, and so it goes for little, but they have no mercy on such illnesses as fevers or catarrhs or lung diseases, which to us appear to be beyond the control of the individual. They are only more lenient towards the diseases of the young – such as measles, which they think to be like sowing one's wild oats – and look over them as pardonable indiscretions if they have not been too serious, and if they are atoned for by complete subsequent recovery.

The Erewhonians regard death with less abhorrence than disease. If it is an offence at all, it is one beyond the reach of the law, which is therefore silent on the subject.

Samuel Butler, *Erewhon*, 1872

I'm most grieved to think you've had such a time and so much pain with that mysterious illness: worse even than I thought. It puzzles me terribly why these things should come. But do you know what I think? I think it's because one isn't just vulgarly selfish enough, vulgarly *physically* selfish, self-keeping and self-preserving. One wastes one's common flesh too much: then these microbes, which are the pure incarnation of invisible selfishness, pounce on one.

You ask me, do I feel things very much? – and I do. And that's why I too am ill. The hurts, and the bitterness sink in, however much one may reject them with one's spirit. They sink in, and there they lie, inside one, wasting one. What is the matter with us is primarily chagrin. Then the microbes pounce. One ought to be tough and selfish: and one is never tough enough, and never selfish in the proper self-preserving way. Then one is laid low.

D. H. Lawrence, letter to Ottoline Morrell, 24 May 1928

So much are men enured in their miserable estate, that no condition is so poor, but they will accept, so they may continue in the same. Hear Maecenas:

Make me be weak of hand,
Scarce on my legs to stand,
Shake my loose teeth with pain,
'Tis well so life remain.
— Seneca, *Epist.* 101

And Tamburlane cloaked the fantastical cruelty he exercised upon Lazars or Lepers, with a foolish kind of humanity, putting all he could find or hear of to death, (as he said) to rid them from so painful and miserable a life as they lived. For, there was none so wretched amongst them that would not rather have been three times a Leper than not to be at all. And Antisthenes the Stoic, being very sick, and crying out: 'Oh who shall deliver me from my tormenting evils?', Diogenes, who was come to visit him, forthwith presenting him a knife: 'Marry, this,' said he, 'and very speedily, if thou please.' 'I mean not of my life,' replied he, 'but of my sickness.'
Michel de Montaigne, 'Of the resemblance between children and fathers', *Essays*, 1580; tr. John Florio, 1603

He restores the Dictionary
Among the shelves marked Medical,
And sits for nearly an hour
In a dark corner, frozen,
White in the face.

Here the books live, the people
Have submitted to anaesthesia
To write more books, and his trance,
His cataleptic stare,
Are nothing unusual.

Though he is not thinking of Empires,
Prison statistics, Poor Laws,
Ikons, the environment,
Catullus, the bomb, or the Letters
Of Madame de Staël,

But a beautiful woman, wearing
A white maribou jacket,
Who smiles whenever he enters
From pillows, and today is so much
Better, they told him;

For whom a sentence just read
Seems to close her life,
Set it on shelves, and make
The rest of his life a memoir,
An index of her.

Cold seas cover him over;
Till slowly, riding some buoyant
Wave not found in these millions
Of waves of learning, he surfaces
On a thought, a question.

'A disease,' the sentence has said,
'That invariably proves fatal.'
A good description of Life.
Rafted on the thought, he goes back.
The question is, 'How long?'
Michael Burn, 'In the London Library', 1977

Finally, to hinder the description of illness in literature, there is the poverty of the language. English, which can express the thoughts of Hamlet and the tragedy of Lear, has no words for the shiver and the headache. It has all grown one way. The merest schoolgirl, when she falls in love, has Shakespeare or Keats to speak her mind for her; but let a sufferer try to describe a pain in his head to a doctor and language at once runs dry. There is nothing ready made for him. He is forced to coin words himself, and, taking his pain in one hand, and a lump of pure sound in the other (as perhaps the people of Babel did in the beginning), so to crush them together that a brand new word in the end drops out. Probably it will be something laughable. For who of English birth can take liberties with the language? To us it is a sacred thing and therefore doomed to die, unless the Americans, whose genius is so much happier in the making of new words than in the disposition of the old, will come to our help and set the springs aflow. Yet it is not only a new language that we need, more primitive, more sensual, more obscene, but a new hierarchy of the passions; love must be deposed in favour of a temperature of 104; jealousy give place to the pangs of sciatica; sleeplessness play the part of villain, and the hero become a white liquid with a sweet taste – that mighty Prince with the moths' eyes and the feathered feet, one of whose names is Chloral.

Virginia Woolf, 'On Being Ill', 1930

Illnesses, Greater and Lesser

That seventeenth-century poets were chiefly interested in fever as a metaphor for the excitations arising from love – as it were, a more acceptable way of saying 'in heat' – lends support to Virginia Woolf's thesis. Or else, recovering from a less figurative fever, they would promptly tender their thanks to God, generally careful to acknowledge that his Son had suffered more painfully and with less reason.

Later writers have been readier to blame the drains than either the rigours of love or the inherited and inescapable sinfulness affirmed by Milton. And on occasion, as in the case of Hardy, ready to blame God or whatever power might be for sheer uncaringness or absenteeism. It was left, prudently, to a fictitious Arab physician to suggest that the Son of God was not a miracle-worker but a clever Nazarene practitioner with an enviable new cure for epilepsy. The Near East was to the fore in medicine; the remarkable Lady Mary Wortley Montagu witnessed a form of inoculation against smallpox in Turkey, and introduced the idea into England, where it met with the resistance she had envisaged.

There follows an assortment of ailments, varying in nature and in gravity, and depicted variously with wit and verve, insight, resourcefulness, comic pedantry, solemnity, pathos, and courage. J. B. S. Haldane commented that while a secondary function of his poem 'Cancer's a Funny Thing' was to voice gratitude towards the medical and nursing staff of hospitals, its primary aim was to persuade cancer patients to have early operations and to be cheerful about it. This aim would have been better served, he added, if his muse, 'rather a slow old lady', hadn't produced an addendum too late for publication. The supplementary passage, to follow the fourth line of the poem as printed here, is this:

> Yet, thanks to modern surgeon's skills,
> It can be killed before it kills

> Upon a scientific basis
> In nineteen out of twenty cases.

Only anticipation of the question forming in the reader's mind could induce the editor to record that Haldane died of his cancer not long afterwards. He had allowed for that one case out of twenty.

To kindness and knowledge, Proust wrote, we only make promises, but pain we obey. If anything is truly inexpressible, then it must be pain; in its manifestations it is often described as simply indescribable. Thus the victim's account of its intensity never quite convinces: only his death can do that, Camus said. 'Human life is everywhere a state in which much is to be endured,' according to Johnson, 'and little to be enjoyed.' Yet he could not tolerate Soame Jenyns's excogitated theory, orthodoxly Christian though it was in tendency, that the pain of the individual somehow yields some indefinable larger benefit or serves some general good. Like life, pain was to be endured as best one could, but not to be enjoyed or endorsed, for whatever reason, by whatever being or class of beings.

===

> O wrangling schooles, that search what fire
>   Shall burne this world, had none the wit
> Unto this knowledge to aspire,
>   That this her feaver might be it?
>   Donne, from 'A Feaver', c.1602

> Now she burnes, as well as I,
> Yet my heat can never dye;
> She burnes that never knew desire,
> She that was ice, she now is fire.
> She whose cold heart chaste thoughts did arme
> So as Love's flames could never warme
> The frozen bosome where it dwelt,
> She burnes, and all her beauties melt;
> She burnes, and cryes, 'Love's fires are milde;
> Fevers are God's, and he's a childe.'
> Love, let her know the difference

'Twixt the heat of soule and sense.
Touch her with thy flames divine,
So shalt thou quench her fire, and mine.

> Thomas Carew, 'Song to my Mistres,
> she burning in a Feaver', 1640

When Sorrowes had begyrt me round,
  And Paines within and out,
When in my flesh no part was found,
  Then didst thou rid me out.

My burning flesh in sweat did boyle,
  My aking head did break;
From side to side for ease I toyle,
  So faint I could not speak.

Beclouded was my Soul with fear
  Of thy Displeasure sore,
Nor could I read my Evidence
  Which oft I read before.

Hide not thy face from me, I cry'd,
  From Burnings keep my soul;
Thou know'st my heart, and hast me try'd;
  I on thy Mercyes rowl.

O, heal my Soul, thou know'st I said,
  Tho' flesh consume to nought;
What tho' in dust it shall bee lay'd,
  To Glory't shall bee brought.

Thou heard'st, thy rod thou didst remove,
  And spar'd my Body frail,
Thou shew'st to me thy tender Love,
  My heart no more might quail.

O, Praises to my mighty God,
  Praise to my Lord, I say,

Who hath redeem'd my Soul from pitt:
Praises to him for Aye!
Anne Bradstreet, 'For Deliverance from a feaver', c.1657

As I have just escaped from a physician and a fever which confined me five days to bed, you wont expect much 'allegrezza' in the ensuing letter. – In this place there is an indigenous distemper, which, when the wind blows from the Gulph of Corinth (as it does five months out of six) attacks great and small, and makes woeful work with visitors. – Here be also two physicians, one of whom trusts to his Genius (never having studied) the other to a campaign of eighteen months against the sick of Otranto, which he made in his youth with great effect. – When I was seized with my disorder, I protested against both these assassins, but what can a helpless, feverish, toasted and watered poor wretch do? In spite of my teeth & tongue, the English Consul, my Tartar, Albanians, Dragoman forced a physician upon me, and in three days vomited and clystered me to the last gasp. – In this state I made my epitaph, take it,

Youth, Nature, and relenting Jove
To keep my *lamp in* strongly strove,
But *Romanelli* was so stout
He beat all three – and *blew* it *out.* –

But Nature and Jove being piqued at my doubts, did in fact at last beat Romanelli, and here I am well but weakly, at your service.
Lord Byron, letter to Francis Hodgson, 3 October 1810

I think more of this little implement on account of its agency in saving the Colony at Plymouth in the year 1623. edward Winslow heard that Massasoit was sick and like to die. He found him with a houseful of people about him, women rubbing his arms and legs, and friends 'making such a hellish noise' as they probably thought would scare away the devil of sickness. Winslow gave him some conserve, washed his mouth, *scraped his tongue*, which was in a horrid state, got down some drink, made him some broth, dosed him with an infusion of strawberry leaves and sassafras root, and had the satisfaction of seeing him rapidly recover. Massasoit, full of grati- tude, revealed the plot which had been formed to destroy the colonists, whereupon the Governor ordered Captain Miles Standish to see to them; who thereupon, as everybody remembers, stabbed Pecksuot with his own knife, broke up the plot, saved the colony, and thus rendered Massachusetts and the Massachusetts Medical Society a possibility, as they now are a fact before us. So much for this parenthesis of the tongue-scraper, which helped to save the young colony from a much more serious scrape, and may save the Union yet, if a Presidential candidate should happen to be taken sick as Massasoit was, and his tongue wanted cleaning, – which process would not hurt a good many politicians, with or without a typhoid fever.

> Oliver Wendell Holmes, 'Currents and Counter-currents in
> Medical Science', 1860, *Medical Essays*

January 1863. Union Hotel Hospital, Georgetown, DC
Up at six, dress by gaslight, run through my ward and throw up the windows, though the men grumble and shiver; but the air is bad enough to breed a pestilence; and as no notice is taken of our frequent appeals for better ventilation, I must do what I can. Poke up the fire, add blankets, joke, coax, and command; but continue to open doors and windows as if life depended upon it. Mine does, and doubtless many another, for a more perfect pestilence-box than this house I never saw, – cold, damp, dirty, full of vile odours from wounds, kitchens, wash rooms, and stables . . .
Ordered to keep my room, being threatened with pneumonia. Sharp pain in the side, cough, fever, and dizziness. A pleasant prospect for a lonely soul five hundred miles from home! Sit and sew on the boys' clothes, write letters, sleep, and read; try to talk and keep merry, but fail decidedly, as day after day goes, and I feel no better. Dream awfully, and wake unrefreshed, think of home, and wonder if I am to die here, as Mrs R., the matron, is likely to do. Feel too miserable to care much what becomes of me. Dr S. creaks up twice a day to feel my pulse, give me doses, and ask if I am at all consumptive, or some other cheering question. Dr O. examines my

lungs and looks sober. Dr J. haunts the room, coming by day and night with wood, cologne, books, and messes, like a motherly little man as he is. Nurses fussy and anxious, matron dying, and everything very gloomy. They want me to go home, but I *won't* yet . . .

On the 21st I suddenly decided to go home, feeling very strangely, and dreading to be worse. Mrs R. died, and that frightened the doctors about me; for my trouble was the same, – typhoid pneumonia . . .

Had a strange, excited journey of a day and a night, – half asleep, half wandering, just conscious that I was going home; and, when I got to Boston, of being taken out of the car, with people looking on as if I was a sight. I daresay I was all blowzed, crazy, and weak. Was too sick to reach Concord that night, though we tried to do so. Spent it at Mr Sewall's; had a sort of fit; they sent for Dr H., and I had a dreadful time of it.

Next morning felt better, and at four went home. Just remember seeing May's shocked face at the depot, Mother's bewildered one at home, and getting to bed in the firm belief that the house was roofless, and no one wanted to see me.

And I shall never forget the strange fancies that haunted me, I shall amuse myself with recording some of them.

The most vivid and enduring was the conviction that I had married a stout, handsome Spaniard, dressed in black velvet, with very soft hands, and a voice that was continually saying, 'Lie still, my dear!' This was Mother, I suspect; but with all the comfort I often found in her presence, there was blended an awful fear of the Spanish spouse, who was always coming after me, appearing out of closets, in at windows, or threatening me dreadfully all night long. I appealed to the Pope, and really got up and made a touching plea in something meant for Latin, they tell me. Once I went to heaven, and found it a twilight place, with people darting through the air in a queer way, – all very busy, and dismal, and ordinary. Miss Dix, W. H. Channing, and other people were there; but I thought it dark and 'slow', and wished I hadn't come.

A mob at Baltimore breaking down the door to get me, being hung for a witch, burned, stoned, and otherwise maltreated, were some of my fancies. Also being tempted to join Dr W. and two of the nurses in worshipping the Devil. Also tending millions of rich men who never died or got well.

February. Recovered my senses after three weeks of delirium, and was told I had had a very bad typhoid fever, had nearly died, and was still very sick. All of which seemed rather curious, for I remembered nothing of it. Found a queer, thin, big-eyed face when I looked in the glass; didn't know myself at all; and when I tried to walk discovered that I couldn't, and cried because my legs wouldn't go.

Never having been sick before, it was all new and very interesting when I got quiet enough to understand matters. Such long, long nights; such feeble, idle days; dozing, fretting about nothing; longing to eat, and no mouth to do it with, – mine being so sore, and full of all manner of queer sensations, it was nothing but a plague. The old fancies still lingered, seeming so real I believed in them, and deluded Mother and May with the most absurd stories, so soberly told that they thought them true . . . Had all my hair, a yard and a half long, cut off, and went into caps like a grandma. Felt badly about losing my one beauty. Never mind, it might have been my head, and a wig outside is better than a loss of wits inside.

Louisa May Alcott, journal

My privy and well drain into each other
  After the custom of Christendie . . .
Fevers and fluxes are wasting my mother.
  Why has the Lord afflicted me?
The Saints are helpless for all I offer –
  So are the clergy I used to fee.
Henceforward I keep my cash in my coffer,
  Because the Lord has afflicted me.

Rudyard Kipling, 'Medieval', from 'Natural Theology', 1919

Fur hoffens we talkt o' my darter es died o' the fever at fall:
An' I thowt 'twur the will o' the Lord, but Miss Annie she said it wur
  draäins . . .

Alfred, Lord Tennyson, from 'The Village Wife', 1880

The inflammatory boils and buboes in the groins and axillae were recognized at once as prognosticating a fatal issue, and those were past all hope of recovery in whom they arose in numbers all over the body. It was not till towards the close of the plague that they ventured to open, by incision, these hard and dry boils, when matter flowed from them in small quantity, and thus by compelling nature to a critical suppuration, many patients were saved. Every spot which the sick had touched, their breath, their clothes, spread the contagion; and, as in all other places, the attendants and friends who were either blind to their danger or heroically despised it, fell a sacrifice to their sympathy. Even the eyes of the patient were considered as sources of contagion, which had the power of acting at a distance, whether on account of their unwonted lustre or the distortion which they always suffer in plague, or whether in conformity with an ancient notion, according to which the sight was considered as the bearer of a demoniacal enchantment. Flight from infected cities seldom availed the fearful, for the germ of the disease adhered to them, and they fell sick, remote from assistance, in the solitude of their country houses.

Thus did the plague spread over England with unexampled rapidity, after it had first broken out in the county of Dorset, whence it advanced through the counties of Devon and Somerset, to Bristol, and thence reached Gloucester, Oxford, and London. Probably few places escaped, perhaps not any; for the annals of contemporaries report that throughout the land only a tenth part of the inhabitants remained alive . . . this estimate is evidently too high. Smaller losses were sufficient to cause those convulsions, whose consequences were felt for some centuries, in a false impulse given to civil life, and whose indirect influence, unknown to the English, has, perhaps, extended even to modern times.

J. F. C. Hecker, *The Black Death in the Fourteenth Century*, 1832;
tr. B. G. Babington

Notice to be given of the Sickness

The master of every house, as soon as any one in his house complaineth, either of blotch or purple, or swelling in any part of his body, or falleth otherwise dangerously sick, without apparent cause

of some other disease, shall give knowledge thereof to the examiner
of health within two hours after the said sign shall appear.

Every visited House to be marked

That every house visited be marked with a red cross of a foot long in
the middle of the door, evident to be seen, and with these usual
printed words, that is to say, 'Lord, have mercy upon us', to be set
close over the same cross, there to continue until lawful opening of
the same house.

Lord Mayor's Orders, City of London, June 1665; in Daniel Defoe,
A Journal of the Plague Year, 1722

Was there no milder way but the Small Pox,
The very filth'ness of *Pandora's Box*?
So many Spots, like *naeves*, our *Venus* soil?
One Jewel set off with so many a Foil?
Blisters with pride swell'd, which thro's flesh did sprout
Like Rose-buds, stuck i' th'Lily-skin about.
Each little Pimple had a Tear in it,
To wail the fault its rising did commit:
Who, Rebel-like, with their own Lord at strife,
Thus made an Insurrection 'gainst his Life.
Or were these Gems sent to adorn his Skin,
The Cab'net of a richer Soul within?
No Comet need foretell his Change drew on,
Whose Corpse might seem a *Constellation*.

John Dryden, from 'Upon the Death of the Lord Hastings', 1650

. . . we passd this afternoone through the Gate which divides the
Valois from the Dutchy of *Savoy*, into which we now were entering,
& so thro *Montei* ariv'd that evening to *Beveretta*, where being
extreamely weary, & complaining of my head, & little accommo-
dation in the house, I caus'd one of our Hostesses daughters to be
removed out of her bed, & went immediately into it, whilst it was yet
warme, being so heavy with paine & drowsinesse, that I would not
stay to have the sheetes chang'd; but I shortly after pay'd dearely for

my impatience, falling sick of the Small Pox so soone as I came to *Geneva*; for by the smell of franc Incense, & the tale the good-woman told me, of her daughters having had an Ague, I afterwards concluded she had ben newly recoverd of the Small Pox: The paine of my head & wearinesse making me not consider of any thing, but how to get to bed so soone as ever I alighted, as not able any longer to sit on horseback . . .

But being now no more able to hold up my head, I was constrain'd to keepe my Chamber, imagining that my very eyes would have droped out, & this night felt such a stinging all about me that I could not sleepe: In the morning I was very ill: yet for all that, the *Doctor* (whom I had now consulted, & was a very learned old man . . .) perswaded me to be let bloud, which he accknowledg'd to me he should not have don, had he suspected the Small Pox, which brake out a day after; for he also purg'd me, & likewise applied *Hirudines* [leeches] *ad anum*, & God knows what this had produc'd if the spots had not appeard: for he was thinking of blouding me againe: Wherefore now they kept me warme in bed for 16 daies, tended by a vigilant Swisse Matron whose monstrous Throat, when I sometimes awake'd out of unquiet slumbers, would affright me: After the pimples were come forth, which were not many, I had much ease, as to paine, but infinitly afflicted with the heate & noysomenesse; But by Gods mercy, after five weekes keping my Chamber, being purg'd, . . . *Monsieur Le Chat* (my *Physitian*) to excuse his letting me bloud, told me it was so burnt & vitious, as it would have prov'd the *Plague* or spoted feavor, had he proceeded by any other method.

John Evelyn, Diary, c.May–July 1646

Adrianople [Edirne, Turkey], 1 April 1717

A propos of Distempers, I am going to tell you a thing that I am sure will make you wish your selfe here. The Small Pox so fatal and so general amongst us is here entirely harmless by the invention of engrafting (which is the term they give it). There is a set of old Women who make it their business to perform the Operation. Every Autumn in the month of September, when the great Heat is abated, people send to one another to know if any of their family has a mind to have the small pox. They make partys for this purpose, and when

they are met (commonly 15 or 16 together) the old Woman comes
with a nutshell full of the best sort of small pox and asks what veins
you please to have open'd. She immediately rips open that you offer
to her with a large needle (which gives you no more pain than a
common scratch) and puts into the vein as much venom as can lye
upon the head of her needle, and after binds up the little wound with
a hollow bit of shell, and in this manner opens 4 or 5 veins. The
Grecians have commonly the superstition of opening one in the
Middle of the forehead, in each arm and on the breast to mark the
sign of the cross, but this has a very ill Effect, all these wounds
leaving little Scars, and is not done by those that are not superstitious, who chuse to have them in the legs or that part of the arm
that is conceal'd. The children or young patients play together all the
rest of the day and are in perfect health till the 8th. Then the fever
begins to seize 'em and they keep their beds 2 days, very seldom 3.
they have very rarely above 20 or 30 in their faces, which never
mark, and in 8 days' time they are as well as before their illness.
Where they are wounded there remains running sores during the
Distemper, which I don't doubt is a great releife to it. Every year
thousands undergo this Operation, and the French Ambassador says
pleasantly that they take the Small Pox here by way of diversion as
they take the Waters in other Countrys. There is no example of any
one that has dy'd in it, and you may beleive I am very well satisfy'd
of the safety of the Experiment since I intend to try it on my dear
little Son. I am Patriot enough to take pains to bring this usefull
invention into fashion in England, and I should not fail to write to
some of our Doctors very particularly about it if I knew any one of
'em that I thought had Virtue enough to destroy such a considerable
branch of their Revenue for the good of Mankind, but that
Distemper is too beneficial to them not to expose to all their
Resentment the hardy wight that should undertake to put an end to
it. Perhaps if I live to return I may, however, have courrage to war
with 'em.

Lady Mary Wortley Montagu, letter to Sarah Chiswell

There is a dread disease which so prepares its victim, as it were, for
death; which so refines it of its grosser aspect, and throws around

familiar looks unearthly indications of the coming change – a dread disease in which the struggle between soul and body is so gradual, quiet, and solemn, and the result so sure, that day by day, and grain by grain, the mortal part wastes and withers away, so that the spirit grows light and sanguine with its lightening load, and feeling immortality at hand, deems it but a new term of mortal life – a disease in which death and life are so strangely blended that death takes the glow and hue of life, and life the gaunt and grisly form of death – a disease which medicine never cured, wealth warded off, or poverty could boast exemption from – which sometimes moves in giant strides, and sometimes at a tardy, sluggish pace, but, slow or quick, is ever sure and certain.

Charles Dickens, *Nicholas Nickleby*, 1839

I saw him steal the light away
        That haunted in her eye:
It went so gently none could say
More than that it was there one day
        And missing by-and-by.

I watched her longer, and he stole
        Her lily tincts and rose;
All her young sprightliness of soul
Next fell beneath his cold control,
        And disappeared like those.

I asked: 'Why do you serve her so?
        Do you, for some glad day,
Hoard these her sweets – ?' He said, 'O no,
They charm not me; I bid Time throw
        Them carelessly away.'

Said I: 'We call that cruelty –
        We, your poor mortal kind.'
He mused. 'The thought is new to me.
Forsooth, though I men's master be
        Theirs is the teaching mind!'

Thomas Hardy, 'God's Education', 1909

19 February 1918

I woke up early this morning and when I opened the shutters the full round sun was just risen. I began to repeat that verse of Shakespeare's: 'Lo, here the gentle lark weary of rest', and bounded back into bed. The bound made me cough – I spat – it tasted strange – it was bright red blood. Since then I've gone on spitting each time I cough a little more. Oh, yes, of course I'm frightened. But for two reasons only. I don't want to be ill, I mean 'seriously', away from Jack [John Middleton Murry]. Jack is the first thought. 2nd, I don't want to find this is real consumption, perhaps it's going to gallop – who knows? – and I shan't have my work written. *That's what matters.* How unbearable it would be to die – leave 'scraps', 'bits' . . . nothing real finished . . .

I *knew* this would happen. Now I'll say why. On my way here, in the train from Paris to Marseilles I sat in a carriage with two women. They were both dressed in black. One was big, one little. The little spry one had a sweet smile and light eyes. She was extremely pale, had been ill – was come to repose herself. The big one, as the night wore on, wrapped herself up in a black shawl – so did her friend. They shaded the lamp and started (trust 'em) talking about illnesses. I sat in the corner feeling damned ill myself.

Then the big one, rolling about in the shaking train, said what a *fatal place* this coast is for anyone who is even threatened with lung trouble. She reeled off the most hideous examples, especially one which froze me finally, of an American 'belle et forte avec une simple bronchite' who came down here to be cured and in three weeks had had a severe haemorrhage and *died.* 'Adieu mon mari, adieu mes beaux enfants.'

This recital, in that dark moving train, told by that big woman swathed in black, had an effect on me that I wouldn't own and never mentioned. I knew the woman was a fool, hysterical, morbid, *but I believed her*; and her voice has gone on somewhere echoing in me ever since.

21 June 1918

The man in the room next to mine has the same complaint as I. When I wake in the night I hear him turning. And then he coughs. And I cough. And after a silence I cough. And he coughs again. This goes on for a long time. Until I feel we are like two roosters calling to each other at false dawn. From far-away hidden farms.

Katherine Mansfield, *Journal*, ed. John Middleton Murry, 1927

I wish I had the voice of Homer
To sing of rectal carcinoma,
Which kills a lot more chaps, in fact,
Than were bumped off when Troy was sacked.

I noticed I was passing blood
(Only a few drops, not a flood)
So pausing on my homeward way
From Tallahassee to Bombay
I asked a doctor, now my friend,
To peer into my hinder end,
To prove or to disprove the rumour
That I had a malignant tumour.
They pumped in $BaSO_4$
Till I could really stand no more,
And, when sufficient had been pressed in,
They photographed my large intestine.
In order to decide the issue
They next scraped out some bits of tissue.
(Before they did so, some good pal
Had knocked me out with pentothal,
Whose action is extremely quick,
And does not leave me feeling sick.)
The microscope returned the answer
That I had certainly got cancer.
So I was wheeled to the theatre
Where holes were made to make me better.
One set is in my perineum
Where I can feel, but can't yet see 'em.
Another made me like a kipper
Or female prey of Jack the Ripper.
Through this incision, I don't doubt,
The neoplasm was taken out,

Along with colon, and lymph nodes
Where cancer cells might find abodes.
A third much smaller hole is meant
To function as a ventral vent:
So now I am like two-faced Janus
The only* god who sees his anus.
I'll swear, without the risk of perjury,
It was a snappy bit of surgery.
My rectum is a serious loss to me,
But I've a very neat colostomy,
And hope, as soon as I am able,
To make it keep a fixed time-table.

So do not wait for aches and pains
To have a surgeon mend your drains;
If he says 'cancer' you're a dunce
Unless you have it out at once.
For if you wait it's sure to swell,
And may have progeny as well.
My final word, before I'm done,
Is 'Cancer can be rather fun.'
Thanks to the nurses and Nye Bevan
The NHS is quite like heaven
Provided one confronts the tumour
With a sufficient sense of humour.
I know that cancer often kills,
But so do cars and sleeping pills;
And it can hurt one till one sweats,
So can bad teeth and unpaid debts.
A spot of laughter, I am sure,
Often accelerates one's cure;
So let us patients do our bit
To help the surgeons make us fit.

* *In India there are several more*
With extra faces, up to four,

But both in Brahma and in Shiva
I own myself an unbeliever.
J. B. S. Haldane, 'Cancer's a Funny Thing', 1964

One day Trousseau [Dr Armand Trousseau, 1801–67] asked Dieulafoy to feel a swelling on his leg, saying: 'Now tell me what that is . . . And I want a serious diagnosis!'

'But it's a . . .'

'Yes, it's a . . .' – and he used the scientific term – 'and on top of that I've got cancer . . . Yes, I've got cancer . . . And now, keep that to yourself, and thank you.'

And he went on living as if he did not know that he was condemned to die within a short time, seeing his patients and inviting friends to musical evenings at his home, serene and impenetrable. But he found himself growing weaker. He accordingly got rid of his carriage but went on seeing his patients at home.

However, for all his courage and determination, the change taking place in him was obvious to everyone and the rumour spread that he had cancer. Mothers promptly came rushing to see him, saying brutally: 'Is it true what they are saying, that you are going to die? But what about my child? What's to become of my daughter when she reaches puberty?' Trousseau smiled, asked them to sit down, and dictated copious advice to them . . .

Finally he could no longer stay on his feet and had to take to his bed. There he received his friends, carefully shaved and exquisitely groomed, like a man who was suffering from a slight indisposition. Soon he began to suffer appalling pain. It was only then that he asked for injections of morphine, but in infinitesimal doses, which gave him peace and calm for no more than a few minutes. Then he would come back to his painful life, pull himself together and say to the doctor friend beside him: 'Let's do some intellectual gymnastics and talk about . . .' And he would mention some medical thesis, determined to keep his mental faculties intact to the very end . . .

When he was on the point of dying, he asked his daughter to come closer, took her hand and sighed: 'As long as I hold your hand I shall still be alive . . . After that, I don't know where I shall be.'

Edmond de Goncourt, *The Goncourt Journal*, 3 January 1883;
tr. Robert Baldick

Gwen Evans, singer and trainer of singers,
    who, in 1941, warbled
an encore (Trees) at Porthcawl Pavilion
    lay in bed, not ½ her weight and dying.
Her husband, Tudor, drew the noise of curtains.

Then, in the artificial dark, she whispered,
    'Please send for Professor Mandlebaum.'
She raised her head pleadingly from the pillow,
    her horror-movie eyes thyrotoxic.
'Who?' Tudor asked, remembering, remembering.

Not Mandlebaum, not that renowned professor
    whom Gwen had once met on holiday;
not that lithe ex-Wimbledon tennis player
    and author of *Mediastinal Tumours*;
not that swine Mandlebaum of 1941?

Mandlebaum doodled in his hotel bedroom.
    For years he had been in speechless sloth.
But now for Gwen and old times' sake he, first-class,
    alert, left echoing Paddington for
a darkened sickroom and two large searching eyes.

She sobbed when he gently took her hand in his.
    'But my dear why are you crying?'
'Because, Max, you're quite unrecognizable.'
    'I can't scold you for crying about that,'
said Mandlebaum and he, too, began to weep.

They wept together (and Tudor closed his eyes)
    Gwen, singer and trainer of singers,
because she was dying; and he, Mandlebaum,
    ex-physician and ex-tennis player,
because he had become so ugly and so old.
    Dannie Abse, 'The silence of Tudor Evans', 1977

I used to pepper my poetics with sophisticated allusions to *dear*
Opera and *divine* Art (one was constantly reminded of A. du C.

Dubreuil's libretto for Piccinni's *Iphigenia in Tauris*; one was
constantly reminded of Niccolò di Bartolomeo da Foggia's bust of a
crowned woman, doubtless an allegory of the Church, from the
pulpit of Ravello cathedral, ca. 1272) but suddenly these are
hopelessly inadequate. Where is the European cultural significance
of tubes stuck up the nose, into the veins, up the arse? A tube is stuck
up my prick, and a bladder carcinoma diagnosed. One does *not*
recall Piccinni.

                                            Peter Reading, C, 1984

I am about to discuss the disease called 'sacred'. It is not, in my
opinion, any more divine or more sacred than other diseases, but has
a natural cause, and its supposed divine origin is due to men's
inexperience, and to their wonder at its peculiar character. Now
while men continue to believe in its divine origin because they are at
a loss to understand it, they really disprove its divinity by the facile
method of healing which they adopt, consisting as it does of
purifications and incantations. But if it is to be considered divine just
because it is wonderful, there will be not one sacred disease but
many, for I will show that other diseases are no less wonderful and
portentous, and yet nobody considers them sacred. For instance,
quotidian fevers, tertians and quartans seem to me to be no less
sacred and god-sent than this disease, but nobody wonders at them.
Then again one can see men who are mad and delirious from no
obvious cause, and committing many strange acts; while in their
sleep, to my knowledge, many groan and shriek, others choke,
others dart up and rush out of doors, being delirious until they wake,
when they become as healthy and rational as they were before,
though pale and weak; and this happens not once but many times.

My own view is that those who first attributed a sacred character
to this malady were like the magicians, purifiers, charlatans and
quacks of our own day, men who claim great piety and superior
knowledge. Being at a loss, and having no treatment which would
help, they concealed and sheltered themselves behind superstition,
and called this illness sacred, in order that their utter ignorance
might not be manifest. They added a plausible story, and established
a method of treatment that secured their own position. They used

purifications and incantations; they forbade the use of baths, and of many foods that are unsuitable for sick folk . . . These observances they impose because of the divine origin of the disease, claiming superior knowledge and alleging other causes, so that, should the patient recover, the reputation for cleverness may be theirs; but should he die, they may have a sure fund of excuses, with the defence that they are not at all to blame, but the gods.

Hippocrates, *The Sacred Disease,* on epilepsy; tr. W. H. S. Jones

'Tis but a case of mania – subinduced
By epilepsy, at the turning-point
Of trance prolonged unduly some three days:
When, by the exhibition of some drug
Or spell, exorcization, stroke of art
Unknown to me and which 'twere well to know,
The evil thing out-breaking all at once
Left the man whole and sound of body indeed, –
But, flinging (so to speak) life's gates too wide,
Making a clear house of it too suddenly,
The first conceit that entered might inscribe
Whatever it was minded on the wall
So plainly at that vantage, as it were,
(First come, first served) that nothing subsequent
Attaineth to erase those fancy-scrawls
The just-returned and new-established soul
Hath gotten now so thoroughly by heart
That henceforth she will read or these or none.
And first – the man's own firm conviction rests
That he was dead (in fact they buried him)
– That he was dead and then restored to life
By a Nazarene physician of his tribe:
– 'Sayeth, the same bade, 'Rise', and he did rise.
'Such cases are diurnal,' thou wilt cry.
Not so this figment! – not, that such a fume,
Instead of giving way to time and health,
Should eat itself into the life of life,
As saffron tingeth flesh, blood, bones and all!

For see, how he takes up the after-life.
The man — it is one Lazarus a Jew,
Sanguine, proportioned, fifty years of age,
The body's habit wholly laudable,
As much, indeed, beyond the common health
As he were made and put aside to show.
Think, could we penetrate by any drug
And bathe the wearied soul and worried flesh,
And bring it clear and fair, by three days' sleep!
Whence has the man the balm that brightens all?
This grown man eyes the world now like a child . . .

    Thou wilt object — Why have I not ere this
Sought out the sage himself, the Nazarene
Who wrought this cure, inquiring at the source,
Conferring with the frankness that befits?
Alas! it grieveth me, the learned leech
Perished in a tumult many years ago,
Accused, — our learning's fate, — of wizardry,
Rebellion, to the setting up a rule
And creed prodigious as described to me . . .
The other imputations must be lies:
But take one — though I loathe to give it thee,
In mere respect for any good man's fame.
(And after all, our patient Lazarus
Is stark mad; should we count on what he says?
Perhaps not: though in writing to a leech
'Tis well to keep back nothing of a case.)
This man so cured regards the curer, then,
As — God forgive me! — who but God himself,
Creator and sustainer of the world,
That came and dwelt in flesh on it awhile!

    Robert Browning, from 'An Epistle Containing the Strange
Medical Experience of Karshish, the Arab Physician', 1855

The stairs, which the prince ran up from under the gateway, led to
the corridors of the ground and first floors, along which were the
rooms of the hotel. This staircase, as in all old houses, was of stone.

Dark and narrow, it twisted round a thick, stone column. On the first half landing there was a cavity in the column, something like a niche, not more than a yard wide and about eighteen inches deep. But there was enough room for a man to stand there. Dark as it was, the prince, on reaching the landing, immediately noticed that a man was hiding in the niche. The prince suddenly wanted to pass by without looking to the right. He had already taken one step, but could not restrain himself, and turned round.

Those two eyes – *the same two eyes* – suddenly met his own. The man who was hiding in the niche, had also taken a step forward. For a second they stood face to face and almost touching each other. Suddenly the prince seized him by the shoulders, turned him round towards the staircase, nearer to the light: he wanted to see his face clearly.

Rogozhin's eyes glittered and a frenzied smile contorted his face. He raised his right hand and something flashed in it. The prince did not try to stop him. All he remembered was that he seemed to have shouted:

'Parfyon, I don't believe it!'

Then suddenly some gulf seemed to open before him: a blinding *inner* light flooded his soul. The moment lasted perhaps half a second, yet he clearly and consciously remembered the beginning, the first sound of the dreadful scream, which burst from his chest of its own accord and which he could have done nothing to suppress. Then his consciousness was instantly extinguished and complete darkness set in.

He had an epileptic fit, the first for a long time. It is a well-known fact that epileptic fits, the *epilepsy* itself, come on instantaneously. At that instant the face suddenly becomes horribly distorted, especially the eyes. Spasms and convulsions seize the whole body and the features of the face. A terrible, quite incredible scream, which is unlike anything else, breaks from the chest; in that scream everything human seems suddenly to be obliterated, and it is quite impossible, at least very difficult, for an observer to imagine and to admit that it is the man himself who is screaming. One gets the impression that it is someone inside the man who is screaming. This, at any rate, is how many people describe their impression; the sight of a man in an epileptic fit fills many others with absolute and unbearable horror, which has something mystical about it. It must be assumed that it was this impression of sudden horror, accompanied by all the other terrible impressions of the moment, that paralysed Rogozhin, and so saved the prince from the inevitable blow of the knife with which he had been attacked. Then, before he had time to realize that it was a fit, seeing that the prince had recoiled from him and suddenly fallen backwards down the stairs, knocking the back of his head violently against the stone step, Rogozhin rushed headlong downstairs and, avoiding the prostrate figure and scarcely knowing what he was doing, ran out of the hotel.

Twisting and writhing in violent convulsions, the sick man's body slipped down the steps, of which there were no fewer than fifteen, to the bottom of the staircase.

Fyodor Mikhailovich Dostoevsky, *The Idiot*, 1869;
tr. David Magarshack

Among the newer patients was a schoolmaster named Popoff, a lean and silent man, with his equally lean and silent wife. They sat together at the 'good' Russian table; and one day, while the meal was in full swing, the man was seized with a violent epileptic fit, and with that oft-described demoniac unearthly shriek fell to the floor, where he lay beside his chair, striking about him with dreadfully distorted arms and legs. To make matters worse, it was a fish dish that had just been handed, and there was ground for fear that Popoff, in his spasm, might choke on a bone. The uproar was indescribable. The ladies, Frau Stöhr in the lead, with Mesdames Salomon, Redisch, Hessenfeld, Magnus, Iltis, Levi, and the rest following hard upon, were taken in a variety of ways, some of them almost as badly as Popoff. Their yells resounded. Everywhere were twitching eyelids, gaping mouths, writhing torsos. One of them elected to faint, silently. There were cases of choking, some of them having been in the act of chewing and swallowing when the excitement began. Many of the guests at the various tables fled, through any available exit, even actually seeking the open, though the weather was very cold and damp. The whole occurrence, however, took a peculiar cast, offensive even beyond the horror of it, through an association of ideas due to Dr Krokowski's latest lecture.

In the course of his exposition of love as a power making for disease, the psychoanalyst had touched upon the 'falling sickness'. This affliction, which, in pre-analytic times, he said, men had by turns interpreted as a holy, even a prophetic visitation, and as a devilish possession, he went on to treat of, half poetically, half in ruthlessly scientific terminology, as the equivalent of love and an orgasm of the brain. In brief, he had cast such an equivocal light upon the disease that his hearers were bound to see, in Popoff's seizure, an illustration of the lecture, an awful manifestation and mysterious scandal. The flight on the part of the ladies was, accordingly, a disguised expression of modesty. The Hofrat himself had been present at the meal; he, with Fraülein von Mylendonk and one or two more robust guests, carried the ecstatic from the room, blue, rigid, twisted, and foaming at the mouth as he was; they put him down in the hall, where the doctors, the Directress, and other people could be seen hovering over the unconscious man, whom they afterwards bore away on a stretcher. But a short time thereafter Herr Popoff, quite happy and serene, with his equally serene and happy wife, was to be seen sitting at the 'good' Russian table, finishing his meal as though nothing had happened.

Thomas Mann, *The Magic Mountain*, 1924; tr. H. T. Lowe-Porter

February 15th 1824

Upon February 15th – (I write on the 17th of the same month) I had a strong shock of a Convulsive description but whether Epileptic – Paralytic – or Apoplectic is not yet decided by the two medical men who attend me – or whether it be of some other nature (if such there be). It was very painful and had it lasted a moment longer must have extinguished my mortality – if I can judge by sensations. – I was speechless with the features much distorted – but *not* foaming at the mouth – they say – and my struggles so violent that several persons – two of whom, Mr Parry the Engineer and my Servant Tita the Chasseur, are very strong men – could not hold me. – It lasted about ten minutes – and came on immediately after drinking a tumbler of Cider mixed with cold water in Col. Stanhope's apartments. – This is the first attack that I have had of this kind to the best of my belief. I never heard that any of my family were liable to the same – though my mother was subject to *hysterical* affections. Yesterday (the 16th) Leeches were applied to my temples. I had previously recovered a good deal – but with some feverish and variable symptoms; – I bled profusely – and as they went too near the temporal Artery, there was some difficulty in stopping the blood – even with the Lunar Caustic – this however after some hours was accomplished about eleven o'clock at night – and this day (the 17th) though weakly I feel tolerably convalescent. –

With regard to the presumed cause of this attack – as far as I know there might be several – the state of the place and of the weather permits little exercise at present; – I have been violently agitated with more than one passion recently – and a good deal occupied politically as well as privately, and amidst conflicting parties – politics – and (as far as regards public matters) circumstances; – I have also been in an anxious state with regard to things which may be only interesting to my own private feelings – and perhaps not uniformly so temperate as I may generally affirm that I was wont to be. – How far any or all of these may have acted on the mind or body of One who had already undergone many previous changes of place and passion during a life of thirty-six years I cannot tell – nor – but I am interrupted by the arrival of a report from a party returned from reconnoitring a Turkish Brig of War just stranded on the Coast – and which is to be attacked the moment we can get some guns to bear upon her. – I shall hear what Parry says about it – here he comes. –

Byron, *Journal in Cephalonia*

The paralytic, who can hold her cards,
But cannot play them, borrows a friend's hand
To deal and shuffle, to divide and sort,
Her mingled suits and sequences; and sits,
Spectatress both and spectacle, a sad
And silent cipher, while her proxy plays.
Others are dragg'd into the crowded room
Between supporters; and, once seated, sit,
Through downright inability to rise,
Till the stout bearers lift the corpse again.

These speak a loud memento. Yet ev'n these
Themselves love life, and cling to it, as he
That overhangs a torrent to a twig.
They love it, and yet loathe it; fear to die,
Yet scorn the purposes for which they live.
Then wherefore not renounce them? No — the dread,
The slavish dread of solitude, that breeds
Reflection and remorse, the fear of shame,
And their invet'rate habits, all forbid.

William Cowper, The Task, 1785

It happens. Will it go on? —
My mind a rock,
No fingers to grip, no tongue,
My god the iron lung

That loves me, pumps
My two
Dust bags in and out,
Will not

Let me relapse
While the day outside glides by like ticker tape.
The night brings violets,
Tapestries of eyes,

Lights,
The soft anonymous
Talkers: 'You all right?'
The starched, inaccessible breast.

Dead egg, I lie
Whole
On a whole world I cannot touch,
At the white, tight

Drum of my sleeping couch
Photographs visit me —

My wife, dead and flat, in 1920 furs,
Mouth full of pearls,

Two girls
As flat as she, who whisper 'We're your daughters.'
The still waters
Wrap my lips,

Eyes, nose and ears,
A clear
Cellophane I cannot crack.
On my bare back

I smile, a buddha, all
Wants, desire
Falling from me like rings
Hugging their lights.

The claw
Of the magnolia,
Drunk on its own scents,
Asks nothing of life.

                              Sylvia Plath, 'Paralytic', 1963

Dear friends, there is no cause for so much sympathy.
I shall certainly manage from time to time to take my walks abroad.
All that matters is an active mind, what is the use of feet?
By land one can ride in a carrying-chair; by water, be rowed in a
    boat.

  Po Chü-I, 'Illness', c.842 (when he was paralysed); tr. Arthur Waley

Guess what it is, my daughter, the thing which comes the fastest in
the world and goes away the most slowly, which brings you closest
to convalescence and takes you the furthest from it, which permits
you to touch the most agreeable condition in the world and most
prevents you from enjoying it, which inspires you with the most

beautiful hopes in the world and most completely removes their realization. Can't you guess? Do you give up? It is rheumatism. I have been ill with it for twenty-three days; since the fourteenth I have been free from fever and pains; and in that blissful state, believing myself capable of walking, which is all I desire, I find myself swollen all over, the feet, the legs, the hands, the arms; and this swelling, which is termed my healing, and which in fact it is, is the very cause of my impatience, and would be that of my merit, were I a good woman. However I believe it is over, and that in a couple of days I shall be able to walk. Lamerchin gives me that hope: *o che spero!* I receive letters of congratulation on my good health from all sides, and with good reason. I have purged myself once with M. Delorme's powder, which worked wonders; I shall take it again; it is the true cure for all these sorts of illness: after this, I have been promised eternal well-being; may it be God's will! The first step I shall take will be in the direction of Paris . . . Before sealing this packet I shall ask my swollen fingers for permission to write a few words to you; I find they do not agree; perhaps they will in an hour or two.

from Charles de Sévigné

If my mother had trusted herself to the treatment prescribed by the good man, and taken his powder every month, as he wanted, she would not have succumbed to this malady, which comes solely from dreadful repletion of humours; but to advise her to try it was like proposing to murder her. Yet this so terrible remedy, whose name makes people tremble, which is made from antimony, a kind of emetic, purges much more gently than a glass of spring water, causes not the slightest colic, not the slightest pain, and has no other effect than to render the head clear and light, and capable of composing verses, should one so wish.

> Mme de Sévigné, letter to her daughter, 3 February 1676;
> dictated to her son, with a postscript by him

Alas! my friend, I fear the voice of the bard will soon be heard among you no more! For these eight or ten months I have been ailing, sometimes bed-fast and sometimes not; but these last three months I have been tortured with an excruciating rheumatism, which has reduced me to nearly the last stage. You actually would not know me if you saw me. Pale, emaciated, and so feeble as occasionally to need help from my chair – my spirits fled! fled! – but I can no more on the subject – only the medical folks tell me that my last and only chance is bathing, and country quarters, and riding. The deuce of the matter is this: when an exciseman is off duty, his salary is reduced to 35£. instead of 50£. What way, in the name of thrift, shall I maintain myself, and keep a horse in country quarters, with a wife and five children at home, on 35£.? I mention this, because I had intended to beg your utmost interest, and that of all the friends you can muster, to move our Commissioners of Excise to grant me the full salary; I dare say you know them all personally. If they do not grant it me, I must lay my account with an exit truly *en poëte* – if I die not of disease, I must perish with hunger.

Robert Burns, letter to Alexander Cunningham, 7 July 1796

When you offered me money assistance, little did I think I should want it so soon. A rascal of a haberdasher, to whom I owe a considerable bill, taking it into his head that I am dying, has commenced a process against me, and will infallibly put my emaciated body into jail. Will you be so good as to accommodate me, and that by return of post, with ten pounds? O, James! did you know the pride of my heart, you would feel doubly for me. Alas! I am not used to beg. The worst of it is, my health was coming about finely; you know, and my physician assured me, that melancholy and low spirits are half my disease: guess, then, my horrors since this business began. If I had it settled, I would be, I think, quite well in a manner. How shall I use the language to you, O do not disappoint me! but strong necessity's curst command . . .

Forgive me for once again mentioning by return of post; – save me from the horrors of a jail!

I do not know what I have written. The subject is so horrible, I dare not look it over again. Farewell.

Burns, letter to his cousin, James Burnes, 12 July 1796

And so rose in the morning in perfect good ease, but only strain I put myself to to shit, more than I needed. But continued all the morning well; and in the afternoon had a natural easily and dry Stoole, the first I have had these five days or six, for which God be praised; and so am likely to continue well, observing for the time to come, when any of this pain comes again:

1. To begin to keep myself warm as I can.

2. Strain as little as ever I can backwards, remembering that my pain will come by and by, though in the very straining I do not feel it.

3. Either by physic forward or by clyster backward, or both ways, to get an easy and plentiful going to stool and breaking of wind.

4. To begin to suspect my health immediately when I begin to become costive and bound, and by all means to keep my body loose, and that to obtain presently after I find myself going to the contrary.

Samuel Pepys, Diary, 13 October 1663

Sept. 24, 1790. Nancy was taken very ill this Afternoon with a pain within her, blown up so as if poisoned, attended with a vomiting. I supposed it proceeded in great measure from what she eat at Dinner and after. She eat for Dinner some boiled Beef rather fat and salt, a good deal of a nice rost duck, and a plenty of boiled Damson Pudding. After Dinner by way of Desert, she eat some green-gage Plumbs, some Figgs, and Rasberries and Cream. I desired her to drink a good half pint Glass of warm Rum and Water which she did and soon was a little better – for Supper she had Water-gruel with a Couple of small Table Spoonfuls of Rum in it, and going to bed I gave her a good dose of Rhubarb and Ginger. She was much better before she went to bed – And I hope will be brave to Morrow.

Sept. 25. Nancy thank God Much better this Morning – The Rhubarb made her rise earlier than usual. She dined on a rost Neck of Mutton and supped on Water-gruel and at night quite hearty and well.

The Revd James Woodforde, The Diary of a Country Parson

I have not been in worse trim for writing this twelvemonth. If you saw me sitting here with my lean and sallow visage, you would wonder how those long bloodless bony fingers could be made to move at all – even tho' the aching brain were by miracle enabled to supply them with materials in sufficient abundance. I have been sick, very sick, since Monday last – indeed I have scarcely been *one day* right, since I came back to this accursed, stinking, reeky mass of stones and lime and dung. I was better somewhat yesterday – for I swallowed salts the day before to supersaturation; but today the *guts* are all wrong again, the headache, the weakness, the black despondency are overpowering me. I fear those paltry viscera will fairly dish me at last. And do but think what a thing it is! that the etherial spirit of a man should be overpowered and hag-ridden by what? by two or three feet of sorry tripe full of –––. Were it by moral suffering that one sunk – by oppression, love or hatred or the thousand ways of heartbreak – it might be tolerable, there might at least be some dignity in the fall; but here! – I conjure thee Jack to watch over thy health as the most precious of earthly things. I believe at this moment I would consent to become as ignorant as a Choctaw – so I were as sound of body.

Carlyle, letter to his brother John Aitken,
from Edinburgh, 10 February 1821

7 December 1826. Again a very disturbed night scarce sleeping an hour yet well when I rose in the morning. I did not do above a leaf today because I had much to read. But I am up to one 4th of the vol. of 400 pages which I began on the 1st December current; the 31st must and shall see the end of vol. VI. I had a book sent me by a very clever woman in defence of what she calls the rights of her sex among which she seems to claim the privilege of getting her husband with child. Clever though. I hope she will publish it.

8 December. Another restless and deplorable knight – night I should say – faith either spelling will suit. I can tell my bowels that if they do not conduct themselves as bowels of compassion I will put the Doctor on them right or wrong.

Sir Walter Scott, *Journal*

Young women. You may depend on it your dear Papa is not very comfortable in mind nor pens nor paper when he begins at you in this hand writing. He got up this morning at 7 quite cheerfully and well, and lighting the candle of the mantelpiece saw before him 'The pills immediately the Draught two hours after the pills.' Like a good boy he took the pills instantly at 7, the Draught at 9. It was Rhubarb, w^h· your dear Father hates like poison. But que voulez vous? He was committed already by having swallowed the pill, don't you see? It is now 12 o'clock. He is nauseated, uncomfortable all over, with the dreadful idea that the pill will have its effect about 5 o'clock, and at 7 he is to be at dinner at M^r· Heath's at Richmond. Fancy having to get up abruptly, and leave the table!

William Makepeace Thackeray, letter to his daughters,
Anne and Harriet, 4 December 1858

The extraordinary attraction I felt towards the study of the intricacies of living structure nearly proved fatal to me at the outset. I was a mere boy – I think between thirteen and fourteen years of age – when I was taken by some older student friends of mine to the first post-mortem examination I ever attended. All my life I have been most unfortunately sensitive to the disagreeables which attend anatomical pursuits; but on this occasion, my curiosity overpowered all other feelings, and I spent two or three hours in gratifying it. I did not cut myself, and none of the ordinary symptoms of dissection poison supervened, but poisoned I was somehow, and I remember sinking into a strange state of apathy. By way of a last chance I was sent to the care of some good, kind people, friends of my father's, who lived in a farmhouse in the heart of Warwickshire. I remember staggering from my bed to the window on the bright spring morning after my arrival, and throwing open the casement. Life seemed to come back on the wings of the breeze; and, to this day, the faint odour of wood-smoke, like that which floated across the farmyard in the early morning, is as good to me as the 'sweet south upon a bed of violets'. I soon recovered; but for years I suffered from occasional paroxysms of internal pain, and from that

time my constant friend, hypochondriacal dyspepsia, commenced
his half century of co-tenancy of my fleshly tabernacle.

> Thomas Henry Huxley, from 'Autobiography', 1889.
> Here, 'hypochondriacal' refers to the hypochondrium,
> the upper region of the abdomen

Now, as I before hinted, I have no objection to any person's religion,
be it what it may, so long as that person does not kill or insult any
other person, because that other person don't believe it also. But
when a man's religion becomes really frantic; when it is a positive
torment to him; and, in fine, makes this earth of ours an uncomfortable inn to lodge in; then I think it high time to take that individual
aside and argue the point with him.

And just so I now did with Queequeg. 'Queequeg,' said I, 'get into
bed now, and lie and listen to me.' I then went on, beginning with the
rise and progress of the primitive religions, and coming down to the
various religions of the present time, during which time I laboured to
show Queequeg that all fasts, voluntary or otherwise, were excessi-
vely bad for the digestion.

I then asked Queequeg whether he himself was ever troubled with
dyspepsia; expressing the idea very plainly, so that he could take it
in. He said no; only upon one memorable occasion. It was after a
great feast given by his father the king, on the gaining of a great
battle wherein fifty of the enemy had been killed by about two
o'clock in the afternoon, and all cooked and eaten that very evening.

> Herman Melville, *Moby Dick*, 1851

Twenty-two feet of wonders
Twenty-two feet of woes:
Why we're obliged to have so many yards of them
Nobody really knows.

Sometimes they lie retentive,
Sometimes they're wild and free,
Sometimes they writhe and get madly expulsive
The moment you're out to tea.

Entrails don't care for travel,
Entrails don't care for stress:
Entrails are better kept folded inside you
For outside, they make a mess.

Entrails put hara-kiri
High on their list of hates:
Also they loathe being spread on the carpet
While someone haruspicates.

Twenty-two feet of wonders
Twenty-two feet of woes:
Why we're obliged to have so many yards of them
Nobody really knows.

                    Connie Bensley, 'Entrails', 1987

Eunuchs are not subject to gout, nor do they grow bald.
Women do not get gout except after the menopause.
A youth does not suffer from gout until after sexual intercourse.
                    Hippocrates, *Aphorisms*

My Disease is probably anomalous. If it can be called anything, by a
lucky Guess, it may be called irregular scrofulous Gout . . . What
gouty Medicines are there that I have not used? What gouty
regimen? Have I not wholly abandoned wine, spirits, & all fer-
mented Liquors? And taken Ginger in superabundance? 'Tis true, I
have not taken Dr Beddoes's North American Fruit – nor do I intend
to do it . . . My Disease, whatever it may be called, consists in an
undue sensibility with a deficient irritability – muscular motion is
languid with me, & venous action languid – my nerves are unduly
vivid – the consequence is, a natural tendency to obstructions in the
glands, &c; because glandular secretion requires the greatest vigour
of any of the secretories. My only medicine is a universal & regular
Stimulus – Brandy, Laudanum, &c &c make me well, during their
first operation; but the secondary Effects increase the cause of the
Disease. Heat in a hot climate is the only regular & universal

Stimulus of the external world; to which if I can add Tranquillity, the equivalent, & Italian climate, of the world within, I do not despair to be a healthy man.

Samuel Taylor Coleridge, letter to Robert Southey, 17 February 1803

I am pretty well, except gout, asthma, and pains in all the bones, and all the flesh, of my body. What a very singular disease gout is! It seems as if the stomach fell down into the feet. The smallest deviation from right diet is immediately punished by limping and lameness, and the innocent ankle and blameless instep are tortured for the vices of the nobler organs. The stomach having found this easy way of getting rid of inconveniences, becomes cruelly despotic, and punishes for the least offences. A plum, a glass of champagne, excess in joy, excess in grief, – any crime, however small, is sufficient for redness, swelling, spasms, and large shoes.

We are tolerably well here; the gout is never far off though not actually present – It is the only Enemy that I do not wish to have at my feet.

Sydney Smith, letters to Lady Carlisle, 5 September 1840,
and Lady Grey, 24 August 1841

The pigeons flutter'd fieldward, one and all,
I saw the swallows wheel, and soar, and dive;
The little bees hung poised before the hive,
Even Partlet hoised herself across the wall:
I felt my earth-bound lot in every limb,
And, in my envious mood, I half-rebell'd;
When lo! an insect cross'd the page I held,
A little helpless minim, slight and slim;
Ah! sure, there was no room for envy there,
But gracious aid and condescending care;
Alas! my pride and pity were misspent,
The atom knew his strength, and rose in air!

My gout came tingling back, as off he went,
A wing was open'd at me everywhere!
Charles Tennyson Turner, 'Gout and Wings', 1873

My dear Gosse,

Forgive this cold-blooded machinery – for I have been of late a stricken man, and still am not on my legs; though judging it a bit urgent to briefly communicate with you on a small practical matter. I have had quite a Devil of a summer, a very bad and damnable July and August, through a renewal of an ailment that I had regarded as a good deal subdued, but that descended upon me in force just after I last saw you and then absolutely raged for many weeks. (I allude to a most deplorable tendency to chronic pectoral, or, more specifically, anginal, pain; which, however, I finally, about a month ago, got more or less the better of, in a considerably reassuring way.) I was but beginning to profit by this comparative reprieve when I was smitten with a violent attack of the atrocious affection known as 'Shingles' – my impression of the nature of which had been vague and inconsiderate, but to the now grim shade of which I take off my hat in the very abjection of respect. It has been a very horrible visitation, but I am getting better; only I am still in bed and have to appeal to you in this graceless mechanical way.

Henry James, letter dictated to Edmund Gosse, 7 October 1912

I am suffering from my old complaint, the Hay-fever (as it is calld). My fear is of perishing by deliquescence. – I melt away in Nasal and Lachrymal profluvia. My remedies are warm Pediluvium, Cathartics, topical application of a watery solution of Opium to eyes, ears, and the interior of the nostrils. The membrane is so irritable, that light, dust, contradiction, an absurd remark, the sight of a dissenter, – anything, sets me a-sneezing and if I begin sneezing at 12, I don't leave off till two o'clock – and am heard distinctly in Taunton when the wind sets that way at a distance of 6 miles. Turn your mind to this little curse. If Consumption is too powerful for Physicians at least they should not suffer themselves to be outwitted by such little upstart disorders as the Hay-fever.

Sydney Smith, letter to Dr Henry Holland, 8 June 1835

For the present we are all in sad taking with Influenza. People speak about it more than they did about Cholera; I do not know whether they die more from it. Miss Wilson, not having come to close quarters with it, has her mind sufficiently at leisure to make philosophical speculations about its gender! She primly promulgates her opinion that Influenza is masculine; my Husband, for the sake of argument, I presume (for I see not what other interest he has in it), protests that Influenza is feminine; for me who have been laid up with it for two weeks and upwards, making lamentations of Jeremiah (not without reason), I am not prejudiced either way, but content myself with sincerely wishing it were neuter.

Jane Welsh Carlyle, letter to John Sterling, 1 February 1837

22 January 1829. I suppose I am turning to my second childhood for not only am I filld drunk or made stupid at least with one bottle of wine but I am disabled from writing by chillblains on my fingers, a most babyish complaint. They say that the character is indicated by the hand writing. If so mine is crabbed enough.

Scott, *Journal*

Montaigne – for him the body of knowledge
Was his own, to be suffered or studied
Like a local custom – had one too, I read
In bed, his diary more alert and all-gathering
The more I lose touch with it, or everything.
Even the gardenia on the neighbour's sill
That for three nights running a nightingale
Has tended with streamsprung song –
The senses competing with a giddy vulgarity –
Draws a blank. The San Vio vesper bells
Close in, fade, close in, then fade
To the congestion of voices from the street.

Why 'clear as a bell'? Even as the time-release
Capsule I'm waiting on is stuffed with pellets
The bell must first be choked with the changes

To be rung, all there at once, little explosions
Of feeling, the passages out of this world.

These pills clear a space, as if for assignment
Undercover. Last week's liver seared in oil
And sage, the mulberry gelato on the Zattere . . .
Neither smell nor taste make it back.
And what of the taste for time itself,
Its ravelled daybook and stiff nightcap,
What it clears from each revisited city,
Depths the same, no inch of surface unchanged?
I can see to that. The gouged pearl pattern
Of light on the canals, the grimy medallioned
Cavities of the facings, or goldleaf phlegm
Around a saint's head. It's always something
About the body. For Montaigne the cure
Was 'Venetian turpentine' – grappa, no doubt –
Done up in a wafer on a silver spoon.
The next morning he noticed the smell
Of March violets in his urine.

                              How dependent
One becomes on remedies, their effects familiar
As a flower's perfumed throat, or a bird's
Thrilled questioning, like the trace
Of a fingertip along that throat, or now
Between the lines of a book by someone well
I'd taken up to read myself asleep with.
            J. D. McClatchy, 'A Cold in Venice', 1986

                              Portland, Maine
                              29 March 1868
With the return of snow, nine days ago, the 'true American' (which
had lulled) came back as bad as ever. I have coughed from two or
three in the morning until five or six, and have been absolutely
sleepless. I have had no appetite besides, and no taste. Last night
here I took some laudanum, and it is the only thing that has done me

good. But the life in this climate is so very hard. When I did manage to get from Boston to New Bedford, I read with my utmost force and vigour. Next morning, well or ill, I must turn out at seven to get back to Boston on my way here . . . I have just now written to Dolby (who is in New York) to see my doctor there, and ask him to send me some composing medicine that I can take at night, inasmuch as without sleep I cannot get through. However sympathetic and devoted the people are about me, they *can not* be got to comprehend that one's being able to do the two hours with spirit when the time comes round, may be coexistent with the consciousness of great depression and fatigue. I don't mind saying all this, now that the labour is so nearly over.

> Boston, Mass.
> 7 April 1868

Longfellow and all the Cambridge men urged me to give in. I have been very near doing so, but feel stronger today. I cannot tell whether the catarrh may have done me any lasting injury in the lungs or other breathing organs, until I shall have rested and got home. I hope and believe not. Consider the weather. There have been two snowstorms since I wrote last, and today the town is blotted out in a ceaseless whirl of snow and wind.

I cannot eat (to anything like the ordinary extent) and have established this system: At seven in the morning, in bed, a tumbler of new cream and two tablespoonsful of rum. At twelve, a sherry cobbler and a biscuit. At three (dinner time), a pint of champagne. At five minutes to eight, an egg beaten up with a glass of sherry. Between the parts, the strongest beef tea that can be made, drunk hot. At a quarter past ten, soup, and anything to drink that I can fancy. I don't eat more than half a pound of solid food in the whole four-and-twenty hours, if so much . . .

I am tremendously 'beat', but I feel really and unaffectedly so much stronger today, both in my body and hopes, that I am much encouraged. I have a fancy that I turned my worst time last night.

> Dickens, letters to his daughter, Mamie

A boil is of no practical value. It is said that everything has its use, but this certainly does not apply to boils. They are of no use; and few people consider them ornamental. They do not improve your personal appearance, and they do not add to your comfort. We are told, on good authority, that in many cases they must be looked upon as salutary, as being the means adopted by Nature to rid the system of morbid matters that irritate the constitution. This may be, but a boil is a violent remedy. Most people, if they had the choice, would prefer a less energetic means of having the system cleared out. Scientific doctors usually call them *furunculi*, but even then they are rather painful.

> The Family Physician, by Physicians and Surgeons of the
> Principal London Hospitals, 1883

Yesterday I had a small operation on the cheek, for my abscess; my face is swaddled in bandages and looks pretty grotesque. As if all the putrescences and infections that preceded our birth and will repossess us at our death were not enough, during our life we are nothing but corruption and putrefaction, successive, alternate, one overrunning the other. Today you lose a tooth, tomorrow a hair, a sore opens, an abscess forms, blisters are raised on you, drains are inserted. Add to all this corns on your feet, bad natural smells of every kind and flavour, and you have a most inspiring picture of the human person. To think that one loves all this! that one loves oneself and that I, for one, have the nerve to look at myself in the mirror without bursting into laughter. Isn't the mere sight of an old pair of boots profoundly sad, bitterly melancholy! When you think of all the steps you have taken in them, going you don't remember where, of all the weeds you have trodden on, all the mud you have picked up, the cracked leather seems to tell you: ' . . . and now, you fool, go and buy another pair, varnished, shining, creaking; they will end up as I did, as you will one day, when you have soiled lots of boot-tops and sweated inside lots of uppers.'

> Gustave Flaubert, letter to Louise Colet, 14 December 1846

I let out 4 ounces of Blood, which was perhaps too much at my greate Age, to try if it would help me, hithertoo tormented with the Haemerrhoids: it was very faulty blood, much serum, & I had that

Evening no reliefe, but at night a kind of Aguish fit: The next day easier & on the next Sonday, I was able to go to Evening prayer: God be praised.

> Evelyn, *Diary*, 10 August 1703

Was rather uneasy today on Account of being afraid that I have got the Piles coming or something else – unless it is owing to my eating a good deal of Peas Pudding two or three days ago with a Leg of Pork.

> Woodforde, *The Diary of a Country Parson*,
> 28 February 1782

(21 December 1672) At home all day vertiginous, took conserves of Rosemary flowers. Took two aloes Rosata pills, ointment in eye from Mr Colwall. (22) Mr Moor here, had been at Portsmouth, told me of a woman in the Tower cured diver of the vertigo by stone horse dung. Mr Gidley let me blood 7 ounces. Bloody windy and melancholly, gave him ½ crown. The vertigo continued but upon snuffing ginger I was much relievd by blowing out of my nose a lump of thick gelly. Went abroad (23) in the morn returned home very guiddy. Refresht by eating Dinner, in the afternoon pretty well. Consulted Dr Godderd, he advisd amber and ale with sage and rosemary, bubbels, caraways and nutmeg steepd and scurvy grasse. (24) Very ill and giddy in the afternoon but pretty well before. I tooke a clyster after which working but once I was very ill and giddy. The worst night I ever yet had, melancholly and giddy, shooting in left side of my head above ear. (25) Christmas day. Slept from 7 to 10, rose pretty well. Upon eating broth, very giddy . . . Eat plumb broth, went pretty well to bed but slept but little and mightily refresht upon cutting off my hair close to my head and supposed I had been perfectly cured but I was somewhat guiddy (26) next day and tooke Dr Godderds 3 pills which wrought 14 times towards latter end. I was again very giddy and more after eating, which continued till I had taken a nap for ½ howr about 5 when I was very melancholly but upon drinking ale strangely inlivernd and refresht after which I slept pretty well and pleasantly. Dreamt of riding and eating cream.

> *The Diary of Robert Hooke, M.A., M.D., F.R.S.*

Chocolate is no longer what it used to be for me: fashion has swept me away, as it always does. All those who praised chocolate to me now condemn it: they curse it, they hold it responsible for all the ills one suffers; it is the source of palpitations and the vapours; it charms for a while, and suddenly sets you on fire with a persistent fever that leads to your death; finally, my child, the great master who lived on it declares himself its enemy: you will know whether I can be of a different opinion. In God's name, don't try to defend it; remember, it is no longer in vogue in the beau monde.

Mme de Sévigné, letter to her daughter, 15 April 1671

My dear Davy
With legs astraddle & bebolster'd back
Alack! alack!
I received your letter just in time to break up some speculations on the Hernia Humoralis, degenerating into Sarcocele, 'in which (after a long paragraph of Horrors) the Patient is at last carried off in great misery.' – From the week that Stoddart left me to the present I have been harassed by a succession of Indispositions, inflamed eyes, swoln eyelids, boils behind my ear, &c &c – Somewhat more than 3 weeks ago I walked to Grasmere, & was wet thro' – I changed immediately – but still the next day I was taken ill, & by the Lettre de cachet of a Rheumatic Fever sentenced to the Bed-bastille – the Fever left me, and on the Friday before last I was well enough to be conveyed home in a chaise – but immediately took to my bed again – a most excruciating pain on the least motion, but not without motion, playing Robespierre & Marat in my left Hip & the small of my back – but alas! worse than all, my left Testicle swelled, without pain indeed, but distressing from its weight; from a foolish shame-facedness almost peculiar to Englishmen I did not shew it to our doctor till last Tuesday night. On examination it appeared that a Fluid had collected between the Epididymis & the Body of the Testicle (*how* learned a Misfortune of this kind makes one) – Fomentations & fumigations of Vinegar having no effect, I applied Sal ammoniac dissolved in verjuice, & to considerable purpose; but the smart was followed by such a frantic & intolerable *Itching* over the whole surface of the Scrotum, that I am convinced it is the

identical Torment which the Damned suffer in Hell, & that Jesus, the good-natured one of the Trinity, had it built of Brimstone, in a pang of pity for the poor Devils. – In all the parts thro' which the Spermatic Cord passes, I have dull & obtuse pains – and on removing the suspensory Bandage the sense of weight is terrible. – I never knew before what it was to be truly weak in body – I have such pains in the Calves of my Legs – yet still my animal spirits bear me up – tho' I am so weak that even from sitting up to write this note to you I seem to sink in upon myself in a ruin, like a Column of Sand informed & animated only by a Whirl-blast of the Desert. Pray, my dear Davy! did you rectify the red oil which rises over after the Spirit of Hartshorn is gotten from the Horns, so as to make that animal oil of Diphelius? And is it true what Hoffman asserts, that 15 or 20 drops will exert many times the power of opium both in degree & duration, without inducing any after-fatigue?

Coleridge, letter to Humphry Davy, 11 January 1801

The Sorrows of a Poet Laureate

I am grieved to hear about your eyes and must again regret that I have nothing to write on of the cool verdant kind nor could I procure it I suppose nearer than at Southampton. One cannot live without bore and bother of all kinds, daily frettings, which of course affect all the nerves, optic and others.

Since I came here my house-troubles have been so great (servant-troubles I mean, these all quarrelling among themselves and unkindly to their mistress who wanted great kindness in her then-condition) that in spite of pure air and frequent outings I have got some 15 *new* specks in my right eye: these all occur together, like a group of dark Pleiads something in this position

not pleasant, rolling round as the eye rolls and damaging these splendid sea-views considerably. I cannot help thinking that these have resulted solely from house-bother and from having been put out, as they say, 3 or 4 times a day for at least 4 months. 'Muscae volitantes' I believe do not lead to amaurosis, which if true is a comfort. The only advice I can give you or I believe that any Doctor could give is 'Keep your mind easy' but it is just that advice which is the hardest to follow.

> Tennyson, letter to his aunt, Elizabeth Russell,
> 24 March 1854

I am laid up with a bad foot and cannot stir out. The nail of the great toe having shot out a spur low down into the flesh causing an inflammation, I have twice had to undergo a rather cruel surgical operation owing to this abnormal fancy of the nail.

> To his son, Hallam, c.1 May 1857

I had a dreadful journey home. Sneezing every moment all the way and both eyes streaming with tears: nothing excites my hay fever so much as the dust of a train. When I got out at Southampton, some one of the officials at the station said 'Sir, you look like a miller: brush the gentleman, Jacob.' So Jacob brushed me.

> To Charles Richard Weld, 28 June 1858

My complaint against the time and my office of Poet Laureate is not so much that I am deluged with verse as that no man ever thinks of sending me a book of prose – hardly ever. I am like a man receiving perpetual parcels of currants and raisins and barley sugar and never a piece of bread.

> To Arthur Helps, 1 March 1858

My head has ached so for two days (not my temper, I assure you), that I thought it was beheading itself.

> Elizabeth Barrett Browning, letter to Richard Hengist Horne,
> 4 November 1841

He is of opinion that there is some inconceivable benefit in pain abstractly considered; that pain however inflicted, or wherever felt, communicates some good to the general system of being, and that every animal is some way or other the better for the pain of every other animal . . .

But that he may not be thought to conceive nothing but things inconceivable, he has at last thought on a way by which human sufferings may produce good effects. He imagines that as we have not only animals for food, but choose some for our diversion, the same privilege may be allowed to some beings above us, *who may deceive, torment, or destroy us for the ends only of their own pleasure or utility.* This he again finds impossible to be conceived, *but that impossibility lessens not the probability of the conjecture, which by analogy is so strongly confirmed.*

I cannot resist the temptation of contemplating this analogy, which I think he might have carried further very much to the advantage of his argument. He might have shewn that these *hunters whose game is man* have many sports analogous to our own. As we drown whelps and kittens, they amuse themselves now and then with sinking a ship, and stand round the fields of *Blenheim* or the walls of *Prague*, as we encircle a cockpit. As we shoot a bird flying, they take a man in the midst of his business or pleasure, and knock him down with an apoplexy. Some of them, perhaps, are virtuosi, and delight in the operations of an asthma, as a human philosopher in the effects of the air pump. To swell a man with a tympany is as good sport as to blow a frog. Many a merry bout have these frolic beings at the vicissitudes of an ague, and good sport it is to see a man tumble with an epilepsy, and revive and tumble again, and all this he knows not why. As they are wiser and more powerful than we, they have more exquisite diversions, for we have no way of procuring any sport so brisk and so lasting as the paroxysms of the gout and stone which undoubtedly must make high mirth, especially if the play be a little diversified with the blunders and puzzles of the blind and deaf. We know not how far their sphere of observation may extend. Perhaps now and then a merry being may place himself in such a situation as to enjoy at once all the varieties of an epidemical disease, or amuse his leisure with the tossings and contortions of every possible pain exhibited together.

Samuel Johnson, review of Soame Jenyns's
A Free Inquiry into the Nature and Origin of Evil, 1757

'Pain, who made thee?' thus I said once
To the grim unpitying monster,
As, one sleepless night, I watched him
Heating in the fire his pincers.

'God Almighty; who dare doubt it?'
With a hideous grin he answered:
'I'm his eldest best-beloved son,
Cut from my dead mother's bowels.'

'Wretch, thou liest'; shocked and shuddering
To the monster I replied then;
'God is good, and kind, and gracious;
Never made a thing so ugly.'

'Tell me then, since thou know'st better,
Whose I am, by whom begotten';
'Hell's thy birthplace, and the Devil
Both thy father and thy mother.'

'Be it so; to me the same 'tis
Whether I'm God's son or grandson,
And to thee not great the difference
Once thy flesh between my tongs is.'

'Spare me, spare me, Pain'; I shrieked out,
As the red-hot pincers caught me;
'Thou art God's son; aye thou'rt God's self;
Only take thy fingers off me.'

James Henry, 'Pain', 1854

Dread Mother of Forgetfulness
   Who, when Thy reign begins,
Wipest away the Soul's distress,
   And memory of her sins.

The trusty Worm that dieth not —
   The steadfast Fire also,
By Thy contrivance are forgot
   In a completer woe.

Thine are the lidless eyes of night
   That stare upon our tears,
Through certain hours which in our sight
   Exceed a thousand years.

Thine is the thickness of the Dark
   That presses in our pain,
As Thine the Dawn that bids us mark
   Life's grinning face again.

Thine is the weariness outworn
   No promise shall relieve,
That says at eve, 'Would God 'twere morn!'
   At morn, 'Would God 'twere eve!'

And when Thy tender mercies cease
   And life unvexed is due,
Instant upon the false release
   The Worm and Fire renew.

Wherefore we praise Thee in the deep,
   And on our beds we pray
For Thy return that Thou may'st keep
   The Pains of Hell at bay!
          Kipling, 'Hymn to Physical Pain', 1932

On the other hand, when my grandmother did not have morphine, her pain became unbearable; she perpetually attempted a certain movement which it was difficult for her to perform without groaning. To a great extent, suffering is a sort of need felt by the organism to make itself familiar with a new state, which makes it uneasy, to adapt its sensibility to that state . . . When my grandmother was in pain the sweat trickled over the pink expanse of her brow, glueing to it her white locks, and if she thought that none of us was in the room she would cry out: 'Oh, it's dreadful!' but if she caught sight of my mother, at once she employed all her energy in banishing from her face every sign of pain, or – an alternative stratagem – repeated the same plaints, accompanying them with explanations which gave a different sense, retrospectively, to those which my mother might have overheard:

'Oh! My dear, it's dreadful to have to stay in bed on a beautiful sunny day like this when one wants to be out in the air; I am crying with rage at your orders.'

But she could not get rid of the look of anguish in her eyes, the sweat on her brow, the convulsive start, checked at once, of her limbs.

'There is nothing wrong. I'm complaining because I'm not lying very comfortably. I feel my hair is untidy, my heart is bad, I knocked myself against the wall.'

Marcel Proust, *Remembrance of Things Past: The Guermantes Way II*,
1921; tr. C. K. Scott Moncrieff

After great pain, a formal feeling comes –
The Nerves sit ceremonious, like Tombs –
The stiff Heart questions was it He, that bore,
And Yesterday, or Centuries before?

The Feet, mechanical, go round –
Of Ground, or Air, or Ought –
A Wooden way
Regardless grown,
A Quartz contentment, like a stone –

This is the Hour of Lead –
Remembered, if outlived,
As Freezing persons, recollect the Snow –
First – Chill – then Stupor – then the letting go –

Emily Dickinson (1830–86),
'After great pain, a formal feeling comes'

Eyes, Ears, and Teeth

Deteriorating sight obliged Pepys to discontinue his secret diary, but he found some slight consolation: as things were, there would be little to record in future that wasn't fit for all to know. Consolations or compensations have always been proposed for poor vision and hardness of hearing. Proverbial wisdom has it that the happiest marriage is between a deaf man and a blind woman, and the gift of sight – 'a queer thing for upsetting a man' – did little for Martin and Mary Doul in Synge's play, *The Well of the Saints*, except destroy their dreams. On the other hand, while claiming there was 'a triple sight in blindness keen', Keats left the details vague; and all Beethoven could recommend to himself in his deafness was patience and resignation.

Comedy of a kind is more likely to occur in the vicinity of the dentist's chair. Teeth can inflict horrible pain, besides mortification, but they can be removed fairly expeditiously, they can be spared, or even replaced. Solyman Brown was an American, a Swedenborgian clergyman, and a practising dentist. If his competence in dentistry equalled his nimbleness as a versifier then George Eliot and Henry James could have benefited from his attention. Whether we would be happy with a dentist as well-informed and voluble as Günter Grass's, is a moot point; one implication of this episode is that there was never a concerned and caring person who couldn't be distracted by his own little local toothache.

These days dental treatment is much easier to endure than it was not so long ago. 'Suddenly there was a fearful blow, a violent shaking as if his neck were broken, accompanied by a quick cracking, crackling noise.' That could have happened much later than 1875, when the dentist's name was Brecht, the crown broke off, and the root had to be pulled out separately. But that Mann's Senator Thomas Buddenbrook should die in the street after a

bungled extraction was more a moral and social portent than a
medical phenomenon. 'Goodness, people don't die of a bad tooth!'

Light, the prime work of God, to me is extinct,
And all her various objects of delight
Annulled, which might in part my grief have eased,
Inferior to the vilest now become
Of man or worm; the vilest here excel me,
They creep, yet see; I, dark in light exposed
To daily fraud, contempt, abuse and wrong,
Within doors, or without, still as a fool,
In power of others, never in my own;
Scarce half I seem to live, dead more than half.
O dark, dark, dark, amid the blaze of noon,
Irrecoverably dark, total eclipse
Without all hope of day!
O first-created beam, and thou great Word,
'Let there be light, and light was over all':
Why am I thus bereaved thy prime decree?
The sun to me is dark
And silent as the moon,
When she deserts the night,
Hid in her vacant interlunar cave.
Since light so necessary is to life,
And almost life itself, if it be true
That light is in the soul,
She all in every part, why was the sight
To such a tender ball as th'eye confined?
So obvious and so easy to be quenched,
And not, as feeling, through all parts diffused,
That she might look at will through every pore?

Milton, *Samson Agonistes*, 1671

13 December 1666. In mighty great pain in back still. But I perceive
it changes its place – and doth not trouble me at all in making of

water; and that is my joy, so that I believe it is nothing but a strain. And for these three or four days I perceive my overworking of my eyes by candlelight doth hurt them, as it did the last winter. That by day I am well and do get them right – but then after candlelight they begin to sore and run – so that I entend to get some green spectacles.

24 *December*. I do truly find that I have overwrought my eyes, so that now they are become weak and apt to be tired, and all excess of light makes them sore, so that now, to the candlelight I am forced to sit by, adding the snow upon the ground all day, my eyes are very bad, and will be worse if not helped; so my Lord Brouncker doth advise me, as a certain cure, to use Greene Spectacles, which I will do.

31 *July 1668*. The month ends mighty sadly with me, my eyes being now past all use almost; and I am mighty hot upon trying the late printed experiment of paper Tubes.

16 *February 1669*. And so to the office, where busy all the afternoon, though my eyes mighty bad with the light of the candles last night; which was so great as to make my eyes sore all this day, and doth teach me, by a manifest experiment, that it is only too much light that doth make my eyes sore. Nevertheless, with the help of my Tube, and being desirous of easing my mind of five or six days Journall, I did adventure to write it down from ever since this day sennit, and I think without hurting my eyes any more than they were before; which was very much. And so home to supper and to bed.

31 *May 1669*. And thus ends all that I doubt I shall ever be able to do with my own eyes in the keeping of my journall, I being not able to do it any longer, having done now so long as to undo my eyes almost every time that I take a pen in my hand; and therefore, whatever comes of it, I must forbear; and therefore resolve from this time forward to have it kept by my people in longhand, and must therefore be contented to set down no more than is fit for them and all the world to know; or if there be anything (which cannot be much, now my amours to Deb are past, and my eyes hindering me in almost all other pleasures), I must endeavour to keep a margin in my

book open, to add here and there a note in shorthand with my own hand. And so I betake myself that course which is almost as much as to see myself go into my grave – for which, and all the discomforts that will accompany my being blind, the good God prepare me.

Pepys, Diary

Mar. 11, 1791. The Stiony on my right Eye-lid still swelled and inflamed very much. As it is commonly said that the Eye-lid being rubbed by the tail of a black Cat would do it much good if not entirely cure it, and having a black Cat, a little before dinner I made a trial of it, and very soon after dinner I found my Eye-lid much abated of the swelling and almost free from Pain. I cannot therefore but conclude it to be of the greatest service to a Stiony on the Eye-lid. Any other Cats Tail may have had the above effect in all probability – but I did my Eye-lid with my own black Tom Cat's Tail.

Mar. 15. My right Eye again, that is, its Eye-lid much inflamed again and rather painful. I put a plaistor to it this morning, but in the Aft. took it of again, as I perceived no good from it.

Mar. 16. My Eye-lid is I think rather better than it was, I bathed it with warm milk and Water last night. I took a little Rhubarb going to bed to night. My Eye-lid about Noon rather worse owing perhaps to the warm Milk and Water, therefore just before Dinner I washed it well with cold Water and in the Evening appeared much better for it.

Woodforde, The Diary of a Country Parson

On the 29th and 30th of June, 1899, I took my examinations for Radcliffe College. The first day I had elementary Greek and advanced Latin, and the second day Geometry, Algebra and advanced Greek.

The college authorities would not permit Miss Sullivan to read the examination papers to me; so Mr Eugene C. Vining, one of the instructors at the Perkins Institution for the Blind, was employed to copy the papers for me in braille. Mr Vining was a perfect stranger to me, and could not communicate with me except by writing in braille. The Proctor also was a stranger, and did not attempt to communicate with me in any way; and, as they were both unfamiliar with my speech, they could not readily understand what I said to them.

However, the braille worked well enough in the languages; but when it came to Geometry and Algebra, it was different. I was sorely perplexed, and felt quite discouraged, and wasted much precious time, especially in Algebra. It is true that I am perfectly familiar with all literary braille – English, American, and New York Point; but the method of writing the various signs used in Geometry and Algebra in the three systems is very different, and two days before the examinations I knew only the English method. I had used it all through my school work, and never any other system.

In Geometry, my chief difficulty was, that I had always been accustomed to reading the propositions in Line Print, or having them spelled into my hand; and somehow, although the propositions were right before me, yet the braille confused me, and I could not fix in my mind clearly what I was reading. But, when I took up Algebra, I had a harder time still – I was terribly handicapped by my imperfect knowledge of the notation. The signs, which I had learned the day before, and which I thought I knew perfectly, confused me. Consequently my work was painfully slow, and I was obliged to read the examples over and over before I could form a clear idea what I was required to do. Indeed, I am not sure now that I read all the signs correctly, especially as I was much distressed, and found it very hard to keep my wits about me.

> Helen Keller, 'How I passed my Entrance Examinations for
> Radcliffe College', letter to John Hitz, Volta Bureau for the Increase
> and Diffusion of Knowledge relating to the Deaf, 11 November 1899

O my fellow men, who consider me, or describe me as, unfriendly, peevish or even misanthropic, how greatly do you wrong me. For you do not know the secret reason why I appear to you to be so. Ever since my childhood my heart and soul have been imbued with the tender feeling of goodwill; and I have always been ready to perform even great actions. But just think, for the last six years I have been afflicted with an incurable complaint which has been made worse by incompetent doctors. From year to year my hopes of being cured have gradually been shattered and finally I have been forced to accept the prospect of a *permanent infirmity* (the curing of which may perhaps take years or may even prove to be impossible). Though endowed with a passionate and lively temperament and even fond of the distractions offered by society I was soon obliged to seclude myself and live in solitude. If at times I decided just to ignore my infirmity, alas! how cruelly was I then driven back by the intensified sad experience of my poor hearing. Yet I could not bring myself to say to people: 'Speak up, shout, for I am deaf.' Alas! how could I possibly refer to the impairing *of a sense* which in me should be more perfectly developed than in other people, a sense which at one time I possessed in the greatest perfection, even to a degree of perfection such as assuredly few in my profession possess or have ever possessed – Oh, I cannot do it; so forgive me, if you ever see me withdrawing from your company which I used to enjoy. Moreover my misfortune pains me doubly, inasmuch as it leads to my being misjudged. For me there can be no relaxation in human society, no refined conversations, no mutual confidences. I must live quite alone and may creep into society only as often as sheer necessity demands; I must live like an outcast. If I appear in company I am overcome by a burning anxiety, a fear that I am running the risk of letting people notice my condition . . . how humiliated I have felt if somebody standing beside me heard the sound of a flute in the distance and *I heard nothing*, or if somebody heard *a shepherd sing* and again I heard nothing – Such experiences almost made me despair, and I was on the point of putting an end to my life – The only thing that held me back was *my art*. For indeed it seemed to me impossible to leave this world before I had produced all the works that I felt the urge to compose; and thus I have dragged on this miserable existence – a truly miserable existence, seeing that I have such a sensitive body that any fairly sudden change can plunge me from the best spirits into the worst of humours – *Patience* – that is the virtue, I am told, which I must now choose for my guide; and I now possess it – I hope that I shall persist in my resolve to endure to the end, until it pleases the inexorable Parcae to cut the thread; perhaps my condition will improve, perhaps not; at any rate I am now resigned – At the early age of twenty-eight I was obliged to become a

philosopher, though this was not easy; for indeed this is more
difficult for an artist than for anyone else – Almighty God, who look
down into my innermost soul, you see into my heart and you know
that it is filled with love for humanity and a desire to do good.
  Ludwig van Beethoven, from 'The Heiligenstadt Testament', addressed
    to his brothers Carl and Johann, 6 October 1802; tr. Emily Anderson

The specialist said: 'Let's leave it at that, couldn't be better.
The treatment's completed: you're deaf. The fact of the matter
Is you've completely lost the faculty.'
And not having heard, he understood perfectly.

– 'Well, thank you sir, for having condescended
        To make a fine coffin of my head.
From now on, I'll be able to understand everything
        On trust, with legitimate vaunting . . .

Like window-shopping – But beware the jealous eye, in the place
Of the nailed-up ear! . . . – No – Why bother to defy?
. . . If in the face of ridicule I've whistled too high,
Below the belt it will sling mud in my face! . . .

I'm a dumb puppet, on a trite string! –
Tomorrow, a friend could take my hand, along the avenue,
Calling me: a bloody post . . . , or more kindly, nothing;
And I would answer 'Not bad, thanks, and you!'

If someone trumpets me a word, I go mad to understand;
If another is silent: would that be through pity? . . .
Always, like a rebus, I work to land
One word askew . . . – No. – So they've forgotten me!

– Or – the reverse of the coin – some officious being
Whose blubber lip makes the motion of grazing,
Believes he's conversing . . . While in torment
I put on an imbecile smile – with an air of discernment!

– Over my soul a dunce's cap in wool a shade of donkey!
And – for an ass – the hardest knock . . . Gee-up! – That good lady,
The vinegary Lemonade-seller, Passion-trader in addition!
Can come and drool her blessed compassion
Into my *Eustachian tube*, in full hue and cry,
While I'm unable even to tread on her corn, as an outcry!

– Foolish as a virgin and stand-offish as a leper,
I am there, but absent . . . They say: Is that a doddering
Old idiot, a muzzled poet, some crab in a temper? . . . –
A shrug of the shoulders: 'deaf' is the meaning.

– An acoustic Tantalus' hysterical suffering!
I can't apprehend the words I see flying;
Impotent fly-catcher, eaten by a mosquito,
A free butt where everyone can have a go.

O celestial music: to hear, on plaster,
A shell scrape! a razor,
A knife grinding in a cork! . . . a stage couplet!
A living bone being sawn! a gentleman! a sonnet! . . .

– Nothing – I babble to myself . . . Words that I toss into the air
Off the cuff, and not knowing if it's in Hindi I declare . . .
Or perhaps in goose language, like a clarinet sounded
By a blind man muddling the stops, with perceptions muted.

– Go then, pendulum, distracted in my head, boozed!
Beat with a swing this fine tom-tom, a tinny piano so flat
It makes the female voice like a cuckoo's!
Like a door bell . . . sometimes: a circling gnat . . .

– Go to bed, heart! and stop flapping your wings.
In the dark lantern let's snuff out the candle,
And, I no longer know where – all that used to be vibrating
There – dungeon where someone has just turned the handle.

– Meditative Idol, for me be dumb,
Both, the one through the other, forgetting phraseology,

You won't say a word: I'll keep mum . . .
And then nothing will be able to tarnish our colloquy.
    Tristan Corbière, 'Deaf Man's Rhapsody', 1873; tr. Val Warner

When I waked up, just at daybreak, he was setting there with his
head down betwixt his knees, moaning and mourning to himself. I
didn't take notice, nor let on. I knowed what it was about. He was
thinking about his wife and his children, away up yonder, and he
was low and homesick; because he hadn't ever been away from
home in his life; and I do believe he cared just as much for his people
as white folks does for their'n . . .

But this time I somehow got to talking to him about his wife and
young ones; and by and by he says:

'What makes me feel so bad dis time, 'uz bekase I hear sumpn over
yonder on de bank like a whack, er a slam, while ago, en it mine me
er de time I treat my little 'Lizabeth so ornery. She warn't on'y 'bout
fo' year ole, en she tuck de sk'yarlet-fever, en had a powful rough
spell; but she got well, en one day she was a-stannin' aroun, en I says
to her, I says:

"Shet de do'."

She never done it; jis' stood dah, kiner smilin' up at me. It make
me mad; en I says agin, mighty loud, I says:

"Doan' you hear me? – shet de do'!"

She jis' stood de same way, kiner smilin' up. I was a-bilin'! I says:

"I lay I *make* you mine!"

En wid dat I fetch' her a slap side de head dat sont her a-spralin'.
Den I went into de yuther room, en 'uz gone 'bout ten minutes; en
when I come back, dah was dat do' a-stannin' open *yit*, en dat chile
stannin' mos' right in it, a-lookin' down and mournin', en de tears
runnin' down. My, but I *wuz* mad. I was a-gwyne for de chile, but
jis' den – it was a do' dat open innerds – jis' den, 'long come de wind
en slam it to, behine de chile, ker-*blam*! – en my lan', de chile never
move'! My breff mos' hop outer me; en I feel so – so – I doan' know
how I feel. I crope out, all a-tremblin', en crope aroun' en open de
do' easy en slow, en poke my head in behine de chile, sof' en still, en
all uv a sudden, I says *pow*! jis' as loud as I could yell. *She never
budge*! Oh, Huck, I bust out a-cryin' en grab her up in my arms, en
say, "Oh, de po' little thing! de Lord God Amighty fogive po' ole

Jim, kaze he never gwyne to fogive hisself as long's he live!" Oh, she
was plumb deef en dumb, Huck, plumb deef en dumb – en I'd ben a-
treat'n her so!'

Mark Twain, *The Adventures of Huckleberry Finn*, 1884

Having peculiar reverence for this creature
Of the numinous imagination, I am come
To visit her church and stand before the altar
Where her image, hewn in pathetic stone,
Exhibits the handiwork of her executioner.

There are the axemarks. Outside, in the courtyard,
In shabby habit, an Italian nun
Came up and spoke: I had to answer, 'Sordo'.
She said she was a teacher of deaf children
And had experience of my disorder.

And I have had experience of her order,
Interpenetrating chords and marshalled sound;
Often I loved to listen to the organ's
Harmonious and concordant interpretation
Of what is due from us to the creation.

But it was taken from me in my childhood
And those graduated pipes turned into stone.
Now, having travelled a long way through silence,
Within the church in Trastevere I stand
A pilgrim to the patron saint of music.

And am abashed by the presence of this nun
Beside the embodiment of that legendary
Virgin whose music and whose martyrdom
Is special to this place: by her reality.
She is a reminder of practical kindness,

The care it takes to draw speech from the dumb
Or pierce with sense the carapace of deafness;
And so, of the plain humility of the ethos

That constructed, also, this elaborate room
To pray for bread in; they are not contradictory.
David Wright, 'By the Effigy of St Cecilia', 1965

At the very end of the war, Dad was called before the Blackford
County Selective Service Board. Most of the men had known the
Walker family all their lives, but the board was desperate for
recruits. At one point Dad was writing a note to an officer when
someone behind him slapped a hand down on the table. My father
started and whirled around. Like most deaf people, Dad is sensitive
to vibrations, not because his ability to feel them is heightened but
because he pays more attention to the sensations he receives. Also,
although he describes himself as 'stone deaf', there is virtually no
one who has an absolutely flat audiogram. Somewhere there is some
tiny perception of something akin to noise in everyone. For Dad, it
happens to be a very loud bang, just like the one on the draft board's
table. When another officer banged, Dad jumped again. The board
required medical reports no matter how well its members knew the
young man, but because their suspicions were aroused about the
severity of Dad's deafness, they forced him to see several doctors.
Finally – according to family legend – it was not deafness but his
very flat feet that kept him from being drafted.

Every day after I left for school, Mom would lock the doors around
the house – a wise procedure since she wouldn't hear if an intruder
entered – and every day just before I came home from grade school
at 3 pm, she'd unlock the front door. Actually, I wasn't even aware
that this was her habit until the one and only time she forgot. That
day I'd gotten off the bus at the corner and run home because I was
desperate to go to the bathroom. The door was locked when I
arrived. Standing on tiptoe on the front porch and leaning way over
toward the window, I could see Mom's back as she mixed a cake in
the kitchen. She was intent on the cookbook and the cake. I banged
on the door, on the window, I waved my arms wildly, hoping to
make a shadow. She didn't look up. I ran around to the backyard.
The dog was barking like crazy as I hammered on the doors, looking
for a window that might be open, but it was winter and everything
was shut tight. I kept running around the house, trying to get in.

After what seemed like an eternity, Mom glanced at the clock, started, and ran to the door to open it. I rushed past her. Immediately she knew what the matter was. She came running behind to help. It was too late. I was wearing French-blue tights, my very first pair. Standing outside in the cold, pounding on the door, I was angry at Mom for having forgotten me, furious that I could see her but couldn't get her attention. I was ready to complain bitterly. Then I looked up at her woebegone face. I saw that she felt worse than I did.

I began losing my own hearing when I was thirteen. I didn't tell a soul about it. I was too terrified.

First my sisters' voices and the television volume became ever so slightly fuzzy. Then I was feeling the vibrations on my violin more than I was hearing the notes. From fuzzy I went to indistinct, from indistinct to thinking a glass bowl was over my head. I was sure the whole thing was a temporary aberration, perhaps psychosomatic, perhaps a hysterical reaction – one aunt was always warning me that reading too much would take its toll. Within a week the problem was affecting my school-work. After a few more days, when it was obvious I was getting worse, not better, I told Mom and Dad. They looked at me strangely. Mom took me to the doctor the next day . . .

Inside his office, Dr Marsh, a vague, dishevelled man, looked in my ears, then got up and left the room. My worst fears were suddenly confirmed. At least I already knew sign language, I comforted myself. But I was already so protective of my sisters and my parents, so charged with the weight of grown-up responsibilities, that I was fretting over just how the family would get along if I went completely deaf.

Dr Marsh came back with a pan full of soapy water and a giant syringe.

'What are you going to do to me?'

'Ear wax,' he grunted.

'What?'

He said it louder. I signed to Mom. She'd been acting as if she weren't all that concerned about my hearing problem, but now she leaned forward, a worried look in her eyes, concentrating heavily on my hands, one eyebrow raised. With the diagnosis, she leaned back, obviously relieved and a little amused.

After a few soapy squirts – it sounded like Niagara Falls inside my head – my hearing was miraculously restored.

'Use Q-Tips with baby oil,' Dr Marsh said.

I'd watched Mom and Dad inserting cotton swabs into their ears, but I'd read so much about puncturing the tympanic membrane that I was scared to put anything in there. It was all right for Mom and Dad, I thought; they didn't have anything to lose. After my bout of deafness, I swabbed regularly.

Lou Ann Walker, *A Loss For Words*, 1987

The country air did not restore me to my former health. I was listless, and growing more so. I could not endure the milk; I had to give it up. Water was the fashionable panacea then; I set about it, and so imprudently that it came near to curing me, not of my ills, but of my life. Every morning, as soon as I was up, I went to the spring with a large goblet and, while strolling about, I drank the equivalent of two bottles of it in succession. I gave up wine with my meals altogether. Like most mountain water, the water I drank was rather hard and difficult to pass. In short, I managed so well that in under two months I completely ruined my stomach, which till then had been excellent. No longer able to digest my food, I realized there was no further hope of a cure. At that same time something happened to me as remarkable in itself as in its consequences, the which will cease only when I do.

One morning when I was no worse than usual, as I was setting a small table on its feet, I felt throughout my whole body a sudden and barely conceivable upheaval. I can only compare it to a kind of storm, arising in my blood and at once seizing on all my limbs. My arteries started to pound with such force that not only did I feel their beating but I even heard it, particularly that of the carotids. A loud noise in the ears joined in, and this noise was triple or quadruple: that is, a deep and muffled buzzing, a clearer murmuring as of running water, a high-pitched whistling, as well as the pounding I have just mentioned, whose beat I could easily count without feeling my pulse or touching my body. This internal noise was so great that it took away the sharpness of ear I used to have, making me not totally deaf but hard of hearing, as I have been ever since.

My surprise can be imagined, and my alarm. I thought I was as good as dead; I took to my bed; the doctor was called; tremblingly, I described my condition, believing it past cure. I think he thought so too; but he obeyed his calling. He strung together long explanations for me, of which I could understand nothing; then, in pursuance of his sublime theory, he commenced *in anima vili* the experimental treatment it pleased him to try. This was so painful, so loathsome, and so useless, that I soon abandoned it; and at the end of several weeks, seeing that I was neither better nor worse, I left my bed and resumed ordinary life, with my pounding arteries and my buzzings, which have not left me for a minute since that time, thirty years ago.

Till then I had been a sound sleeper. The total deprivation of sleep which attended all these symptoms, and which has continued without cease to the present day, finally convinced me that I had little time to live. The conviction suspended for a time my worry over getting cured. Unable to prolong my life, I resolved to make the most of what little remained; and this was rendered possible thanks to a curious favour of nature which, in my baleful state, exempted me from the pains I should have expected. I was troubled by the noise, but did not suffer much from it; the only other inconveniences accompanying it were insomnia at nights and, at all times, a shortness of breath, not amounting to asthma, which I was conscious of only when I wanted to run or exert myself a little.

This misfortune, which ought to have killed my body, merely killed my passions, and I thank heaven every day for the happy effect it has had on my soul. I can truly say that I began to live only when I considered myself a dead man. Setting their true value on the things I was about to leave behind, I began to concern myself with nobler duties, as if anticipating those I should soon have to perform and which I had sadly neglected up till then.

Jean-Jacques Rousseau, The Confessions; of the year 1738

So it's come to this! Not only when you've
Just brought out a book, and not quite
Faintly praising: more like a hissing,

Not especially faint, and minus respite.
   In sweeter terms, it's what you still remember
Fondly: the long continuous chirring
Of cicadas, through the night, in one or other
Long-left place — that tropic velvet,
That fecund heat — making a second, more stirring
Sort of silence. But what enhances darkness
By day grows merely stupid.
   Or you might say, a distant soughing,
A sea whose waves unbrokenly are breaking;
Or some well-mannered but unfaltering wind
Through brittle grass; or gas escaping.
   Or tittle-tattle's buzz: a new biography
In the offing, rending of veils and shrouds?
(For truth is great and shall prevail,
If stiffened with pornography.)
   Or else, at speed, a tape of all the words
That ever were, stripped of all their affect.
Tools of the trade reduced to rusty susurration,
Ancient arid bookstacks calcining unchecked.
   But this is mere imagination
(A presence which itself is hissing, darkly
Whispering in the wings, without remission,
And lucidly, alas) —
And you no better than the class of ass
Who bores his doctor with prodigious symptoms!
   Still, something's cooking. A pullulation
Of micro-organisms, non-readers all the lot,
All ranters? Then it's when the ululation
Ceases that you start to worry. Or you stop.
                    D. J. Enright, 'Writer's Tinnitus', 1986

            Deaf, giddy, helpless, left alone,
            To all my Friends a Burthen grown,
            No more I hear my Church's Bell,
            Than if it rang out for my Knell:
            At Thunder now I no more start,

Than at the Rumblings of a Cart:
Nay, what's incredible, alack!
I hardly hear a Woman's Clack.
    Swift, 'On his own Deafness', 1734

If sloth or negligence the task forbear
Of making cleanliness a daily care;
If fresh ablution, with the morning sun,
Be quite forborne or negligently done;
In dark disguise insidious tartar comes,
Incrusts the teeth and irritates the gums,
Till vile deformity usurps the seat
Where smiles should play and winning graces meet,
And foul disease pollutes the fair domain,
Where health and purity should ever reign.
   Solyman Brown, *Dentologia: A Poem on the Diseases of the*
            Teeth, and their Proper Remedies, 1833

28 December 1787

The cold and dark weather was gloomy, and for two days I had been troubled with one of my foreteeth being half broken off yet the root of the broken part not separated from the gum. It was a mouldering memento of my mortality.

5 January 1788

The half of my foretooth which was loose came out a day or two ago, but it did not affect me so much as I supposed it would have done.

                    James Boswell, *Journals*

My curse upon your venom'd stang,
That shoots my tortur'd gums alang:
And thro' my lugs gies monie a twang,   *ears*
      Wi' gnawing vengeance;
Tearing my nerves wi' bitter pang,
      Like racking engines!

When fevers burn, or ague freezes,
Rheumatics gnaw, or colic squeezes,
Our neighbour's sympathy may ease us,
        Wi' pitying moan;
But thee – thou hell o' a' diseases,
        Ay mocks our groan!

Adown my beard the slavers trickle!
I throw the wee stools o'er the mickle,
As round the fire the giglets keckle   *giggling girls*
        To see me loup;   *leap*
While, raving mad, I wish a heckle   *steel flax-comb*
        Were in their doup.   *backside*

O' a' the numerous human dools,   *sorrows*
Ill har'sts, daft bargains, cutty-stools, *stool of repentance*
Or worthy friends rak'd i' the mools,   *the grave*
        Sad sight to see!
The tricks o' knaves, or fash o' fools,
        Thou bear'st the gree.   *prize*

Where'er that place be priests ca' hell,
Whence a' the tones o' mis'ry yell
And ranked plagues their numbers tell,
        In dreadfu' raw,   *row*
Thou, Toothache, surely bear'st the bell
        Amang them a'!

O thou grim mischief-making chiel,   *fellow*
That gars the notes of discord squeel,   *makes*
Till daft mankind aft dance a reel
        In gore a shoe-thick; –
Gie a' the faes o' Scotland's weal   *foes*
        A towmont's Toothache!   *twelvemonths'*
Burns, 'Address to the Toothache', 1795–6

Wednesday, 15 September 1813

Going to Mr Spence's was a sad business and cost us many tears; unluckily we were obliged to go a second time before he could do more than just look. We went first at half-past twelve and afterwards at three; papa with us each time; and alas! we are to go again tomorrow. Lizzy is not finished yet. There have been no teeth taken out, however, nor will be, I believe, but he finds *hers* in a very bad state, and seems to think particularly ill of their durableness. They have all been cleaned, *hers* filed, and are to be filed again. There is a very sad hole between two of her front teeth.

Thursday – after dinner

The poor Girls & their Teeth! – I have not mentioned them yet, but we were a whole hour at Spence's, & Lizzy's were filed & lamented over again & poor Marianne had two taken out after all, the two just beyond the Eye teeth, to make room for those in front. – When her doom was fixed, Fanny, Lizzy & I walked into the next room, where we heard each of the two sharp hasty Screams. – Fanny's teeth were cleaned too – & pretty as they are, Spence found something to do to them, putting in gold and talking gravely – & making a considerable point of seeing her again before winter; – he had before urged the expediency of L. and M.s being brought to Town in the course of a couple of Months to be further examined, & continued to the last to press for their all coming to him. – My B^r would not absolutely promise. – The little girls' teeth I can suppose in a critical state, but I think he must be a Lover of Teeth & Money & Mischeif to parade about Fanny's. – I would not have had him look at mine for a shilling a tooth & double it. – It was a disagreable hour.

Jane Austen, letters to Cassandra Austen

17 June 1853

Mr Barclay put an end to my pain in ten minutes by stopping my hollow tooth, and moreover consoled me by telling me that I need feel no anxiety about the state of my teeth in general. So I am radiant with benevolence, as it is so easy to be when one is perfectly comfortable.

25 June 1853

When I was reading your congratulations that my teeth were 'settled' I was racked with pain, and the next day I had the tooth which *Mr Barclay had stopped* taken out by another dentist – a man with 'bowels' who will risk giving chloroform. I was quite unconscious during the extraction and only began to protest that I would not submit to the operation when the tooth was lying on the table before me.

George Eliot, letters to Caroline Bray and Sara Hennell

I had a tooth out the other day, curious and interesting like a little lifetime – first, the long drawn drag, then the twist of the hand and the crack of doom! The dentist seized my face in his two hands and exclaimed, 'Bravo, Miss James!' and Katharine and Nurse shaking of knee and pale of cheek went on about my 'heroism' whilst I, serenely wadded in that sensational paralysis which attends all the simple, rudimentary sensations and experiences common to man, whether tearing of the flesh or of the affections, laughed and laughed at 'em. As long as one doesn't break in two in the middle, I never have been able to see where the 'heroism' comes in. Harry [Henry James] had a most eccentric accident in Florence. The evening he arrived he was seized after dinner with a very severe pain in his throat; having had a bad toothache he supposed it had to do with that. The next day he spent with the dentist, and went in the afternoon from the hotel to stay with Dr Baldwin, his throat becoming more and more sore so that he immediately said to the Doctor, 'You must look at my throat' – 'Why, you have got something sticking in it and it's green!' He tugged and tugged and brought out a long haricot vert which had wound itself about the root of his tongue, which was already beginning to ulcerate. Think of the dentist, gazing into his mouth all the morning, not having seen a green object.

The Diary of Alice James, 15 September 1890

In May 1988 the papers reported the case of a dentist who was struck off the register for wreaking havoc on people's teeth because he couldn't see what he was doing, and for misappropriating thousands of pounds by carrying out unnecessary treatment. Mrs —, a secretary, stated that she had been given ten fillings during one session. Mr — told the disciplinary hearing that on occasion he had treated patients while wearing the wrong glasses and his vision had been blurred and distorted. The General Dental Council found him guilty of serious professional misconduct and fined him £18,300.

Press reports

While I copiously rinsed, he entertained me with anecdotes. He told me about a certain Scribonius Largus who invented a tooth powder for Messalina, first wife to the Emperor Claudius: burned hartshorn plus Chiot resin and sal ammoniac. When he admitted that Pliny already mentions a popular good fortune powder made of crushed milk-teeth, my mother's words once again knocked in my ear: 'Here, my boy, I'm putting them in green cotton. One day they'll bring you good fortune . . .'

My dentist attributed my bearable but persistent toothache to bone and gum recession which exposed the sensitive necks of my teeth. When another anecdote failed to go over with me – 'Pliny's recommendation for toothache: sprinkle the ashes of a mad dog's skull in your ear' – he pointed his scraper over his shoulder: 'Perhaps we ought to turn on . . .' – But I insisted on the pain: A cry. A lament that is never adjourned. ('Forgive me if my mind seems to be wandering.')

My student rode his bicycle through the picture. 'You and your toothache. But what's going on in the Mekong Delta? Have you read?'

'Yes, Scherbaum, I've read. Bad. Very very bad. But I must admit that this ache, this draught that always hits the same nerve, this pain, which isn't even so bad, but which I can localize and which never stirs from the spot, affects me, shakes me and lays me bare more than the photographed pain of this world, which for all its enormity is abstract because it doesn't hit my nerve.'

'Doesn't it make you angry or at least sad?'

'I often try to be sad.'

'Doesn't it make you indignant, the injustice of it?'

'I do my best to be indignant.'

Scherbaum dissolved. (He lodged his bicycle in the bicycle shed.)
My dentist was there in normal listening volume: 'If it hurts, make a
sign please.'

'It hurts all right. It aches here in front.'

'That's the tartar on your exposed necks.'

'Christ, it hurts.'

'We'll take some Arantil later.'

'May I rinse, Doc, just a little rinse?'

What was it he said? 'Enemy Number One is tartar. While we walk,
hesitate, yawn, tie our tie, digest and pray, our saliva never ceases to
produce it. It forms a deposit that ensnares the tongue. Always
looking for incrustations, the tongue is drawn to rough surfaces and
provides nourishment that reinforces our enemy, tartar. It chokes
our tooth necks with its crust. It is consumed with blind hatred for
enamel. Because you can't fool me. One look is enough: Your tartar
is your calcified hate. Not only the microflora in your oral cavity, but
also your muddled thoughts, your obstinate squinting backwards,
the way you regress when you mean to progress, in other words, the
tendency of your diseased gums to form germ-catching pockets, all
that – the sum of dental picture and psyche – betrays you: stored-up
violence, murderous designs. – Rinse, rinse, don't mind me! There
will still be plenty of tartar . . .'

I deny all that. As a teacher of German and history, I have a deep-
seated horror of violence.

Günter Grass, *Local Anaesthetic*, 1969; tr. Ralph Manheim

Venerable Mother Toothache
Climb down from the white battlements,
Stop twisting in your yellow fingers
The fourfold rope of nerves;
And tomorrow I will give you a tot of whisky
To hold in your cupped hands,
A garland of anise-flowers,
And three cloves like nails.

And tell the attendant gnomes
It is time to knock off now,
To shoulder their little pickaxes,
Their cold-chisels and drills.
And you may mount by a silver ladder
Into the sky, to grind
In the cracked polished mortar
Of the hollow moon.

By the lapse of warm waters,
And the poppies nodding like red coals,
The paths on the granite mountains,
And the plantation of my dreams.

John Heath-Stubbs, 'A Charm Against the Toothache', 1954

Doctors and Cures

Cur'd yesterday of my Disease,
I died last night of my Physician,

wrote Matthew Prior in 1714. Power can corrupt, and so can ignorance, and no doubt some of the abuse heaped on the medical profession over the ages has been justified. But in large part the hostility or mockery expressed behind the backs of doctors is intimately linked with the fear, docility, and even abjectness displayed in front of them. John Brown touches lightly on the situation in speaking of 'the bitter-sweet joking' to which we resort in the face of those with whom (as he euphemistically puts it) we have close dealings. However, John Brown was himself a doctor, in Edinburgh.

Bacon remarks temperately that there is a wisdom beyond 'the Rules of Physicke': a man's own observation of what does him good and what harms him. The thought is echoed by Proust: inherent in the body is an instinct for what is beneficial to it, just as in the heart there is an instinct for what is our moral duty, and no authorization by doctors of medicine or of divinity can replace those instincts. 'We know that cold baths are bad for us, we like them, we can always find a doctor to recommend them.'

In this respect (or lack of it) psychiatrists or 'soul-doctors' have ousted physicians of late; but it still comes as a surprise in the annals of literature, where practitioners feature variously as bogymen, quacks, and figures of fun, to encounter lines like those of Johnson on his friend Robert Levet, whom Boswell described condescendingly as 'an obscure practiser in physick among the lower people', as it might be a GP working in the National Health Service:

When fainting nature call'd for aid,
    And hov'ring death prepar'd the blow,
His vig'rous remedy display'd
    The power of art without the show.

In La Bruyère, to whom the last word is given here, the god
Aesculapius, representing the medical profession (though presumably not obliged to earn a living from it), turns the tables on one class
of patients. But that doctors are only human, and so are their cures,
is best conveyed by the dignified sentence with which Hippocrates
begins his *Aphorisms*: 'Life is short, the Art is long, opportunity is
fleeting, experiment deceptive, and judgement difficult.'

══════

With us ther was a DOCTOUR OF PHISYK,
In al this world ne was ther noon him lyk
To speke of phisik and of surgerye;
For he was grounded in astronomye.
He kepte his pacient a ful greet del
In houres, by his magik naturel.
Wel coude he fortunen the ascendent
Of his images for his pacient.
He knew the cause of everich maladye,
Were it of hoot or cold, or moiste, or drye,
And where engendred, and of what humour;
He was a verrey parfit practisour.
The cause y-knowe, and of his harm the rote,
Anon he yaf the seke man his bote.
Ful redy hadde he his apothecaries,
To sende him drogges and his letuaries,
For ech of hem made other for to winne;
Hir frendschipe nas nat newe to biginne.
Wel knew he th'olde Esculapius,
And Deiscorides, and eek Rufus,
Old Ypocras, Haly, and Galien;
Serapion, Razis, and Avicen;
Averrois, Damascien, and Constantyn;
Bernard, and Gatesden, and Gilbertyn.
Of his diete mesurable was he,
For it was of no superfluitee,
But of greet norissing and digestible.
His studie was but litel on the bible.

> In sangwin and in pers he clad was al,
> Lyned with taffata and with sendal;
> And yet he was but esy of dispence;
> He kepte that he wan in pestilence.
> For gold in phisik is a cordial,
> Therfore he lovede gold in special.
>
> Geoffrey Chaucer, 'Prologue', *The Canterbury Tales*,
> c.1387 onwards

Aesop, an author of exceeding rare excellence, and whose graces few discover, is very pleasant in representing this kind of tyrannical authority unto us, which they [physicians] usurp upon poor souls, weakened by sickness, and overwhelmed through fear. For he reporteth how a sick man, being demanded by his Physician what operation he felt by the Physic he had given him, 'I have sweat much,' answered he. 'That is good,' replied the Physician. Another time he asked him again how he had done since. 'I have had a great cold and quivered much,' said he. 'That is very well,' quoth the Physician again. The third time he demanded of him how he felt himself, he answered, 'I swell and puff up as it were with the dropsy.' 'That's not amiss,' said the Physician. A familiar friend of his coming afterward to visit him, and to know how he did, 'Verily,' said he, 'my friend, I die with being too well.'

> Montaigne, 'Of the resemblance between children and fathers'

Géronte. There's just one thing that puzzles me, and that is the location of the liver and of the heart. It seems to me that you place them otherwise than where they are – the heart is on the left side, and the liver on the right.
Sganarelle. Yes, that was formerly the case. But we have changed all that, and now we practise medicine according to an entirely new method.

Sganarelle. We must find out what is wrong with her.
Thibaut. She's bad with hypocrisy, sir.
Sganarelle. With hypocrisy?

Thibaut.   Aye, that's to say she's all swelled up, and they say there's lots of seriosities in her insides, and that her liver, her belly, or her spleen, as you'd call it, instead of making blood, makes nowt but water. Every other day she has the quotigian fever, with lassitudes and pains in the muzzles of the legs. You can hear phlegms in her throat what are all set to choke her, and now' n' then she's taken with syncoles and conversions, so as I reckon as 'ow she's going. In our village there's a pothecary, saving yer reverence, 'e's given her no end of stuff, and it's cost me more'n dozen good crowns in enemies, beggin' yer pardon, in apostumes what he's made her swaller, and infections of hyacinth, and cordial portions. But all this, as folks say, is nowt but a load of eyewash. He wanted to give her some sort of physic called antimoony wine, but I was afeard it 'ud send her to join her fathers. They do say as 'ow them big doctors kill off I don't know 'ow many poor souls with that there concoction.

Molière, Le Médecin Malgré Lui, 1666

There PHYSIC fills the space, and far around,
Pile above pile her learned works abound:
Glorious their aim – to ease the labouring heart;
To war with death, and stop his flying dart;
To trace the source whence the fierce contest grew,
And life's short lease on easier terms renew;
To calm the frenzy of the burning brain;
To heal the tortures of imploring pain;
Or, when more powerful ills all efforts brave,
To ease the victim no device can save,
And smooth the stormy passage to the grave.
   But man, who knows no good unmixed and pure,
Oft finds a poison where he sought a cure;
For grave deceivers lodge their labours here,
And cloud the science they pretend to clear . . .
   What thought so wild, what airy dream so light,
That will not prompt a theorist to write?
What art so prevalent, what proofs so strong,
That will convince him his attempt is wrong?
One in the solids finds each lurking ill,

Nor grants the passive fluids power to kill;
A learned friend some subtler reason brings,
Absolves the channels, but condemns their springs;
The subtile nerves, that shun the doctor's eye,
Escape no more his subtler theory . . .
Some have their favourite ills, and each disease
Is but a younger branch that kills from these;
One to the gout contracts all human pain;
He views it raging in the frantic brain,
Finds it in fevers all his efforts mar,
And sees it lurking in the cold catarrh;
Bilious by some, by others nervous seen,
Rage the fantastic demons of the spleen;
And every symptom of the strange disease
With every system of the sage agrees.

> George Crabbe, *The Library*, 1781

Your short neck is rather an Argumt. for a Vomit now and then than
against it for no long-necked Animal can vomit, & Vomits are the
best Preservative from Apoplexies after little Phlebotomies.

> Dr George Cheyne, letter to Samuel Richardson, 1739

I read once of a man who was cured of a dangerous illness by eating
his doctor's prescription which he understood was the medicine
itself. So William Sefton Moorhouse [in New Zealand] imagined he
was being converted to Christianity by reading Burton's *Anatomy of
Melancholy*, which he had got by mistake for Butler's *Analogy* [*of
Religion*], on the recommendation of a friend. But it puzzled him a
good deal.

> Samuel Butler (1835–1902), *Notebooks*

I stayed three months with the Licentiate Sédillo, without complaining of bad nights. At the end of that time he fell sick. The distemper
was a fever; and it inflamed the gout. For the first time in his life,
which had been long, he called in a physician. Doctor Sangrado was

sent for; the Hippocrates of Valladolid. Dame Jacintha was for
sending for the lawyer first, and touched that string; but the patient
thought it was time enough, and had a little will of his own upon
some points. Away I went therefore for Doctor Sangrado; and
brought him with me. A tall, withered, wan executioner of the sisters
three, who had done all their justice for at least these forty years!
This learned forerunner of the undertaker had an aspect suited to his
office: his words were weighed to a scruple; and his jargon sounded
grand in the ears of the uninitiated. His arguments were mathemati-
cal demonstrations: and his opinions had the merit of originality.

After studying my master's symptoms, he began with medical
solemnity. The question here is, to remedy an obstructed perspiration. Ordinary practitioners, in this case, would follow the old
routine of salines, diuretics, volatile salts, sulphur and mercury; but
purges and sudorifics are a deadly practice! Chemical preparations
are edged tools in the hands of the ignorant. My methods are more
simple, and more efficacious. What is your usual diet? I live pretty
much upon soups, replied the canon, and eat my meat with a good
deal of gravy. Soups and gravy! exclaimed the petrified doctor. Upon
my word, it is no wonder you are ill. High living is a poisoned bait; a
trap set by sensuality, to cut short the days of wretched man. We
must have done with pampering our appetites: the more insipid, the
more wholesome. The human blood is not a gravy! Why then, you
must give it such a nourishment, as will assimilate with the particles
of which it is composed. You drink wine, I warrant you? Yes, said
the licentiate, but diluted. Oh! finely diluted, I dare say, rejoined the
physician. This is licentiousness with a vengeance! A frightful course
of feeding! Why you ought to have died years ago. How old are you?
I am in my sixty-ninth year, replied the canon. So I thought, quoth
the practitioner, a premature old age is always the consequence of
intemperance. If you had only drank clear water all your life, and
had been contented with plain food, boiled apples for instance, you
would not have been a martyr to the gout, and your limbs would
have performed their functions with lubricity. But I do not despair of
setting you on your legs again, provided you give yourself up to my
management. The licentiate promised to be upon his good behaviour.

Sangrado then sent me for a surgeon of his own choosing, and took from him six good porringers of blood, by way of a beginning, to remedy this obstinate obstruction. He then said to the surgeon; Master Martin Onez, you will take as much more three hours hence, and tomorrow you will repeat the operation. It is a mere vulgar error, that the blood is of any use in the system; the faster you draw it off, the better. A patient has nothing to do but to keep himself quiet; with him, to live is merely not to die; he has no more occasion for blood than a man in a trance; in both cases, life consists exclusively in pulsation and respiration. When the doctor had ordered these frequent and copious bleedings, he added a drench of warm water at very short intervals, maintaining that water in sufficient quantities was the grand secret in the materia medica. He then took his leave, telling Dame Jacintha and me with an air of confidence, that he would answer for the patient's life, if his system was fairly pursued. The housekeeper, though protesting secretly against this new practice, bowed to his superior authority. In fact, we set on the kettles in a hurry; and, as the physician had desired us above all things to give him enough, we began with pouring down two or three pints at as many gulps. An hour after, we beset him again; then, returning to the attack time after time, we fairly poured a deluge into his poor stomach. The surgeon, on the other hand, taking out the blood as we put in the water, we reduced the old canon to death's door, in less than two days.

This venerable ecclesiastic, able to hold it out no longer, as I pledged him in a large glass of his new cordial, said to me in a faint voice – Hold, Gil Blas, do not give me any more, my friend. It is plain death will come when he will come, in spite of water; and, though I have hardly a drop of blood in my veins, I am no better for getting rid of the enemy. The ablest physician in the world can do nothing for us, when our time is expired. Fetch a notary; I will make my will. At these last words, pleasing enough to my fancy, I affected to appear unhappy; and concealing my impatience to be gone: Sir, said I, you are not reduced so low, thank God, but you may yet recover. No, no, interrupted he, my good fellow, it is all over. I feel the gout shifting, and the hand of death is upon me. Make haste, and go where I told you. I saw, sure enough, that he changed every moment: and the case was so urgent, that I ran as fast as I could, leaving him in Dame Jacintha's care, who was more afraid than myself of his dying without a will. I laid hold of the first notary I could find; Sir, said I, the Licentiate Sédillo, my master, is drawing near his end; he wants to settle his affairs; there is not a moment to be lost. The notary was a dapper little fellow, who loved his joke; and enquired who was our physician. At the name of Doctor Sangrado, hurrying on his cloak and hat: For mercy's sake! cried he, let us set off with all possible speed; for this doctor dispatches business so fast, that our fraternity cannot keep pace with him. That fellow spoils half my jobs.

Lesage, *Gil Blas*, 1715–35; tr. Tobias Smollett

The captain of the Thunder *has ordered the sick list to be brought to the quarterdeck, for the patients to be reviewed*

This inhuman order shocked us extremely, as we knew it would be impossible to carry some of them on the deck, without imminent danger of their lives; but, as we likewise knew it would be to no purpose for us to remonstrate against it, we repaired to the quarterdeck in a body, to see this extraordinary muster . . . When we appeared upon deck, the captain bade the doctor, who stood bowing at his right hand, look at these lazy lubberly sons of bitches, who were good for nothing on board but to eat the king's provision, and encourage idleness in the skulkers. The surgeon grinned approbation, and taking the list, began to examine the complaints of each, as they could crawl to the place appointed. The first who came under his cognizance was a poor fellow just freed of a fever, which had weakened him so much, that he could hardly stand. Mr Mackshane (for that was the doctor's name) having felt his pulse, protested he was as well as any man in the world; and the captain delivered him over to the boatswain's mate, with orders that he should receive a round dozen at the gangway immediately, for counterfeiting himself sick: but before the discipline could be executed, the man dropped down on the deck, and had well nigh perished under the hands of the executioner. The next patient to be considered, laboured under a quartan ague, and being then in his interval of health, discovered no other symptoms of distemper than a pale meagre countenance, and emaciated body; upon which, he was declared fit for duty, and turned over to the boatswain: but being resolved to disgrace the doctor, died upon the forecastle next day, during his cold fit. The third complained of a pleuritic stitch, and spitting of blood; for which Doctor Mackshane prescribed exercise at the pump, to promote expectoration: but whether this was improper for one in his situation, or that it was used to excess, I know not; for in less than half an hour he was suffocated with a deluge of blood that issued from his lungs. A fourth, with much difficulty, climbed to the quarterdeck, being loaded with a mon-strous ascites or dropsy, that invaded his chest so much, he could scarce fetch his breath; but his disease being interpreted into fat, occasioned by idleness and excess of eating, he was ordered, with a view to promote perspiration, and enlarge his chest, to go aloft immediately: it was in vain for this unwieldy wretch to allege his utter incapacity; the boatswain's driver was commanded to whip him up with a cat-o'-nine-tails: the smart of this application made him exert himself so much, that he actually arrived at the puttock shrouds; but when the enormous weight of his body had nothing else to support it than his weakened arms, either out of spite or necessity, he quitted his hold, and plumped into the sea, where he must have been drowned, had not a sailor, who was in a boat alongside, saved his life, by keeping him afloat till he was hoisted on board by a tackle . . . On the whole, the number of the sick was reduced to less than a dozen; and the authors of this reduction were applauding themselves for the services they had done to their king and country . . .

Tobias Smollett, Roderick Random, 1748

Sir Patrick Cullen. Ah yes. It's very interesting. What is it the old cardinal says in Browning's play? 'I have known four and twenty leaders of revolt.' Well, I've known over thirty men that found out how to cure consumption. Why do people go on dying of it, Colly? Devilment, I suppose. There was my father's old friend George Boddington of Sutton Coldfield. He discovered the open-air cure in eighteen-forty. He was ruined and driven out of his practice for only opening the windows; and now we won't let a consumptive patient have as much as a roof over his head. Oh, it's very *very* interesting to an old man.

Sir Colenso Ridgeon.   You old cynic, you don't believe a bit in my discovery.

Sir Patrick.   No, no: I don't go quite so far as that, Colly. But still, you remember Jane Marsh?

Ridgeon.   Jane Marsh? No . . .

Sir Patrick.   You mean to tell me you don't remember the woman with the tuberculous ulcer on her arm?

Ridgeon.   Oh, your washerwoman's daughter. Was her name Jane Marsh? I forgot.

Sir Patrick.   Perhaps you've forgotten also that you undertook to cure her with Koch's tuberculin.

Ridgeon.   And instead of curing her, it rotted her arm right off. Yes: I remember. Poor Jane! However, she makes a good living out of that arm now by showing it at medical lectures.

Sir Patrick.   Still, that wasn't quite what you intended, was it?

Ridgeon.   I took my chance of it.

Sir Patrick.   Jane did, you mean.

Ridgeon.   Well, it's always the patient who has to take the chance when an experiment is necessary. And we can find out nothing without experiment.

Sir Patrick.   What did you find out from Jane's case?

Ridgeon.   I found out that the inoculation that ought to cure sometimes kills.

George Bernard Shaw, The Doctor's Dilemma, 1906

I haven't done much, in fact only two patients in twenty-five years. And when they come they're usually the difficult ones. Both mine had been virgins in their forties, married twenty years or more.

One had a bloody great fibroid there and she thought it was an immaculate conception or something. I examined her and thought, 'Oh Gawd, she's VI (virgo intacta). Oh Gawd, what do we do now?' 'Well,' I said, 'I think you've got something.' I thought she'd got an ovarian cyst actually, but she'd got a fibroid. Anyway, she had a hysterectomy and nothing there had been used at all!

And the other one, I did try some psychosexual counselling but it

was a total disaster and the husband lit off with someone else so I
thought, 'Well, perhaps I'm not cut out for this.'

A GP on sex counselling; from Jonathan Gathorne-Hardy,
Doctors: The Lives and Works of GPs, 1984

'Whence come disease and healing?' asked the Prophet Moses of
God.

'From me,' was the reply.

'What purpose then do doctors serve?'

'They earn their living and cultivate hope in the heart of the
patient until I either take away his life or give him back his health.'
Thus it was written in Nozhat el Majalis.

Alberto Denti di Pirajno, *A Cure for Serpents: An Italian
Doctor in North Africa*, 1955

As to . . . wise men's pleasantries about doctors and their drugs, we
all know what they mean, and what they are worth; they are the
bitter-sweet joking human nature must have at those with whom it
has close dealings – its priests, its lawyers, its doctors, its wives and
husbands; the very existence of such expressions proves the
opposite; it is one of the luxuries of disrespect . . .

To part pleasantly . . . three good old jokes: – The Visigoths
abandoned an unsuccessful surgeon to the family of his deceased
patient, *'ut quod de eo facere voluerint, habeant potestatem'* [with
permission to do what they wanted with him]. Montaigne, who is
great upon doctors, used to beseech his friends, that if he felt ill they
would let him *get a little stronger* before sending for the doctor!
Louis the Fourteenth, who, of course, was a slave to his physicians,
asked his friend Molière what he did with his doctor. 'Oh, Sire,' said
he, 'when I am ill I send for him. He comes, we have a chat, and
enjoy ourselves. He prescribes. I don't take it – and I am cured!'

John Brown, 'Our Gideon Grays', *Horae Subsecivae*, first series, 1858

I feel not in me those sordid and unchristian desires of my
profession; I do not secretly implore and wish for Plagues, rejoyce at

Famines, revolve Ephemerides and Almanacks in expectation of maligant Aspects, fatal Conjunctions, and Eclipses. I rejoyce not at unwholesome Springs, nor unseasonable Winters: my Prayer goes with the Husbandman's; I desire every thing in its proper season, that neither men nor the times be put out of temper. Let me be sick my self, if sometimes the malady of my patient be not a disease unto me. I desire rather to cure his infirmities than my own necessities. Where I do him no good, methinks it is scarce honest gain; though I confess 'tis but the worthy salary of our well-intended endeavours. I am not only ashamed, but heartily sorry, that, besides death, there are diseases incurable: yet not for my own sake, or that they be beyond my Art, but for the general cause and sake of humanity, whose common cause I apprehend as mine own.

Sir Thomas Browne, Religio Medici, 1642

As for the Passions and Studies of the Minde: Avoid Envie; Anxious Feares; Anger fretting inwards; Subtill and knottie Inquisitions; Joyes and Exhilarations in Excesse; Sadnesse not Communicated. Entertaine Hopes; Mirth rather than Joy; Varietie of Delights rather than Surfet of them; Wonder and Admiration, and therefore Novelties; Studies that fill the Minde with Splendide and Illustrious Objects, as Histories, Fables, and Contemplations of Nature. If you flie Physicke in *Health* altogether, it will be too strange for your Body, when you shall need it. If you make it too familiar, it will worke no Extraordinary Effect, when Sicknesse commeth. I commend, rather, some Diet, for certaine Seasons, than frequent Use of *Physicke*, except it be growen into a Custome. For those Diets alter the Body more, and trouble it lesse. Despise no new Accident in your Body, but aske Opinion of it . . .

Physicians are some of them so pleasing, and conformable to the Humor of the Patient, as they presse not the true Cure of the Disease; and some other are so Regular, in proceeding according to Art for the Disease, as they respect not sufficiently the Condition of the Patient. Take one of a Middle Temper; or if it may not be found in one Man, combine two of either sort.

Sir Francis Bacon, 'Of Regiment of Health', 1597

You that would last long, list to my song,
Make no more coil, but buy of this oil.
Would you be ever fair? and young?
Stout of teeth? and strong of tongue?
Tart of palate? quick of ear?
Sharp of sight? of nostril clear?
Moist of hand? and light of foot?
(Or I will come nearer to't)
Would you live free from all diseases?
Do the act your mistress pleases;
Yet fright all achès from your bones?
Here's a medicine for the nones.

Ben Jonson, 'Mountebank's Song', *Volpone*, 1606

For I bless God in all gums & balsams & every thing that
    ministers relief to the sick.
For the Sun's at work to make me a garment & the Moon is at
    work for my wife.

For the bite of an Adder is cured by its grease & the malice
    of my enemies by their stupidity.

For to worship naked in the Rain is the bravest thing for
    the refreshing & purifying the body.

For TEA is a blessed plant and of excellent virtue. God give
    the Physicians more skill and honesty!
For nutmeg is exceeding wholesome and cherishing, neither does
    it hurt the liver.

For the Fern is exceeding good & pleasant to rub the teeth.
For a strong preparation of Mandragora is good for the gout.
For the Bark was a communication from God and is sovereign.

– Poor Jeoffry! poor Jeoffry! the rat has bit thy throat.
For I bless the name of the Lord Jesus that Jeoffry is better.

For the divine spirit comes about his body to sustain it in
   compleat cat.

Let Elasah rejoice with Olibanum White or Male Frankinsense
   from an Arabian tree, good against Catarrhs and Spitting
   blood from which Christ Jesus deliver me.
Let Adna rejoice with Gum Opopanax from the wounded root of a
   species of panace Heracleum a tall plant growing to be two
   or three yards high with many large wings of a yellowish
   green – good for old coughs and asthmas.

For I prophecy that men will be much stronger in the body.
For I prophecy that the gout, and consumptions will be curable.

Let Ruston, house of Ruston rejoice with Fulviana Herba, ab
   inventore good to provoke urine.

Let Shield, house of Shield rejoice with Reseda herb dissolving
   swelling, and imposthumes.

Let Farmer, house of Farmer rejoice with Merios an herb growing
   at Meroe leaf like lettuce & good for dropsy.
Christopher Smart, from *Jubilate Agno*, written between 1758 and 1763

Now of all motions that is the best which is produced in a thing by
itself, for it is most akin to the motion of thought and of the
universe; but that motion which is caused by others is not so good,
and worst of all is that which moves the body, when at rest, in parts
only and by some external agency. Wherefore of all modes of
purifying and re-uniting the body the best is gymnastic; the next best
is a surging motion, as in sailing or any other mode of conveyance
which is not fatiguing; the third sort of motion may be of use in a
case of extreme necessity, but in any other will be adopted by no
man of sense: I mean the purgative treatment of physicians; for
diseases unless they are very dangerous should not be irritated by
medicines, since every form of disease is in a manner akin to the
living being, whose complex frame has an appointed term of life. For

not the whole race only, but each individual – barring inevitable accidents – comes into the world having a fixed span, and the triangles in us are originally framed with power to last for a certain time, beyond which no man can prolong his life. And this holds also of the constitution of diseases; if any one regardless of the appointed time tries to subdue them by medicine, he only aggravates and multiplies them. Wherefore we ought always to manage them by regimen, as far as a man can spare the time, and not provoke a disagreeable enemy by medicines.

Plato, ?429–347 BC, Timaeus; tr. Benjamin Jowett

> By Chase our long-liv'd Fathers earned their Food;
> Toil strung the Nerves, and purifi'd the Blood:
> But we, their Sons, a pamper'd Race of Men,
> Are dwindl'd down to threescore Years and ten.
> Better to hunt in Fields, for Health unbought,
> Than fee the Doctor for a nauseous Draught.
> The Wise, for Cure, on Exercise depend;
> God never made his Work, for Man to mend.

Dryden, from 'To my honour'd Kinsman, John Driden,
of Chesterton', 1700

Exercise is bunk. If you are healthy, you don't need it: if you are sick, you shouldn't take it.

Attributed to Henry Ford (1863–1947)

But refuse profane and old wives' fables, and exercise thyself rather unto godliness.

For bodily exercise profiteth little: but godliness is profitable unto all things, having promise of the life that now is, and of that which is to come.

I Timothy, 4

To Dr LEWIS

Dear Dick,

I have done with the waters; therefore your advice comes a day too late – I grant that physic is no mystery of your making. I know it is a mystery in its own nature; and, like other mysteries, requires a strong gulp of faith to make it go down – Two days ago, I went into the King's Bath, by the advice of our friend Ch—, in order to clear the strainer of the skin, for the benefit of a free perspiration; and the first object that saluted my eye, was a child full of scrophulous ulcers, carried in the arms of one of the guides, under the very noses of the bathers. I was so shocked at the sight, that I retired immediately with indignation and disgust – Suppose the matter of those ulcers, floating on the water, comes in contact with my skin, when the pores are all open, I would ask you what must be the consequence? – Good Heaven, the very thought makes my blood run cold! we know not what sores may be running into the water while we are bathing, and what sort of matter we may thus imbibe; the king's-evil, the scurvy, the cancer, and the pox; and, no doubt, the heat will render the *virus* the more volatile and penetrating. To purify myself from all such contamination, I went to the duke of Kingston's private Bath, and there I was almost suffocated for want of free air; the place was so small, and the steam so stifling.

After all, if the intention is no more than to wash the skin, I am convinced that simple element is more effectual than any water impregnated with salt and iron; which, being astringent, will certainly contract the pores, and leave a kind of crust upon the surface of the body. But I am now as much afraid of drinking, as of bathing; for, after a long conversation with the Doctor, about the construction of the pump and the cistern, it is very far from being clear with me, that the patients in the Pump-room don't swallow the scourings of the bathers. I can't help suspecting, that there is, or may be, some regurgitation from the bath into the cistern of the pump. In that case, what a delicate beveridge is every day quaffed by the drinkers; medicated with the sweat and dirt, and dandriff; and the abominable discharges of various kinds, from twenty different diseased bodies, parboiling in the kettle below. In order to avoid this filthy composition, I had recourse to the spring that supplies the

private baths on the Abbey-green; but I at once perceived something
extraordinary in the taste and smell; and, upon inquiry, I find that
the Roman baths in this quarter, were found covered by an old
burying ground, belonging to the Abbey; through which, in all
probability, the water drains in its passage; so that as we drink the
decoction of living bodies at the Pump-room, we swallow the
strainings of rotten bones and carcasses at the private bath – I vow
to God, the very idea turns my stomach! – Determined, as I am,
against any farther use of the Bath waters, this consideration would
give me little disturbance, if I could find any thing more pure, or less
pernicious, to quench my thirst; but, although the natural springs of
excellent water are seen gushing spontaneous on every side, from the
hills that surround us, the inhabitants, in general, make use of well-
water, so impregnated with nitre, or alum, or some other villainous
mineral, that it is equally ungrateful to the taste, and mischievous to
the constitution. It must be owned, indeed, that here, in Milsham-
street, we have a precarious and scanty supply from the hill; which is
collected in an open bason in the Circus, liable to be defiled with
dead dogs, cats, rats, and every species of nastiness, which the
rascally populace may throw into it, from mere wantonness and
brutality . . .

Yours,

Bath Matt. Bramble

Smollett, *Humphry Clinker*, 1771

It is very kind of you to think of such a poor forlorn body as myself.
The perpetual panic and horror of the last two years had steeped my
nerves in poison: now I am left a beggar but I am or shall be shortly
somewhat better off in nerves. I am in a Hydropathy Establishment
near Cheltenham (the only one in England conducted on pure
Priessnitzan principles). I have had four crisises (one larger than had
been seen for two or three years in Gräfenberg [where Vincenz
Priessnitz practised] – indeed I believe the largest but one that has
been seen). Much poison has come out of me, which no physic ever
would have brought to light . . . I have been here already upwards
of two months. Of all the uncomfortable ways of living sure an
hydropathical is the worst: no reading by candlelight, no going near

a fire, no tea, no coffee, perpetual wet sheet and cold bath and alternation from hot to cold: however I have much faith in it.

Tennyson, letter to Edward FitzGerald, 2 February 1844

Tennyson is emerged half-cured, or half-destroyed, from a water establishment: has gone to a new Doctor who gives him iron pills; and altogether this really great man thinks more about his bowels and nerves than about the Laureate wreath he was born to inherit. Not but he meditates new poems; and now the Princess is done, he turns to King Arthur – a worthy subject indeed – and has consulted some histories of him, and spent some time in visiting his traditionary haunts in Cornwall. But I believe the trumpet can wake Tennyson no longer to do *great* deeds; I may mistake and prove myself an owl; which I hope may be the case. But how are we to expect heroic poems from a valetudinary? I have told him he should fly from England and go among savages.

Edward FitzGerald, letter to Edward Byles Cowell, November 1848

Six hours a day I lay me down
Within this tub but cannot drown.

The ice cap at my rigid neck
Has served to keep me with the quick.

This water, heated like my blood,
Refits me for the true and good.

Within this primal element
The flesh is willing to repent.

I do not laugh; I do not cry;
I'm sweating out the will to die.

My past is sliding down the drain;
I soon will be myself again.

Theodore Roethke, 'Meditation in Hydrotherapy', 1937

Never, never, never, was that little watering-place aware of anything
– the little watering-place with its vulgar municipal council elected
by avaricious mountaineers whose only lightness lay in their light-
opera costume.

Ah, why isn't everything light opera! . . . Why doesn't everything
revolve to the tune of that English waltz 'Myosotis'! . . .

Little town, little town of my heart.

Now invalids no longer walk round and round the Springs,
holding their carefully graduated glasses. Now baths are the thing –
water at 25 degrees centigrade – then a stroll and a nap; baths for
neurotics, and especially for women and for the womanly who are in
such bad shape.

You see them wandering about, these good neurotics, dragging
feet that will never again waltz to the delicate formal air of
'Myosotis', or pushed about on the frayed leather of their wheel-
chairs. You see them suddenly leave their seats during concerts at the
Casino, emitting those peculiar sounds of involuntary swallowing;
you see them whirl around in the course of their walks, bringing
their hands to their necks as if some joker had just slashed them with
a razor. You meet them in the woods, their disturbed faces
twitching, strewing bits of torn letters in the antediluvian ravines.
These are the neurotics, children of too brilliant a century; you find
them everywhere.

Here, as elsewhere, the kindly sun, lover of snakes, cemeteries,
and wax dolls, also attracts a few consumptives, slow of step but
dear to the dilettante . . .

The Entertainment Committee does a fine job: Venetian evenings,
balloon ascensions (the balloonist is always called Karl Securius),
merry-go-rounds, seances of spiritualism and anti-spiritualism – all
to the accompaniment of a valiant little band that nothing in the
world could prevent from trooping to the Springs at half past seven
every morning to play its overture for the day. Then in the afternoon
under the acacias of the Promenade – O solos of the little harpist
who dresses in black, blanches her face with powder, and lifts her
eyes to the roof of the bandstand, hoping to be snatched away by
some exotic invalid whose soul trembles like her harp strings! . . .

At twilight when the band is playing and one yawns a bit, lifting
one's eyes to this eternal circle of trim green hills and to the people

strolling round and round with pale, intense smiles, one has indeed the maddening sensation of being in a luxurious prison, with its green exercise ground, and that the prisoners are invalids suffering from a romantic past, banished here far from the serious capitals where Progress continues on its merry way.

Jules Laforgue, 'The Miracle of the Roses', 1887; tr. William Jay Smith

Who will assert that, had the populace of Paris satisfied their hunger at the ever-furnished table of vegetable nature, they would have lent their brutal suffrage to the proscription-list of Robespierre? Could a set of men, whose passions were not perverted by unnatural stimuli, look with coolness on an *auto da fé*? Is it to be believed that a being of gentle feelings, rising from his meal of roots, would take delight in sports of blood? Was Nero a man of temperate life? Could you read calm health in his cheeks, flushed with ungovernable propensities of hatred for the human race? . . . Surely the bile-suffused cheek of Bonaparte, his wrinkled brow, and yellow eye, the ceaseless inquietude of his nervous system, speak no less plainly the character of his unresting ambition than his murders and his victories. It is impossible, had Bonaparte descended from a race of vegetable feeders, that he could have had either the inclination or the power to ascend the throne of the Bourbons . . .

By all that is sacred in our hopes for the human race, I conjure those who love happiness and truth to give a fair trial to the vegetable system . . .

The pleasures of taste to be derived from a dinner of potatoes, beans, peas, turnips, lettuces. with a dessert of apples, gooseberries, strawberries, currants, raspberries, and in winter, oranges, apples and pears, is far greater than is supposed . . .

The most valuable lives are daily destroyed by diseases that it is dangerous to palliate and impossible to cure by medicine. How much longer will man continue to pimp for the gluttony of Death, his most insidious, implacable, and eternal foe?

Percy Bysshe Shelley, Notes on *Queen Mab*, 1813

The mistakes made by doctors are innumerable. They err habitually on the side of optimism as to treatment, of pessimism as to the outcome. 'Wine? In moderation, it can do you no harm, it is always a tonic . . . Sexual enjoyment? After all it is a natural function. I allow you to use, but not to abuse it, you understand. Excess in anything is wrong.' At once, what a temptation to the patient to renounce those two life-givers, water and chastity.

Proust, Cities of the Plain II, 1922; tr. Scott Moncrieff

A young gentleman had a small pimple on his leg, to which a little ointment was applied, and in a day or two the surrounding parts were covered with similar pimples; these, being treated with similar applications, spread until the whole leg was covered with them. Then I was consulted and asked what was to be done. 'Nothing.' 'How is that?' 'Can anything be easier?' I said: 'Do nothing to the leg.' 'Then the stocking will stick to it.' 'Let no stocking be worn. Put a pair of trousers on the boy.' The advice was taken and the leg dried and healed up directly.

John Hunter (1728–93), in a lecture

The man's an imbecile. Even supposing that that doesn't prevent his being a good doctor, which I hesitate to believe, it does prevent his being a good doctor for artists, for men of intelligence. People like you must have suitable doctors, I would almost go so far as to say treatment and medicines specially adapted to themselves. Cottard will bore you, and that alone will prevent his treatment from having any effect. Besides, the proper course of treatment cannot possibly be the same for you as for any Tom, Dick or Harry. Nine-tenths of the ills from which intelligent people suffer spring from their intellect. They need at least a doctor who understands their disease. How do you expect that Cottard should be able to treat you; he has made allowances for the difficulty of digesting sauces, for gastric trouble, but he has made no allowance for the effect of reading Shakespeare. So that his calculations are inaccurate in your case, the balance is upset; you see, always the little bottle-imp bobbing up again.

Proust, Within a Budding Grove, 1919; tr. Scott Moncrieff.
The writer Bergotte is speaking to the narrator

When a lot of different remedies are proposed for a disease, then it means the disease can't be cured.

Anton Chekhov, *The Cherry Orchard*, 1903

> Nor bring, to see me cease to live,
> Some doctor full of phrase and fame,
> To shake his sapient head and give
> The ill he cannot cure a name.
>
> Matthew Arnold, from 'A Wish', 1865

Tho' MEDICINE makes not so plain an appeal to the vulgar,
Yet she lags not a whit: her pregnant theory touches
Deeper discoveries, her more complete revolution
Gives promise of wider benefits in larger abundance.
  Where she nam'd the disease she now separates the bacillus;
Sets the atoms of offence, those blind and sickly bloodeaters,
'Neath lens and daylight, forcing their foul propagations,
Which had ever prosper'd in dark impunity unguess'd,
Now to behave in sight, deliver their poisonous extract
And their strange self-brew'd, self-slaying juice to be handled,
Experimented upon, set aside and stor'd to oppose them . . .
And yet in all mankind's disappointed history, now first
Have his scouts push'd surely within his foul enemies' lines,
And his sharpshooters descried their insidious foe,
Those swarming parasites, that barely within the detection
Of manifold search-light, have bred, swimming unsuspected
Thro' man's brain and limbs, slaying with loathly pollution
His beauty's children, his sweet scions of affection,
In fev'rous torment and tears, his home desolating
Of their fair innocence, breaking his proud passionate heart,
And his kindly belief in GOD's good justice arraigning.
  With what wildly directed attack, what an armory illjudged,
Has he (alas, poor man), with what cumbrous machination
Sought to defend himself from their Lilliputian onslaught;
Aye discharging around him, in obscure night, at a venture,
Ev'ry missile which his despair confus'dly imagin'd;
His simples, compounds, specifics, chemical therapeutics,

Juice of plants, whatever was nam'd in lordly Salerno's
Herbaries and gardens, vipers, snails, all animal filth,
Incredible quackeries, the pretentious jugglery of knaves,
Green electricities, saints' bones and priestly anointings.
Fools! that oppose his one scientific intelligent hope!
Grant us an hundred years, and man shall hold in abeyance
These foul distempers, and with this world's benefactors
Shall PASTEUR obtain the reward of saintly devotion,
His crown heroic, who fought not destiny in vain.
          Robert Bridges, from *Poems in Classical Prosody*, 1, 1903

When the cure for a disease is discovered
Those who have died of the illness
Ought to rise again
And go on living
All the rest of their days
Until they fall sick with another disease
Whose cure has not yet been discovered.
    Marin Sorescu, 'Cure', 1975; tr. Joana Gebbett-Russell

At last I took it into my head to etch once more . . . I soon bit the
plate [i.e. applied the acid] and had a proof taken. Unluckily the
composition was without light and shade, and I now tormented
myself to bring in both; but as it was not quite clear to me what was
really the essential point, I could not finish. Up to this time I had
been quite well, after my own fashion; but now a disease attacked
me which had never troubled me before. My throat, namely, had
become completely sore, and particularly what is called the *uvula*
very much inflamed; I could only swallow with great pain, and the
physicians did not know what to make of it. They tormented me
with gargles and hair-pencils, but could not free me from my misery.
At last it struck me that I had not been careful enough in the biting of
my plates, and that by often and passionately repeating it, I had
contracted this disease, and had always revived and increased it. To
the physicians this cause was plausible and very soon certain on my
leaving my etching and biting, and that so much the more readily as

the attempt had by no means turned out well, and I had more reason
to conceal than to exhibit my labours; for which I consoled myself
the more easily, as I very soon saw myself free from the troublesome
disease.

Goethe, *Poetry and Truth*

I may give an instance, when a joke was more and better than itself.
A comely young wife, the 'cynosure' of her circle, was in bed,
apparently dying from swelling and inflammation of the throat, an
inaccessible abscess stopping the way; she could swallow nothing;
everything had been tried. Her friends were standing round the bed
in misery and helplessness. 'Try her wi' a compliment,' said her
husband, in a not uncomic despair. She had genuine humour, as well
as he; and as physiologists know, there is a sort of mental tickling
which is beyond and above control, being under the reflex system,
and instinctive as well as sighing. She laughed with her whole body
and soul, and burst the abscess, and was well.

John Brown, 'Preface', *Horae Subsecivae*

It meant a lot of work, indeed it did. You were always out – late at
night often. I've done forty, fifty visits a day. But we all accepted it.
You knew nothing else. We went into medicine knowing that's what
life meant. But there was a lot to recommend it, you know. There
was, there was indeed. You got to know your patients intimately
and they either trusted you or they didn't, and went elsewhere. You
knew all the little bits and bobs about their body.

And of course you were a friend. They came with all manner of
problems. Whether little Johnny should go in the police force, or
would he make a good doctor or priest or what have you.

They didn't mind what you said once you'd got to know them. I
remember this old thing who was always getting me out, always
ailing. I'd been here many years by this time. I went out once again,
and she said, 'I don't want to bother you, but every bone in my body
is aching.' I said, 'If I were you, I'd get down on my knees and thank
God I wasn't a herring.'

And you were the *family* doctor. You knew them all so well.

Well, you used your placebos. We had a lot. White aspirins, green aspirins and blue ones. We had a mixture of lactose, you know, milk sugar which was dissolved. Some we put some stuff in it to give it a horrible taste, some we didn't . . . We made them in the surgery – your mixtures, your concoctions, your infusions. You name them, they were all there, all used . . .

Did any of those linctuses help? Strychnine in the tonic? I don't know. But, you know, there's such a thing as the *vis medicatrix naturae* – the healing force of nature. Old Sir John Craven always said to us – 'Remember, 90 per cent of your patients will get better whether you treat them or not. Never give them anything that may be likely to harm them; 7 per cent or 8 per cent will require a little attention and some skill; 2 per cent are going to die anyway. But the healing force of nature is the one thing you've got to remember.' A lot of truth in that.

Two doctors talking of their practices in the 1930s; from *Doctors*
by Jonathan Gathorne-Hardy

An author has defined sickness as 'a function that leads to death', as opposed to a normal function that sustains life. I do not need to say that this definition of sickness seems to me pure fantasy. All functions have as their object the sustaining of life and tend constantly to restore the physiological condition when it is disturbed. The tendency persists in all morbid conditions, and it is this that already constituted for Hippocrates the healing power of nature.

Claude Bernard, the physiologist, *Leçons sur le diabète et la glycogenèse animale*, 1877

Instead of taking up the position obvious for a physiologist that the heart is merely 'a squeezing pump destined to distribute the fluid which nourishes and stimulates the functions of all the bodily organs', he undertook to justify the association of the word *heart* in literature and common speech with the emotions. He pointed out that although the characteristic movement of the heart is the earliest as well as the latest manifestation of life, and is independent of nervous stimulus, nevertheless the nervous system exercises a negative control over its beating . . . A strong nerve stimulus, such as may be provoked by terror or deep emotion, will stop the heart long enough to prevent the arrival of blood in the brain, and the result will be fainting. A milder stimulus will stop the heart more briefly, imperceptibly except to the physiologist, but the function will be resumed with an increase of tempo, fluttering, or palpitation, which will send more blood to the brain, and result in a blush. Bernard therefore considered the use of such expressions as 'a heart broken with grief', 'a heavy heart', 'a heart beating with love', 'to love with the whole heart', etc., as thoroughly sound on physiological grounds.

J. M. D. Olmsted and E. Harris Olmsted, *Claude Bernard
and the Experimental Method in Medicine*, 1952

An example of the therapeutic force of love was noted by Bertram Woods in his *The Healing Ministry*: the story of the French Communist, Louis Olivari, who suffered from paralysis. As a good Marxist, he despised Lourdes and all it stood for; but he eventually went there, on the insistence of his wife, and cynically watched the antics of his fellow pilgrims. One of them, a boy, noticed this, and called on him to pray. Olivari, moved in spite of himself, called out 'God, if you exist, cure that boy: his need is greater than mine.' As he spoke, Olivari felt faint, and when he was pulled out of the water he found that he was no longer paralysed; he could walk again. It was as if the first unselfish thought had sent a current through his body, instructing nerves and muscles which had long been out of use that they could begin to function again – that their fuel supply, the life force, had once more started to flow.

Brian Inglis, *Fringe Medicine*, 1964

And my husband said, when he was a-dying – 'Mary,' he said, 'the Elixir, and the Pills, and the Cancer Cure will support you, for they've a great name in all the country round, and you'll pray for a blessing on them.' And so I have done, Mr Lyon; and to say they're not good medicines, when they've been taken for fifty miles round by high and low, and rich and poor, and nobody speaking against 'em but Dr Lukin, it seems to me it's a flying in the face of Heaven; for if it was wrong to take the medicines, couldn't the blessed Lord have stopped it? . . .

And when everybody gets their due, and people's doings are spoke of on the house-tops, as the Bible says they will be, it'll be known what I've gone through with those medicines – the pounding, and the pouring, and the letting stand, and the weighing – up early and down late – there's nobody knows yet but One that's worthy to know; and the pasting o' the printed labels right side upwards. There's few women would have gone through with it; and it's reasonable to think it'll be made up to me; for if there's promised and purchased blessings, I should think this trouble is purchasing 'em.

For as for curing, how can anybody know? There's no physic'll cure without a blessing, and *with* a blessing I know I've seen a mustard plaister work when there was no more smell nor strength in the mustard than so much flour. And reason good – for the mustard had lain in paper nobody knows how long – so I'll leave you to guess.

George Eliot, *Felix Holt*, 1866; Mrs Holt speaking

I was born in 1944. In the thirties, my father had been a painter and decorator, plumber, electrician, publican and boxer, but when I was growing up, he was a Spiritualist and a faith healer, talking about his negro spirit-guide, Massa, and explaining how he knew when people were cured because he felt burning coals in the palms of his hands. Inspiration ran in the family. My father would explain how he dreamed about the ill and how, for instance, in the case of Bobby Bowen's hand, paralysed after a pit accident, he'd worked on the fingers for days without success until, in a dream, the answer had come. Asleep, he'd felt a terrible pain in his upper arm. After that, he ignored the hand and massaged Bobby's arm until he felt the sensation of burning coals. The fingers, however, still didn't function and the hospital was going to amputate on the following Wednesday. 'You're better,' my father said. The miner left the house gloomily but returned in half an hour with the fingers working. He had gone to the lavatory and pressed the flush absent-mindedly with the damaged hand. There was a click and the fingers worked.

Craig Raine, from 'A Silver Plate', 1982

Both in health and in sickness, I have willingly seconded and given myself over to those appetites that pressed me. I allow great authority to my desires and propensions. I love not to cure one evil by another mischief. I hate those remedies that importune more than sickness. To be subject to the colic [i.e. 'stone'], and to be tied to abstain from the pleasure I have in eating of oysters, are two mischiefs for one. The disease pincheth us on the one side, the rule on the other. Since we are ever in danger to misdo, let us rather hazard ourselves to follow pleasure.

Experience hath also taught me this, that we lose ourselves with impatience. Evils have their life, their limits; their diseases and their health. The constitution of diseases is framed by the pattern of the constitution of living creatures. They have their fortunes limited even at their birth, and their days allotted them. He that shall imperiously go about, or by compulsion (contrary to their courses), to abridge them, doth lengthen and multiply them; and instead of appeasing, doth torment and wring them . . . A man must give sicknesses their passage: and I find that they stay least with me, because I allow them their swinge, and let them do what they list. And contrary to common received rules, I have without aid or art rid myself of some that are deemed the most obstinately lingering and unremovably obstinate. Let nature work: let her have her will: she knoweth what she hath to do, and understands herself better than we do. But such a one died of it, will you say; so shall you doubtless, if not of that, yet of some other disease . . . I have suffered rheums, gouty defluxions, relaxations, pantings of the heart, megraines and other suchlike accidents, to grow old in me, and die their natural death; all of which have left me, when I half enured and framed myself to foster them. They are better conjured by courtesy, than by bragging or threats.

Montaigne, 'Of Experience'

Irene travels at great expense to Epidaurus, visits Aesculapius in his
temple, and consults him on her various ailments. To begin with she
complains that she feels weary and worn out; and the god declares
that this is because of the great distance she has just come. She says
that she has no appetite in the evenings; the oracle orders her not to
eat much. She adds that she is subject to insomnia; he advises not to
take to her bed except at nights. She asks him why she is growing
heavy, and what the remedy is; the oracle replies that she should get
up before noon and use her legs for walking from time to time. She
states that wine isn't good for her: the oracle tells her to drink water;
that she suffers from indigestion: he proposes that she should diet.
'My eyesight is failing,' Irene says. 'Get some glasses,' says Aesculapius. 'I'm failing myself,' she continues, 'I'm not as strong and
healthy as I was.' 'That,' the god says, 'is because you are ageing.'
'But what way is there of curing this lassitude?' 'The quickest way,
Irene, is to die, as your mother and your grandmother have done.'
'Son of Apollo,' Irene cries, 'what advice are you giving me? Is that
all the wisdom men speak of, for which the whole world reveres
you? What have you told me that is exceptional or mysterious? And
didn't I already know all those remedies you have advised?' 'Then
why did you not make use of them,' the god replies, 'without coming
so far to find me, and shortening your days by a long journey?'

Jean de La Bruyère, Les Caractères, 1688

Hospitals and Patients

Sir Thomas More's vision of the hospital as rather superior to a home from home is somewhat utopian; and Marian, in Elizabeth Barrett Browning's verse novel, being the child of tramps, a drunken father and a vengeful mother who proposed to sell her to the squire, might be thought to have an aberrant prehistory.

Elsewhere patients have been regarded as trouble-makers, if not potential criminals. The Guy's Hospital ruling that they should be made to do the humbler everyday chores, resembling the 'community service' now dished out to petty offenders against the law, may conceivably make a come-back. A common complaint among patients these days is that they are considered dead stupid, not fit for rational discourse; according to one observer, the hardest thing to put up with in hospitals is the assumption that because you have lost your gall bladder, you have also lost your mind.

R. D. Laing, however, has brooded over the fact that during years of practice as a psychiatrist he hardly ever saw a patient outside an institution – a mental hospital, a unit, a clinic, or a prison. Patients, both in-patients and out-patients, are patients because of what they were like before they became patients, but 'whatever were they like when they were not yet patients?'

When Sir Thomas Browne declares that he counted the world not an inn but a hospital, we accept the inference. We wouldn't generally think of hospitals as taverns, nor as love-nests. The prevailing response, as this section shows, is a mixed one, of trepidation and resentment, admiration and gratitude.

Though Fanny Burney, remaining conscious, was able to lend her nervous surgeons a hand (she was after all the wife of a French general), for the invention of anaesthetics more sophisticated than a sharp blow to the head, inadvertent fainting, or a glass of rum, we can feel only one simple whole-hearted emotion.

Closed like confessionals, they thread
Loud noons of cities, giving back
None of the glances they absorb.
Light glossy grey, arms on a plaque,
They come to rest at any kerb:
All streets in time are visited.

Then children strewn on steps or road,
Or women coming from the shops
Past smells of different dinners, see
A wild white face that overtops
Red stretcher-blankets momently
As it is carried in and stowed,

And sense the solving emptiness
That lies just under all we do,
And for a second get it whole,
So permanent and blank and true.
The fastened doors recede. *Poor soul*,
They whisper at their own distress;

For borne away in deadened air
May go the sudden shut of loss
Round something nearly at an end,
And what cohered in it across
The years, the unique random blend
Of families and fashions, there

At last begin to loosen. Far
From the exchange of love to lie
Unreachable inside a room
The traffic parts to let go by
Brings closer what is left to come,
And dulls to distance all we are.

Philip Larkin, 'Ambulances', 1961

But first and chiefly of all, respect is had to the sick, that be cured in the hospitals. For in the circuit of the city, a little without the walls, they have four hospitals, so big, so wide, so ample, and so large, that they may seem four little towns, which were devised of that bigness partly to the intent that the sick, be they never so many in number, should not lie too thronged or strait, and therefore uneasily and incommodiously: and partly that they which were taken and held with contagious diseases, such as be wont by infection to creep from one to another, might be laid apart far from the company of the residue. These hospitals be so well appointed, and with all things necessary to health so furnished, and moreover so diligent attendance through the continual presence of cunning physicians is given, that though no man be sent thither against his will, yet notwithstanding there is no sick person in all the city, that had not rather lie there, than at home in his own house.

Sir Thomas More, *Utopia*, 1516; tr. Ralph Robinson, 1551

All Patients admitted into this Hospital must, before they be received into the Ward, be clean from Vermin and furnished with a Change of Body-Linen, Stockings, Neck-cloth, Stock, or Handkerchief, and to pay to the Sister Two Shillings and Ninepence, for *Two Towels, a Tin Pot, a Knife, a Spoon, an Earthen Plate, and five pairs of Sheets*, and if any Part of the Number of Sheets is not expended during their Continuance, the Sister shall return Three-pence per Pair; and if any more is used they shall pay Three-pence per Pair . . .

If any Patient curse or swear, or use any prophane or Lewd Talking, and it be proved on them by two Witnesses, such Patient shall, for the first Offence, lose their next Day's Diet, and for the second Offence lose two Day's Diet, and the third be discharged . . . If any Patient be found strolling about the Streets, or frequenting Publick-Houses, or Brandy Shops, they forfeit their next Day's Diet. If any Patient do privately bring into this Hospital any Spirituous Liquors, such as are not allowed by the Doctors or Surgeons, or fetch such Liquors for any other Patient, both the Patient bringing and the Patient sending are to be discharged . . . If any Patient be found

guilty of any Indecency, or commit any Nuisance in the Squares of
the Hospital, they shall lose their next Day's Diet.

If any Patient that is able neglect or refuse to assist their fellow
Patients that are weak, or confined to their Beds, or to assist when
called on by the Sister, Nurse or Watch, in cleaning the Ward,
helping down with their Stools, fetching Coals, or any other
necessary Business relating to their Ward, or shall absent themselves
at the Time they know such Business must be done, they shall, for
the first Offence, forfeit their next Day's Diet; and for the second
Offence, and persisting therein, they shall be discharged by the
Steward.

Benjamin Harrison Jr, Treasurer of Guy's Hospital, 1797

She stirred; – the place seemed new and strange as death.
The white strait bed, with others strait and white,
Like graves dug side by side, at measured lengths,
And quiet people walking in and out
With wonderful low voices and soft steps,
And apparitional equal care for each,
Astonished her with order, silence, law:
And when a gentle hand held out a cup,
She took it, as you do at sacrament,
Half awed, half melted, – not being used, indeed,
To so much love as makes the form of love
And courtesy of manners. Delicate drinks
And rare white bread, to which some dying eyes
Were turned in observation. O my God,
How sick we must be, ere we make men just!
I think it frets the saints in heaven to see
How many desolate creatures on the earth
Have learnt the simple dues of fellowship
And social comfort, in a hospital,
As Marian did. She lay there, stunned, half tranced,
And wished, at intervals of growing sense,
She might be sicker yet, if sickness made
The world so marvellous kind, the air so hushed,

And all her wake-time quiet as a sleep;
For now she understood (as such things were),
How sickness ended very oft in heaven,
Among the unspoken raptures. Yet more sick,
And surelier happy. Then she dropped her lids,
And, folding up her hands as flowers at night,
Would lose no moment of the blessed time.

Elizabeth Barrett Browning, *Aurora Leigh*, 1856

Bearing the bandages, water and sponge,
Straight and swift to my wounded I go,
Where they lie on the ground after the battle brought in,
Where their priceless blood reddens the grass the ground,
Or to the rows of the hospital tent, or under the roof'd hospital,
To the long rows of cots up and down each side I return,
To each and all one after another I draw near, not one do I miss,
An attendant follows holding a tray, he carries a refuse pail,
Soon to be fill'd with clotted rags and blood, emptied and fill'd
    again . . .

From the stump of the arm, the amputated hand,
I undo the clotted lint, remove the slough, wash off the matter and
    blood,
Back on his pillow the soldier bends with curv'd neck and side-
    falling head,
His eyes are closed, his face is pale, he dares not look on the bloody
    stump,
And has not yet look'd on it.

I dress a wound in the side, deep, deep,
But a day or two more, for see the frame all wasted and sinking,
And the yellow-blue countenance see.

I dress the perforated shoulder, the foot with the bullet-wound,
Cleanse the one with a gnawing and putrid gangrene, so sickening,
    so offensive,

While the attendant stands behind aside me holding the tray and
  pail.

I am faithful, I do not give out,
The fractur'd thigh, the knee, the wound in the abdomen,
These and more I dress with impassive hand, (yet deep in my breast a
  fire, a burning flame.)

Thus in silence in dreams' projections,
Returning, resuming, I thread my way through the hospitals,
The hurt and wounded I pacify with soothing hand,
I sit by the restless all the dark night, some are so young,
Some suffer so much, I recall the experience sweet and sad,
(Many a soldier's loving arms about this neck have cross'd and
  rested,
Many a soldier's kiss dwells on these bearded lips.)
                    Walt Whitman, from 'The Wound-Dresser', 1865

His fingers wake, and flutter; up the bed.
His eyes come open with a pull of will,
Helped by the yellow mayflowers by his head.
The blind-cord drawls across the window-sill . . .
What a smooth floor the ward has! What a rug!
Who is that talking somewhere out of sight?
Why are they laughing? What's inside that jug?
'Nurse! Doctor!' – 'Yes; all right, all right.'

But sudden evening muddles all the air –
There seems no time to want a drink of water,
Nurse looks so far away. And here and there
Music and roses burst through crimson slaughter.
He can't remember where he saw blue sky.
More blankets. Cold. He's cold. And yet so hot.
And there's no light to see the voices by;
There is no time to ask – he knows not what.
                    Wilfred Owen, 'Conscious', 1917/18

This is the time of day when we in the Men's Ward
   Think 'One more surge of the pain and I give up the fight',
When he who struggles for breath can struggle less strongly:
   This is the time of day which is worse than night.

A haze of thunder hangs on the hospital rose-beds,
   A doctors' foursome out on the links is played,
Safe in her sitting-room Sister is putting her feet up:
   This is the time of day when we feel betrayed.

Below the windows, loads of loving relations
   Rev in the car-park, changing gear at the bend,
Making for home and a nice big tea and the telly:
   'Well, we've done what we can. It can't be long till the end.'

This is the time of day when the weight of bedclothes
   Is harder to bear than a sharp incision of steel.
The endless anonymous croak of a cheap transistor
   Intensifies the lonely terror I feel.
           John Betjeman, 'Five o'Clock Shadow', 1966

The Sabbath bells renew the inviting peal;
Glad music! yet there be that, worn with pain
And sickness, listen where they long have lain,
In sadness listen. With maternal zeal
Inspired, the Church sends ministers to kneel
Beside the afflicted; to sustain with prayer,
And soothe the heart confession hath laid bare –
That pardon, from God's throne, may set its seal
On a true Penitent. When breath departs
From one disburthened so, so comforted,
His Spirit Angels greet; and ours be hope
That, if the Sufferer rise from his sick-bed,
Hence he will gain a firmer mind, to cope
With a bad world, and foil the Tempter's arts.
      William Wordsworth, 'Visitation of the Sick', 1845

They sought me out, the ancient consolations,
    now that I lay helpless in their reach,
with well-greased shoes and oily conversation,
    hoping to net me on that painful beach;

helpless indeed I lay, in that white bed, hands outspread,
    legs useless down the length before my eyes,
and could not care a deal for anything they said,
    kind though they thought themselves and wise.

Jamaican nurses spoke of Christ, wheelchair conversions,
    souls brought to God who'd never seen the light;
quietly I nodded when I could, without aspersions,
    was grateful that they cared to help me fight.

Catholic nurses said they'd pray for me, raising
    their rosaries, promising *aves* every day;
a priest put up a meaningless blessing, praising
    a courage I did not have, and went away.

The Church of England would have liked discussion,
    seeing I'd admitted myself: 'religion none'.
I held my own a while but without passion
    and asked to be excused a dialectic run.

And all the while I lay, under the words and attempted curing,
    seeking inside not out for a human grace
that would give me a strength and a courage for enduring
    against great odds in a narrow place.
                          Molly Holden, 'Hospital', 1968

                    Sunset: the blaze of evening burns
                    through curtains like a firelit ghost.
                    Kröte, dreaming of snow, returns
                    to something horrible on toast

                    slapped at him by a sulky nurse
                    whose boy-friend's waiting. Kröte loves

food. Is this food? He finds it worse
than starving, as he cuts and shoves

one nauseating mouthful down.
Kröte has managed to conceal
some brandy in his dressing-gown.
He gulps it fast, until the real

sunset's a field of painted light
and his white curtains frame a stage
where he's the hero and must fight
his fever. He begins to rage

fortissimo in German, flings
the empty bottle on the floor;
roars for more brandy, thumps and sings.
Three nurses crackle through the door

and hold him down. He struggles, then
submits to the indignities
nurses inflict, and sleeps again,
dreaming he goes, where the stiff trees

glitter in silence, hand in hand
with a young child he does not know,
who walking makes no footprint and
no shadow on soft-fallen snow.
  Gwen Harwood, 'Hospital Evening', 1968

My experience of hospital was of pervasive kindness, including the
poignant kindness of patient to patient.

A large public ward runs to a timetable apparently designed to
keep all patients short of sleep. Shortage of food may be added.
These days a menu sheet is distributed on which you may tick the
box that allows you to opt for a vegetarian meal. The system does
not work if you were not present the day before to make your future
option or were undergoing medical treatment elsewhere when the
sheets were distributed in the ward. In any case, carnivores and
vegetarians alike found the food disgusting

The deprivations visited on the patient reduce his emotional stamina for his dealings with the most rigorously hierarchical society to be found in Britain since the middle ages. The most cheerful social layer is the next-to-lowest, only just above the patients: the ancillary workers, who reign alone at mealtimes.

Indian files of medical students practised their gavel technique one by one on the reflexes of my knees. Swarms at a time of medical students settled about my bed. I was asked to walk about the ward for them, which I did leaning on the umbrella I had taken into hospital, and they were asked to note that my way of walking was 'highly characteristic'. I did not know what of.

I was rushed through a series of tests: of the responses of my nerves, of my vision; electrodes were glued to my scalp; I was dunked in a brain scanner.

A better read patient would, I dare say, have guessed what tentative diagnosis the tests were designed to confirm or deny.

I was told that I had multiple sclerosis: or, rather, that the results of all the tests thoroughly conformed with my having it – a presumably legalistic formula that reminded me of my sending down. My college wrote during a vacation to say not that I had been sent down but that I should be if I attempted to return to Oxford when the new term began.

The remnants of my ancient Greek told me that sclerosis was a thickening. I did not realize that the thickening in question was of the very nerves. Neither did I know that the cause of the disease is one of the puzzles of medicine. I asked the doctors what caused it. 'You had a very severe illness in childhood.' 'No, I didn't.' 'You mean you don't remember. You were too young at the time.' 'I mean I specifically and explicitly remember that I was exceptionally healthy as a child and that my parents repeatedly and specifically told me that that was so from the moment I was born.'

Brigid Brophy, 'A Case-Historical Fragment of Autobiography', 1986

To make a man sleep that he may be treated or cut take the gall of a swine three spoonfuls and take the juice of hemlock root three

spoonfuls and of vinegar three spoonfuls and mingle all together and
then put them in a vessel of glass to hold to the sick man that thou
wilt treat or cut and take thereof a spoonful and add it to a gallon of
wine or of ale and if thou wilt make it strong add two spoonfuls
thereof and give him to drink and he shall sleep soon treat him and
cut him then as thou wilt.

From a fifteenth-century manuscript, MS no. 136 of the
Medical Society of London

Before

Behold me waiting – waiting for the knife.
A little while, and at a leap I storm
The thick, sweet mystery of chloroform,
The drunken dark, the little death-in-life.
The gods are good to me: I have no wife,
No innocent child, to think of as I near
The fateful minute; nothing all-too dear
Unmans me for my bout of passive strife.
Yet am I tremulous and a trifle sick,
And, face to face with chance, I shrink a little:
My hopes are strong, my will is something weak.
Here comes the basket? Thank you. I am ready.
But, gentlemen my porters, life is brittle:
You carry Caesar and his fortunes – steady!

After

Like as a flamelet blanketed in smoke,
So through the anaesthetic shows my life;
So flashes and so fades my thought, at strife
With the strong stupor that I heave and choke
And sicken at, it is so foully sweet.
Faces look strange from space – and disappear.
Far voices, sudden loud, offend my ear –
And hush as sudden. Then my senses fleet:
All were a blank, save for this dull, new pain
That grinds my leg and foot; and brokenly
Time and the place glimpse on to me again;

And, unsurprised, out of uncertainty,
I wake – relapsing – somewhat faint and fain,
To an immense, complacent dreamery.

                                        W. E. Henley, 1875

*On 30 September 1811 Fanny Burney (Madame d'Arblay) under-
went a mastectomy in Paris. She was then fifty-nine. This extract is
taken from a long and remarkable account of the operation which
she wrote, over a period of some four months, for her sister Esther.
Fanny Burney made a good recovery, and lived until 1840. Antoine
Dubois and Dominique-Jean Larry were respectively the leading
obstetrician of the time and Surgeon in Chief to Napoleon's Grande
Armée. The only approach to an anaesthetic available was a wine
cordial.*

M. Dubois now tried to issue his commands *en militaire*, but I
resisted all that were resistable – I was compelled, however, to
submit to taking off my long robe de Chambre, which I had meant to
retain – Ah, then, how did I think of My Sisters! – not one, at so
dreadful an instant, at hand, to protect – adjust – guard me . . .
– My distress was, I suppose, apparent, though not my Wishes, for
M. Dubois himself now softened, & spoke soothingly. Can *You*, I
cried, feel for an operation that, to *You*, must seem so trivial? –
Trivial? he repeated – taking up a bit of paper, which he tore,
unconsciously, into a million of pieces, '*oui – c'est peu de chose –
mais – *' he stammered, & could not go on. No one else attempted to
speak, but I was softened myself, when I saw even M. Dubois grow
agitated, while Dr Larry kept always aloof, yet a glance shewed me
he was pale as ashes. I knew not, positively, then, the immediate
danger, but every thing convinced me danger was hovering about
me, & that this experiment could alone save me from its jaws. I
mounted, therefore, unbidden, the Bed stead – & M. Dubois placed
me upon the Mattress, & spread a cambric handkerchief upon my
face. It was transparent, however, & I saw, through it, that the Bed
stead was instantly surrounded by the 7 men & my nurse. I refused
to be held; but when, Bright through the cambric, I saw the glitter of

polished Steel – I closed my Eyes. I would not trust to convulsive fear the sight of the terrible incision. A silence the most profound ensued, which lasted for some minutes, during which, I imagine, they took their orders by signs, & made their examination – Oh what a horrible suspension! – I did not breathe – & M. Dubois tried vainly to find any pulse. This pause, at length, was broken by Dr Larry, who, in a voice of solemn melancholy, said 'Qui me tiendra ce sein? – '

No one answered; at least not verbally; but this aroused me from my passively submissive state, for I feared they imagined the whole breast infected – feared it too justly, – for, again through the Cambric, I saw the hand of M. Dubois held up, while his fore finger first described a straight line from top to bottom of the breast, secondly a Cross, & thirdly a circle; intimating that the WHOLE was to be taken off. Excited by this idea, I started up, threw off my veil, &, in answer to the demand 'Qui me tiendra ce sein?', cried 'C'est moi, Monsieur!' & I held My hand under it, & explained the nature of my sufferings, which all sprang from one point, though they darted into every part. I was heard attentively, but in utter silence, & M. Dubois then re-placed me as before, &, as before, spread my veil over my face. How vain, alas, my representation! immediately again I saw the fatal finger describe the Cross – & the circle – Hopeless, then, desperate, & self-given up, I closed once more my Eyes, relinquishing all watching, all resistance, all interference, & sadly resolute to be wholly resigned.

My dearest Esther, – & all my dears to whom she communicates this doleful ditty, will rejoice to hear that this resolution once taken, was firmly adhered to, in defiance of a terror that surpasses all description, & the most torturing pain. Yet – when the dreadful steel was plunged into the breast – cutting through veins – arteries – flesh – nerves – I needed no injunctions not to restrain my cries. I began a scream that lasted unintermittingly during the whole time of the incision – & I almost marvel that it rings not in my Ears still! so excruciating was the agony. When the wound was made, & the instrument was withdrawn, the pain seemed undiminished, for the air that suddenly rushed into those delicate parts felt like a mass of minute but sharp & forked poniards, that were tearing the edges of the wound – but when again I felt the instrument – describing a curve – cutting against the grain, if I may so say, while the flesh resisted in a manner so forcible as to oppose & tire the hand of the operator, who was forced to change from the right to the left – then, indeed, I thought I must have expired. I attempted no more to open my Eyes, – they felt as if hermettically shut, & so firmly closed, that the Eyelids seemed indented into the Cheeks. The instrument this second time withdrawn, I concluded the operation over – Oh no! presently the terrible cutting was renewed – & worse than ever, to separate the bottom, the foundation of this dreadful gland from the parts to which it adhered – Again all description would be baffled – yet again all was not over, – Dr Larry rested but his own hand, & – Oh Heaven! – I then felt the Knife <rack>ling against the breast bone – scraping it! – This performed, while I yet remained in utterly speechless torture, I heard the Voice of Mr Larry, – (all others guarded a dead silence) in a tone nearly tragic, desire every one present to pronounce if any thing more remained to be done; The general voice was Yes, – but the finger of Mr Dubois – which I literally *felt* elevated over the wound, though I saw nothing, & though he touched nothing, so indescribably sensitive was the spot – pointed to some further requisition – & again began the scraping! – and, after this, Dr Moreau thought he discerned a peccant attom – and still, & still, M. Dubois demanded attom after attom . . .

To conclude, the evil was so profound, the case so delicate, & the precautions necessary for preventing a return so numerous, that the operation, including the treatment & the dressing, lasted 20 minutes! a time, for sufferings so acute, that was hardly supportable – However, I bore it with all the courage I could exert, & never moved, nor stopt them, nor resisted, nor remonstrated, nor spoke – except once or twice, during the dressings, to say 'Ah Messieurs! que je vous plains! – ' for indeed I was sensible to the feeling concern with which they all saw what I endured, though my speech was principally – *very* principally meant for Dr Larry. Except this, I uttered not a syllable, save, when so often they re-commenced, calling out 'Avertissez moi, Messieurs! avertissez moi! – ' Twice, I believe, I fainted; at least, I have two total chasms in my memory of this transaction, that impede my tying together what passed. When all was done, & they lifted me up that I might be put to bed, my strength was so totally annihilated, that I was obliged to be carried,

& could not even sustain my hands & arms, which hung as if I had
been lifeless; while my face, as the Nurse has told me, was utterly
colourless. This removal made me open my Eyes – & I then saw my
good Dr Larry, pale nearly as myself, his face streaked with blood,
& its expression depicting grief, apprehension, & almost horrour.
*She ended the letter: 'I am at this moment quite Well . . . Read,
therefore, this Narrative at your leisure, & without emotion – for all
has ended happily.'*

Fanny Burney

Our old friend Turgenev is a real man of letters. He has just had a
cyst removed from his stomach, and he told Daudet, who went to see
him a few days ago: 'During the operation I thought of our dinners
and I searched for the words with which I could give you an exact
impression of the steel cutting through my skin and entering my
flesh . . . something like a knife cutting a banana.'

Edmond de Goncourt, The Goncourt Journal, 25 April 1883

One night she had fallen quiet, and as we hoped, asleep; her eyes
were shut. We put down the gas, and sat watching her. Suddenly she
sat up in bed, and taking a bedgown which was lying on it rolled up,
she held it eagerly to her breast – to the right side. We could see her
eyes bright with a surprising tenderness and joy, bending over this
bundle of clothes. She held it as a woman holds her sucking child;
opening out her nightgown impatiently, and holding it close, and
brooding over it, and murmuring foolish little words, as over one
whom his mother comforteth, and who is sucking, and being
satisfied. It was pitiful and strange to see her wasted dying look, keen
and yet vague – her immense love. 'Preserve me!' groaned James,
giving way. And then she rocked back and forward, as if to make it
sleep, hushing it, and wasting on it her infinite fondness. 'Wae's me,
doctor; I declare she's thinkin' it's that bairn.' 'What bairn?' 'The
only bairn we ever had; our wee Mysie, and she's in the Kingdom,
forty years and mair.' It was plainly true: the pain in the breast,
telling its urgent story to a bewildered, ruined brain; it was misread
and mistaken; it suggested to her the uneasiness of a breast full of

milk, and then the child; and so again once more they were together, and she had her ain wee Mysie in her bosom.

John Brown, 'Rab and his Friends', *Horae Subsecivae*

'Try and sit quietly, Mother. The more you fidget, the longer a time it seems. Should be your turn soon.'

'Which one is it today, Doris? Which X-ray are they doing today?'

'I told you, stomach. It's stomach today.'

'Oh yes.' But it doesn't really matter. Stomach today, liver yesterday, kidneys the day before. Who would think a person had so many vital organs? It seems an impertinence to me, that these doctors should expose and peer at my giblets.

'Mrs Shipley next. Is Mrs Shipley here, please?'

We rise and follow the voice and the beckoning arm.

'You stay here, Doris. Leave me be. I can manage perfectly well alone.'

'No, I think I'd better—'

Luckily the nurse comes out to speed us, grasps my elbow, steers me like a car, waves Doris politely back. Looking both disappointed and relieved, Doris picks up her magazine once more.

What sort of dungeon is this, and what is happening? They've put me on the table, as before, but now the lights are out and I am falling, falling through darkness as one does only in dreams.

'What're you doing? What's going on?'

'Just relax, Mrs Shipley. We're only going to tilt you forward, you see, until you're almost in a standing position.'

'No, I don't see. I don't see at all. Why not ask me to stand up, then, if that's what you want?'

A subdued titter from the creamy-voiced nurse, and now my annoyance almost obliterates my apprehension. Isn't she the saucy piece? She should try being tipped like a tea-tray and see how she'd feel about it. You'd hear no snicker then. She'd likely shriek the place down, that's the type she is.

The mechanism stops. I haven't fallen after all. The nurse puts something in my hand – a glass with a bent straw.

'Drink as much as you feel you comfortably can.' A male voice, intent on reassurance.

'What is it? What's this stuff?'

'Barium,' the unseen doctor says, a trace abruptly. 'Drink up, Mrs Shipley – we must get on with these.'

Barium – someone has said something about it to me, I'm certain, but what? I sip. It's thick and glutinous, like chalk and oil. I gag on it, and then I recall what the other doctor said. I force the stuff back down my throat. If only there were someone to speak with. Are they human, those around me, hidden in the dark?

'My doctor – Doctor Tappen – no, no, I mean the other man, the one I go to now – he said this stuff would taste just like a milk-shake.'

I intend it only as a pleasantry, hoping they may speak, explain, say something. But I've bungled it. My voice, shakily complaining, falters and fades.

'Is that so?' says the X-ray presence in a bored and abstract voice. Then, an impatient tapping out of words, 'Drink a little more, please.'

It goes through my head now that the pit of hell might be similar to this. It's not the darkness of night, for eyes can become used to that. Another sort of darkness flourishes here – a darkness absolute, not the colour black, which can be seen, but a total absence of light. That's hell all right, and Rome is perfectly correct in that if nothing else.

Red and green flecks appear and disappear, but even they are somehow not so much lights as illustrations in darkness. Momentarily they dazzle my eyes but illuminate nothing. There are voices, though, and these should mean that people are beside me, but I have the feeling that only the voices exist, only the vocal chords, the unbodied mouths babbling and plotting somewhere in the middle of this vault's dark air. The air is cool and stagnant, and I feel I have been kept in storage here too long. Perhaps when I'm let out, launched into wind and sun, I may disintegrate entirely, like the flowers found on ancient young Tutankhamen's tomb, that crumbled when time flooded in through the broken door.

I sip again and force myself to swallow. Again and again, until I start to retch.

'I can't – I can't—'

'Stop, then. Perhaps that'll do for now.'

'I'm going to be sick. Oh—'

'Try to keep it down,' the X-ray says, calm as Lucifer. 'If you don't, you'll have it all to take again. You wouldn't like that, would you?'

My eyes stop watering and my constricted throat is eased by my fury.

'Would *you*?' I snap.

'No. No, I wouldn't.'

'Well, why ask me if I would, then, for pity's sake?'

From the infinite gloom comes, unexpectedly, a sigh.

'We're only doing our best, Mrs Shipley,' the doctor says.

And then I see it's true, and he's a human, and overworked no doubt, and I'm difficult, and who's to blame for any of it?

'I only wish my stomach or whatever it is could be left alone,' I say, more to myself than to him. 'I can't see that it matters much what's wrong with it. It's been digesting for getting on a century. Maybe it's tired – who'd wonder at it?'

'I know,' he says. 'Sometimes one feels that way.'

So sudden is his gentleness that it accomplishes the opposite of what he intended and now I'm robbed even of endurance and can only lean here mutely, waiting for whatever they'll perform upon me.

Margaret Laurence, *The Stone Angel*, 1964

If being a successful visitor is an art, so is being a successful patient; something which, after long practice, I pride myself on having mastered . . .

On admission I did, indeed, put a foot wrong, when my surgeon came to see me. Noticing the flowers friends had already despatched before my arrival, he commented that the previous occupant of the room must have left his flowers behind him. 'No, these are all for me,' I said. 'I think that my friends were afraid their floral tributes might arrive too late for the funeral.'

I was trying to be gallant, but from the faces of both the surgeon and the sister accompanying him, it was clear that to them my remark had been in deplorable taste. It was as though someone had entered my study, had seen the pile of the typescript of my latest novel and commented, 'That's going to be quite a weight for the dustman.'

After that bad beginning, however, I felt that I did well. Naturally strong-willed, even obdurate, I had at once turned myself, on stepping across the threshold of the hospital, into a secretly frightened and bewildered but outwardly plucky child, pathetically trusting that somehow all these clever, kind adults would do their best for him. The adults at once responded and did indeed do their best.

For that best, I am full of gratitude and wonder. One particular memory, of all my hospital memories, many gruesome, sticks with me. It was late on the second night after my operation; I was attempting to be sick on a totally empty stomach, irrationally convinced that I would tear my stitches apart; and in the dim light three beautiful young nurses, all looking as though they were the ghosts of 'stunners' painted by Rossetti a century ago, were attempting to support and calm me. 'Take it easy . . . It's all right . . . That's it . . .' Most of us, if we had to minister to an old codger while he was attempting to bring up his guts, would show some distaste, as well as concern. There was no distaste whatever, only a patient tenderness, on the faces around me.

The sadness comes when one realizes the tenderness is not something personal, a tribute to some quality in oneself, but merely professional. As one gets better, so inevitably the manner of one's nurses – now concerned with other patients in crisis – becomes brisker, more peremptory. One's temperature is taken once a day, one's blood pressure ceases to be taken. A head appears around a door. 'Everything's all right, Mr King?' 'Yes, thank you.' 'Well, don't hesitate to ring if you want anything.' The head disappears.

Francis King, 'Questions of life, death and hospital visitors',
The Independent, 5 December 1988

I don't know what kind of pneumonia I had, but it ran around inside me like a dervish. Actually, I think I had a new disease, just discovered this winter, called Pulmonary Alveolar Proteinosis. You get it from inhaling modern products, like detergents, insecticides, plastics, and therapeutic drugs. For all I know to the contrary you can get it from watching television. Anyway, it leaves its victims either dead or wishing they were . . .

I am also an old student of hospital nuttiness. When I start for a hospital, the first things I pack in my overnight case (ahead of pajamas and bathrobe) are (1) a piece of strong cord about six feet long, (2) a jack-knife, and (3) a pint of whisky. I immediately on arriving tie one end of the cord to that crazy bed-spanning table, and the other end to the headboard. Then when a nurse comes in the room and pushes the table out of reach, I can recapture it by pulling the string.

You are right about the beds – they should go up and down hydraulically, like any sensible barber chair. I always got out of bed, the last thing at night after the nurse had fixed everything to suit herself, and tucked the sheets and blankets in around myself so I wouldn't fall out while asleep. It would have been like falling off the Chrysler Building. One thing I learned years ago about hospitals is, you should *never* stay in bed. I've never yet used a bedpan. Always leap back and forth to the bathroom. Two years ago I had a hernia operation one morning, and went to the bathroom under my own steam in the afternoon, to prevent them from pulling a catheter on me. I managed to start the old bladder going by dashing cold water from the tap all over my frontside. Damn near fainted, but made it back to bed before anybody discovered me.

Another thing I discovered, that time, was that there is a gadget in every hospital setup called a 'colon lavage', and it is exactly the right size and shape for cooling splits of champagne. I always notify a rich friend the minute I get into a hospital and ask for a few splits. Then I swipe ice from the bedside water pitcher, fill the colon lavage, and keep a split cooling. You have to know these things, otherwise you die.

E. B. White, letter to Eleanor and Arthur Brittingham, Jr, 4 May 1958

Once I saw a girl of about eighteen with magnificent hair that hung in thick tresses all the way to her feet; she was nicely plump and had splendid white skin. Apart from her charming features, she was obviously of good breeding. At the moment she was suffering from a very bad toothache. Her hair was in great disorder and where it hung over her forehead it was damp with tears. Quite unconscious of this she kept pressing her hand against her flushed cheek, which made a delightful effect.

On another occasion I saw a girl in an unlined robe of soft white material, an attractive trouser-skirt, and a bright aster cloak. She had a terrible pain in her chest. Her fellow ladies-in-waiting visited her one after another, while outside her room a crowd of young noblemen had come to enquire about her. 'How dreadfully sad!' they exclaimed. 'Has she ever suffered from this before?' In fact none of them seemed particularly concerned, except one who, being the girl's lover, was obviously very distressed about her illness. Since their relations were secret, he was frightened of attracting attention and, though he entered her room, he did not dare come too close. I found it fascinating to watch him standing there, his eyes full of anxiety.

She bound back her beautiful long hair and sat up in bed, saying that she was going to be sick. It was painful to see how ill she looked, yet there was something charming about her appearance.

The Empress, having heard about the girl's condition, sent a priest who was known for his skill in performing the Sacred Readings. He installed himself behind a curtain of state and started to intone his sutras. Since it was a very small room, it was impossible to provide screens and curtains for all the ladies who had come to visit their friend and who now wanted to hear the recitation. They were therefore clearly exposed to view and, while the priest read the scriptures, he kept glancing in their direction, which no doubt earned him a heavy load of guilt.

Sei Shōnagon, *The Pillow Book*, c.1000; tr. Ivan Morris

He told me too the most curious and amusing things that he had noticed during the long periods he had spent in hospital with various protracted illnesses, including hydrarthrosis. He gave me some delightful details about love in hospital and how affairs were conducted in [the Hospital of] Saint-Louis. It was all arranged during Mass. There, the patients of an amorous nature, the women dressed up to the best of their ability in their grey coats, the men wearing their cotton caps with a conquering air, used to sit in the seats nearest the aisle, along which a nurse walked up and down.

They would pick the side which would allow them to display an undamaged profile, for many of them were suffering from scrofula in an advanced stage, and each person would hold his missal in such a way as to show the number of his bed, which was marked on it. Seats along the aisle cost five sous each.

Edmond de Goncourt, *The Goncourt Journal*, 9 January 1884

The paper [given at a medical meeting in London] concerned a woman patient in a hospital . . . The treatment consisted of psychotherapy, explained here as 'a general rational approach', and 'desensitization', which meant encouraging her to undergo the activities she feared, and so overcome her aversion. One of the things she was averse to, as shown on a list passed round by the psychologist [a behaviourist], was 'Being kissed', and a second list showed that 'Kissing' – along with such phobias as 'Going into a cinema' and 'Being left alone in a restaurant' – had been treated by desensitization. When the lecture was over and it was time for questions, the chairman beamed at us all and asked the psychologist what this desensitization to kissing involved – the number of treatments wasn't recorded, but the course had lasted 42 days. The psychologist explained that 'she remembered she had fallen in love with one of the male patients . . . We took advantage of this to get the co-operation of the other patient to overcome her aversion to being kissed.'

The psychoanalyst, who had been sitting with an inscrutable expression, said mildly: 'May I ask if it is part of the pharmacopoeia of the hospital to encourage male patients to kiss female patients?'

'She was doing it anyway,' said the psychologist. 'We couldn't stop her.' . . .

What surprised the analyst was the fact that the woman fell in love, 'a momentous achievement', yet this wasn't mentioned till after the paper had been given, and then only by chance. 'For you and for your whole measurement,' he said, 'this is something irrelevant and secondary that is not even embodied in your paper.'

'I don't really know how to answer you,' said the psychologist. 'We move in different cultures.'

Paul Ferris, *The Doctors*, 1965

We drew lots, who would go and see him.
It was me. I got up from our table.
It was almost time for visiting hours.

He said nothing in reply to my greeting.
I tried to take his hand — he pulled it back
like a hungry dog who wouldn't give up a bone.

He seemed ashamed of dying.
I don't know what you say to someone like him.
As in a photomontage, our eyes would not meet.

He didn't ask me to stay or go.
He didn't ask about anyone at our table.
Not about you, Bolek. Not about you, Tolek. Not about you,
    Lolek.

My head began to ache. Who was dying for whom!
I praised medicine and the three violets in the glass.
I talked about the sun and thought dark thoughts.

How good there's a staircase to run down.
How good there's a gate to be opened.
How good you're all waiting for me at our table.

The smell of a hospital makes me sick.
        Wisława Szymborska, b.1923, 'Report from the Hospital';
                tr. Magnus J. Krynski and Robert A. Maguire

Language, the oldest but still the most reliable guide to a people's
true sentiments, starkly reveals the intimate connection between
illness and indignity. In English, we use the same word to describe an
expired passport, an indefensible argument, an illegitimate legal
document, and a person disabled by disease. We call each of them
invalid. To be an invalid, then, is to be an invalidated person, a
human being stamped *not valid* by the invisible but invincible hand

of public opinion. While invalidism carries with it the heaviest burden of indignity, some of the stigma adheres to virtually all illness, to virtually any participation in the role of patient.

Thomas Szasz, *The Theology of Medicine*, 1979

Whoever gives an invalid advice acquires a feeling of superiority over him, whether the advice is taken or rejected. For this reason susceptible and proud invalids hate their advisers even more than their illness.

Friedrich Nietzsche, *Human, All Too Human*, 1878

He had received from nature a robust and happy constitution, one indeed that was scarcely to be impaired by intemperance. He even pretended, among his friends, that he never followed a single prescription in the whole course of his life. However, in this he was one day detected on the parade; for boasting there of his contempt and utter disuse of medicine, unluckily the water of two blisters, which Dr Oliver had prescribed, and which he then had upon each leg, oozed through his stockings, and betrayed him. His aversion to physic, however, was frequently a topic of raillery between him and Dr Cheyne, who was a man of some wit and breeding. When Cheyne recommended his vegetable diet, Nash would swear that his design was to send half the world grazing like Nebuchadnezzar. 'Ay,' Cheyne would reply, 'Nebuchadnezzar was never such an infidel as thou art. It was but last week, gentlemen, that I attended this fellow in a fit of sickness; there I found him rolling up his eyes to heaven and crying for mercy: he would then swallow my drugs like breast milk; yet you now hear him, how the old dog blasphemes the faculty.'

Oliver Goldsmith, *Life of Richard* [Beau] *Nash*, 1762.

Nov. 23rd, 1848

'I told you Emily was ill in my last letter. She has not rallied yet. She is *very* ill. I believe if you were to see her your impression would be that there is no hope. A more hollow, wasted, pallid aspect I have not beheld. The deep tight cough continues; the breathing after the least exertion is a rapid pant; and these symptoms are accompanied by pains in the chest and side. Her pulse, the only time she allowed it to be felt, was found to beat 115 per minute. In this state she resolutely refuses to see a doctor; she will give no explanation of her feelings; she will scarcely allow her feelings to be alluded to. Our position is, and has been for some weeks, exquisitely painful. God only knows how all this is to terminate. More than once I have been forced boldly to regard the terrible event of her loss as possible, and even probable. But nature shrinks from such thoughts. I think Emily seems the nearest thing to my heart in the world.'

When a doctor had been sent for, and was in the very house, Emily refused to see him. Her sisters could only describe to him what symptoms they had observed; and the medicines which he sent she would not take, denying that she was ill.

Dec. 10th, 1848

'. . . Hope and fear fluctuate daily. The pain in her side and chest is better; the cough, the shortness of breath, the extreme emaciation continue. I have endured, however, such tortures of uncertainty on this subject that at length I could endure it no longer; and as her repugnance to see a medical man continues immutable, – as she declares "no poisoning doctor" shall come near her, – I have written, unknown to her, to an eminent physician in London, giving as minute a statement of her case and symptoms as I could draw up, and requesting an opinion. I expect an answer in a day or two. I am thankful to say, that my own health at present is very tolerable. It is well such is the case; for Anne, with the best will in the world to be useful, is really too delicate to do or bear much. She, too, at present has frequent pains in the side . . .'

But Emily was growing rapidly worse. I remember Miss Brontë's shiver at recalling the pang she felt when, after having searched in the little hollows and sheltered crevices of the moors for a lingering spray of heather – just one spray, however withered – to take in to Emily, she saw that the flower was not recognized by the dim and indifferent eyes. Yet, to the last, Emily adhered tenaciously to her habits of independence. She would suffer no one to assist her. Any effort to do so roused the old stern spirit. One Tuesday morning, in

December, she arose and dressed herself as usual, making many a pause, but doing everything for herself, and even endeavouring to take up her employment of sewing: the servants looked on, and knew what the catching, rattling breath and the glazing of the eye too surely foretold; but she kept at her work; and Charlotte and Anne, though full of unspeakable dread, had still the faintest spark of hope. On that morning Charlotte wrote thus — probably in the very presence of her dying sister: —

Tuesday

'I should have written to you before, if I had had one word of hope to say; but I have not. She grows daily weaker. The physician's opinion was expressed too obscurely to be of use. He sent some medicine, which she would not take. Moments so dark as these I have never known. I pray for God's support to us all. Hitherto He has granted it.'

The morning drew on to noon. Emily was worse: she could only whisper in gasps. Now, when it was too late, she said to Charlotte, 'If you will send for a doctor, I will see him now.' About two o'clock she died.

Mrs Gaskell, *The Life of Charlotte Brontë*, 1857

I remember the smile of the Indian.
I told him
                Fine, finished,
you are cured
and he sat there smiling sadly.
Any painter could paint it
the smile of a man resigned
saying
                Thank you, doctor,
you have been kind
and then, as in melodrama,
                How long
have I to live?
The Indian smiling, resigned,
all the fatalism of the East.

So one starts again, also smiling,
                    All is well
you are well, you are cured.
And the Indian still smiling
his assignations with death
still shaking his head, resigned.
                    Thank you
for telling me the truth, doctor.
Two months? Three months?

And beginning again
        and again
whatever I said, thumping the table,
however much I reassured him
the more he smiled the conspiratorial
smile of a damned, doomed man.

Dannie Abse, from 'The smile was', 1968

It is a small thing that the patient knows of his own state; yet some
things he *does* know better than his physician.

Coleridge, *Table Talk*, 19 April 1830

The germ is nothing; the terrain is everything.

Attributed to Louis Pasteur on his death-bed, 1895

Let us have medicos of our own maturity,
For callow practitioners incline to be casual
        with a middle-aged party.

Doctors in their thirties are loath to labour
        over sick men in their sixties.
Such are near their natural end: respect nature.

To save us suffering, or them their pains,
        physicians in their fifties
Are prepared to surrender us senior citizens.

Let our medical attendants be of compatible years,
Who will think of us as in certain ways their peers,

Who know what we possibly still have to live for,
Why we are not unfailingly poised to withdraw.

Yet for the giving of enemas or injections,
    let there be youthful nurses
With steady hands, clear heads, and other attractions.

Whether physicians or patients, we all can appreciate
A pretty miss, or (it may be) her male associate.

Then permit us to be appreciative and appreciated
A little, in our final fruition, however belated.

Anonymous patient, c.1985

A man does not know whose hands will stroke from him the last
bubbles of his life. That alone should make him kinder to strangers.

Richard Selzer, Mortal Lessons, 1981

Philosophers and Kings

In his reference to philosophers and the toothache, Shakespeare was not suggesting that the literary style of philosophers is divinely exquisite, but rather that they write as if they were gods, above human suffering. And it isn't exactly their pushing away or putting to rout of accident and suffering that he has in mind, but the assurance with which they say 'pish!' to such paltry phenomena. Before his death, the Marxist philosopher whom Czeslaw Milosz calls Tiger in *Native Realm* had been reading only Proust's *Remembrance of Things Past* and Hegel's *Aesthetics*: 'He joked that Hegel was so difficult he had made him sick.' Milosz believes that the joke was more of a confession than anyone realized, for the heart is unable to keep up with the mind as it strives to discover the will of God in the current of history.

It is good to hear that the author of *The Decline and Fall of the Roman Empire* never abused his relatively rude health, even if he sounds rather like Rousseau, that nonpareil and medical prodigy, piously boasting (see p.212) that he never exploited his peculiar and arcane natural advantage.

In his notes on James I, Sir Theodore Turquet de Mayerne diagnosed an excess of black bile ('melancholy') arising from obstructed liver and spleen, plus arthritis and nephritis. The passage is taken from *George III and the Mad-Business*, whose authors believe that James, as well as George, may have suffered from porphyria, a disease of the body's metabolism. It was George III, a year before he died, whom Shelley described as 'an old, mad, blind, despised, and dying king'. Byron's later account raised the adjectival score: 'this old, blind, mad, helpless, weak, poor worm'.

Besides its insights into the future Kaiser Bill, the correspondence between Queen Victoria and her daughter demonstrates both the burden of royalty and the democracy of disease. Monarchs are men like the rest of us, and the human machine is fragile, Voltaire informed the King of Prussia:

> Great King, for you the stomach is
> As was the heel for Achilles.

And 'They told me I was every thing,' said King Lear: ''tis a lie, I am not ague-proof.'

———————

One of Kant's foibles was the meticulous regularity of his habits. He went to bed exactly at ten and arose precisely at five, and up to 1790 he went for a walk at three-thirty, on the minute. To guard against chill he kept his study as nearly as possible to a temperature of seventy-five degrees.

He detested sweat as a sort of watery excrementation. He would not wear garters for fear of impeding the circulation in his legs and was driven to a great extremity, it appears, to find a substitute. The best he could do was to contrive an affair consisting of a watch-spring in a wheel around which was wound an elastic cord divided at each loose end to form a 'Y'. On either side of the trousers in front was a 'watch-pocket' with a small hole in the bottom. The gadget was placed in a pocket and the loose ends of the cord drawn through and down to the stocking where they were attached by hooks. We are told on good authority that the contraption was not an unqualified success . . .

He became increasingly unsteady on his legs, and one day early in his seventy-ninth year he fell while walking in the street. Although he suffered no physical injury, he seemed content thereafter to avoid all unnecessary physical exertion. A few months later he was so unsteady that he could scarcely get about his home. While sitting, he was likely to fall forward, especially if he dozed, which he was very likely to do. On one occasion he nodded into some lighted candles which set his nightcap afire, and he suffered minor burns of the hands in removing the *chapeau flamboyant* . . .

Wasianski, who had tried to enforce a dietary regime of his own conception, blamed the fall on the fact that the old professor had surreptitiously obtained and eaten some bread and English cheese the previous day. Poor Kant had achieved transcendental philosophy only to have transcendental dietetics thrust upon him.

Philip Marshall Dale, Medical Biographies, 1952

When I was a psychiatric resident at Metropolitan Hospital in New York City [1963–5] the consultant on ward rounds used as a criterion for diagnosing a man schizophrenic that he could not understand what he was talking about. A fellow resident, now on the faculty of the Harvard Psychiatry Dept., commented that he had real difficulty understanding what Hegel was talking about. Would the consultant, if he had similar difficulty and indeed could not fathom Hegel, thereby diagnose Hegel as schizophrenic? The consultant psychiatrist replied: 'I certainly would.'

Dr Leon Redler, quoted in R. D. Laing's
Wisdom, Madness and Folly, 1985

In early 1889 Nietzsche caused a commotion in Turin when he threw his arms around an old cart-horse and prevented it from being flogged by its driver. (In a more cerebral moment he had remarked that while we do not regard animals as moral beings, we ought to ask ourselves whether animals are likely to regard us as moral beings.) Postcards he sent to his friends were signed 'The Crucified' and 'Dionysos'; and to Jakob Burckhardt he wrote, 'Dear Professor, finally I would much rather have been a Basle professor than God. But I didn't dare carry my private egoism so far as to omit on its account the creation of the world . . . I have had Caiaphas placed in chains, last summer I too was being crucified by German doctors in a most wearisome manner.'

Writing from Jena in March 1890, Nietzsche's mother told his friend Franz Overbeck of a walk during which they met an officer returning from the firing-range. Nietzsche went up to him, saying 'Once an artilleryman myself, now a professor and overworked.' At her request the officer shook hands with him before parting. 'He understood at once,' she added.

Speculating on the causes of Nietzsche's final breakdown, Overbeck observed that quite possibly he didn't bring madness into life with him, but it grew out of his way of life. Quoting Dryden's line, 'Great wits are sure to madness near allied', Coleridge insisted that, all the same, great genius is divided from madness by an impassable mountain. He was thinking of the products, Dryden of the producers.

Drawn from J. P. Stern, *A Study of Nietzsche*, 1979

For there was never yet philosopher
That could endure the toothache patiently,
However they have writ the style of gods
And made a push at chance and sufferance.
William Shakespeare, *Much Ado about Nothing*, 1598–9

After toothache or
sexual rejection, the
epics are supposed
to come: instead, sexual
rejection and toothache recur.
Peter Porter, from ' "Talking Shop" Tanka', 1978

The violence and variety of my complaints, which had excused my frequent absence from Westminster School, at length engaged Mrs Porten [his aunt], with the advice of physicians, to conduct me to Bath: at the end of the Michaelmas vacation (1750) she quitted me with reluctance, and I remained several months under the care of a trusty maid-servant. A strange nervous affection, which alternately contracted my legs, and produced, without any visible symptoms, the most excruciating pain, was ineffectually opposed by the various methods of bathing and pumping. From Bath I was transported to Winchester, to the house of a physician; and after the failure of his medical skill, we had again recourse to the virtues of the Bath waters. During the intervals of these fits, I moved with my father to Buriton and Putney; and a short unsuccessful trial was attempted to renew my attendance at Westminster School. But my infirmities could not be reconciled with the hours and discipline of a public seminary; and instead of a domestic tutor, who might have watched the favourable moments, and gently advanced the progress of my learning, my father was too easily content with such occasional teachers as the different places of my residence could supply. I was never forced, and seldom was I persuaded, to admit these lessons: yet I read with a clergyman at Bath some odes of Horace, and several episodes of Virgil, which gave me an imperfect and transient enjoyment of the Latin poets. It might now be apprehended that I should continue for life an illiterate cripple; but, as I approached my sixteenth year, nature displayed in my favour her mysterious energies: my constitution was fortified and fixed; and my disorders, instead of growing with my growth and strengthening with my strength, most wonderfully vanished. I have never possessed or abused the insolence of health: but since that time few persons have been more exempt from real or imaginary ills; and, till I am admonished by the gout, the reader will no more be troubled with the history of my bodily complaints.

Edward Gibbon, *Memoirs of my Life and Writings*

My life consists, and basically always has consisted, of attempts at writing, mostly unsuccessful. But when I didn't write, I was at once flat on the floor, fit for the dustbin . . .

Just as I am thin, and I am the thinnest person I know (and that's saying something, for I am no stranger to sanatoria), there is also nothing to me which, in relation to writing, one could call super-fluous, superfluous in the sense of overflowing. If there is a higher power that wishes to use me, or does use me, then I am at its mercy, if no more than as a well-prepared instrument. If not, I am nothing, and will suddenly be abandoned in a dreadful void . . .

My mode of life is devised solely for writing, and if there are any changes, then only for the sake of perhaps fitting in better with my writing; for time is short, my strength is limited, the office is a horror, the apartment is noisy, and if a pleasant, straightforward life is not possible then one must try to wriggle through by subtle manoeuvres. The satisfaction gained by manoeuvring one's time-table successfully cannot be compared to the permanent misery of knowing that fatigue of any kind shows itself better and more clearly in writing than anything one is really trying to say. For the past six weeks, with some interruptions in the last few days, due to unbearable weakness, my timetable has been as follows: from 8 to 2 or 2.30 in the office, then lunch till 3 or 3.30, after that sleep in bed (usually only attempts: for a whole week I saw nothing but Montenegrins in my sleep, in extremely disagreeable clarity, which gave me headaches, I saw every detail of their complicated dress) till 7.30, then ten minutes of exercises, naked at the open window, then an hour's walk – alone, with Max, or with another friend, then dinner with my family . . . ; then at 10.30 (but often not till 11.30) I sit down to write, and I go on, depending on my strength, inclination, and luck, until 1, 2, or 3 o'clock, once even till 6 in the morning. Then again exercises, as above, but of course avoiding all exertions, a wash, and then, usually with a slight pain in my heart and twitching stomach muscles, to bed. Then every imaginable effort to get to sleep – i.e., to achieve the impossible, for one cannot sleep (Herr K. even demands dreamless sleep) and at the same time be thinking about one's work and trying to solve with certainty the one question that certainly is insoluble, namely, whether there will be a letter from you the next day, and at what time. Thus the night consists of two parts: one wakeful, the other sleepless, and if I were to tell you about it at length and you were prepared to listen, I should never finish. So it is hardly surprising if, at the office the next morning, I only just manage to start work with what little strength is left. In one of the corridors along which I always walk to reach my typist, there used to be a coffinlike trolley for the moving of files and documents, and each time I passed it I felt as though it had been made for me, and was waiting for me.

> Franz Kafka, letter to Felice Bauer, 1 November 1912;
> tr. James Stern and Elisabeth Duckworth

My dear Edith,

I have been much touched by your solicitude, but till now absolutely too 'bad' to write – to do anything but helplessly, yearningly languish and suffer and surrender. I have had a perfect Hell of a Time – since just after Xmas – nearly 15 long weeks of dismal, dreary, interminable illness (with occasional slight pickings-up followed by black relapses). But the tide, thank the Powers, has at last definitely turned and I am on the way to getting not only better, but, as I believe, creepily and abjectly well. I sent my Nurse (my second) flying the other day, after ten deadly weeks of her, and her predecessor's, aggressive presence and policy, and the mere relief from that overdone discipline has done wonders for me. I must have patience, much, yet – but my face is toward the light, which shows, beautifully, that I look ten years older, and with my bonny tresses ten degrees whiter (like Marie Antoinette's in the Conciergerie). However, if I've lost all my beauty and (by my expenses) most of my money, I rejoice I've kept my friends, and I shall come and show you *that* appreciation yet. I am so delighted that you and the Daughterling had your go at Italy – even though I was feeling so preeminently un-Italian. The worst of that Paradise is indeed that one returns but to Purgatories at the best. Have a little patience yet with your still struggling but all clinging

Henry James

Henry James, letter to Mrs Bigelow, 19 April 1910

James the First, King of Great Britain, was born at Edinburgh in the year 1566, on June 19th, at half-past eleven in the mornng, and is now 57 years. He had a drunken wct-nurse and was suckled for about a year. He has a very steadfast brain, which was never disturbed by the sea, by drinking wine, or by driving in a coach . . .

Air. – His Majesty bears all changes of air fairly well, in damp weather with a south wind he is attacked by catarrh.

Food. – As regards food there is nothing wrong except that he eats no bread . . . He eats fruit at all hours of the day and night.

Drink. – In drink he errs as to quality, quantity, frequency, time and order. He . . . drinks beer, ale, Spanish wine, sweet French wine . . . and sometimes Alicante wine.

Exercise and rest. – The King used to indulge in most violent exercise in hunting. Now he is quieter and lies and sits more, which is due to the weakness of his knees.

Former illnesses and present inclination to various morbid conditions. – The King did not walk to the sixth year of his age . . . owing to the bad milk of his drunken nurse . . . Between the second and fifth year he had smallpox and measles.

Sleep and waking. – By nature he is a poor sleeper and often at night calls for the servant to read to him aloud.

Affections of the mind. – He is easily and quickly disturbed . . . Sometimes he is melancholy from the spleen exciting disorders.

Excreta. – He blows his nose and sneezes often . . . His stomach is easily made sick if he retains undigested food or bile . . . He then vomits vehemently, so that for two or three days afterwards his face is dotted with red spots. Wind from the stomach precedes illness and he is constipated . . .

Colic. – Very frequently he laboured under painful colic and flatus (an affliction from which his mother also suffered) . . . with vomiting and diarrhoea, preceded by melancholy and nocturnal rigors . . . Fasting, sadness, cold at night produced it . . .

Diarrhoea. – He has been liable to diarrhoea all his life, attacks are usually ushered in by lowness of spirits, heavy breathing, dread of everything and other symptoms . . . pain in the chest, palpitation, sometimes hiccough. In 1610 his life was in acute danger with persistent vomiting. In 1612 after the death of his son another fit of melancholy with the same symptoms, and again in 1619 . . .

In 1619 the attack was accompanied by arthritic and nephritic pains, he lost consciousness, breathing was laboured, great fearfulness and dejection, intermittent pulse and his life was in danger for eight days. It was the most dangerous illness the King ever had. In 1623 an attack lasted only two or three days but was very severe. It was followed by arthritis and he could not walk for months.

Fever. – He rarely has fever and if he has it does not last long and is ephemeral.

Nephritis. – For many years past, after hunting, he often had turbid urine and red like Alicante wine (which are His Majesty's own words) but without pain. In July 1613 he passed blood-red urine with frequent severe vomiting, pain in the left kidney and other nephritic symptoms. Later in the year they recurred and again in 1615 when they were even worse.

Arthritis. – Many years ago he had such pain and weakness in the foot that it was left with an odd twist when walking. For several weeks he had to give up all exercise and had to stay in bed or in a chair. In 1616 this weakness continued for more than four months. The following year the pain spread from the foot to both ankles, knees, and shoulders and hands. The pain is acute, and followed by weakness.

Three times in his life he was seized with excruciating pain in his thighs which, as if by spasms of the muscles and tendons, most pertinaciously twitched at night. The leanness, and so to say atrophy, of his legs are apparently due to the intermission of exercise not calling forth the spirits and nourishment to the lower limbs.

As to remedies. – The King laughs at medicine, and holds it so cheap that he declares physicians of very little use and hardly necessary. He asserts the art of medicine to be supported by mere conjectures, and useless because uncertain.

From the manuscript notes of Sir Theodore Turquet de Mayerne,
1573–1655

31 *May 1663.* The King of France was given out to be poisoned and dead; but it proves to be the meazles and is well, or likely to be soon well again.

Pepys, *Diary*

The Sons of Art all Med'cines tried,
And every Noble remedy applied,
With emulation each essay'd
His utmost skill, nay more they pray'd:
Never was losing game with better conduct play'd.
Death never won a stake with greater toil,
Nor e'er was Fate so near a foil:
But, like a fortress on a Rock,
Th'impregnable Disease their vain attempts did mock;
They mined it near, they batter'd from afar
With all the Cannon of the Med'cinal War;
No gentle means could be essay'd,
'Twas beyond parley when the siege was laid:
The extremest ways they first ordain,
Prescribing such intolerable pain
As none but *Caesar* could sustain;
Undaunted *Caesar* underwent
The malice of their Art, nor bent
Beneath what e'er their pious rigour could invent.
In five such days he suffer'd more
Than any suffer'd in his reign before;
More, infinitely more, than he
Against the worst of Rebels could decree,
A Traitor, or twice pardon'd Enemy.
Now Art was tir'd without success,
No Racks could make the stubborn malady confess . . .

Death and despair was in their looks,
No longer they consult their memories or books;
Like helpless friends, who view from shore
The labouring Ship and hear the tempest roar,
    So stood they with their arms across;
Not to assist; but to deplore
        Th'inevitable loss.
                Dryden, from 'Threnodia Augustalis. Sacred to the
                        Happy Memory of King Charles II', 1685

In the afternoon I was received by His Majesty in a very unusual manner, of which I had not the least expectation. The look of his eyes, the tone of his voice, every gesture and his whole deportment represented a person in a most furious passion of anger. 'One medicine had been too powerful; another had only teased him without effect. The importation of senna ought to be prohibited, and he would give orders that in future it shall never be given to any of the royal family.' With a frequent repetition of this and similar language he detained me three hours. His pulse was much quickened; but I did not number the strokes.

    – Sir George Baker, 22 October 1788

Dr Warren, in some set of fine phrases, is to tell His Majesty that he is stark mad, and must have a strait-waistcoat. I am glad that I am not chosen to be that Rat who is to put the bell about the Cat's neck. For if it should please God to . . . restore His Majesty to his senses . . . I should not like to stand in the place of that man who has moved such an Address to the Crown.

    – George Selwyn, 20 November 1788

He was as deranged as possible . . . Among his extravagancies of the moment he had at this time hid part of the bedclothes under his bed, had taken off his nightcap, and got a pillowcase round his head, and the pillow in the bed with him, which he called Prince Octavius [his youngest son, who died at the age of four in 1783], who he said was to be new born this day.

— Robert Fulke Greville, 25 December 1788

From *George III and the Mad-Business*, by Ida Macalpine and Richard Hunter, 1969

To speak frankly, our profession has never struck me as a pleasant one when conducted among the great, and I have always found it better for us to stick to the ordinary public. They are accommodating. You don't have to account to anyone for your actions; and as long as you follow the accepted rules of the art, you need not worry over what may ensue. But what is troublesome about the great is that, when they fall ill, they insist on their doctors curing them.

M. Diafoirus, in Molière, *Le Malade Imaginaire*, 1673

A correspondence between Queen Victoria and her eldest daughter, the Crown Princess of Prussia

From the Queen   20 December 1871

Doctor Gull is a very clever, and the fashionable, doctor; but he is a very clever man besides, and a good, religious, courageous one — who is as anxious for dear Bertie's [the Prince of Wales] moral welfare as for his physical well doing. We all feel that if God has spared his life it is to enable him to lead a new life — and if this great warning is not taken, and the wonderful sympathy and devotion of the whole nation does not make a great change in him, it will be worse than before and his utter ruin.

23 December 1871

His progress is terribly slow. Broken sleep — wandering (yesterday morning a great deal) and great prostration. The nerves have received a terrible shock and will take long recovering. Another person, a woman who helped in the kitchen, has now got the fever. I think the house [Sandringham] very unhealthy — drainage and ventilation — bad; bad smells in some rooms — of gas and drains. It would never do to let the children go back there.

30 December 1871

I wish I could give you a really satisfactory report of dear Bertie –
but I cannot. He has the most dreadful pain in his leg which comes
on in violent spasms – and the temperature is very high which if it
were merely pain would not be the case. There is, as Sir William
Jenner (who has been here since the 26th) says, no cause of alarm but
for anxiety. The breathing is not good – and always hurried when he
talks or moves. The leg can hardly be moved and he had a most
restless night . . . They fear some deep seated inflammation somewhere and certainly it is very anxious.

From The Crown Princess   1 January 1872

I am in great pain this evening from neuralgia in my face, my right
cheek and ear. I had not got rid of my cold and having to go twice
today to the Emperor's Palace, which was so fearfully hot that I had
not a dry thread upon me and then coming out into the cold air, has
brought this on.

From the Queen   7 January 1872

Dear Bertie seems, though of course very weak and obliged to take
great care, to go on well and steadily though slowly. The rise of
temperature, which still occurs every afternoon, lessens each day a
little; the pain in the leg is also much better and the lung likewise
improved. One only trembles lest he should commit any imprudence
– which will become more likely when once he is no longer entirely
under the care of the doctors.

10 January 1872

Dear Bertie is going on quite well. You ask me several questions all
of which I can't answer.

    1. his appetite – it is good but I don't think so very large.
    2. he is grown very thin – and his weight has lessened
       immensely.
    3. his hair comes off dreadfully and has been cut quite short.

From the Crown Princess   31 January 1872

Many affectionate thanks for your kind wishes for Willy's [the
future Kaiser] birthday. His future is indeed a great anxiety – I only
trust he may be fit for it in every way. His poor arm is a sad

disadvantage to him – a hindrance to his education – and will not be
without influence on the development of his character – he will
never be manly and independent like other boys – and never feel at
his ease, he cannot do any single thing in the way of amusement or
bodily exercise that they can. It always was and continues to me a
great grief – those who only see him occasionally have not an idea
how it affects everything. I cannot help thinking it very hard and
very cruel. His appearance seems to me to grow more awkward as
the limb gets stiffer – but that is not of vital importance, though it
makes his manner shy and sheepish and all his movements so
awkward. He is really a good boy on the whole – and can be so
pleasant and amiable . . .

From the Queen   21 February 1872
Our dear Bertie is not as well as was supposed. His leg is swelled (not
painful) from a stoppage and thickening of the veins – and he must
not walk and must be very careful to keep it up a great deal. It is still
uncertain if Bertie can go on the 27th to this dreadful affair at St
Paul's [the Thanksgiving Service for his recovery]. It will be a great,
great trial and what I don't like is religion being made a vehicle for a
great show!! However, that could not it seems be avoided.

                                                   28 February 1872
I am thankful to say that yesterday was a day of triumph – really
most marvellous! Such touching affection and loyalty cannot be seen
anywhere I think . . . Millions must have been out and the decora-
tions were really beautiful – the cheering deafening. It was the first
time since Bertie was a boy that he had ever been with me on a great
public occasion – and such an occasion – even in former happier
days – perhaps there never has been; he looked ill and was very lame
but was touched by the immense loyalty and really touching
affection shown. From the highest to the poorest 'rags' there was but
one and the same feeling! It was of course very fatiguing – bowing
all this time, but still it was so very gratifying that one could not feel
tired. My head aches rather but not very much today.
          Darling Child, Private Correspondence of Queen Victoria
                and the Crown Princess of Prussia, 1871–1878,
                              ed. Roger Fulford, 1976

The Prince of Wales has had a rough time recently; so rough, it is reported, that there are times when he is so tense that his muscles lock. Although the description of his symptoms, should they be accurate, sound horrific, his problem seems to be no more than carpo-pedal spasms, a common symptom of the hyperventilation syndrome: over-breathing or panting respirations often induced in patients stressed by anxiety, fatigue or grief.

If somebody breathes more quickly than nature intended, the carbon dioxide in the blood is flushed out, with subsequent changes in blood acidity. This results, if sufficiently severe, in a tight contraction of the muscles of the hands and feet, which go into a spasm. At the same time, the patient often notices numbness around the mouth, pins and needles generally, and a feeling of faintness which may even lead to an actual faint.

Alarming as these changes are, the symptom which really worries the sufferer is an associated chest pain and tightness, so that he (or more often she) wonders if they are to suffer a coronary thrombosis or a stroke. The more anxious patients become, the faster they breathe, and the worse the symptoms.

Rather than rushing to consult distant experts on stress diseases, the easier, but rather undignified way to resolve the situation is for the patient to find a paper bag, put it over his mouth and nose (rather like a carriage horse having its lunch-time oats) and re-breathe the expired carbon dioxide. The usually recommended first aid drill is to take ten deliberate, slow breaths into the bag, pause for a few minutes, and then repeat the process, breathing into the bag intermittently until all the symptoms have gone. A plastic bag should, of course, never be used.

Dr Thomas Stuttaford, 'Medical Briefing', *The Times*, 14 April 1988

For the most part, a constitutional monarch is a *damaged* common man; not forced to business by necessity as a despot often is, but yet spoiled for business by most of the temptations which spoil a despot. History, too, seems to show that hereditary royal families gather from the repeated influence of their corrupting situation some dark taint in the blood, some transmitted and growing poison which hurts their judgements, darkens all their sorrow, and is a cloud on half their pleasure. It has been said, not truly, but with a possible approximation to truth, 'that in 1802 every hereditary monarch was insane'.

Walter Bagehot, The English Constitution, 1867

Intellectual and Spiritual Frets

These distresses include instances of seemingly arbitrary, undeserved suffering as in Coleridge and Clare, the sense of purposeless-
ness as in Mill, and of guilt as in the Reverend Dimmesdale. For
reasons of his own, the sinister physician is interested in the
psychosomatic nature of the clergyman's malady; the clergyman, in
his own judgement, more needs the Divine than a prying physician.

The seventeenth-century poets represent spiritual woes as physical disorders, infections obviously caught from Satan, in Edward
Taylor's view, and God as the physician-in-chief: 'I ope my Case to
thee'. Thackeray sounds a refreshing note when he declares with
some pride that he is too humble to suppose the supernatural powers
engrossed in his physical condition – having a tooth out is just
having a tooth out. And especially refreshing in comparison with
Margery Kempe, who is confident that for better or for worse she
has the exclusive and full-time attention of the Almighty.

To social and political ills there is no end, the poor are still with us
and so are persecution and oppression. They have been amply
documented, and here I include only two passages under these
heads.

The concluding excerpt from Pascal ('Marques de la grandeur de
l'homme') carries a measure of good cheer, if not pride, latent even
in the words from Lamentations with which it ends. Later in
Chapter 3, in Jeremiah's list of afflictions ('He hath also broken my
teeth with gravel stones'), it is said, 'This I recall to my mind,
therefore have I hope.'

═══════════

But yesternight I prayed aloud
In anguish and in agony,
Up-starting from the fiendish crowd

Of shapes and thoughts that tortured me:
A lurid light, a trampling throng,
Sense of intolerable wrong,
And whom I scorned, those only strong!
Thirst of revenge, the powerless will
Still baffled, and yet burning still!
Desire with loathing strangely mixed
On wild or hateful objects fixed.
Fantastic passions! maddening brawl!
And shame and terror over all!
Deeds to be hid which were not hid,
Which all confused I could not know
Whether I suffered, or I did:
For all seemed guilt, remorse or woe,
My own or others still the same
Life-stifling fear, soul-stifling shame.

So two nights passed: the night's dismay
Saddened and stunned the coming day.
Sleep, the wide blessing, seemed to me
Distemper's worst calamity.
The third night, when my own loud scream
Had waked me from the fiendish dream,
O'ercome with sufferings strange and wild,
I wept as I had been a child;
And having thus by tears subdued
My anguish to a milder mood,
Such punishments, I said, were due
To natures deepliest stained with sin, –
For aye entempesting anew
The unfathomable hell within,
The horror of their deeds to view,
To know and loathe, yet wish and do!
Such griefs with such men well agree,
But wherefore, wherefore fall on me?
To be beloved is all I need,
And whom I love, I love indeed.

Coleridge, from 'The Pains of Sleep', 1816

I am – yet what I am, none cares or knows;
   My friends forsake me like a memory lost:
I am the self-consumer of my woes –
   They rise and vanish in oblivion's host,
Like shadows in love's frenzied stifled throes,
   And yet I am, and live – like vapours tost

Into the nothingness of scorn and noise,
   Into the living sea of waking dreams,
Where there is neither sense of life or joys,
   But the vast shipwreck of my life's esteems,
Even the dearest that I love the best
   Are strange – nay, rather, stranger than the rest.

I long for scenes where man hath never trod,
   A place where woman never smiled or wept,
There to abide with my Creator, God,
   And sleep as I in childhood sweetly slept,
Untroubling and untroubled where I lie,
   The grass below – above the vaulted sky.
                      John Clare, 'I Am', 1846

'Let me ask, as your friend, as one having charge, under Providence, of your life and physical well-being, hath all the operation of this disorder been fairly laid open and recounted to me?'

'How can you question it?' asked the minister. 'Surely it were child's play to call in a physician and then hide the sore!'

'You would tell me, then, that I know all?' said Roger Chillingworth, deliberately, and fixing an eye bright with intense and concentrated intelligence on the minister's face. 'Be it so! But, again! He to whom only the outward and physical evil is laid open, knoweth, oftentimes, but half the evil which he is called upon to cure. A bodily disease, which we look upon as whole and entire within itself, may, after all, be but a symptom of some ailment in the spiritual part. Your pardon once again, good Sir, if my speech give the shadow of offence. You, Sir, of all men whom I have known, are he whose body is the closest conjoined, and imbued, and identified, so to speak, with the spirit whereof it is the instrument.'

'Then I need ask no further,' said the clergyman, somewhat hastily rising from his chair. 'You deal not, I take it, in medicine for the soul!'

'Thus, a sickness,' continued Roger Chillingworth, going on, in an unaltered tone, without heeding the interruption, but standing up and confronting the emaciated and white-cheeked minister, with his low, dark, and misshapen figure, – 'a sickness, a sore place, if we may call it so, in your spirit hath immediately its appropriate manifestation in your bodily frame. Would you, therefore, that your physician heal the bodily evil? How may this be unless you first lay open to him the wound or trouble in your soul?'

'No, not to thee! not to an earthly physician!' cried Mr Dimmesdale, passionately, and turning his eyes, full and bright, and with a kind of fierceness, on old Roger Chillingworth. 'Not to thee! But, if it be the soul's disease, then do I commit myself to the one Physician of the soul! He, if it stand with His good pleasure, can cure, or He can kill. Let Him do with me as, in His justice and wisdom, He shall see good. But who art thou, that meddlest in this matter? that dares thrust himself between the sufferer and his God?'

Nathaniel Hawthorne, The Scarlet Letter, 1850

Others, I am not the first,
Have willed more mischief than they durst:
If in the breathless night I too
Shiver now, 'tis nothing new.

More than I, if truth were told,
Have stood and sweated hot and cold,
And through their reins in ice and fire
Fear contended with desire.

Agued once like me were they,
But I like them shall win my way
Lastly to the bed of mould
Where there's neither heat nor cold.

But from my grave across my brow
Plays no wind of healing now,
And fire and ice within me fight
Beneath the suffocating night.

A.E. Housman, *A Shropshire Lad*, XXX, 1896

Macbeth.   Canst thou not minister to a mind diseas'd,
     Pluck from the memory a rooted sorrow,
     Raze out the written troubles of the brain,
     And with some sweet oblivious antidote
     Cleanse the stuff'd bosom of that perilous stuff
     Which weighs upon the heart?
Doctor.   Therein the patient
     Must minister to himself.

Shakespeare, *Macbeth*, 1605–6

28 November 1826.   When we returnd home were astounded with the news of Colonel Huxley's death and the manner of it. A quieter, more inoffensive, mild and staid mind I never knew. He was free from all those sinkings of the imagination which render those who are liable to them the victims of occasional low spirits. All belonging to this gifted as it is calld but often unhappy class must have felt at times that but for the dictates of religion or the natural recoil of the mind from the idea of dissolution there have been times when they would have been willing to throw away life as a child does a broken toy. I am sure I know one who has often felt so. But poor Huxley was none of these; he was happy in his domestic relations and on the very day on which the rash deed was committed was to have embarkd for rejoining his wife and child whom I so lately saw anxious to impart to him their improved prospects – O Lord, What are we? – Lords of Nature – why a tile drops from a house top which an elephant would not feel more than the fall of a sheet of pasteboard and there lies his Lordship. Or something of inconceivably minute origin, the pressure of a bone or the inflammation of a particle of the brain, takes place and the emblem of the Deity destroys himself or some one else. We hold our health and our reason on terms slighter than one would desire were it in their choice to hold an Irish cabbin.

29. Awakd from horrid dreams to reconsideration of the sad
reality – he was such a kind, obliging, assiduous creature. I thought
he came to my bedside to expostulate with me how I could believe
such a scandal – and I thought I detected that it was but a spirit who
spoke by the paleness of his look and the blood flowing from his
cravat. I had the night-mare in short, and no wonders.

I felt stupefied all this day but wrote the necessary letters
notwithstanding. Walter, Jane and Mrs Jobson dined with us – but I
could not gather my spirits. But it is nonsense and contrary to my
system which is of the Stoic school and I think pretty well maintaind.
It is the only philosophy I know or can practise – but it cannot
always keep the helm.

> Scott, *Journal*; Colonel Thomas Huxley was the
> husband of Scott's niece, Jessie

I was in a dull state of nerves, such as everybody is occasionally
liable to; unsusceptible to enjoyment or pleasurable excitement; one
of those moods when what is pleasure at other times, becomes
insipid or indifferent; the state, I should think, in which converts to
Methodism usually are, when smitten by their first 'conviction of
sin'. In this frame of mind it occurred to me to put the question
directly to myself: 'Suppose that all your objects in life were realized;
that all the changes in institutions and opinions which you are
looking forward to, could be completely effected at this very instant:
would this be a great joy and happiness to you?' And an irrepressible
self-consciousness distinctly answered, 'No!' At this my heart sank
within me: the whole foundation on which my life was constructed
fell down. All my happiness was to have been found in the continual
pursuit of this end. The end had ceased to charm, and how could
there ever again be any interest in the means? I seemed to have
nothing left to live for . . .

In vain I sought relief from my favourite books; those memorials
of past nobleness and greatness from which I had always hitherto
drawn strength and animation. I read them now without feeling, or
with the accustomed feeling *minus* all its charm; and I became
persuaded, that my love of mankind, and of excellence for its own
sake, had worn itself out. I sought no comfort by speaking to others

of what I felt. If I had loved any one sufficiently to make confiding my griefs a necessity, I should not have been in the condition I was. I felt, too, that mine was not an interesting, or in any way respectable distress. There was nothing in it to attract sympathy. Advice, if I had known where to seek it, would have been most precious. The words of Macbeth to the physician often occurred to my thoughts. But there was no one on whom I could build the faintest hope of such assistance . . .

These were the thoughts which mingled with the dry heavy dejection of the melancholy winter of 1826–7. During this time I was not incapable of my usual occupations. I went on with them mechanically, by the mere force of habit. I had been so drilled in a certain sort of mental exercise, that I could still carry it on when all the spirit had gone out of it. I even composed and spoke several speeches at the debating society, how, or with what degree of success, I know not. Of four years continual speaking at that society, this is the only year of which I remember next to nothing. Two lines of Coleridge, in whom alone of all writers I have found a true description of what I felt, were often in my thoughts, not at this time (for I had never read them), but in a later period of the same mental malady:

> Work without hope draws nectar in a sieve,
> And hope without an object cannot live.

In all probability my case was by no means so peculiar as I fancied it, and I doubt not that many others have passed through a similar state; but the idiosyncrasies of my education had given to the general phenomenon a special character, which made it seem the natural effect of causes that it was hardly possible for time to remove. I frequently asked myself, if I could, or if I was bound to go on living, when life must be passed in this manner. I generally answered to myself, that I did not think I could possibly bear it beyond a year. When, however, not more than half that duration of time had elapsed, a small ray of light broke in upon my gloom. I was reading, accidentally, Marmontel's *Mémoires*, and came to the passage which relates his father's death, the distressed position of the family, and the sudden inspiration by which he, then a mere boy, felt and made them feel that he would be everything to them – would supply the place of all that they had lost. A vivid conception of the scene and its feelings came over me, and I was moved to tears. From this moment my burden grew lighter. The oppression of the thought that all feeling was dead within me, was gone. I was no longer hopeless: I was not a stock or a stone. I had still, it seemed, some of the material out of which all worth of character, and all capacity for happiness, are made. Relieved from my ever present sense of irremediable wretchedness, I gradually found that the ordinary incidents of life could again give me some pleasure; that I could again find enjoyment, not intense, but sufficient for cheerfulness, in sunshine and sky, in books, in conversation, in public affairs; and that there was, once more, excitement, though of a moderate kind, in exerting myself for my opinions, and for the public good. Thus the cloud gradually drew off, and I again enjoyed life.

John Stuart Mill, Autobiography, 1873

Lydgate seemed to think the case worth a great deal of his attention. He not only used his stethoscope (which had not become a matter of course in practice at that time), but sat quietly by his patient and watched him. To Mr Casaubon's questions about himself, he replied that the source of the illness was the common error of intellectual men – a too eager and monotonous application: the remedy was, to be satisfied with moderate work, and to seek variety of relaxation. Mr Brooke, who sat by on one occasion, suggested that Mr Casaubon should go fishing, as Cadwallader did, and have a turning-room, make toys, table-legs, and that kind of thing.

'In short you recommend me to anticipate the arrival of my second childhood,' said poor Mr Casaubon, with some bitterness. 'These things,' he added, looking at Lydgate, 'would be to me such relaxation as tow-picking is to prisoners in a house of correction.'

'I confess,' said Lydgate, smiling, 'amusement is rather an unsatisfactory prescription. It is something like telling people to keep up their spirits. Perhaps I had better say, that you must submit to be mildly bored rather than to go on working.'

'Yes, yes,' said Mr Brooke. 'Get Dorothea to play backgammon with you in the evenings. And shuttlecock, now – I don't know a finer game than shuttlecock for the daytime. I remember it all the fashion. To be sure, your eyes might not stand that, Casaubon. But you must unbend, you know. Why, you might take to some light study: conchology, now: I always think that must be a light study. Or get Dorothea to read you light things, Smollett – *Roderick Random*, *Humphry Clinker*: they are a little broad, but she may read anything now she's married, you know. I remember they made me laugh uncommonly – there's a droll bit about a postilion's breeches. We have no such humour now. I have gone through all these things, but they might be rather new to you.'

'As new as eating thistles,' would have been an answer to represent Mr Casaubon's feelings. But he only bowed resignedly, with due respect to his wife's uncle, and observed that doubtless the works he mentioned had 'served as a resource to a certain order of mind'.

George Eliot, Middlemarch, 1871–2

Hang this thinking, at last! what good is it? oh, and what evil!
Oh, what mischief and pain! like a clock in a sick man's chamber,
Ticking and ticking, and still through each covert of slumber
    pursuing.
  What shall I do to thee, O thou Preserver of men? Have
    compassion;
Be favourable, and hear! Take from me this regal knowledge;
Let me, contented and mute, with the beasts of the fields, my
    brothers,
Tranquilly, happily lie, – and eat grass, like Nebuchadnezzar!

Arthur Hugh Clough, Amours de Voyage, 1849

                    These beauteous forms,
        Through a long absence, have not been to me
        As is a landscape to a blind man's eye:
        But oft, in lonely rooms, and 'mid the din
        Of towns and cities, I have owed to them,
        In hours of weariness, sensations sweet,

Felt in the blood, and felt along the heart;
And passing even into my purer mind,
With tranquil restoration: — feelings too
Of unremembered pleasure: such, perhaps,
As have no slight or trivial influence
On that best portion of a good man's life,
His little, nameless, unremembered, acts
Of kindness and of love. Nor less, I trust,
To them I may have owed another gift,
Of aspect more sublime; that blessed mood
In which the burthen of the mystery,
In which the heavy and the weary weight
Of all this unintelligible world,
Is lightened; — that serene and blessed mood,
In which the affections gently lead us on, —
Until, the breath of this corporeal frame
And even the motion of our human blood
Almost suspended, we are laid asleep
In body, and become a living soul:
While with an eye made quiet by the power
Of harmony, and the deep power of joy,
We see into the life of things.
                                        If this
Be but a vain belief, yet, oh! how oft —
In darkness and amid the many shapes
Of joyless daylight; when the fretful stir
Unprofitable, and the fever of the world,
Have hung upon the beatings of my heart —
How oft, in spirit, have I turned to thee,
O sylvan Wye! thou wanderer thro' the woods,
How often has my spirit turned to thee!
          Wordsworth, from 'Lines composed a few miles
                              above Tintern Abbey', 1798

Oh thou great Power! in whom I move,
For whom I Live, to whom I Die,
Behold me through thy beams of Love,

Whilst on this Couch of Tears I lie;
  And cleanse my sordid Soul within
  By thy Christ's Blood, the Bath of Sin.

No hallowed Oyls, no grains I need,
No Rags of Saints, no purging Fire;
One Rosie drop from David's Seed
Was Worlds of Seas to quench thine Ire.
  O Precious Ransome! which once paid,
  That *Consummatum est* was said;

And said by him that said no more,
But seal'd it with his Sacred Breath:
Thou, then, that hast dispong'd my Score,
And dying wast the Death of Death,
  Be to me now, on Thee I call,
  My Life, my Strength, my Joy, my All!
    Sir Henry Wotton, 'A Hymn to my God,
      in a night of my late sickness', 1638

        O do not use me,
After my sinnes! look not on my desert,
But on thy glorie! then thou wilt reform
And not refuse me: for thou only art
The mightie God, but I a sillie worm;
        O do not bruise me!

        O do not urge me!
For what account can thy ill steward make?
I have abus'd thy stock, destroy'd thy woods,
Suckt all thy magazens: my head did ake,
Till it found out how to consume thy goods;
        O do not scourge me!

        O do not blinde me!
I have deserv'd that an Egyptian night
Should thicken all my powers; because my lust

Hath still sow'd fig-leaves to exclude thy light:
But I am frailtie, and already dust;
          O do not grinde me!

          O do not fill me
With the turn'd viall of thy bitter wrath!
For thou hast other vessels full of bloud,
A part whereof my Saviour empti'd hath,
Ev'n unto death: since he died for my good,
          O do not kill me!

          But O reprieve me!
For thou hast life and death at thy command;
Thou art both *Judge* and *Saviour, feast* and *rod*,
Cordiall and *Corrosive*: put not thy hand
Into the bitter box; but O my God,
          My God, relieve me!
        George Herbert, 'Sighs and Grones', 1633

When I lie within my bed,
Sick in heart and sick in head,
And with doubts discomforted,
        Sweet Spirit, comfort me!

When the house doth sigh and weep,
And the world is drown'd in sleep,
Yet mine eyes the watch do keep,
        Sweet Spirit, comfort me!

When the artless doctor sees
No one hope, but of his fees,
And his skill runs on the lees,
        Sweet Spirit, comfort me!

When his potion and his pill
Has, or none, or little skill,

Meet for nothing, but to kill,
　　Sweet Spirit, comfort me!

When the passing bell doth toll,
And the Furies in a shoal
Come to fright a parting soul,
　　Sweet Spirit, comfort me!

When the tapers now burn blue,
And the comforters are few,
And that number more than true,
　　Sweet Spirit, comfort me!

When the priest his last hath pray'd,
And I nod to what is said,
'Cause my speech is now decay'd,
　　Sweet Spirit, comfort me!

Robert Herrick, from 'Litany to the Holy Spirit', 1647

The Fiery Darts of Satan stob my heart,
　　His Punyards Thrusts are deep, and venom'd too.
His Arrows wound my thoughts, Words, Works, each part
　　They all a-bleeding ly by th'Stobs, and rue.
　　His Aire I breath in, poison doth my Lungs.
　　Hence come Consumptions, Fevers, Head pains, Turns.

Yea, Lythargy, the Apoplectick Stroke,
　　The Catochee, Soul Blindness, Surdity,
Ill Tongue, Mouth Ulcers, Frog, the Quinsie Throate,
　　The Palate Fallen, Wheezings, Pleurisy,
　　Heart Ach, the Syncopee, bad stomach tricks,
　　Gaul Tumors, Liver grown, spleen evill's Cricks,

The Kidny toucht, the Iliak, Colick Griefe,
　　The Ricats, Dropsy, Gout, the Scurvy, Sore,
The Miserere Mei. O Reliefe
　　I want and would, and beg it at thy doore.
　　O! Sun of Righteousness, thy Beams bright, hot
　　Rafter a Doctor's, and a Surgeon's Shop.

I ope my Case to thee, my Lord: mee in
  Thy glorious Bath of Sun Shine, Bathe and Sweate.
So rout Ill Humors: and thy purges bring.
  Administer in Sunbeame, Light and Heate.
  Pound some for Cordiall powders very small
  To Cure my Kidnies, Spleen, my Liver, Gaul.

And with the same refresh my Heart, and Lungs,
  From Wasts, and Weakness. Free from Pleurisy,
Bad Stomach, Iliak, Colick Fever, Turns,
  From Scurvy, Dropsy, Gout, and Leprosy,
  From Itch, Botch Scab. And purify my Blood
  From all Ill Humors: So make all things good.
    Edward Taylor, from 'With Healing in His Wings', 1705

  Be near me when my light is low,
    When the blood creeps, and the nerves prick
    And tingle; and the heart is sick,
  And all the wheels of Being slow.

  Be near me when the sensuous frame
    Is rack'd with pangs that conquer trust;
    And Time, a maniac scattering dust,
  And Life, a Fury slinging flame.
        Tennyson, In Memoriam A.H.H., 1850

  And almost every one when age,
    Disease, or sorrows strike him,
  Inclines to think there is a God,
    Or something very like Him.
  Clough, from ' "There is no God," the
        wicked saith', Dipsychus, 1850

Did Heaven send the little boys out of the shop to knock you down
and give you 100 days of pain, & years of lameness? Was it specially
concerned in punishing chastising trying blessing smashing saving

those Jews, who were under the tower of Siloam when it fell? A brick
may have knocked a just man's brains out: and a beam fallen so as to
protect a scoundrel who happened to be standing under. The bricks
and beams fell according to the laws w^h. regulate bricks in tumbling
– So with our diseases, we die because we are born; we decay
because we grow. I have a right to say O Father give me submission
to bear cheerfully (if possible) & patiently my sufferings but I can't
request any special change in my behalf from the ordinary processes,
or see any special Divine *animus* superintending my illnesses or
wellnesses. Those people seem to me presumptuous who are forever
dragging the Awful Divinity into a participation with their private
concerns. In health, disease, birth, life, death, here, hereafter, I am
His subject & creature, He lifts me up and sets me down certainly –
so He orders my beard to grow . . . I am well. Amen. I am ill. Amen.
I die. Amen always. I can't say that having a tooth out is a blessing or
a punishment for my sins – I say it's having a tooth out.

Thackeray, letter to his mother, February 1859

In delusional insanity, paranoia, as they sometimes call it, we may
have a *diabolical* mysticism, a sort of religious mysticism turned
upside down. The same sense of ineffable importance in the smallest
events, the same texts and words coming with new meanings, the
same voices and visions and leadings and missions, the same
controlling by extraneous powers; only this time the emotion is
pessimistic: instead of consolations we have desolations; the meanings are dreadful; and the powers are enemies to life. It is evident
that from the point of view of their psychological mechanism, the
classic mysticism and these lower mysticisms spring from the same
mental level, from that great subliminal or transmarginal region of
which science is beginning to admit the existence, but of which so
little is really known. That region contains every kind of matter:
'seraph and snake' abide there side by side.

William James, *The Varieties of Religious Experience*, 1902

Afterwards God punished her with many great and divers sicknesses. She had the flux a long time, until she was anointed,

expecting to be dead. She was so feeble that she could not hold a spoon in her hand. Then Our Lord Jesus Christ spoke to her soul and said she should not die yet. Then she recovered again a little while.

And anon afterwards she had a great sickness in her head, and later, in her back, so that she feared to have lost her wits therethrough.

Afterwards, when she was recovered of all these sicknesses, in a short time there followed another sickness, which was set in her right side, lasting the time of eight years, less eight weeks, at divers times. Sometimes she had it once a week, continuing for thirty hours, sometimes twenty, sometimes ten, sometimes eight, sometimes four and sometimes two, so hard and so sharp that she must void what was in her stomach, as bitter as if it were gall, neither eating nor drinking while the sickness endured, but ever groaning till it was gone.

Then she would say to Our Lord: — 'Ah! Blissful Lord, why wouldst Thou become Man, and suffer so much pain for my sins, and for all men's sins, that shall be saved; and we so unkind, O Lord, to Thee; and I, most unworthy, cannot suffer this little pain. Ah! Lord, because of Thy great pain, have mercy on my little pain.'

On a Good Friday, as the said creature beheld priests kneeling on their knees and other worshipful men with torches burning in their hands before the Sepulchre, devoutly representing the lamentable death and doleful burying of Our Lord Jesus Christ after the good custom of Holy Church, the memory of Our Lady's Sorrows, which she suffered when she beheld His Precious Body hanging on the Cross, and then buried before her sight, suddenly occupied the heart of this creature drawing her mind wholly into the Passion of Our Lord Christ Jesus, Whom she beheld in her ghostly eyes in the sight of her soul as verily as though she had seen His Precious Body beaten, scourged and crucified with her bodily eyes, which sight and ghostly beholding wrought by grace so fervently in her soul, wounding her with pity and compassion, so that she sobbed, moaned and cried, and spreading her arms abroad, said with a loud voice, 'I die! I die!' so that many men wondered and marvelled what ailed her.

And the more she tried to keep herself from crying, the louder she cried, for it was not in her power to take it or leave it, but as God would send it.

Then a priest took her in his arms and bore her into the Prior's Cloister to let her take the air, supposing she would not otherwise have endured it, her labour was so great.

Then she waxed all livid like lead, and sweated full sore.

This manner of crying lasted ten years, as has been written before, and every Good Friday in all the aforesaid years she was weeping and sobbing five or six hours together, and therewith cried full loud many times, so that she could not restrain herself therefrom, and this made her full feeble and weak in her bodily might.

> Margery Kempe, c.1373–after 1438, *The Book of Margery Kempe*;
> modernized by W. Butler-Bowdon

Now again I blessed the condition of the Dog and Toad, and counted the estate of everything that *God* had made far better than this dreadful state of mine, and such as my companions' was: yea, gladly would I have been in the condition of Dog or Horse, for I knew they had no Soul to perish under the everlasting weights of Hell for sin, as mine was like to do. Nay, and though I saw this, felt this, and was broken to pieces with it, yet that which added to my sorrow was, that I could not find that with all my Soul I did desire deliverance. That Scripture did also tear and rend my Soul in the midst of these distractions. *The wicked are like the troubled Sea which cannot rest, whose waters cast up mire and dirt: There is no peace to the wicked, saith my God*, Isa. 57: 20,21.

. . . About this time, I did light on the dreadful story of that miserable mortal, *Francis Spira*; a book that was to my troubled spirit as salt, when rubbed into a fresh wound; every sentence in that book, every groan of that man, with all the rest of his actions in his dolours, as his tears, his prayers, his gnashing of teeth, his wringing of hands, his twining and twisting, languishing and pining away under that mighty hand of God that was upon him, was as knives and daggers in my Soul; especially that sentence of his was frightful to me, *Man knows the beginning of sin, but who bounds the issues thereof?* Then would the former sentence, as the conclusion of all, fall like a hot thunderbolt again upon my Conscience; *for you know how that afterwards, when he would have inherited the blessing, he was rejected; for he found no place of repentance, though he sought it carefully with tears.*

Then was I struck into a very great trembling, insomuch that at some times I could for whole days together feel my very body as well as my mind to shake and totter under the sense of the dreadful Judgement of God, that should fall on those that have sinned that most fearful and unpardonable sin. I felt also such a clogging and heat at my stomach by reason of this my terror, that I was, especially at some times, as if my breastbone would have split in sunder. Then I thought of that concerning *Judas, who, by his falling headlong, burst asunder, and all his bowels gushed out,* Acts 1: 18 . . . Thus did I wind, and twine, and shrink under the burden that was upon me; which burden also did so oppress me, that I could neither stand nor go, nor lie either at rest or quiet.

John Bunyan, *Grace Abounding to the Chief of Sinners,* 1666

I had such a universal terror that I woke at night with a start, thinking that the Pantheon was tumbling on the Polytechnic school, or that the school was in flames, or that the Seine was pouring into the Catacombs, and that Paris was being swallowed up. And when these impressions were past, all day long without respite I suffered an incurable and intolerable desolation, verging on despair. I thought myself, in fact, rejected by God, lost, damned! I felt something like the suffering of hell. Before that I had never even thought of hell. My mind had never turned in that direction. Neither discourses nor reflections had impressed me in that way. I took no account of hell. Now, and all at once, I suffered in a measure what is suffered there.

But what was perhaps still more dreadful is that every idea of heaven was taken away from me: I could no longer conceive of anything of the sort. Heaven did not seem to me worth going to. It was like a vacuum; a mythological elysium, an abode of shadows less real than the earth. I could conceive no joy, no pleasure in inhabiting it. Happiness, joy, light, affection, love – all these words were now devoid of sense . . . There was my great and inconsolable grief! I neither perceived nor conceived any longer the existence of happiness or perfection. An abstract heaven over a naked rock. Such was my present abode for eternity.

A. Gratry, *Souvenirs de ma jeunesse*, 1874; tr. William James in
The Varieties of Religious Experience

Daemonomania differs widely from the mental disease called Theomania. In the latter state of insanity the patient fancies that he is placed in communication with the Deity or his angels; in the former, he feels convinced that he has become the prey of the destroyer of mankind.

The sufferings which daemoniacs say they endure must be excruciating; so powerful is moral influence over our physical sensations. They will tell you that the devil is drawing them tight, and suffocating them with a cord; that he is pinching and lacerating their entrails, burning and tearing their heart, pouring hot oil or molten lead in their veins, while internal flames are consuming them. Their strength exhausted, their digestive functions impaired, their appearance soon becomes miserable in the extreme, their countenances pale and haggard: the wretched creatures endeavour to conceal themselves in their scanty meals, or their attempts to enjoy a broken slumber; they are persuaded that they no longer possess a corporeal existence that requires refection or repose – the evil spirit has borne away their bodies, the devil requires no earthly support; they even deny their sex: they are doomed to live for ever in constant agony. One of them asserts, with horrid imprecations, that she has been the devil's wife for a million of years, and had borne him a numerous family; her body is nothing but a sack made of a devil's skin, and filled with their offspring in the shape of devouring snakes, toads, and venomous reptiles. She exclaims that her husband constantly urges her to commit murder, theft, and every imaginable crime; and sometimes with bitter tears supplicates her keeper to put on a strait-waistcoat, to prevent her from doing evil.

It has been generally remarked that cases of daemonomania are more common amongst women than in men. Their greater susceptibility to nervous affections, their warmth of imagination and strong passions, which habit and education compel them to restrain, produce a state of concentration that must cause increased excitement, and render them more liable to those terrific impressions that constitute the disease. These terrors, from false notions of the Deity, make them anticipate in this world the sufferings denounced in the next. One woman has been known to become daemonomaniac after an intense perusal of the Apocalypse, and another by the constant reading of the works of Thomas à Kempis. Women, moreover, at certain periods are subject to great mental depression, which they have not the power to relieve by exciting pursuits, like men . . . Zacutus relates the case of a daemoniac who was cured by a person who appeared to her in the form of an angel, to inform her that her sins had been forgiven: it is possible that stratagems of a similar nature might prevail. I attended a monomaniac lady in Paris, who fancied herself in Jerusalem on the eve of its destruction. She furiously opposed all endeavours to move her from her residence; and it was only by personating a Jewish rabbi, and offering to take her to New Jerusalem as a place of refuge, that she consented to accompany me in a carriage to a *maison de santé* near the capital. Here imagination subdued imagination. I have had the pleasure to hear that ever since I thus succeeded in breaking a link in the morbid association of her fancies, her state of mind rapidly improved, and that she is now restored to perfect sanity.

J. G. Millingen, Curiosities of Medical Experience, 1837

Oh, once I had a lovely fatherland.
   The oaks grew tall
Up to the sky, the gentle violets swayed.
   I dreamt it all.

I felt a German kiss, heard German words
   (Hard to recall
How good they rang) – the words *Ich liebe dich!*
   I dreamt it all.

Heinrich Heine, from 'Abroad', 1834; tr. Hal Draper

Heard at the station –
Words they use in my home town.
Ah, to go back there . . .
Ishikawa Takuboku (1885–1912)

I was the love that chose my mother out;
    I joined two lives and from the union burst;
My weakness and my strength without a doubt
    Are mine alone for ever from the first:
It's just the very same with a difference in the name
    As 'Thy will be done.' You say it if you durst!

They say it daily up and down the land
    As easy as you take a drink, it's true;
But the difficultest go to understand,
    And the difficultest job a man can do,
Is to come it brave and meek with thirty bob a week,
    And feel that that's the proper thing for you.

It's a naked child against a hungry wolf;
    It's playing bowls upon a splitting wreck;
It's walking on a string across a gulf
    With millstones fore-and-aft about your neck;
But the thing is daily done by many and many a one;
    And we fall, face forward, fighting, on the deck.
        John Davidson, from 'Thirty Bob a Week', 1894

At four in the morning
the milkwoman was knocking,
in plain clothes, threatening
she wouldn't leave us anything,
at most remove the empties,
if I didn't produce the receipt.

It was somewhere in my jacket,
but in any case I knew

what the outcome would be:
she'd take away yesterday's curds,
she'd take the cheese and the eggs,
she'd take our flat away,
she'd take away our child.

If I don't produce the receipt,
if I fail to find the receipt,
the milkwoman will cut our throats.

Piotr Sommer, 'Papers', 1982; tr. the author

The greatness of man is great in that he knows himself miserable. A tree does not know itself to be miserable.

So it is misery to know oneself miserable; but it is greatness to know that one is miserable.

Without consciousness, one is not miserable: a ruined house is not. Only man is miserable. *I am the man that hath seen affliction.*

Blaise Pascal (1623–62), *Pensées*

Strange Complaints, Mishaps, Embarrassments

The items in this section, concerning unnatural ills to which the flesh and the spirit are heir, embrace the pathetic, the intriguing, the inspiring, the humiliating, the unseemly, the ludicrous, and the downright odd. Perhaps only the case of reversed evolution is wholly beyond belief; and we may have second thoughts there, in view of Dog Walker's Elbow, Space Invaders' Wrist, the reported measurements of tapeworms, and the case, treated by Jonathan Gathorne-Hardy's father, of a naval rating who complained of constipation accompanied by unusual symptoms. On examination, a Gloy pot was found embedded in his rectum. 'I sat on it, sir,' the rating confessed.

In his entry for 6 April 1668 Pepys tells an unsavoury story of how Robert Carnegie, Earl of Southesk, having discovered that his wife was 'too kind' to the Duke of York, deliberately infected himself and passed the pox on to Lady Carnegie, so that she might communicate it to the Duke, and thence to the Duchess. Since that time all the Duchess's children proved sickly and infirm: 'which is the most pernicious and foul piece of revenge that ever I heard of'. Less foul in the telling, because fantastic-symbolic, is the tale in Grass's *Dog Years* of Matern touring post-war Germany and conscientiously infecting the female relatives of former Nazi Party functionaries with gonorrhoea, 'the milk of vengeance' he calls it.

It has been noted that Goethe's chilling poem, long excluded from the official canon, has acquired a new relevance. 'Sheer caution will make us think twice.'

=======

Dr P. was a musician of distinction, well known for many years as a singer, and then, at the local School of Music, as a teacher. It was here, in relation to his students, that certain strange problems were first observed. Sometimes a student would present himself, and Dr P. would not recognize him; or, specifically, would not recognize his face. The moment the student spoke, he would be recognized by his voice. Such incidents multiplied, causing embarrassment, perplexity, fear – and, sometimes, comedy. For not only did Dr. P. increasingly fail to see faces, but he saw faces when there were no faces to see: genially, Magoo-like, when in the street, he might pat the heads of water-hydrants and parking-meters, taking these to be the heads of children; he would amiably address carved knobs on the furniture, and be astounded when they did not reply. At first these odd mistakes were laughed off as jokes, not least by Dr P. himself. Had he not always had a quirky sense of humour, and been given to Zen-like paradoxes and jests? His musical powers were as dazzling as ever; he did not feel ill – he had never felt better; and the mistakes were so ludicrous – and so ingenious – that they could hardly be serious or betoken anything serious . . .

There was a hint of a smile on his face. He also appeared to have decided that the examination was over, and started to look round for his hat. He reached out his hand, and took hold of his wife's head, tried to lift it off, to put it on. He had apparently mistaken his wife for a hat! His wife looked as if she was used to such things . . .

How does he do anything, I wondered to myself? What happens when he's dressing, goes to the lavatory, has a bath? I followed his wife into the kitchen and asked her how, for instance, he managed to dress himself. 'It's just like the eating,' she explained. 'I put his usual clothes out, in all the usual places, and he dresses without difficulty, singing to himself. He does everything singing to himself. But if he is interrupted and loses the thread, he comes to a complete stop, doesn't know his clothes – or his own body. He sings all the time – eating songs, dressing songs, bathing songs, everything. He can't do anything unless he makes it a song.' . . .

That was four years ago – I never saw him again, but I often wondered how he apprehended the world, given his strange loss of image, visuality, and the perfect preservation of a great musicality. I think that music, for him, had taken the place of image . . . In *The World as Representation and Will* Schopenhauer speaks of music as 'pure will'. How fascinated he would have been by Dr P., a man who had wholly lost the world as representation, but wholly preserved it as music or will.

And this, mercifully, held to the end – for despite the gradual advance of his disease (a massive tumour or degenerative process in the visual parts of his brain) Dr P. lived and taught music to the last days of his life.

Oliver Sacks, *The Man Who Mistook His Wife For a Hat*, 1985

The Italians have discovered a new incurable syndrome that strikes down those who have too intimate a contact with Michelangelo or Leonardo or Caravaggio.

Art lovers, carried out at Florence's galleries at the rate of one a month, paralysed by rapture, are part of a new clinical phenomenon; victims of the so-called Stendhal syndrome. So far there has been no government health warning.

The syndrome is named after the nineteenth-century French writer who in his book *Rome, Naples and Florence* noted the extraordinary physical reaction that follows from hypersensitivity to art works. Clinical psychologists in Rome and Venice have been noting the phenomenon in those who collapse after visiting the Sistine Chapel or the Titian masterpieces in Venice.

But Florence, with one of the world's most important collections, is where most visitors seem prone to Stendhal syndrome. The central hospital claims that 107 victims have been registered in the past eight years. Compared with the millions of tourists, that is statistically negligible, but clinically significant, says Professor Graziella Magherini. The Florence authorities are preparing a lengthy analysis of the phenomenon.

The syndrome strikes like this: the art lover stands in front of Michelangelo's *David*, or his *Pietà*, or Leonardo da Vinci's *Adoration of the Magi* or *Bacchus* by Caravaggio. He (most victims are males) stands impervious to the shock troops of Japanese tourists. Even the Germans do not bother him. Suddenly he starts to writhe, shudder and blacks out. Stretchers carry out the new victim.

Within a few days the art lover is fit to travel again. Comparison of medical notes with the tourist's doctor's at home show that he set out to Italy in good health and the Florence psychiatrists at least are convinced that the nervous breakdown was brought on by an excess of beauty.

Roger Boyes, 'Warning: Art can damage your health',

The Times, 2 May 1987

The gloomy December days drag on lazily under a dark-grey smoky sky. Although I have discovered Swedenborg's explanation concerning the character of my sufferings, I cannot bring myself once for all to bend under the hand of the Powers. My disposition to make objections asserts itself, and I continually refer the real causes of my suffering to external things, especially the malice of men. Attacked day and night by 'electric streams', which compress my chest and stab my heart, I quit my torture-chamber, and visit the tavern where I find friends. Fearing sobriety, I drink ceaselessly, as the only way of procuring sleep at night. Shame and disgust, however, combined with restlessness, compel me to give this up, and for some evenings I visit the Temperance Café called the 'Blue Band'. But the company one meets with there depresses me – bluish, pale, and emaciated faces, terrible and malicious eyes, and a silence which is not the peace of God.

My health constantly gets worse, for there are cracks in the wall so that smoke penetrates into my room. Today when I walked in the street the pavement moved under my feet like the deck of a ship swaying up and down. Only with considerable difficulty can I make the ascent to the Garden of the Luxembourg. My appetite grows continually less, and I only eat in order to still the pangs of hunger.

An occurrence which has often happened since my arrival in Paris has caused me to make various reflections. Inside my coat, on the left side, exactly over the heart, there is heard a regular ticking; it reminds me of the ticking noise in walls produced by the insect called, in Sweden, 'the carpenter' and also the 'death-watch', believed to presage somebody's death. I thought at first it was my watch, but found it was not so, as the ticking continued after I had laid the watch aside. It is not the buckle of my suspenders, nor the lining of my vest. I accept the explanation of the death-watch, as it suits me best.

August Strindberg, *Legends*, 1898; tr. anon.

Miss R. was born in New York City in 1905, the youngest child of a large, wealthy and talented family. Her childhood and schooldays were free of serious illness, and were marked, from their earliest days, by a love of merriment, games and jokes . . . Between 1922 and 1926, Miss R. lived in the blaze of her own vitality, and lived more than most people in the whole of their lives. And this was as well, for at the age of twenty-one she was suddenly struck down by a virulent form of *encephalitis lethargica* – one of its last victims before the epidemic vanished. 1926, then, was the last year in which Miss R. really *lived* . . .

The acute phase announced itself by nightmares of a grotesque and terrifying and premonitory nature. Miss R. had a series of dreams about one central theme: she dreamed she was imprisoned in an inaccessible castle, but the castle had the form and shape of herself; she dreamed of enchantments, bewitchments, entrance-ments; she dreamed that she had become a living, sentient statue of stone; she dreamed that the world had come to a stop; she dreamed that she had fallen into a sleep so deep that nothing could wake her; she dreamed of a death which was different from death. Her family had difficulty waking her the next morning, and when she awoke there was intense consternation: 'Rose,' they cried, 'Wake up! What's the matter? Your expression, your position . . . You're so still and so strange.' Miss R. could not answer, but turned her eyes to the wardrobe-mirror, and there she saw that her dreams had come true . . .

Her state changed little after the age of thirty, and when I first saw her in 1966, my findings coincided with the original notes from her admission. Indeed, the old staff-nurse on her ward, who had known her throughout, said: 'It's uncanny, that woman hasn't aged a day in the thirty years I've known her. The rest of us get older – but Rosie's the same.' It was true: Miss R. at sixty-one looked thirty years younger; she had raven-black hair, and her face was unlined, as if she had been magically preserved by her trance or her stupor . . .

She continues to look much younger than her years; indeed, in a fundamental sense, she *is* much younger than her age. But she is a Sleeping Beauty whose 'awakening' was unbearable to her, and who will never be awoken again.

Sacks, *Awakenings*, 1973

In the literature of morbidity occasional reference was made to a disorder called bulimia, or pathological craving for food; and I had of course met with numerous instances of related oral disturbances, such as perverted appetite or addiction to a specific food. As a matter of fact, one of the most amusing incidents of my career concerned a case in this category. It happened at the Federal Penitentiary in Atlanta, where I had been sent on a special assignment during the first years of the war. One day I received a note from an inmate requesting an answer to the engaging question, 'Do you think I will get ptomaine poisoning from eating tomatoes on top of razor blades?' I showed this provocative communication to my colleagues in the Clinic who thought, as I did, that someone was pulling my leg. In reply, therefore, I wrote the questioner that the outcome of such a meal depended on whether the razor blades were used or new. Much to my chagrin, a few days later the X-ray technician called me into his office and exhibited two pictures on the stereoscopic viewer, inviting me to look at the 'damnedest thing you ever saw'. I looked. In the area of the stomach I saw a number of clearly defined, oblong shadows. 'What the heck are those?' I asked. 'What do they look like to you?' he responded. I looked again. 'To me,' I said, 'they look like – well, I'll be damned! Razor blades!'

We called the inmate from the hall where he had been sitting hunched over on a bench, moaning with pain. When he saw me, he complained, 'I did what you said. I only ate new blades like you told me . . . Now look what's happened!'

'Musta been the tomatoes, then,' was the technician's dry comment.

When the surgeons went to work on this man they discovered him to be a veritable walking hardware store. I was present in the operating room when they opened him up, and my eyes bulged with amazement as they carefully removed piece after piece of the junk he later told us he had been swallowing for many years. Somewhere in my private collection of psychological curiosa, I have a photograph of the debris collected from this man's interior. It shows not only numerous fragments of razor blades, but also two spoons, a coil of wire, some bottle caps, a small screwdriver, a few bolts, about five screws, some nails, many bits of coloured glass and a couple of twisted metallic objects no one can identify.

> Robert Lindner, *The Fifty-Minute Hour: A Collection of True Psychoanalytic Tales*, 1954

Continental medicine has always favoured unusual methods of taking drugs. Hormone creams, which are still popular in France, can cause unexpected side-effects in a patient's spouse. Four doctors in Rouen have written to *The Lancet* describing the troubles which can arise when somebody shares a bed with a patient using a hormone-impregnated cream.

One man whose wife had been prescribed an oestrogen skin cream started to develop breasts. Another man, not satisfied with the anatomy provided by nature, used a testosterone impregnated cream. It is not recorded whether his stature improved, but his wife began to grow a beard.

> Dr Thomas Stuttaford, 'Medical Briefing', *The Times*, 10 March 1988

In later life, an odd disease
afflicted my great-uncle; no cellular morbidities
as such were manifest, no diminution in faculties –
there were postural changes, a growing addiction to berries,
a fondness for flints – then, of several psychoses
one came to dominate, an obsession with phylogenies;
he spoke less, read more, frequented the reading-rooms of reference
     libraries.
As the syndrome progressed, arms hanging loose to his knees,
small bum in the air, he prowled the anthropological laboratories
of redbrick universities,
convinced he was The Missing Link; these
embarrassing peculiarities
were never remarked upon; idiosyncrasies

in such purlieus are not uncommon. Even when in the trees
of Kensington Gardens he gambolled, ingesting bananas, the park
  police
were not unduly concerned. At afternoon teas
in Sloane Square, great-aunt Maude would give technical summaries
to enquiring family and friends (whose less interesting maladies
by tacit agreement were never pursued at length). By slow degrees
his sense of frustration increased; his contemporaries
were polite, but unimpressed. He was in his late nineties
when recognized at last in one of the appendices
of Leakey's standard work; great-aunt was in ecstasies –
he became much sought-after at Chelsea cocktail parties.
But the old man, having seen his salvation, was now lost in reveries;
he, a latter-day simian, wished only to depart in peace;
he searched no more for fleas.

He eventually died in a fall from the frieze
of the British Museum, a merciful release
for a passing elderly widow. His obsequies
were unmarked by further irregularities.

Ivor C Treby, 'a descent of man', 1981

The censorious game is an ancient medical tradition – some doctors
are still uncertain whether they approve of sex – but the commonest
version played today was shaped during the 1950s, with the coming
of the hula hoop. Doctors discovered then that if they issued gloomy
warnings about what hooping could do to the spine, not only did
they get their letters into their professional journals but their names
into the sort of newspapers read by their patients.

They needed little further encouragement and recently, for
instance, we've had grave pronouncements about Jogger's Nipple,
Break-dancing Neck, Crab-eater's Lung, Swim-goggle Headache,
and Amusement Slide Anaphylaxis. Indeed, in the index of the *New
England Journal of Medicine*, which has become the official journal
of the game, you can find Cyclist's Pudendum, Dog Walker's Elbow,
Space Invaders' Wrist, Unicyclist's Sciatica, Jeans Folliculitis, Jogger's Kidney, Flautist's Neuropathy, and Urban Cowboy's Rhabdo-

myolosis – a painful nastiness in the muscles caused by riding mechanical bucking broncos in amusement arcades . . .

Some sort of prize must surely go to the three punctilious Swiss who, in December 1984, reported yet another jogging hazard: bird attacks by the European Buzzard (*Buteo buteo*). Drs Itin, Heanel and Stalder from Kantonsspital Liestal described how the attacks came during the buzzard breeding season and how 'the birds attacked by diving from behind and continuing to dive as long as the joggers were in motion'. Sadly they didn't speculate on what was passing through the buzzards' minds at the time.

Michael O'Donnell, Doctor! Doctor!, 1986

Some of the most fantastic pages of medical history tell of the terrible things that can happen to the human frame when it is attacked by worms. At one time there seems to have been an international competition as to who could produce the longest tape worm. Vienna started off with a mere twenty-four-footer. Paris countered with one measuring thirty-four-point-five metres and weighing a kilogram. But, it is alleged, victory was finally won by a St Petersburg peasant who presented his proud country with 238 feet of tape worm. Older reports of 800-yarders were dismissed as being 'erroneous' by writers on this choice subject.

There was even a disease, presumed to have killed such illustrious personages as Herod the Great, Emperor Galerius and Philip II of Spain, called 'eaten by Worms'. Gibbon gives a good description of Galerius dying of this illness. 'His body, swelled by an intemperate course of life to an unwieldy corpulence, was covered with ulcers and devoured by immense swarms of those insects who have given their names to this loathsome disease.' In all probability he was referring to filariasis.

Eric Jameson, The Natural History of Quackery, 1961

To *Lond: Royal Society*, where Dr *Tyson* produced a *Lumbricus Latus*, which a Patient of his voided, of 24 foote in length, it had severall joynts, at lesse than one inch asunder, which on examin-ation prov'd so many mouthes & stomaches in number *400* by which it adhered to & sucked the nutrition & juice of the Gutts, & by impairing health, fills it selfe with a white Chyle, which it spewed-out, upon diping the worme in spirit of Wine; nor was it otherwise possible a Creature of that prodigious length should be nourish'd, & so turgid, with but one mouth at that distance: The part or joynt towards the head was exceeding small: We ordered the Doctor to print the discourse made upon it: The Person who voided it, indured such torment in his bowels, that he thought of killing himselfe. There were likewise the Anatomies of other Wormes bred in humane bodys, which, *though* strangly small, were discoverd apparently to be *male* & *female*, had their *Penis*, *Uterus*, *Ovaries* and seminal Vessels &c: so as no likely hood of aequivocal generations. There was also produced *Millipedes* newly voided by Urine, *per penem*, it having it seemes stuck in the neck of the blader and yard, giving a most intollerable itching to the patient; but the difficulty was, how it could possibly passe-through the bloud and the *Heart*, & other minute *ductus's* & strainers through the kidnies to the blader; which being looked on as impossible, was believed to be produced by an Egg in the blader; The person who voided it, having ben prescribed *Millipedes* against suppression of Urine: &c.

Evelyn, Diary, 9 August 1682

Hydrophobia is a kind of madness, well known in every village, which comes by the biting of a mad dog, or scratching . . . so called because the parties affected cannot endure the sight of water, or any liquor, supposing still they see a mad dog in it. And which is more wonderful, though they be very dry (as in this malady they are), they will rather die than drink . . . To such as are so affected, the fear of water begins at 14 days after they are bitten, to some again not till 40 or 60 days after: commonly, saith *Heurnius*, they begin to rave, fly water and glasses, to look red, and swell in the face, about 20 days after (if some remedy be not taken in the mean time) to lie awake, to be pensive, sad, to see strange visions, to bark and howl, to fall into a swoon, and oftentimes fits of the falling sickness. Some say, little things like whelps will be seen in their urine. If any of these signs appear, they are past recovery.

Burton, The Anatomy of Melancholy

When they pushed open the great doors of the barn, and entered into that cool empty space, which would have held two companies at a pinch, it had seemed to offer them the pleasantest lodging they had known for months: it was as lofty as a church, the roof upheld by unwrought beams and rafters, the walls pierced with narrow slits for light and air, and the floor thick-littered with fine, dry straw. Some panicky fowls flew up into their faces, and then fled precipitately as they took possession. They slipped off their equipment and wet tunics, and unrolled their puttees before sprawling at ease.

'Cushy place, this,' said Shem contentedly. 'Wonder what the village is like, it would be all right if we were billeted here for a week; that is, unless we're going on to some decent town.'

'Some bloody thing's bitin' my legs,' said Martlow after a few minutes.

'Mine, too,' said Bourne. 'What the hell . . . ?'

'I'm alive with the buggers,' said Pritchard angrily.

Men were scratching and cursing furiously, for the straw swarmed with hen-fleas, which seemed to bite them in a hundred different places at one and the same time. Compared with these minute black insects of a lively and vindictive disposition, lice were merely caressing in their attentions; and the amount of profane blasphemy which broke from the surprised and discomfited men was of an unusual fervour. For the moment they were routed, scratching themselves savagely with dirty fingernails; and then gradually the bites decreased, and they seemed, with the exception of an occasional nip, to have become immune, hen-fleas apparently preferring a more delicate pasture. They caught one or two with considerable difficulty, and examined them curiously: after all, they were not so repulsive as the crawling, white, crab-like lice, which lived and bred, hatching in swarms, on the hairy parts of one's body. These were mere raiding pleasure-seekers, and when the first onset had spent its force, the fitful skirmishes which succeeded it were endurable.

Frederic Manning, *The Middle Parts of Fortune*, 1929; on the Somme

I remember the night my mother
was stung by a scorpion. Ten hours
of steady rain had driven him
to crawl beneath a sack of rice.
Parting with his poison – flash
of diabolic tail in the dark room –
he risked the rain again.
The peasants came like swarms of flies
and buzzed the Name of God a hundred times
to paralyse the Evil One.
With candles and with lanterns
throwing giant scorpion shadows
on the sun-baked walls
they searched for him: he was not found.
They clicked their tongues.
With every movement that the scorpion made
his poison moved in Mother's blood, they said.
May he sit still, they said.
May your suffering decrease
the misfortunes of your next birth, they said.
May the sum of evil
balanced in this unreal world
against the sum of good
become diminished by your pain.
May the poison purify your flesh
of desire, and your spirit of ambition,
they said, and they sat around
on the floor with my mother in the centre,
the peace of understanding on each face.
More candles, more lanterns, more neighbours,
more insects, and the endless rain.
My mother twisted through and through
groaning on a mat.
My father, sceptic, rationalist,
trying every curse and blessing,
powder, mixture, herb and hybrid.
He even poured a little paraffin
upon the bitten toe and put a match to it.

I watched the flame feeding on my mother.
I watched the holy man perform his rites
to tame the poison with an incantation.
After twenty hours
it lost its sting.

My mother only said
Thank God the scorpion picked on me
and spared my children.
                    Nissim Ezekiel, 'Night of the Scorpion', 1965

18 November 1870. Went into the Tump to see young Meredith who has had his jaw locked for six months, a legacy of mumps. He has been to Hereford Infirmary where they kept him two months, gave him chloroform and wrenched his jaws open gradually by a screw lever. But they could not do him any good.

8 April 1875. A sad accident lately befell the poor strange Solitary, the Vicar of Llanbedr Painscastle. He was sitting by the fire in his little lone hut at Cwm Cello that lies in the bosom of Llanbedr Hill when he either dropped heavily asleep or had a fit and fell full upon the fire. Before he could recover himself his stomach, bowels and thighs were dreadfully burnt, and he has had to stay away from Church for three Sundays. Yet he will let neither doctor nor nurse come near him. The poor solitary.
                    The Revd Francis Kilvert, *Diary*

In 1843 Isambard Kingdom Brunel, the famous engineer, was entertaining children by pretending to pass a half-sovereign through his ear into his mouth, when he accidentally inhaled the coin. He could feel it moving in his windpipe whenever he coughed. Several attempts were made to remove it by tracheotomy but without success. Six weeks after the mishap Brunel had a table constructed which could be moved into a vertical position. He caused himself to be strapped to the table, which was then stood on end and shaken.

After a fit of coughing, he heard with great satisfaction the coin clinking against his teeth.

Retold

Westminster Hotel, New York

Did I tell you that the severity of the weather, and the heat of the intolerable furnaces, dry the hair and break the nails of strangers? There is not a complete nail in the whole British suite, and my hair cracks again when I brush it. (I am losing my hair with great rapidity, and what I don't lose is getting very grey.)

Dickens, letter to Georgina Hogarth, 12 January 1868

At dawn I sighed to see my hairs fall;
At dusk I sighed to see my hairs fall.
For I dreaded the time when the last lock should go . . .
They are all gone and I do not mind at all!
I have done with that cumbrous washing and getting dry;
My tiresome comb for ever is laid aside.
Best of all, when the weather is hot and wet,
To have no top-knot weighing down on one's head!
I put aside my messy cloth wrap;
I have got rid of my dusty tasselled fringe.
In a silver jar I have stored a cold stream,
On my bald pate I trickle a ladle full.
Like one baptized with the Water of Buddha's Law,
I sit and receive this cool, cleansing joy.
Now I know why the priest who seeks Repose
Frees his heart by first shaving his head.

Po Chü-I, 'On his Baldness', 832; tr. Arthur Waley

Hypnotized by the brazen eye of an eagle, part of a lectern presented by a rival for the churchwardenship, Augustus Carp Senior has tripped over the talons and subsequently been dropped twice while being borne to the vestry.

For not only was it discovered by the three doctors, who were immediately summoned to attend upon him, that his right knee was displaying evidences of incipient synovitis, but the three falls, to which he had been subjected between the lectern and the vestry, had resulted in extremely severe contusions of both his larger gluteal muscles.

The problem before the physicians was thus an exceptionally difficult one. For while the condition of his knee demanded that he should lie upon his back, that of his gluteal muscles was even more imperative in demanding a position precisely opposed to this. After a considerable argument, therefore, it was finally decided that for the first week or ten days the position to be assumed should be a face downwards one, with a protective cage over the contused muscles. By this means any painful pressure that might have been exerted by the bed-clothes was avoided – an additional protection being afforded by two discs of lint, previously spread with a cooling ointment. For the purposes of nourishment, which was to be ample and sustaining, my father was then to be drawn towards the end of the bed, his head being allowed to project to a sufficient distance to permit of nutriment being inserted from below. Owing to his weight, this, of course, necessitated the erection of a pulley with straps passing under his arm-pits, a return pulley with straps passing round his ankles coming into play at the end of each meal. Even with such assistance, however, my poor father's plight remained an exceedingly deplorable one; and it is scarcely to be wondered at that, from time to time, he betrayed a marked irritability.

Prostrate as he was, however, and already conscious that his career as a sidesman was definitely over, he flung himself almost immediately, and with all the energy left to him, into the necessary preliminaries of the approaching litigation. Day after day, even while still lying on his abdomen, he held prolonged interviews with Mr Balfour Whey, who most considerately lay beneath my father's bed, parallel with the sufferer and looking up into his face. Whether, in the world's history, an action of such importance – for it was fully reported in most of the daily newspapers – was ever arranged in similar circumstances I do not know, although I doubt it. But I have certainly never seen a spectacle more solemn and pathetic than that of these two earnest and horizontal men vertically discussing, across the end of the bedstead, the possible methods of legal procedure.

Sir Henry Howarth Bashford, *Augustus Carp, Esq. By Himself*, 1924

How holy people look when they are seasick! There was a patient Parsee near me who seemed purified once and for ever from all taint of the flesh. Buddha was a low, worldly-minded, music-hall comic singer in comparison. He sat like this for a long time until . . . and he made a noise like cows coming home to be milked on an April evening.

Butler, *Notebooks*

I was going to say, I can only compare it to a Wench kept at home on some gay Day to nurse a fretful infant, and who, having long rocked it in vain, at length rocks it in spite. – But the Rain came suddenly on: & (this too is the second time) brought on almost instantly a stomach & bowel attack . . . After breakfast I found that the two preceding Days had accumulated some sordes in my Stomach; and I drank three half-pints of Salt water – delivered myself of a great deal of mucous stuff with green & yellow Bile – & really ate a better dinner today than I have done these six weeks: tho' I have taken since I have been at sea no animal food in the Solid. – I was not at all seasick, for the first two or three hours I was hot-eyed with fever-smells in my nose – and 4 or 5 times since in very gusty weather, when my stomach has been weak, I have thrown my food in a jerk off my Stomach; but it was by an action seemingly as mechanical as that by which one's glass or teacup is emptied by a thwart blow of the Sea: preceded by no sense of sickness, accompanied with no nausea, no straining, indeed by no sort of sensation, & followed by permanent comfortable feeling – according to the state of my Health. But tho' the rough weather & the incessant Rocking does not disease me, yet this damned Rocking depresses me inconceivably – like Hiccups, or Itching, it is troublesome & impertinent & forces you away from your Thoughts – like the presence & gossip of an old Aunt or long-staying Visitor to two Lovers.

Coleridge, letter to Robert Southey, 16 April 1804; on board the *Speedwell*, off the coast of Portugal

The damned ship lurched and slithered. Quiet and quick
My cold gorge rose; the long sea rolled; I knew

I must think hard of something, or be sick;
   And could think hard of only one thing – *you*!
You, you alone could hold my fancy ever!
   And with you memories come, sharp pain, and dole.
Now there's a choice – heartache or tortured liver!
   A sea-sick body, or a you-sick soul!

Do I forget you? Retchings twist and tie me,
   Old meat, good meals, brown gobbets, up I throw.
Do I remember? Acrid return and slimy,
   The sobs and slobber of a last year's woe.
And still the sick ship rolls. 'Tis hard, I tell ye,
To choose 'twixt love and nausea, heart and belly.

> Rupert Brooke, 'A Channel Passage', 1909

What is strong drink? Let me think – I answer 'tis a thing
From whence the majority of evils spring,
And causes many a fireside with boistcrous talk to ring,
And leaves behind it a deadly sting . . .

Strong drink to the body can do no good;
It defiles the blood, likewise the food,
And causes the drunkard with pain to groan,
Because it extracts the marrow from the bone:

And hastens him on to a premature grave,
Because to the cup he is bound a slave;
For the temptation is hard to thole,
And by it he will lose his immortal soul.

> William McGonagall, from 'A Tribute to Mr Murphy and the
> Blue Ribbon Army', 1890

1 May 1788
Took a glass of brandy at Bedford Arms, Charlotte Street, which did
me some good . . . In the forenoon when thirsty I had drank a bottle
of cider at the old Cider Cellars, and then being somewhat uneasy,

took another glass of brandy at Jupps's in Duke Court . . . I *felt*, as I have formerly done, that intoxication kept up makes me happy; at least not unhappy, but pleased. I dined heartily with my family on roast pork, drank a good deal of small beer and three glasses of port, and enjoyed my existence. How *material* is man! I myself am certainly much so . . . On this first of May, felt a return of a certain warmth which had not disturbed me for some time. I experience all changes of constitution.

2 May 1788
Perceived that in my late intoxication I had sprained my ankle. At home all day.

Boswell, *Journals*

He found Sir Louis in a low, wretched, miserable state. Though he was a drunkard as his father was, he was not at all such a drunkard as was his father. The physical capacities of the men were very different. The daily amount of alcohol which the father had consumed would have burnt up the son in a week; whereas, though the son was continually tipsy, what he swallowed would hardly have had an injurious effect upon the father.

'You are all wrong, quite wrong,' said Sir Louis, petulantly; 'it isn't that at all. I have taken nothing this week past – literally nothing. I think it's the liver.'

Dr Thorne wanted no one to tell him what was the matter with his ward. It was his liver; his liver, and his head, and his stomach, and his heart. Every organ in his body had been destroyed, or was in course of destruction. His father had killed himself with brandy; the son, more elevated in his tastes, was doing the same thing with curaçao, maraschino, and cherry-bounce.

'Do you know as how my master is dying, very like, while you stand there?'

'What is your master's disease?' said Dr Fillgrave, facing Joe, slowly, and still rubbing his hands. 'What ails him? What is the matter with him?'

'Oh; the matter with him? Well, to say it out at once then, he do take a drop too much at times, and then he has the horrors – what is it they call it? delicious beam-ends, or something of that sort.'. . .

The name which Joe had given his master's illness was certainly not a false one. He did find Sir Louis 'in the horrors'. If any father have a son whose besetting sin is a passion for alcohol, let him take his child to the room of a drunkard when possessed by 'the horrors'. Nothing will cure him if not that.

I will not disgust my reader by attempting to describe the poor wretch in his misery: the sunken, but yet glaring eyes; the emaciated cheeks; the fallen mouth; the parched, sore lips; the face, now dry and hot, and then suddenly clammy with drops of perspiration; the shaking hand, and all but palsied limbs; and worse than this, the fearful mental efforts, and the struggles for drink; struggles to which it is often necessary to give way.

Dr Fillgrave soon knew what was to be the man's fate; but he did what he might to relieve it.

Anthony Trollope, Doctor Thorne, 1858

He was awake. What had he done last night? Played the piano? Was it last night? Nothing at all, perhaps, yet remorse tore at his vitals. He needed a drink desperately. He did not know whether his eyes were closed or open. Horrid shapes plunged out of the blankness, gibbering, rubbing their bristles against his face, but he couldn't move. Something had got under his bed too, a bear that kept trying to get up. Voices, a prosopopoeia of voices, murmured in his ears, ebbed away, murmured again, cackled, shrieked, cajoled; voices pleading with him to stop drinking, to die and be damned. Thronged, dreadful shadows came close, were snatched away. A cataract of water was pouring through the wall, filling the room. A red hand gesticulated, prodded him: over a ravaged mountainside a swift stream was carrying with it legless bodies yelling out of great eye-sockets, in which were broken teeth. Music mounted to a screech, subsided. On a tumbled bloodstained bed in a house whose face was blasted away a large scorpion was gravely raping a one-armed Negress. His wife appeared, tears streaming down her face, pitying, only to be instantly transformed into Richard III, who sprang forward to smother him.

Malcolm Lowry (1909–57), Lunar Caustic

He has taught the Universe to realize itself,
and that must have been: very simple.
Surely he has a recovery for me
and that must be after all my complex struggles: *very* simple.

I do, despite my self-doubts, day by day
grow more & more but a little confident
that I will never down a whiskey again
or gin or rum or vodka, brandy or ale.

It is, after all, very very difficult to despair
while the wonder of the sun   this morning
as yesterday & probably tomorrow.
It all is, after all, very simple.

You just never drink again all each damned day.
> John Berryman, 'The Alcoholic in the 3rd Week of the 3rd
> Treatment', c.1971

We curse not wine: The vile excess we blame;
More fruitful than th'accumulated board,
Of pain and misery . . .
    Meantime, I would not always dread the bowl,
Nor every trespass shun. The feverish strife,
Rous'd by the rare debauch, subdues, expels
The loitering crudities that burden life;
And, like a torrent full and rapid, clears
Th'obstructed tubes.
> John Armstrong, MD, *The Art of Preserving Health*, 1744

My introduction to opium arose in the following way. From an early age I had been accustomed to wash my head in cold water at least once a day: being suddenly seized with toothache, I attributed it to some relaxation caused by an accidental intermission of that practice; jumped out of bed; plunged my head into a basin of cold water; and with hair thus wetted went to sleep. The next morning, as I need hardly say, I awoke with excruciating rheumatic pains of the head and face, from which I had hardly any respite for about twenty days. On the twenty-first day, I think it was, and on a Sunday, that I went out into the streets; rather to run away, if possible, from my torments, than with any distinct purpose. By accident I met a college acquaintance who recommended opium. Opium! dread agent of unimaginable pleasure and pain! I had heard of it as I had of manna or of ambrosia, but no further: how unmeaning a sound was it at that time! what solemn chords does it now strike upon my heart! what heart-quaking vibrations of sad and happy remembrances! . . .

Arrived at my lodgings, it may be supposed that I lost not a moment in taking the quantity prescribed. I was necessarily ignorant of the whole art and mystery of opium-taking: and, what I took, I took under every disadvantage. But I took it: – and in an hour, oh! heavens! what a revulsion! what an upheaving, from its lowest depths, of the inner spirit! what an apocalypse of the world within me! That my pains had vanished, was now a trifle in my eyes: – this negative effect was swallowed up in the immensity of those positive effects which had opened before me – in the abyss of divine enjoyment thus suddenly revealed . . . here was the secret of happiness, about which philosophers had disputed for so many ages, at once discovered: happiness might now be bought for a penny, and carried in the waistcoat pocket.

. . . the unimaginable horror which these dreams of Oriental imagery, and mythological tortures, impressed upon me. Under the connecting feeling of tropical heat and vertical sunlights, I brought together all creatures, birds, beasts, reptiles, all trees and plants, usages and appearances, that are found in all tropical regions, and assembled them together in China or Indostan. From kindred feelings, I soon brought Egypt and all her gods under the same law. I was stared at, hooted at, grinned at, chattered at, by monkeys, by paroquets, by cockatoos. I ran into pagodas: and was fixed, for centuries, at the summit, or in secret rooms; I was the idol; I was the priest; I was worshipped; I was sacrificed. I fled from the wrath of Brahma through all the forests of Asia: Vishnu hated me: Siva laid wait for me. I came suddenly upon Isis and Osiris: I had done a deed, they said, which the ibis and the crocodile trembled at. I was buried, for a thousand years, in stone coffins, with mummies and sphinxes, in narrow chambers at the heart of eternal pyramids. I was kissed, with cancerous kisses, by crocodiles; and laid, confounded with all unutterable slimy things, amongst reeds and Nilotic mud.

Opium therefore I resolved wholly to abjure, as soon as I should find myself at liberty to bend my undivided attention and energy to this purpose. It was not however until the 24th of June last that any tolerable concurrence of facilities for such an attempt arrived . . . I persevered in my abstinence for 90 hours; i.e. upwards of half a week. Then I took – ask me not how much: say, ye severest, what would ye have done? then I abstained again: then took about 25 drops: then abstained: and so on.

Meantime the symptoms which attended my case for the first six weeks of the experiment were these: – enormous irritability and excitement of the whole system: the stomach in particular restored to a full feeling of vitality and sensibility; but often in great pain: unceasing restlessness night and day: sleep – I scarcely knew what it was: 3 hours out of the 24 was the utmost I had, and that so agitated and shallow that I heard every sound that was near me: lower jaw constantly swelling: mouth ulcerated: and many other distressing symptoms that would be tedious to repeat; amongst which, however, I must mention one, because it had never failed to accompany any attempt to renounce opium – viz. violent sternutation: this now became exceedingly troublesome: sometimes lasting for 2 hours at once, and recurring at least twice or three times a day. I was not much surprised at this, on recollecting what I had somewhere heard or read, that the membrane which lines the nostrils is a prolongation of that which lines the stomach; whence I believe are explained the inflammatory appearances about the nostrils of dram-drinkers. The sudden restoration of its original sensibility to the stomach expressed itself, I suppose, in this way. It is remarkable also that, during the whole period of years through which I had taken opium, I had never once caught cold (as the phrase is), nor even the slightest cough. But now a violent cold attacked me, and a cough soon after.

A case history, from Thomas De Quincey, *Confessions of an English Opium-Eater*, 1821

— 'Twas nothing, – I did not lose two drops of blood by it — 'twas not worth calling in a surgeon, had he lived next door to us — thousands suffer by choice, what I did by accident. — Doctor *Slop* made ten times more of it, than there was occasion: — some men rise, by the art of hanging great weights upon small wires, — and I am this day (*August* the 10th, 1761) paying part of the price of this man's reputation. — O 'twould provoke a stone, to see how things are carried on in this world! — The chamber-maid had left no ******* *** under the bed: — Cannot you contrive, master, quoth *Susannah*, lifting up the sash with one hand, as she spoke, and helping me up into the window-seat with the other, — cannot you manage, my dear, for a single time, to **** *** ** *** ******?

I was five years old. — *Susannah* did not consider that nothing was well hung in our family, — so slap came the sash down like lightning upon us; — Nothing is left, — cried *Susannah*, – nothing is left – for me, but to run my country. —

My uncle *Toby*'s house was a much kinder sanctuary; and so *Susannah* fled to it.

My father put on his spectacles — looked, — took them off, — put them into the case — all in less than a statutable minute; and without opening his lips, turned about and walked precipitately down stairs: my mother imagined he had stepped down for lint and basilicon; but seeing him return with a couple of large folios under his arm, and *Obadiah* following him with a large reading-desk, she took it for granted 'twas an herbal, and so drew him a chair to the bedside, that he might consult upon the case at his ease.

— If it be but right done, — said my father, turning to the *Section — de sede vel subjecto circumcisionis*, — for he had brought up *Spenser de Legibus Hebroeorum Ritualibus* – and *Maimonides*, in order to confront and examine us altogether. —

— If it be but right done, quoth he: — only tell us, cried my mother, interrupting him, what herbs? — For that, replied my father, you must send for Dr *Slop*.

My mother went down, and my father went on, reading the section as follows,

*	*	*	*	*	*	*	*
*	*	*	*	*	*	*	*
*	*	*	*	— Very well, — said my father,			
*	*	*	*	*	*	*	*
*	*	*	*	*	*	*	*
*	*	— nay, if it has that convenience — and so without					

stopping a moment to settle it first in his mind, whether the *Jews* had it from the *Egyptians*, or the *Egyptians* from the *Jews*, — he rose up, and rubbing his forehead two or three times across with the palm of his hand, in the manner we rub out the footsteps of care, when evil has trod lighter upon us than we foreboded, — he shut the book, and walked down stairs. — Nay, said he, mentioning the name of a different great nation upon every step as he set his foot upon it, — if the EGYPTIANS, — the SYRIANS, — the PHOENICIANS, — the ARABIANS, — the CAPPADOCIANS, — if the COLCHI, and TROGLODYTES did it — if SOLON and PYTHAGORAS submitted, — what is TRISTRAM? — Who am I, that I should fret or fume one moment about the matter?

Laurence Sterne, Tristram Shandy, 1759–67

During the autumn of 1967 Singapore suffered an epidemic of the dread disease known as *koro*, in which the penis retreats into the abdomen, threatening at best a loss of pleasure, at worst a self-inflicted stabbing. Long ago the Hippocratic school of medicine at Cos held that cases showing retraction of the genitalia were hopeless.

Emergency measures resorted to on the present occasion were rough and ready, including weights attached to the all-too-private parts, contraptions made of string and wire and wood, adhesive tape, and even, in desperate cases, skewers and safety-pins. The casualty departments of hospitals were mobbed by panic-stricken victims, some tenaciously hanging on to their snail-like members, others requiring treatment more for the cure than for the disease.

Nothing recedes like recess. Or, in the words of Dennis Bloodworth, the *Observer* correspondent resident there, 'Since worry can cause shrinking and the shrinking in turn causes worry, Singapore has been caught on a spiral of alarm.' Rumour had it that the affliction came from eating the flesh of pigs vaccinated against swine-fever. Chinese citizens were faced with an agonizing choice. Which were they prepared to go without?

The rulers of the country have always looked askance at superstition, wastage, and absenteeism; and besides, panic can have political repercussions. Happily the Singapore Medical Association provided a more acceptable alternative by declaring that the immediate cause of *koro* was a spell of unusually cool weather, exacerbated by natural though unfounded anxiety. After raging for a week or ten days the epidemic died out.

It was whispered subsequently that women had experienced a similar disorder, but there was no hint concerning the means they adopted to discourage their nipples from retracting. Those acquainted with the self-possession and fortitude characteristic of these women would guess that they simply waited for the normal heat of the tropics to reassert itself.

Former resident

The talk at table was about the amusements of Venice. The gentlemen reproached me for my indifference towards the most inviting of all, extolling the graciousness of Venetian courtesans, and declaring that there were none in the world to equal them. Dominique said that I must become acquainted with the most amiable of them, that he would take me to her, and that I should be well satisfied . . . In fact I neither had the intention nor felt the temptation, despite which, by one of those inconsistencies which I can hardly understand myself, I ended by letting them drag me off against my inclination, my heart, my reason, even my will, solely through feebleness, through being ashamed to show my mistrust of them, and, as they say in those parts, *per non parer troppo coglione* [so as not to seem too much of a ninny]. La Padoana, to whose house we went, had a pretty enough face, even beautiful, though not the kind of beauty that pleased me. Dominique left me with her; I sent for *sorbetti*, I got her to sing, and at the end of half an hour I prepared to depart, leaving a ducat on the table. But she was singularly scrupulous in not accepting what she hadn't earned, and I was singularly stupid in relieving her of her scruples. I returned to the palace so convinced I had caught a dose that the first thing I did on arriving was to send for the surgeon and ask for medication. Nothing can exceed the anxiety of spirit I suffered during the next three weeks, without any real discomfort, without any obvious sign to warrant it. I could not imagine how anyone could come away from La Padoana's arms scot-free. The surgeon found the greatest possible difficulty in reassuring me. He managed only by persuading me that I was formed in so peculiar a fashion that I couldn't easily be infected; and while I have exposed myself to that test less than any other man perhaps, the fact that my health has never been impaired in this respect is for me a proof that the surgeon was correct. The knowledge, however, has never made me rash, and, if indeed I have received this advantage from nature, I can say that I have not abused it.

Rousseau, The Confessions; of the year 1744

No peace saith my God for the wicked! no quiet Gestation for me! on Sunday Night the 3rd of Septr. [1776] Mr Thrale told me he had an Ailment & shewed me a Testicle swelled to an immense Size: I had no Notion but of a *Cancer* – Poor Fool! & press'd him to have the best help that could be got – no he would have only Gregory – a drunken crazy Fellow that his Father had known: however when I pressed him with an honest earnestness and kind Voice to have Hawkins, Potts or some eminent hand – he said it was nothing dangerous with a Smile; but that since I had an Aversion to Mr Gregory he would send for one Osborne; a sort of half Quack, whose Name I have sometimes read in the papers as possessing the Receipts of a M. Daran a famous Practitioner in the *Venereal* Way: I now began to understand where I was, and to perceive that my poor Father's Prophecy was verified who said If you marry that Scoundrel he will catch the Pox, and for your Amusement set you to make his Pultices. This is now literally made out; & I am preparing Pultices as he said, and Fomenting this elegant Ailment every Night & Morning for an Hour together on my Knees, & receiving for my Reward such Impatient Expressions as disgreable Confinement happens to dictate. However tis well tis no worse – he has I am pretty sure not given it me, and I am now pregnant & may bring a healthy Boy who knows? All my Concern is lest it *should* after all prove a Schirrus [scirrhus, cancerous tumour] – my Master denies its being the other Thing very resolutely, & says he has felt it ever since he jumped from the Chaise between Rouen & Paris exactly this Time Twelvemonth: if this should be true we are all undone, undone indeed! for it can end in nothing but a Cancer, & I know but too well the Dreadful

Consequence of that most fatal Disease – Yet I will *hope* it may be only a Venereal Complaint, if so there is no Danger to be sure & this Osborne may manage it rightly.

30 Octr.
. . . Be this as it may, I have wronged my poor husband grossly with my wicked Suspicions: it was undoubtedly the leaping from the Chaise in France so long ago that produced the Tumor at first – for he often feels pain I find in the great Muscle of the Thigh which he strain'd at that same fatal Time, & this Disorder in the Scrotum has been coming ever since tho' he never would speak on't. Perhaps he was afraid of my being frighted, perhaps of my suspecting his being tainted with the bad Distemper . . .

13 Decr.
We have been to London for a Week and are returned. Mr Thrale has consulted Hawkins about his Ailment, which turns out a mere Hydrocele, occasioned by the Accident of jumping from the Chaise between Vernon & Paris: Hawkins has let off the Water once, but it is filling again: and he must have it radically cured by the Seton & Caustic after the next Tapping the Surgeons tell him. Upon the whole tis a bad Thing, but better than I thought for every way.

21 Decr.
Mr Thrale's Complaint *was* venereal at last – What need of so many Lyes about it! – I'm sure I care not, so he recovers to hold us all together.

Hester Lynch Thrale, *Family Book*

You were two perilous serpents, reviled with one voice by the poets,
    And for long ages the world shuddered on hearing your names:
Python, and you, Lernaean Hydra! But luckily you're both
    Dead, struck down by the strong hands of adventuresome gods.
Now your fiery breath and your venomous spittle no longer
    Blast our forests and flocks, blight our rich acres of corn.
But, alas! what god in his fury and malice has sent us
    This new monster, this plague born of the poisonous mire?

Nowhere is safe from its creeping intrusion, it lurks in the loveliest
  Gardens, this treacherous worm strikes in the act of our joy!
Hail, Hesperian dragon! at least you bravely and fiercely
  Guarded those apples of gold, out in the uttermost west.
But this creature has nothing to guard, for gardens where he hides,
  And any fruit he has touched, they're not worth guarding at all.
Secretly there in the bushes he squirms, befouling the waters,
  Slavering poison and death into Love's life-giving dew.
Happy Lucretius! you could renounce romantic attachment,
  And without cause for alarm clasp any body you chose.
Slaves brought you your consenting bedmates, lucky Propertius,
  Down from the Aventine Hill, out of the Tarpeian Grove;
And if Cynthia caught you with one, then though you had wronged
    her
  By being faithless, at least nothing was wrong with your health.
Who does not hesitate now to break faith with a tedious mistress?
  Love may not hold us, but sheer caution will make us think twice.
Even at home, who knows! Not a single pleasure is risk-free;
  Who in his own wife's lap now lays a confident head?
Neither in wedlock now nor out of it can we be certain;
  Mutually noxious we are, husband and lover and wife.
Oh for that golden age, when Jove would descend from Olympus,
  Visiting Semele's place, paying Callisto a call!
He himself, in that sacred temple, required a clean welcome
  When he came to its door, entering in amorous might.
What a great fuss would Juno have made, if she'd found that with
    poisoned
  Weapons her husband fought, back in the conjugal bed! –
But we old heathen sinners are not completely abandoned;
  We can still call on one god – he hovers over the earth,
Busy and swift: you all know his name, so pay him due homage!
  He, Jove's messenger-boy, Mercury – he knows the cure.
Though his father's great temples have fallen, with pairs of old
    columns
  Scarcely still marking the place of the majestic old cult,
Yet young Mercury's temple will stand, and his suppliants enter
  Still, while others depart gratefully, world without end.
One petition to you, oh Graces, I offer in private!

Grant this one fervent request, made from the depths of my heart:
Always protect the neat little garden I cherish, and always
  Fend off diseases from me; when I'm invited by Love
And when I trust myself to him, that rogue, may my pleasure be ever
  Carefree, and never with fear, never with danger be mixed!
          Goethe, *Roman Elegies* XVII, 1788–90; tr. David Luke

It looked a suitably seedy establishment. A wooden plaque bearing the doctor's name and qualifications hung against a frosted-glass window.

The doctor himself answered the door. He was finishing what appeared to be a sandwich, the crusts still in his hand.

The surgery was small and gloomy, made colder by a large unlighted gas fire.

X mumbled his fears, striving to inject an element of man-to-man and devil-may-care into his voice.

'And your name is – ?' The doctor reached for a loose sheet of paper.

X hadn't thought of that. Mr X? Hardly. 'John Bee,' he said quickly.

The doctor, a stout man, rocked with laughter. 'So you think you've been stung, Mr Bee?'

'Ha, ha,' said X appreciatively.

'Not a bee sting but a bee stung, eh?' At least the doctor was in a good humour. 'Let's have you then, Mr Bee . . . Come closer to the light . . . Not much to see, is there?'

He explained that he was not exactly the right person, there were proper places for these little problems, the addresses were written up in most public lavatories. In his opinion, but no, he wouldn't pass an opinion, he would only say, what was obvious, that there were no obvious outer signs. Nonetheless he agreed to accept a modest consultation fee.

Back in the street, X remembered an anecdote about a well-known figure in the book world who, preyed on by feelings of guilt, was virtually convinced he had caught a venereal disease. He would go repeatedly to the frosted window of his office, open his fly, and inspect himself for sinister signs. This ended only when a polite letter came from the shop across the street, a popular gents' outfitter, informing him that from their point of view the frosting of his window panes was wholly inadequate.

Anon.

Bear with me friends when ill-defined
The mortal part shall touch the mind
And look not askance at me
And my post-cocious potency.

When the glands set my loins on fire
Urging inordinate desire,
And from the seas 'neath which it lies
A thousand Venuses arise.

When I am contemplating rape
And growing careless of escape
And Lust not art engrosses me —
For who writes old men's poetry?

Then may your minds be set at ease
And learn to pity my disease
Till I with undishonoured head
Join the uncopulating dead.

Oliver St John Gogarty, 'To his Friends when his
Prostate shall have become Enlarged', 1943

Bonadea was that lady who had rescued Ulrich on the night of his unfortunate fisticuffs and the next morning came, heavily veiled, to visit him. He had nicknamed her Bonadea, the Good Goddess, because of the way she had come into his life and also after a goddess of chastity who had a temple in ancient Rome, which by a queer reversal later became a centre of all debaucheries. She did not know that. She liked the sonorous name that Ulrich had given her, and on her visits she wore it like a sumptuously embroidered négligé . . .

She was the wife of a well-respected man and the fond mother of two fine little boys. Her favourite idea was that of the 'paragon'; she applied this expression to people, servants, shops and feelings, whenever she wanted to speak well of them. She was capable of uttering the words 'the true, the good and the beautiful' as often and as naturally as someone else might say 'Thursday'. What was most deeply satisfying to her craving for ideas was the concept of a tranquil, ideal mode of life in a circle formed by husband and children, while far below that there floated the dark realm of 'Lead me not into temptation', the awe of it toning the radiant happiness down into soft lamplight. She had only one fault, and this was that she was liable to be stimulated to a quite uncommon degree by the mere sight of men. She was by no means lustful; she was sensual in the way that other people have other troubles, such as sweating of the hands or blushing easily; it was apparently congenital, and she could never do anything about it. When she got to know Ulrich in circumstances so romantic, so extraordinarily stimulating to the imagination, she had from the first instant been the destined prey of a passion that began as sympathy, after a brief but severe tussle went over into forbidden intimacies, and then continued as an alternation between the pangs of sin and the pangs of remorse.

But Ulrich was only one of heaven alone knows how many cases in her life. Men – as soon as they have grasped the situation – are generally in the habit of treating such nymphomaniac women little better than imbeciles, who can by the most trivial means be tricked into stumbling over the same thing time and time again; for the tender aspects of masculine self-abandonment somewhat resemble the growling of a jaguar over a hunk of meat, and any interruption is taken gravely amiss. The consequence was that Bonadea often led a double life, like that of any citizen who, entirely respectable in the everyday world, in the dark interspaces of his consciousness leads the life of a railway thief; and the moment she held no one in her arms, this quiet, majestic woman began to suffer from self-contempt, which was caused by the lies and degradations to which she had exposed herself in order to be held in someone's arms. When her sensuality was aroused, she was melancholy and kind; indeed, in her mingling of rapture and tears, of crude naturalness and inevitably approaching remorse, in the way that her mania would bolt in panic before the threatening depression that was already lying in wait for her, she had a heightened charm that was exciting in much the same way as a ceaseless tattoo on a darkly muffled drum. But in the lucid intervals, in the state of remorse between two states of weakness during which she felt her helplessness, she was full of the claims of respectability, which did not make it any too easy to get on with her. One had to be truthful and good, to be sympathetic towards all misfortune, to be devoted to the Imperial House, to respect everything respected and in matters of morality to be as sensitive and gentle as at a sick-bed.

> Robert Musil (1880–1942), *The Man Without Qualities*;
> tr. Eithne Wilkins and Ernst Kaiser

In 1821 my being in love resulted in a highly comical virtue: chastity.

In August 1821, in spite of my efforts, Lussinge, Barot and Poitevin, who thought I looked depressed, arranged a delightful evening out . . . Alexandrine appeared and surpassed all expectations. She was a tall and slim girl of seventeen or eighteen, already mature and with the black eyes which I've since found in Titian's portrait of the Duchess of Urbino in the Florence Gallery. Apart from the colour of the hair, Titian's portrait is her. She was quiet and gentle but not at all shy, fairly gay but not unseemly in her behaviour. My friends' eyes goggled at the sight of her. Lussinge offered a glass of champagne, which she refused, and disappeared with her . . . After a dreadfully long interval, a very pale Lussinge returned.

    – Your turn, Beyle, they cried. You've just come home; it's your privilege.

I found Alexandrine on a bed, a little wan, almost in the costume and in the exact position of Titian's Duchess of Urbino.

    – Let's just talk for ten minutes, she said in a lively way. I'm a bit tired, let's chat. My young blood will flare up again soon.

She was adorable, I perhaps had never seen anyone prettier. There wasn't too much licentiousness about her except in the eyes which gradually became suggestively animated again and full (you could say) of passion.

I failed entirely with her; it was a complete *fiasco*. So I had to rely on a substitute which she submitted to. Not quite knowing what to do, I wanted to try this manual expedient again but she refused. She seemed astonished. Considering my situation, I said several quite good things and then went out.

Hardly had Barot taken my place when we heard bursts of laughter although there were three rooms separating him from us . . . Those fellows wanted to persuade me I was dying of shame and that that moment was the unhappiest of my life. I was astonished but nothing more. I don't know why the idea of Métilde had seized hold of me when I entered that room so attractively graced by Alexandrine.

Stendhal, *Memoirs of an Egotist*; tr. David Ellis

VIII

Ready to taste a thousand Joys,
The too transported hapless Swain
Found the vast Pleasure turn'd to Pain;
Pleasure which too much Love destroys:
The willing Garments by he laid,
And Heaven all open'd to his view,
Mad to possess, himself he threw
On the Defenceless Lovely Maid.
But Oh what envying God conspires
To snatch his Power, yet leave him the Desire!

IX

Nature's Support (without whose Aid
She can no Human Being give)
Itself now wants the Art to live;
Faintness its slacken'd Nerves invade:
In vain th'enragèd Youth essay'd
To call its fleeting Vigor back,
No motion 'twill from Motion take;
Excess of Love his Love betray'd:
In vain he Toils, in vain Commands;
Th'Insensible fell weeping in his Hand.

XI

Cloris returning from the Trance
Which Love and soft Desire had bred,
Her timorous Hand she gently laid
(Or guided by Design or Chance)
Upon that Fabulous *Priapus*,
That Potent God, as Poets feign;
But never did young *Shepherdess*,
Gath'ring of Fern upon the Plain,
More nimbly draw her Fingers back,
Finding beneath the verdant Leaves a Snake:

XII

Than *Cloris* her fair Hand withdrew,
Finding that God of her Desires
Disarm'd of all his Awful Fires,
And Cold as Flow'rs bath'd in the Morning Dew.
Who can the *Nymph's* Confusion guess?
The Blood forsook the hinder Place,
And strew'd with Blushes all her Face,
Which both Disdain and Shame express'd:
And from *Lysander's* Arms she fled,
Leaving him fainting on the Gloomy Bed.

XIV

The *Nymph's* Resentments none but I
Can well Imagine or Condole:
But none can guess *Lysander's* Soul,
But those who sway'd his *Destiny*.
His silent Griefs swell up to Storms,
And not one God his Fury spares;
He curs'd his Birth, his Fate, his Stars;
But more the *Shepherdess's* Charms;
Whose soft bewitching Influence
Had Damn'd him to the *Hell* of Impotence.

Aphra Behn, from 'The Disappointment', 1684

The shame in ageing
is not that Desire should fail
(who mourns for something
he no longer needs?): it is
that someone else must be told.
W. H. Auden, from 'Marginalia', 1965–8

Imaginary, Feigned, Psychological

In their assumed roles, Addison and Jerome K. Jerome attribute valetudinarianism or hypochondria to the noxious practice of reading books about disease. So, *in propria persona*, does Tessa Miller. Hence it seems necessary to insist that the present book is designed to have the opposite effect, and to persuade its readers that, compared with what they are reading, they enjoy pretty sound health. Or, at the very least, like Johnson as seen by Boswell in a later section, that whatever degree of eccentricity they may evince, they are still superior to other men and women.

Though the borderline between the two can be uncertain, feigned illness is another matter, one whose purpose may be to preserve health and well-being, and in the promotion of which you need all your wits about you. The Münchhausen syndrome is not easy to sustain, as Volpone discovered, although he might have succeeded in his plots had it not been that some of those involved were no less crooked than he.

As for the 'psychological': the mind being what it is, to say that it's all in the mind is hardly to brush it, whatever it is, aside. The Jesuit priest and poet saw that the mind has mountains, cliffs of fall, frightful, sheer; and the fallen Archangel was speaking humanly when he averred that

> The mind is its own place, and in itself
> Can make a Heav'n of Hell, a Hell of Heav'n.

───────────

I am one of that sickly tribe who are commonly known by the name of Valetudinarians, and do confess to you, that I first contracted this ill habit of body, or rather of mind, by the study of physick. I no sooner began to peruse books of this nature, but I found my pulse was irregular, and scarce ever read the account of any disease that I did not fancy myself afflicted with.

Joseph Addison, 'Valetudinarians', *The Spectator*, 29 March 1711

I remember going to the British Museum one day to read up the treatment for some slight ailment of which I had a touch – hay fever, I fancy it was. I got down the book, and read all I came to read; and then, in an unthinking moment, I idly turned the leaves, and began to indolently study diseases, generally. I forget which was the first distemper I plunged into – some fearful, devastating scourge, I know – and before I had glanced half down the list of 'premonitory symptoms', it was borne in upon me that I had fairly got it.

I sat for a while frozen with horror; and then in the listlessness of despair, I again turned over the pages. I came to typhoid fever – read the symptoms – discovered that I had typhoid fever, must have had it for months without knowing it – wondered what else I had got; turned up St Vitus's dance – found, as I expected, that I had that too – began to get interested in my case, and determined to sift it to the bottom, and so started alphabetically – read up ague, and learnt that I was sickening for it, and that the acute stage would commence in about another fortnight. Bright's disease, I was relieved to find, I had only in a modified form, and, so far as that was concerned, I might live for years. Cholera I had, with severe complications; and diphtheria I seemed to have been born with. I plodded conscientiously through the twenty-six letters, and the only malady I could conclude I had not got was housemaid's knee.

I felt rather hurt about this at first; it seemed somehow to be a sort of slight. Why hadn't I got housemaid's knee? Why this invidious reservation? After a while, however, less grasping feelings prevailed. I reflected that I had every other known malady in the pharmacology, and I grew less selfish, and determined to do without housemaid's knee. Gout, in its most malignant stage, it would appear, had seized me without my being aware of it; and zymosis I had evidently been suffering with from boyhood. There were no more diseases after zymosis, so I concluded there was nothing else the matter with me.

I walked into that reading-room a happy healthy man. I crawled out a decrepit wreck.

I went to my medical man. He is an old chum of mine, and feels my pulse, and looks at my tongue, and talks about the weather, all for nothing, when I fancy I'm ill; so I thought I would do him a good turn by going to him now. 'What a doctor wants,' I said, 'is practice. He shall have me. He will get more practice out of me than out of seventeen hundred of your ordinary, commonplace patients, with only one or two diseases each.' So I went straight up and saw him, and he said:

'Well, what's the matter with you?'

I said:

'I will not take up your time, dear boy, with telling you what is the matter with me. Life is brief, and you might pass away before I had finished. But I will tell you what is *not* the matter with me. I have not got housemaid's knee. Why I have not got housemaid's knee, I cannot tell you; but the fact remains that I have not got it. Everything else, however, I *have* got.'

And I told him how I came to discover it all.

Then he opened me and looked down me, and clutched hold of my wrist, and then he hit me over the chest when I wasn't expecting it – a cowardly thing to do, I call it – and immediately afterwards butted me with the side of his head. After that, he sat down and wrote out a prescription, and folded it up and gave it me, and I put it in my pocket and went out.

I did not open it. I took it to the nearest chemist's, and handed it in. The man read it, and then handed it back.

He said he didn't keep it.

I said:

'You are a chemist?'

He said:

'I am a chemist. If I was a co-operative stores and family hotel combined, I might be able to oblige you. Being only a chemist hampers me.'

I read the prescription. It ran:

1 lb beefsteak, with 1 pt bitter beer every six hours. 1 ten-mile walk every morning. 1 bed at 11 sharp every night. And don't stuff up your head with things you don't understand.

I followed the directions, with the happy result – speaking for myself – that my life was preserved, and is still going on.

Jerome K. Jerome, *Three Men in a Boat*, 1889

'Mr Merdle is dead.'

'I should wish,' said the Chief Butler, 'to give a month's notice.'

'Mr Merdle has destroyed himself.'

'Sir,' said the Chief Butler, 'that is very unpleasant to the feelings of one in my position, as calculated to awaken prejudice; and I should wish to leave immediate.'

'If you are not shocked, are you not surprised, man?' demanded the Physician, warmly.

The Chief Butler, erect and calm, replied in these memorable words. 'Sir, Mr Merdle never was the gentleman, and no ungentlemanly act on Mr Merdle's part would surprise me.' . . .

The report that the great man was dead, got about with astonishing rapidity. At first, he was dead of all the diseases that ever were known, and of several bran-new maladies invented with the speed of Light to meet the demand of the occasion. He had concealed a dropsy from infancy, he had inherited a large estate of water on the chest from his grandfather, he had had an operation performed upon him every morning of his life for eighteen years, he had been subject to the explosion of important veins in his body after the manner of fireworks, he had had something the matter with his lungs, he had had something the matter with his heart, he had had something the matter with his brain. Five hundred people who sat down to breakfast entirely uninformed on the whole subject, believed before they had done breakfast, that they privately and personally knew Physician to have said to Mr Merdle, 'You must expect to go out, some day, like the snuff of a candle', and that they knew Mr Merdle to have said to Physician, 'A man can die but once.' By about eleven o'clock in the forenoon, something the matter with the brain, became the favourite theory against the field; and by twelve the something had been distinctly ascertained to be 'Pressure'.

Pressure was so entirely satisfactory to the public mind, and seemed to make everybody so comfortable, that it might have lasted all day but for Bar's having taken the real state of the case into Court at half-past nine. This led to its beginning to be currently whispered all over London by about one, that Mr Merdle had killed himself. Pressure, however, so far from being overthrown by the discovery, became a greater favourite than ever. There was a general moralizing upon Pressure, in every street. All the people who had tried to make money and had not been able to do it, said, There you were! You no sooner began to devote yourself to the pursuit of wealth, than you got Pressure. The idle people improved the occasion in a similar manner. See, said they, what you brought yourself to by work, work, work! You persisted in working, you overdid it, Pressure ensued, and you were done for! This consideration was very potent in many quarters, but nowhere more so than among the young clerks and partners who had never been in the slightest danger of overdoing it. These one and all declared, quite piously, that they hoped they would never forget the warning as long as they lived, and that their conduct might be so regulated as to keep off Pressure, and preserve them, a comfort to their friends, for many years.

Dickens, Little Dorrit, 1855–7

I went to that doctor because I had been told that he cured nervous diseases by electricity. I thought I might derive from electricity the strength necessary to give up smoking.

The doctor was a stout man and his asthmatic breathing accompanied the clicking of the electrical machine that he set in motion at my very first visit. This was rather a disappointment, for I thought the doctor would make an examination of me and discover what poison it was which was polluting my blood. But he only said that my constitution was sound, and that since I complained of bad digestion and sleeplessness he supposed my stomach lacked acids and that the peristaltic action was weak; he repeated that word so many times that I have never forgotten it. He prescribed me an acid that ruined my inside, for I have suffered ever since from over-acidity.

When I saw that he would never discover the nicotine in my blood himself, I thought I would help him, and suggested that my ill health was probably due to that. He shrugged his great shoulders wearily:

'Peristaltic action – acid. It has nothing to do with nicotine!'

He gave me seventy electric treatments, and I should be having them still if I had not decided I had had enough. I did not hasten to my appointments so much because I expected miraculous results, as because I hoped to persuade the doctor to order me to give up smoking. Things might have turned out very differently if I had had a command like that with which to fortify my resolutions.

This is the description I gave the doctor of my illness:

'I am incapable of studying, and on the few occasions when I go to bed early I lie awake till the first bells begin to ring. And that is why I continue to waver between law and chemistry, because both those sciences oblige one to begin work at a stated time, whereas I never know at what time I shall be able to get up.'

'Electricity cures every form of insomnia,' announced Aesculapius, his eyes fixed as usual on his quadrant instead of on his patient.

I began talking to him about psychoanalysis as if I expected him to understand it; for I was one of the first, though timidly, to dabble in it.

I told him of my troubles with women. I was not satisfied with one or even with many; I desired them all! My excitement as I walked along the streets was intense; whenever I passed a woman, I wanted to possess her. I stared at them insolently, because I wanted to feel as brutal as possible. I undressed them in imagination down to their shoes. I held them in my arms and only let them go when I was sure that I knew every part of them.

I might have spared my breath. All my sincerity was wasted. The doctor snorted:

'I hope the electrical treatment won't cure you of that disease. A fine state of things that would be! I would never touch a high frequency again if I thought that it was going to have that effect.'

He told me what he thought to be a very spicy anecdote. Someone who was suffering from my complaint went to a famous doctor hoping to be cured; but the doctor having treated him with complete success was obliged to leave the town, otherwise the patient would have torn him limb from limb.

'My excitement is not normal,' I yelled. 'It comes from the poison burning in my veins!'

The doctor muttered sympathetically:
'No one is ever satisfied with his lot.'

> Italo Svevo, *Confessions of Zeno*, 1923; tr. Beryl de Zoete

In both real life and fiction, hypochondriacs, like mothers-in-law, are always good for a laugh . . . But to those who suffer from it, hypochondria is no joke. It is a horrible and disabling condition, which gradually dominates and undermines one's life as inexorably as any 'real' disease.

Some years ago, I had a serious illness. It is now completely cured, but I no longer have total confidence in my body. Over the past six months a slight abdominal pain, which my baffled doctor says must be muscular, has been enough to turn me from a cheerful, positive person into a neurotic, underweight, hypochondriac wreck . . .

Anxiety has become a full-time occupation, from waking in the morning till, thankfully, getting to sleep at night, and my fears are fed by the indulgence of an urge endemic to the condition – the compulsive reading of medical books. Our *Penguin Medical Dictionary*, for years barely opened, is now the most-thumbed, dog-eared paperback in the house. It has not, however, yielded the longed-for treasure – some trivial, curable disorder that fits my symptoms – but has instead given further grounds for worry.

In the good old days, if I felt unusually thirsty I assumed I had eaten something salty: now, I brood about diabetes. A cold sore is a potential cancer of the mouth. It is no consolation, as I sit in the bath fearfully examining myself for signs of thinning pubic hair (cirrhosis), to reflect that I must be one of the greatest unqualified experts on disorders of the abdominal organs, heart and lungs.

Hypochondria, like many more reputable illnesses, puts a great strain on the sufferer's family and friends. My husband could not be more supportive, but even he is getting understandably fed up with being greeted, evening after evening, with 'Hello, it was bad this morning but got better at lunch-time . . .', accompanied by requests to feel my pulse/stomach/ankles and make reassuring noises. And is asking him not to flush the lavatory after using it, so that I can compare his urine colour with mine, not perhaps verging on Unreasonable Behaviour?

Tessa Miller, 'Hypochondria: a sick joke?', *The Observer*,
18 January 1987

Some men employ their health, an ugly trick,
In making known how oft they have been sick,
And give us, in recitals of disease,
A doctor's trouble, but without the fees;
Relate how many weeks they kept their bed,
How an emetic or cathartic sped;
Nothing is slightly touch'd, much less forgot,
Nose, ears, and eyes, seem present on the spot.
Now the distemper, spite of draught or pill,
Victorious seem'd, and now the doctor's skill;
And now – alas for unforeseen mishaps!
They put on a damp nightcap and relapse;
They thought they must have died they were so bad –
Their peevish hearers almost wish they had.

Cowper, *Conversation*, 1782

Most of these patients were women, many of them rich, idle, spoiled, and neurotic . . . I was firm, I was stern, I bullied and commanded, I even invented a new disease for them – asthenia. This word, which means no more than weakness or general debility, became a sort of talisman, which procured my entry to more important portals. At afternoon tea in Cadogan Place, or Belgrave Square, Lady Blank would announce to the Honourable Miss Dash – eldest daughter of the Earl of Dot:

'Do you know, my dear, this young Scottish doctor – rather uncivilized, but amazingly clever – has discovered that I'm suffering from asthenia. Yes . . . , asthenia. And for months old Dr Brown-Blodgett kept telling me it was nothing but nerves.'

Having created a disease, it was essential to produce the remedy. At this time the system of medication by intramuscular injection was coming into vogue – a process whereby colloidal suspensions of iron, manganese, strychnine, and other tonic medicaments were introduced to the patient's blood stream, not by the mouth, but through the medium of the hypodermic syringe. Later on, this technique was largely discounted as being in no way superior to the old-fashioned method of oral administration, but at that moment it suited me to perfection . . .

Again and yet again my sharp and shining needle sank into fashionable buttocks, bared upon the finest linen sheets. I became expert, indeed, superlative, in the art of penetrating the worst end of the best society with a dexterity which rendered the operation almost painless . . .

Strange though it may seem, the results of this complex process of hocus-pocus – and I was, I assure you, a great rogue at this period, though perhaps not more so than many of my colleagues – were surprisingly, often amazingly, successful. Asthenia gave these bored and idle women an interest in life. My tonics braced their languid nerves. I dieted them, insisted on a regime of moderate exercise and early hours. I even persuaded two errant wives to return to their long-suffering husbands, with the result that within nine months they had other matters than asthenia to occupy them.

> A. J. Cronin, *Adventures in Two Worlds*, 1952; a London
> practice in the 1920s

> Say, ye, oppressed by some fantastic woes,
> Some jarring nerve that baffles your repose;
> Who press the downy couch, while slaves advance
> With timid eye to read the distant glance;
> Who with sad prayers the weary doctor tease,
> To name the nameless ever new disease;
> Who with mock patience dire complaints endure,
> Which real pain and that alone can cure;
> How would ye bear in real pain to lie,
> Despised, neglected, left alone to die?
>
> Crabbe, *The Village*, 1783

Tullio and I began talking again about his illness, which was his principal distraction. He had studied the anatomy of the leg and foot. He told me with amusement that when one is walking rapidly each step takes no more than half a second, and in that half second no fewer than fifty-four muscles are set in motion. I listened in bewilderment. I at once directed my attention to my legs and tried to discover the infernal machine. I thought I had succeeded in finding it. I could not of course distinguish all its fifty-four parts, but I discovered something terrifically complicated which seemed to get out of order directly I began thinking about it.

I limped as I left the café, and for several days afterwards walking became a burden to me and even caused me a certain amount of pain. I felt as if the whole machine needed oiling. All the muscles seemed to grate together whenever one moved . . . Even today, if anyone watches me walking, the fifty-four movements get tied up in a knot, and I feel as if I shall fall down.

Svevo, Confessions of Zeno

But let not little men triumph upon knowing that Johnson was an HYPOCHONDRIACK, was subject to what the learned, philosophical, and pious Dr Cheyne has so well treated under the title of 'The English Malady'. Though he suffered severely from it, he was not therefore degraded. The powers of his great mind might be troubled, and their full exercise suspended at times; but the mind itself was ever entire . . .

It is a common effect of low spirits or melancholy, to make those who are afflicted with it imagine that they are actually suffering those evils which happen to be most strongly presented to their minds. Some have fancied themselves to be deprived of the use of their limbs, some to labour under acute diseases, others to be in extreme poverty; when, in truth, there was not the least reality in any of the suppositions; so that when the vapours were dispelled, they were convinced of the delusion. To Johnson, whose supreme enjoyment was the exercise of his reason, the disturbance or obscuration of that faculty was the evil most to be dreaded. Insanity, therefore, was the object of his most dismal apprehension; and he fancied himself seized by it, or approaching to it, at the very time when he was giving proofs of a more than ordinary soundness and vigour of judgement.

About this time [1764] he was afflicted with a very severe return of the hypochondriack disorder, which was ever lurking about him. He was so ill, as, notwithstanding his remarkable love of company, to be entirely averse to society, the most fatal symptom of that malady. Dr Adams told me, that, as an old friend, he was admitted to visit him, and that he found him in a deplorable state, sighing, groaning, talking to himself, and restlessly walking from room to room. He then used this emphatical expression of the misery which he felt: 'I would consent to have a limb amputated to recover my spirits.'

Talking to himself was, indeed, one of his singularities ever since I knew him. I was certain that he was frequently uttering pious ejaculations; for fragments of the Lord's Prayer have been distinctly overheard. His friend Mr Thomas Davies, of whom Churchill says,

'That Davies hath a very pretty wife',

when Dr Johnson muttered 'lead us not into temptation', used with waggish and gallant humour to whisper Mrs Davies, 'You, my dear, are the cause of this.'

He had another particularity, of which none of his friends ever ventured to ask an explanation. It appeared to me some superstitious habit, which he had contracted early, and from which he had never called upon his reason to disentangle him. This was his anxious care to go out or in at a door or passage by a certain number of steps from a certain point, or at least so as that either his right or his left foot (I am not certain which) should constantly make the first actual movement when he came close to the door or passage. Thus I conjecture: for I have, upon innumerable occasions, observed him suddenly stop, and then seem to count his steps with a deep earnestness; and when he had neglected or gone wrong in this sort of magical movement, I have seen him go back again, put himself in a proper posture to begin the ceremony, and, having gone through it, break from his abstraction, walk briskly on, and join his companion.

Boswell, *Life of Johnson*, 1791

The world is come upon me, I used to keep it a long way off,
But now I have been run over and I am in the hands of the hospital
     staff.
They say as a matter of fact I have not been run over it's imagination,

But they all admit I shall be kept in bed under observation.
I must say it's very comfortable here, nursie has such nice hands,
And every morning the doctor comes and lances my tuberculous
  glands.
He says he does nothing of the sort, but I have my own feelings
  about that,
And what they are if you don't mind I shall keep under my hat.
My friend, if you call it a friend, has left me; he says I am a deserter
  to ill health,
And that the things I should think about have made off for ever, and
  so has my wealth.
Portentous ass, what to do about him's no strain
I shall quite simply never speak to the fellow again.

Stevie Smith, 'The Deserter', 1950

My body is that part of the world which my thoughts can alter. Even
imagined illnesses can become actual ones. In the rest of the world,
my hypotheses cannot disturb the order of things.

Georg Christoph Lichtenberg, *Sudelbuch*, 1789

The imposter nearly always pretends to be absolutely dumb, and
seldom knows enough about his pretended complaint to see the
necessity of uttering some word or word-like syllable, as the true
aphasic nearly always does. This reminds us of the case of a soldier
who, with the view of obtaining his discharge, pretended that he had
been suddenly struck dumb. He was taken to the doctor, who at
once suspected the real nature of the case. The man was told to try
and say 'Ah', it being explained to him that he would have no
difficulty as it was 'a purely laryngeal sound, unconnected with the
faculty of language'. The effort was successful. He was then told to
say 'No', which, it was explained, was 'a sound of similar character'.
Not seeing the trap, he promptly replied as directed, 'No'. 'Well, my
friend,' said the doctor, 'if you can say "No" you can say anything;
so good day.'

The Family Physician

Volpone feigns extreme sickness in order that rich and covetous
Venetians shall make him their heir in return for being made his. He
desires the young wife of old Corvino; and Mosca, his accomplice,
tells Corvino that in a final effort to keep Volpone alive the college of
physicians has advised that some young woman should be found to
lie in his bed, and that one of the doctors has already offered his
daughter –

> And a virgin, sir. Why? Alas
> He knows the state of's body, what it is;
> That naught can warm his blood, sir, but a fever;
> Nor any incantation raise his spirit;
> A long forgetfulness hath seized that part.
> Besides, sir, who shall know it? Some one, or two . . .

To pre-empt this proposal, Corvino offers his wife. He forces
Celia into Volpone's bedchamber, in pursuance, as he puts it, of 'a
pious work, mere charity, for physic, and honest polity, to assure
mine own'. As Celia is strenuously deploring the affront to her
modesty, Volpone leaps from his couch:

> Why art thou 'mazed, to see me thus revived?
> Rather applaud thy beauty's miracle;
> 'Tis thy great work: that hath, not now alone,
> But sundry times, raised me, in several shapes . . .
>   Nay, fly me not.
> Nor let thy false imagination
> That I was bed-rid, make thee think I am so;
> Thou shalt not find it.
>
>   See Jonson, *Volpone*, for the sequel

How I dreaded the end of school! As soon as I was outside, I slipped
off as fast as I could and took to my heels. Fortunately we did not
live far off; but my enemies lay in wait for me; then, for fear of
ambushes, I contrived immense detours; as soon as the others
became aware of this they changed their tactics and the hunt which

•

had begun as a stalk developed into a chase; there might really have been some fun in it, but I felt that what moved them was not so much love of sport as hatred of me – wretched game that I was. The chief among them was the son of a travelling circus manager – a boy called Lopez, or Tropez, or Gomez, a great athletic brute, who was considerably older than any of us and who made it a point of honour to be at the bottom of the form. I can see him now – his horrid expression, his low forehead and plastered hair, shiny with hair-oil, his floating scarlet tie; it was he who was the leader and *he* really wanted my blood. There were days when I got home in a lamentable state, my clothes torn and muddy, my nose bleeding, my teeth chattering, haggard with fright. My poor mother was at her wits' ends. Then at last, by some merciful Providence, I fell seriously ill and my torture came to an end.

The doctor was sent for. I had small-pox. I was saved!

I was well nursed and looked after and in the normal course of things should soon have been about again. But as my convalescence advanced and the moment drew near for resuming my halter, I felt overwhelmed with horror, the unspeakable horror left me by the recollection of my torments. I saw the ferocious Gomez in my dreams; I fled panting from his pack; I felt again the abominable sensation on my cheek of the dead cat which he had one day picked out of the gutter and rubbed against my face, while the others held my arms; I used to wake up bathed in sweat, but only to a renewal of my terror, as I thought of what Dr Leenhardt had said to my mother – that in a few days I should be well enough to go back to the *lycée*; and my heart quaked within me. But I am not wishing to excuse what follows. I leave it to neurologists to disentangle what was real and what was assumed in the nervous malady that followed my small-pox.

This, I think, is how it began. The first day I was allowed to get up, I felt a kind of giddiness which made me totter on my legs, as was only natural after three weeks in bed. If this giddiness got a little worse, thought I to myself, can I imagine what would happen? Oh, yes; I should feel my head sink backwards; my knees would give way (I was in the little passage that led from my room to my mother's) and I should suddenly collapse on the floor. 'Ha!' said I to myself, 'suppose I were to imitate what I imagine!' And even in the act of

imagining I could feel what a relief, what a respite, it would be to
yield to this suggestion of my nerves. One glance behind me to make
sure of a place where the fall would not hurt too much and . . .

I heard a cry from the next room. It was Marie who came running.
I knew my mother was out; some remains of shame or pity
restrained me when she was there, but I counted on her being told all
about it. After this first trial, encouraged by my success, I grew
bolder, cleverer and more decidedly inspired; I ventured on other
movements; sometimes I invented jerky and abrupt ones; sometimes, on the contrary, they were long drawn out and rhythmically
repeated in a kind of dance. I became extremely expert at these
danses and my repertory was soon fairly varied; one consisted in just
jumping up and down on the same spot; in another, I went
backwards and forwards across the little space between the window
and my bed, on to which I sprang, standing upright, at every return
journey – three jumps in all hit it off exactly; sometimes this lasted
an hour on end. There was another I performed in bed with the
bedclothes thrown off, consisting of a series of high kicks done in
cadence like those of a Japanese juggler.

I have often reproached myself since that time and wondered how
I had the heart to carry on in this way in my mother's presence. But I
must confess that nowadays my self-reproach seems to me less
grounded. These movements of mine, though perhaps conscious,
were barely voluntary. That is to say that at most I might have
controlled them a little. But that gave me the greatest relief. Ah! how
often in later days, when suffering from my nerves, have I regretted
that I was no longer of an age when a pirouette or two . . .

André Gide, *If It Die . . .* , 1926; tr. Dorothy Bussy

A report in the *Journal of the Royal Society of Medicine*, October
1987, concerns a 'Falklands war veteran' who arrived at a London
hospital showing symptoms of a heart attack. It turned out that his
cardiac condition was as false as his claim to have been present at
Goose Green. The Army had not heard of him.

Another hospital, where he claimed he had had a heart operation,
could find no record of him, but he carried numerous surgical scars,
indicating that some hospitals had been fooled into operating

needlessly on him. The man was said to be suffering from a form of Münchhausen's syndrome, the medical term for imaginary illnesses and invented medical histories.

The report states that many hundreds of such cases present themselves at hospitals every year, often using aliases and forged medical records. Some have been so convincing that major operations such as coronary artery bypasses have been performed on them. Others have tampered with equipment used in diagnosis in an attempt to fool the doctors.

A study by heart specialists at the Royal Free Hospital in London has identified thirty-six cases of 'cardiopathia fantastica' in a ten-year period, including one man probably admitted six times under different names. A man of sixty-seven, seemingly in the throes of a heart attack, was given cardiac massage in hospital; the next morning, after examination by doctors, he was discharged as fully recovered. Later the same day he appeared in the emergency department, suffering another heart attack. A nurse told him that one of the same doctors was coming to see him, and he made a speedy recovery.

Medical reports

The effects of fear upon the body are apparent in many other ways. An approach to the door of a dentist by one labouring under toothache has often been found a sure means of banishing violent pain. Fright has frequently cured ague and other disorders of a periodical character; even fits of the gout have been terminated in the same manner. Paralysed muscles, and limbs that were useless, have suddenly been thrown into action, and haemorrhages have as instantaneously been checked. The same causes productive of disease have been found also to effect their cure. Dr Pfeuffer knew a girl in the vicinity of Würzburg, who, after being deaf for several years, instantly regained her hearing upon being made acquainted with the sudden death of her father. Everyone has heard of the treatment proposed by the celebrated Boerhaave, to restrain imitative epilepsy by branding the next who should be affected with a hot iron. Dr Scott relates a case in which a threat to apply a red-hot iron to the feet of a boy who had been frequently attacked with epilepsy upwards of a year, was perfectly successful in preventing the recurrence of the disease.

> Thomas Pettigrew, *On Superstitions connected with the History and Practice of Medicine and Surgery*, 1844

In Brian Inglis's book, *The Diseases of Civilisation*, a London dermatologist recalls the case of a patient who came out in a rash every time he went home to the country at the weekend. It was supposed that he was allergic to some rural substance, but the rash disappeared only when his wife died and he was free to marry the woman with whom he had lived during the week while working in the City. Inglis also cites the case of a woman, allergic to roses, who developed the symptoms when an artificial bloom was offered to her.

> Drawn from Brian Inglis, *The Diseases of Civilisation*, 1981

The surgeon recommended an operation for the removal of the appendix and this was accordingly performed. But after recovery and convalescence the girl again complained of abdominal pain. This time she was advised to consult a surgeon with a view to treatment for adhesions resulting from the first operation. But the second surgeon referred the girl to a psychiatrist from whose inquiries it transpired that the girl's education had been such that she believed it to be possible to become pregnant by being kissed. The first abdominal pain had appeared after the experience of being kissed by an undergraduate during his vacation. After the recovery from the operation the girl was again kissed by the same undergraduate with a similar result.

> J. H. Woodger, *Physics, Psychology and Medicine*, 1956

Annually for the past twenty years and more, hundreds of thousands of people who have been brought up in the belief that sexual promiscuity (or even sexual intercourse before marriage) is wicked, have been pitchforked in their adolescence into communities where such views are ridiculed. The stresses occasioned by the subsequent breaking of taboos must in the aggregate be formidable. If sexual embarrassment can trigger a blush, we can hardly rule out the possibility that it can also trigger irritation in the urethral tract. And just as blushes appear on the face — as if they were a deliberate punishment, because only on the face is the blush such a give-away — may not the same process select the site for urethritis?

Inglis, *The Diseases of Civilisation*

I know one diabetic who when he was hypoglycaemic started eating the flowers in the vase by his bed. Another man, a most respectable chemist, used to rush into the adjacent female ward as soon as his blood sugar fell and make unwelcome advances to the women there. A diabetic houseman I once had, used during a round to become abnormally polite and start saying 'Excuse me sir, I beg your pardon sir', until I could persuade him to eat some sugar.

Richard Asher, 'The Physical Basis of Mental Illness',
Medical Society's Transactions, 1953–4

Nothing can so pierce the soul as the uttermost sigh of the body.

George Santayana, *The Life of Reason*, 1905–6

Melancholy and Love Sickness

Ancient basic theory had it that, just as matter was composed of the four elements, so the human body contained four cardinal fluids or 'humours': Blood, Phlegm, Yellow Bile or Choler, and Black Bile or Melancholy. In health, these humours were present in harmonious blend; sickness was due to an imbalance among them.

Humours could thus determine a person's temperament, both physical and emotional. The prologue to Ben Jonson's *Every Man Out of His Humour* explains that the fluids in question are termed humours because they flow continually in one or another part of the body and are not held together.

> Now thus far
> It may, by metaphor, apply itself
> Unto the general disposition:
> As when some one peculiar quality
> Doth so possess a man, that it doth draw
> All his affects, his spirits, and his powers,
> In their confluctions, all to run one way,
> This may be truly said to be a humour.

The theory offered a rich field for satirical writers, comic dramatists in particular. Humours made splendid copy, and characters marked by a preponderance of one of them, especially those who affected an odious or outlandish eccentricity or gave themselves up to some 'ruling passion', what Pope called 'the Mind's disease', would be given 'pills to purge,/And make them fit for fair societies'. In Jonson's *The Magnetic Lady*, Sir Moth Interest's ruling passion is money, and the doctor diagnoses 'a pursiness, a kind of stoppage,/ Or tumour of the purse, for want of exercise', along with difficulty in putting the hand into the pocket, or what 'we sons of physic do call *chiragra*,/A kind of cramp, or hand-gout'. The cure prescribed entails purging the purse once or twice a week at dice or cards, bleeding the lending vein, and training in pulling out the wallet.

We have noticed in the past a poverty of differentiation between diseases, no doubt a result of crude diagnosis. Fever and gout (the latter seen as nature's paroxysmal way of casting out an excess of humours) were blanket terms. And the spleen, the greensickness (a malady most incident to maids: 'Stay, coward blood, and doe not yield/To thy pale sister beauty's field,' cried Thomas Carew in a poem on the subject), and the vapours, barely distinguishable one from another, probably embraced anaemia, anorexia, indigestion, tuberculosis, laziness, emotional distresses, tight clothing, gender expectations – and never mind the sort of deprivation Lady Mary Wortley Montagu pointed to in her poem and, perhaps, Pope in his depiction of the fantasies generated by spleen.

Spleen indicated melancholy, but encompassed ill temper and moroseness verging on and indeed – because of the delusions attending it – merging into insanity. In milder forms, melancholy was for long a popular ailment, a sign of sensibility, a ladylike condition and a gentlemanly one too. Until it wore out its welcome, and the satirists fell upon it.

The melancholy caused by the onset of love or by love unrequited appealed to poets for obvious reasons: it had a respectable source, safer than the loss of one's religious faith and more exalted than the loss of one's money, and it could accommodate a variety of graceful or quaint symptoms. The lover, Shakespeare remarked, sighed like a furnace and made woeful ballads to his mistress's eyebrow. And Berowne, in *Love's Labour's Lost*, resenting his weakness, protested 'By heaven, I do love, and it hath taught me to rhyme, and to be melancholy.' This malady too, or its literary exploitation, eventually fell into disrepute: one lovesick poet came to sound much like another, and few of them sounded authentic. Here, though indulged sincerely (alas) by Hazlitt, it is dealt with even-handedly by John Armstrong, another doctor-poet, and briskly and robustly by Robert Burton. Hardy puts in a final and good, if ironic, word for it.

What art thou, Spleen, which ev'ry thing dost ape.
   Thou Proteus to abused mankind;
   Who never yet thy real cause could find,
Or fix thee to remain in one continued shape
   Still varying thy perplexing form,
   Now a Dead Sea thou'lt represent,
   A calm of stupid discontent,
Then, dashing on the rocks, wilt rage into a storm.
   Trembling sometimes thou dost appear,
   Dissolved into a panic fear;
   On sleep intruding dost thy shadows spread,
   Thy gloomy terrors round the silent bed,
And crowd with boding dreams the melancholy head;
   Or, when the midnight hour is told,
   And drooping lids thou still dost waking hold,
   Thy fond delusions cheat the eyes:
   Before them antic spectres dance,
Unusual fires their pointed heads advance,
   And airy phantoms rise.
   Such was the monstrous vision seen,
When Brutus (now beneath his cares oppressed,
And all Rome's fortunes rolling on his breast,
   Before Philippi's latest field,
Before his fate did to Octavius lead)
   Was vanquished by the spleen.

Anne Finch, Countess of Winchilsea, from 'The Spleen', *c.* 1702

Umbriel, a dusky melancholy Spright,
As ever sullied the fair face of Light,
Down to the Central Earth, his proper Scene,
Repair'd to search the gloomy Cave of *Spleen*.
   Swift on his sooty Pinions flits the *Gnome*,
And in a Vapour reach'd the dismal Dome.
No cheerful Breeze this sullen Region knows,
The dreaded *East* is all the Wind that blows.
Here, in a Grotto, shelter'd close from Air,
And screen'd in Shades from Day's detested Glare,

She sighs for ever on her pensive Bed,
Pain at her Side, and *Megrim* at her Head.
    Two Handmaids wait the Throne: alike in Place,
But diff'ring far in Figure and in Face.
Here stood *Ill-nature* like an *ancient Maid*,
Her wrinkled Form in *Black* and *White* array'd;
With store of Pray'rs, for Mornings, Nights, and Noons,
Her Hand is fill'd; her Bosom with Lampoons.
    There *Affectation* with a sickly Mien
Shows in her Cheek the Roses of Eighteen,
Practis'd to Lisp, and hang the Head aside,
Faints into Airs, and languishes with Pride;
On the rich Quilt sinks with becoming Woe,
Wrapt in a Gown, for Sickness, and for Show.
The Fair Ones feel such Maladies as these,
When each new Night-dress gives a new Disease.
    A constant *Vapour* o'er the Palace flies;
Strange Phantoms rising as the Mists arise;
Dreadful, as Hermit's Dreams in haunted Shades,
Or bright as Visions of expiring Maids.
Now glaring Fiends, and Snakes on rolling Spires,
Pale Spectres, gaping Tombs, and Purple Fires:
Now Lakes of liquid Gold, *Elysian* Scenes,
And Crystal Domes, and Angels in Machines.
    Unnumber'd Throngs on ev'ry side are seen
Of Bodies chang'd to various Forms by *Spleen*.
Here living *Teapots* stand, one Arm held out,
One bent; the Handle this, and that the Spout:
A Pipkin there like *Homer*'s *Tripod* walks;
Here sighs a Jar, and there a Goose-pie talks;
Men prove with Child, as pow'rful Fancy works,
And Maids turn'd Bottles, call aloud for Corks.

                    Pope, *The Rape of the Lock*, 1714

When the men of this country are once turned of thirty, they regularly retire every year at proper intervals to lie in of the *spleen*. The vulgar, unfurnished with the luxurious comforts of the soft cushion, down bed, and easy chair, are obliged when the fit is on them, to nurse it up by drinking, idleness, and ill-humour . . .

The rich, as they have more sensibility, are operated upon with greater violence by this disorder. Different from the poor, instead of becoming more insolent, they grow totally unfit for opposition. A general here, who would have faced a culverin when well, if the fit be upon him, shall hardly find courage to snuff a candle. An admiral, who could have opposed a broadside without shrinking, shall sit whole days in his chamber, mobbed up in double nightcaps, shuddering at the intrusive breeze, and distinguished from his wife only by his black beard and heavy eyebrows . . .

But those who reside constantly in town owe this disorder mostly to the influence of the weather. It is impossible to describe what a variety of transmutations an east wind shall produce; it has been known to change a Lady of fashion into a parlour couch; an Alderman into a plate of custards; and a dispenser of justice into a rattrap. Even Philosophers themselves are not exempt from its influence; it has often converted a Poet into a coral and bells [teething-ring], and a patriot Senator into a dumbwaiter.

    Oliver Goldsmith, *The Citizen of the World: Letters from a Chinese Philosopher, Residing in London, to his Friends in the East,* 1760–1

    When by its magic lantern spleen
With frightful figures spread life's scene,
And threat'ning prospects urged my fears,
A stranger to the luck of heirs;
Reason, some quiet to restore,
Showed part was substance, shadow more;
With spleen's dead weight though heavy grown,
In life's rough tide I sunk not down,
But swam, till fortune threw a rope,
Buoyant on bladders filled with hope.
    I always choose the plainest food
To mend viscidity of blood.
Hail! water-gruel, healing power,
Of easy access to the poor;
Thy help love's confessors implore,

And doctors secretly adore;
To thee I fly, by thee dilute,
Through veins my blood doth quicker shoot,
And by swift current throws off clean
Prolific particles of spleen . . .

    Hunting I reckon very good
To brace the nerves, and stir the blood,
But after no field-honours itch,
Achieved by leaping hedge and ditch.
While spleen lies soft relaxed in bed,
Hygeia's sons with hound and horn,
And jovial cry awake the morn . . .

    To cure the mind's wrong bias, spleen,
Some recommend the bowling-green;
Some, hilly walks; all, exercise;
Fling but a stone, the giant dies.
Laugh and be well; monkeys have been
Extreme good doctors for the spleen;
And kitten, if the humour hit,
Has harlequined away the fit.

    Since mirth is good on this behalf,
At some partic'lars let us laugh:
Witlings, brisk fools cursed with half sense,
That stimulates their impotence,
Who buzz in rhyme, and, like blind flies,
Err with their wings for want of eyes,
Poor authors worshipping a calf,
Deep tragedies that make us laugh,
A strict dissenter saying grace,
A lect'rer preaching for a place,
Folks, things prophetic to dispense,
Making the past the future tense . . .

    If spleen-fogs rise at close of day,
I clear my ev'ning with a play,
Or to some concert take my way.
The company, the shine of lights,
The scenes of humour, music's flights,
Adjust and set the soul to rights.

Life's moving pictures, well-wrought plays,
To others' griefs attention raise:
Here, while the tragic fictions glow,
We borrow joy by pitying woe;
There, gaily comic scenes delight,
And hold true mirrors to our sight.
Virtue, in charming dress arrayed,
Calling the passions to her aid,
When moral scenes just action join,
Takes shape, and shows her face divine.
   Music has charms, we all may find,
Ingratiate deeply with the mind
When art does sound's high pow'r advance,
To music's pipe the passions dance;
Motions unwilled its pow'r have shown,
Tarantulated by a tune.
Many have held the soul to be
Nearly allied to harmony.
Her have I known indulging grief,
And shunning company's relief,
Unveil her face, and looking round,
Own, by neglecting sorrow's wound,
The consanguinity of sound.
            Matthew Green, from 'The Spleen', 1737

                                    5 March 1653
You make soe reasonable demandes, that 'tis not fitt you should bee
deny'd, you aske my thought's but at one hower. You will think mee
bountifull I hope, when I shall tell you, that I know noe hower when
you have them not; Noe, in Earnest my very dream's are yours, and I
have gott such a habitt of thinking of you, that any other thought
intrudes and grow's uneasy to mee. I drink your health every
morning in a drench that would Poyson a horse I beleeve, and 'tis the
only way I have to perswade my self to take it, 'tis the infusion of
steell, and makes mee soe horridly sick that every day at ten a clock, I
am makeing my will, and takeing leave of all my freind's, you will
beleeve you are not forgot then: They tell mee I must take this ugly

drink a fortnight, and then begin another as Bad, but unlesse you say soe too I doe not thinke I shall, 'tis worse then dyeing, by the halfe.

12 March

I am soe farre from thinking you ill natured for wisheing I might not outlive you, that I should not have thought you at all kinde, if you had done otherwise; Noe, in Earnest I was never soe in love with my life, but that I could have parted with it upon a much lesse occasion then your Death, and 'twill bee noe complement to you, to say it would bee very uneasy to mee then, since 'tis not very pleasant to mee now. Yet you will say, I take great paines to preserve it, as ill as I like it; but noe, I'le sweare 'tis not that I intende in what I doe, all that I ayme at, is but to keep my self from groweing a Beast. They doe soe fright mee with strange Story's of what the Spleen will bring mee to in time, that I am kept in awe with them like a Childe. They tell mee 'twill not leave mee common sence, that I shall hardly bee fitt company for my owne dog's, and that it will ende, either in a Stupidnesse that will make mee uncapable of any thing, or fill my head with such whim's as will make mee rediculous; to prevent this, whoe would not take steel or any thing? though I am partly of your opinion, that 'tis an ill kinde of Phisick. Yet I am confident that I take it the safest way, for I doe not take the powder, as many doe, but onely lay a peece of steel in white wine over night, and drink the infusion next morning, which one would think were nothing, and yet 'tis not to bee imagin'd how sick it makes mee for an hower or two. And, which is the missery, all that time one must be useing some kind of Exercise. Your fellow servant has a blessed time on't, I make her play at Shutlecock with mee, and she is the veryest bungler at it that ever you saw, then am I ready to beate her with the batledore, and grow soe peevish as I grow sick, that I'le undertake she wishes there were noe steel in Englande; but then to recompence the morning I am in good humor all the day after, for Joy that I am well againe. I am tolde, 'twill doe mee good, and am content to beleeve; if it do's not, I am but where I was.

Dorothy Osborne, letters to William Temple

Why will Delia thus retire,
  And idly languish life away?
While the sighing crowd admire,
  'Tis too soon for hartshorn tea.

All those dismal looks and fretting
  Cannot Damon's life restore;
Long ago the worms have ate him,
  You can never see him more.

Once again consult your toilette,
  In the glass your face review:
So much weeping soon will spoil it,
  And no spring your charms renew.

I, like you, was born a woman,
  Well I know what vapours mean:
The disease, alas! is common;
  Single, we have all the spleen.

All the morals that they tell us
  Never cur'd the sorrow yet:
Choose, among the pretty fellows,
  One of honour, youth, and wit.

Prithee hear him every morning,
  At the least an hour or two;
Once again at night returning –
  I believe the dose will do.
Lady Mary Wortley Montagu, 'A Receipt to
                Cure the Vapours', 1748

In old prints melancholy is usually portrayed as a woman, dishevelled, deranged, surrounded by broken pitchers, leaning casks, torn
books. She may be sunk in unpeaceful sleep, heavy limbed, overpowered by her inability to take the world's measure, her compass

and book laid aside. She is very frightening, but the person she frightens most is herself. She is her own disease. Dürer shows her wearing a large ungainly dress, winged, a garland in her tangled hair. She has a fierce frown and so great is her disarray that she is closed in by emblems of study, duty, and suffering: a bell, an hourglass, a pair of scales, a globe, a compass, a ladder, nails. Sometimes this woman is shown surrounded by encroaching weeds, a cobweb undisturbed above her head. Sometimes she gazes out of the window at a full moon, for she is moonstruck. And should melancholy strike a man it will be because he is suffering from romantic love: he will lean his padded satin arm on a velvet cushion and gaze skywards under the nodding plume of his hat, or he will grasp a thorn or a nettle and indicate that he does not sleep. These men seem to me to be striking a bit of a pose, unlike the women, whose melancholy is less picturesque. The women look as if they are in the grip of an affliction too serious to be put into words. The men, on the other hand, appear to have dressed up for the occasion, and are anxious to put a noble face on their suffering. Which shows that nothing much has changed since the sixteenth century, at least in that respect.

Anita Brookner, Look at Me, 1983

Rosalind.   They say you are a melancholy fellow.
Jaques.   I am so. I do love it better than laughing.
Ros.   Those that are in extremity of either are abominable fellows, and betray themselves to every modern censure, worse than drunkards.
Jaq.   Why, 'tis good to be sad and say nothing.
Ros.   Why then, 'tis good to be a post.
Jaq.   I have neither the scholar's melancholy, which is emulation; nor the musician's, which is fantastical; nor the courtier's, which is proud; nor the soldier's, which is ambitious; nor the lawyer's, which is politic; nor the lady's, which is nice; nor the lover's, which is all these: but it is a melancholy of mine own, compounded of many simples, extracted from many objects, and indeed the sundry contemplation of my travels, in which my often rumination wraps me in a most humorous sadness.

Ros.   A traveller! By my faith, you have great reason to be sad. I fear you have sold your own lands to see other men's. Then to have seen much and to have nothing is to have rich eyes and poor hands.
Jaq.   Yes, I have gained my experience.
Ros.   And your experience makes you sad. I had rather have a fool to make me merry than experience to make me sad, and to travel for it too!

Shakespeare, As You Like It, 1599

I have not been well enough to make any tolerable rejoinder to your kind Letter. I will as you advise be very chary of my health and spirits. I am sorry to hear of your relapse and hypochondriac symptoms attending it. Let us hope for the best as you say. I shall follow your example in looking to the future good rather than brooding upon present ill. I have not been so worn with lengthen'd illnesses as you have therefore cannot answer you on your own ground with respect to those haunting and deformed thoughts and feelings you speak of. When I have been or supposed myself in health I have had my share of them, especially within this last year. I may say that for 6 Months before I was taken ill I had not passed a tranquil day. Either that gloom overspread me or I was suffering under some passionate feeling, or if I turn'd to versify that acerbated the poison of either sensation. The Beauties of Nature had lost their power over me. How astonishingly (here I must premise that illness as far as I can judge in so short a time has relieved my Mind of a load of deceptive thoughts and images and makes me perceive things in a truer light) – how astonishingly does the chance of leaving the world impress a sense of its natural beauties on us. Like poor Falstaff, though I do not babble, I think of green fields. I muse with the greatest affection on every flower I have known from my infancy – their shapes and colours are as new to me as if I had just created them with a superhuman fancy. It is because they are connected with the most thoughtless and happiest moments of our Lives. I have seen foreign flowers in hothouses of the most beautiful nature, but I do not care a straw for them. The simple flowers of our spring are what I want to see again.

John Keats, letter to James Rice, 14 February 1820

Sorry you are feeling low in spirits. Don't worry, it is very common with men when they pass forty – or when they draw near forty. Men seem to undergo a sort of *spiritual* change of life, with really painful depression and loss of energy. Even men whose physical health is quite good. So don't fret. Often an *entire* change of scene helps quite a lot. But it's a condition which often drags over several years. Then, in the end, you come out of it with a new sort of rhythm, a new psychic rhythm: a sort of re-birth. Meanwhile, it is what the mystics call the little death, and you have to put up with it. I have had it too, though not so acutely as some men. But then my health is enough to depress the Archangel Michael himself.

> D. H. Lawrence, letter to Mark Gertler, 23 December 1929

He [Johnson] owned, this morning, that one might have a greater aptitude to learn than another, and that we inherit dispositions from our parents. 'I inherited (said he) a vile melancholy from my father, which has made me mad all my life, at least not sober.' – Lady Macleod wondered he should tell this. – 'Madam (said I), he knows that with that madness he is superior to other men.'

> Boswell, *Journal of a Tour to the Hebrides*, 16 September 1773

Love Melancholy and its Cures

Symptoms are either of Body or Mind; of body, Paleness, Leanness, Dryness, &c. *Avicenna* makes *hollow eyes, dryness*, symptoms of this disease, *to go smiling to themselves, or acting as if they saw or heard some delectable object* . . . They pine away, and look ill, with waking, cares, sighs, with groans, griefs, sadness, dulness, want of appetite, &c. A reason of all this, *Jason Pratensis* gives, *because of the distraction of the spirits, the Liver doth not perform his part, nor turns the aliment into blood as it ought; and for that cause the members are weak for want of sustenance, they are lean and pine, as the herbs of my garden do this month of* May, *for want of rain.*

Although it be controverted by some, whether Love-Melancholy may be cured, because it is so irresistible and violent a passion; for, as you know,

> It is an easy passage down to hell,
> But to come back, once there, you cannot well:

yet without question, if it be taken in time, it may be helped, and by many good remedies amended . . . The first rule to be observed in this stubborn and unbridled passion, is exercise and diet. As an idle sedentary life, liberal feeding, are great causes of it, so the opposite, labour, slender and sparing diet, with continual business, are the best and most ordinary means to prevent it. *Minerva, Diana, Vesta*, and the nine *Muses* were not enamoured at all, because they never were idle . . . Those opposite meats which ought to be used are Cowcumbers, Melons, Purselan, Water-Lilies, Rue, Woodbine, Ammi, Lettice; *Agnus castus* [chaste tree, Abraham's balm] before the rest.

Some are of opinion, that to see a woman naked, is able of itself to alter his affection; and it is worthy of consideration, saith *Montaigne*, the Frenchman in his Essays, that the skilfullest masters of amorous dalliance, appoint for a remedy of venereous passions, a full survey of the body . . . Examine all parts of body and mind, I advise thee to enquire of all. See her angry, merry, laugh, weep, hot, cold, sick, sullen, dressed, undressed, in all attires, sites, gestures, passions, eat her meals, &c., and in some of these you will surely dislike her. Yea, not her only let them observe, but her parents, how they carry themselves: for what deformities, defects, incumbrances of body or mind be in them, at such an age, they will likely be subject to, be molested in like manner, they will *patrizare* or *matrizare* [take after their father or mother] . . .

The last refuge and surest remedy, to be put in practice in the utmost place, when no other means will take effect, is, to let them go together, and enjoy one another.

Burton, The Anatomy of Melancholy

> O Rose, thou art sick.
> The invisible worm
> That flies in the night,
> In the howling storm,

Has found out thy bed
Of crimson joy;
And his dark secret love
Does thy life destroy.
William Blake, 'The Sick Rose,' 1794

What meaneth this? When I lie alone,
I toss, I turn, I sigh, I groan;
My bed me seems as hard as stone:
       What meaneth this?

I sigh, I plain continually;
The clothes that on my bed do lie
Always methinks they lie awry:
       What meaneth this?

In slumbers oft for fear I quake;
For heat and cold I burn and shake;
For lack of sleep my head doth ache:
       What meaneth this?

A-mornings then when I do rise
I turn unto my wonted guise;
All day after muse and devise
       What meaneth this?

And if perchance by me there pass
She unto whom I sue for grace,
The cold blood forsaketh my face:
       What meaneth this?

But if I sit near her by,
With loud voice my heart doth cry,
And yet my mouth is dumb and dry:
       What meaneth this?

To ask for help no heart I have,
My tongue doth fail what I should crave,
Yet inwardly I rage and rave:
        What meaneth this?

Thus have I passed many a year
And many a day, though naught appear,
But most of that that most I fear:
        What meaneth this?

Sir Thomas Wyatt (1503–42), 'What meaneth this?'

My love is as a fever, longing still
For that which longer nurseth the disease;
Feeding on that which doth preserve the ill,
Th'uncertain sickly appetite to please.
My reason, the physician to my love,
Angry that his prescriptions are not kept,
Hath left me, and I desperate now approve
Desire is death, which physic did except.
Past cure I am, now reason is past care,
And frantic-mad with evermore unrest;
My thoughts and my discourse as madmen's are,
At random from the truth vainly express'd.
   For I have sworn thee fair, and thought thee bright,
   Who art as black as hell, as dark as night.

                Shakespeare, *Sonnets*, 147, *c.*1598

Corax (a physician). A book! Is this the early exercise
I did prescribe? Instead of following health,
Which all men covet, you pursue disease.
Where's your great horse, your hounds, your set at tennis,
Your balloon-ball, the practice of your dancing,
Your casting of the sledge, or learning how
To toss a pike? All chang'd into a sonnet!

            John Ford, *The Lover's Melancholy*, 1628

Come, *Doctor*, use thy roughest art,
     Thou canst not cruel prove;
Cut, burn, and torture every part,
     To heal me of my *Love*.

There is no danger, if the pain
     Should me to a *Feaver* bring;
Compar'd with *Heats* I now sustain,
     A *Feaver* is so *Cool* a thing,
     (Like drink which feaverish men desire)
That I should hope 'twould almost *quench* my *Fire*.
                    Abraham Cowley, 'The Cure', 1647

Hence *Cupid* with your cheating Toyes,
     Your real Griefs, and painted Joyes,
Your Pleasure which itself destroyes.
     Lovers like men in Fevers burn and rave,
     And only what will injure them do crave.
Men's weakness makes Love so severe,
They give him power by their fear,
And make the Shackles which they wear.
     Who to another does his heart submit,
     Makes his own Idol, and then worships it.
Him whose heart is all his own,
Peace and liberty does crown,
He apprehends no killing frown.
     He feels no raptures which are joyes diseas'd,
     And is not much transported, but still pleas'd.
               Katherine Philips (1631–64), 'Against Love'

Heartwell [*aside*].   O manhood! Where art thou? What am I come to? A woman's toy, at these years! Death, a bearded baby for a girl to dandle! O dotage, dotage! That ever that noble passion, lust, should ebb to this degree! . . .
[*to Silvia*]   Take the symptoms, and ask all the tyrants of thy sex, if their fools are not known by this parti-coloured livery. – I am

melancholic when thou art absent, look like an ass when thou art present, wake for thee when I should sleep, and even dream of thee when I am awake, sigh much, drink little, eat less, court solitude, am grown very entertaining to myself, and (as I am informed) very troublesome to everybody else. If this be not love, it is madness, and then it is pardonable. Nay, yet a more certain sign than all this, I give thee my money.

William Congreve, The Old Bachelor, 1693

She was my life – it is gone from me, and I am grown spectral! . . . If the clock strikes, the sound jars me; a million of hours will not bring back peace to my breast. The light startles me; the darkness terrifies me. I seem falling into a pit, without a hand to help me. She has deceived me, and the earth fails from under my feet: no object in nature is substantial, real, but false and hollow, like her faith on which I built my trust. She came (I knew not how) and sat by my side and was folded in my arms, a vision of love and joy, as if she had dropped from the Heavens to bless me by some especial dispensation of a favouring Providence, and make me amends for all; and now without any fault of mine but too much fondness, she has vanished from me, and I am left to perish. My heart is torn out of me, with every feeling for which I wished to live. The whole is like a dream, an effect of enchantment; it torments me, and it drives me mad. I lie down with it; I rise up with it; and see no chance of repose. I grasp at a shadow, I try to undo the past, and weep with rage and pity over my own weakness and misery . . . I had hopes, I had prospects to come, the flattery of something like fame, a pleasure in writing, health even would have come back with her smile – she has blighted all, turned all to poison and childish tears. Yet the barbed arrow is in my heart – I can neither endure it, nor draw it out; for with it flows my life's-blood.

William Hazlitt, Liber Amoris, 1823

The venom clamours of a jealous woman
Poisons more deadly than a mad dog's tooth.
It seems his sleeps were hinder'd by thy railing,

And thereof comes it that his head is light.
Thou say'st his meat was sauc'd with thy upbraidings;
Unquiet meals make ill digestions;
Thereof the raging fire of fever bred,
And what's a fever but a fit of madness?
Thou say'st his sports were hinder'd by thy brawls;
Sweet recreation barr'd, what doth ensue
But moody and dull melancholy,
Kinsman to grim and comfortless despair,
And at her heels a huge infectious troop
Of pale distemperatures and foes to life?
In food, in sport and life-preserving rest
To be disturb'd, would mad or man or beast;
The consequence is then, thy jealous fits
Hath scar'd thy husband from the use of wits.

Shakespeare, *The Comedy of Errors*, c.1592

I've got dyspepsia from love;
I ache; I've wind around my heart:
why should it trouble me like this?
Can't it excite a different part?

Macedonius the Consul, c.550; tr. Robin Skelton

Not that I deem
Love always dangerous, always to be shunn'd.
Love well repaid, and not too weakly sunk
In wanton and unmanly tenderness,
Adds bloom to Health; o'er ev'ry virtue sheds
A gay, humane, a sweet, and generous grace,
And brightens all the ornaments of man.
But fruitless, hopeless, disappointed, rack'd
With jealousy, fatigu'd with hope and fear,
Too serious, or too languishingly fond,
Unnerves the body and unmans the soul.
And some have died for love; and some run mad;
And some with desperate hands themselves have slain.

Some to extinguish, others to prevent,
A mad devotion to one dangerous Fair,
Court all they meet; in hopes to dissipate
The cares of Love amongst an hundred Brides.
Th'event is doubtful: for there are who find
A cure in this; there are who find it not.

Armstrong, *The Art of Preserving Health*

I said: 'O let me sing the praise
Of her who sweetly racks my days, –
  Her I adore;
Her lips, her eyes, her moods, her ways!'

In miseries of pulse and pang
I strung my harp, and straightway sang
  As none before: –
To wondrous words my quavers rang!

Thus I let heartaches lilt my verse,
Which suaged and soothed, and made disperse
  The smarts I bore
To stagnance like a sepulchre's.

But, eased, the days that thrilled ere then
Lost value; and I ask, O when,
  And how, restore
Those old sweet agonies again!

Hardy, 'He inadvertently cures his Love-pains', 1925

Manias, Phobias, Fantasies, Fears

Among the manifestations of hypochondria in an advanced or obsessional state, imagining oneself to be made of glass appears to have been widespread. (It is certainly more modest, and more rational in view of human fragility, than supposing one is Napoleon or Jesus Christ. All flesh is glass.) The antidote offered by Dr Rush is simple and on the face of it apt, but the Percys' story of Vincentinus shows that it could prove fatal. The self-deceived are not easily deceived by others. 'Men may dye of imaginacioun,' Chaucer said of the carpenter who built an ark against a second great flood. Yet Burton's anecdote of 1609 not only anticipates the Italian doctor's experience in 1926 but could have inspired the treatment he adopted.

The experience of the Hugo family is a different matter altogether: part of a long, tormented history, involving seances and table-rapping (two of the participants lost their reason as a consequence, and one of these died), spirit messages (verses dictated by Shakespeare sounded much like Victor Hugo), the ghost of a 'White Lady', mysteriously swaying beds, and noises inside the walls as if 'dwarfs were ascending and descending a wooden staircase'. Perhaps any house Hugo lived in was bound to be haunted.

Imlac's little speech in the opening passage was inspired by an old astronomer he befriended, who believed himself the regulator of the world's weather and distributor of the seasons, and hence fretted over finding a successor who would be equally impartial and exact in carrying out that crucial duty. The stories taken from *The Anatomy of Melancholy* and the Percy treasure-house – its pseudonymous compilers were Joseph Clinton Robertson and Thomas Byerley – may challenge belief, but are really no more incredible than other incidents recounted here, such as the (well-attested) outbreak or inbreak of *koro* described earlier, or a woman's conviction, reported recently in the press, that two aspirins she had swallowed were actually flying saucers.

Where the bizarre is concerned, it seems that nothing is alien to us humans.

========

'Disorders of intellect,' answered Imlac, 'happen much more often than superficial observers will easily believe. Perhaps, if we speak with rigorous exactness, no human mind is in its right state. There is no man whose imagination does not sometimes predominate over his reason, who can regulate his attention wholly by his will, and whose ideas will come and go at his command. No man will be found in whose mind airy notions do not sometimes tyrannize, and force him to hope or fear beyond the limits of sober probability. All power of fancy over reason is a degree of insanity; but while this power is such as we can control and repress, it is not visible to others, nor considered as any depravation of the mental faculties: it is not pronounced madness but when it comes ungovernable, and apparently influences speech or action.

To indulge the power of fiction, and send imagination out upon the wing, is often the sport of those who delight too much in silent speculation . . .

In time some particular train of ideas fixes the attention, all other intellectual gratifications are rejected, the mind, in weariness or leisure, recurs constantly to the favourite conception, and feasts on the luscious falsehood whenever she is offended with the bitterness of truth. By degrees the reign of fancy is confirmed; she grows first imperious, and in time despotick. Then fictions begin to operate as realities, false opinions fasten upon the mind, and life passes in dreams of rapture or of anguish.'

Samuel Johnson, *Rasselas*, 1759

The fancies of hypochondriacs are frequently of the most extraordinary nature: one patient imagines that he is in such a state of obesity as to prevent his passing through the door of his chamber or his house; another, impressed with the idea that he is made of glass, will not sit down for fear of cracking; a third seems convinced that his head is empty; and an intelligent American, holding a high judicial seat in our West Indies colonies, could not divest himself of the occasional conviction of his being transformed into a turtle.

J. G. Millingen, Curiosities of Medical Experience

Cures of patients who suppose themselves to be glass may easily be performed by pulling a chair upon which they are about to sit from under them, and afterwards showing them a large collection of pieces of glass as the fragments of their bodies.

Dr Benjamin Rush, Medical Inquiries and Observations
upon the Diseases of the Mind, 1812

Marcus Donatus, in his *Hist. Med. Rar.*, records the case of a person of the name of Vincentinus, who believed that he was of such enormous size that he could not go through the door of his apartment. His physician gave orders that he should be forcibly led through it; which was done accordingly, but not without a fatal effect, for Vincentinus cried out, as he was forced along, that the flesh was torn from his bones, and that his limbs were broken off; of which terrible impression he died in a few days, accusing those who conducted him of being his murderers.

Sholto and Reuben Percy, The Percy Anecdotes, 1823

An. 1550, an Advocate of *Paris* fell into such a melancholy fit, that he believed verily he was dead; he could not be persuaded otherwise, or to eat or drink, till a kinsman of his, a Scholar of *Bourges*, did eat before him, dressed like a corse . . . One thinks himself a Giant, another a Dwarf; one is heavy as lead, another is as light as a feather . . . Another thinks he is a nightingale, and therefore sings all the night long; another he is all glass, a pitcher, and will therefore let nobody come near him . . . A Baker in *Ferrara* thought he was composed of butter, & durst not sit in the sun, or come near the fire, for fear of being melted; another thought he was a case of leather, stuffed with wind.

Burton, The Anatomy of Melancholy

In the latter part of his life, and even in his last year, he let nothing enter or leave his body without having it weighed and the debit and credit written down, a practice which led to discussions that were the despair of his doctors. Fever and gout made a series of attacks on him; he made his illness worse by a strict regime, by his solitude, in which he would see no one, not even his closest family, by his restlessness and by his over-attention to detail, which drove him into transports of fury. His doctor was Finot, who was also my family's doctor – what's more, our friend. He couldn't handle Monsieur le Prince. According to what he told us more than once, Finot was most troubled by his patient's refusal to eat – he said that he was dead, and the dead don't eat. Still, he had to have some food or he would die properly. Finally, Finot decided to agree that he had died but to suggest that there were in fact dead people who ate food. Finot offered to show him some, and brought along people who could be relied on, who were well prepared and who claimed to have died but still ate. This ploy worked, but Monsieur le Prince would only eat in the company of Finot. By this means he dined very well. This fantasy lasted quite a long time, though its persistence was the despair of his doctor – yet Finot almost died of laughter as he described the scene and the conversations from the other world that took place at these meals. Monsieur le Prince in fact lived a long time after.

> Duc de Saint-Simon, *Mémoires*; from the year 1709, and concerning
> Henri Jules de Bourbon, Prince de Condé; tr. Michel Petheram

One, by reason of those ascending vapours and gripings rumbling beneath, will not be persuaded but that he hath a serpent in his guts, a viper; another frogs. *Felix Platerus* hath a most memorable example of a countryman of his, that, by chance falling into a pit where frogs and frogs' spawn was, and a little of that water swallowed, began to suspect that he had likewise swallowed frogs' spawn, and with that conceit and fear his phantasy wrought so far, that he verily thought he had young live frogs in his belly, that lived by his nourishment . . . He studied Physick seven years together to cure himself, travelled into *Italy*, *France*, and *Germany* to confer with the best Physicians about it, and, *An.* 1609, asked his counsel amongst the rest; he told him it was wind, his conceit, &c., but no saying would serve: it was no wind, but real frogs: and *do you not hear them croak? Platerus* would have deceived him by putting live frogs into his excrements: but he, being a Physician himself, would not be deceived.

Burton, *The Anatomy of Melancholy*

In *A Cure for Serpents* Dr Alberto Denti di Pirajno tells how, in Misurata (Tripoli) in 1926, he treated Hajj Ahmed 'The Lion' for atrocious stomach pains. Hajj Ahmed believed that these were caused by a serpent which had entered his mouth while he was sleeping; and his dead father had confirmed, in a dream, that it was a male serpent, and particularly malignant.

All native remedies having failed, Hajj Ahmed decided to consult the Christian doctor. The truth of the matter, Dr Denti writes, was that he was undergoing the male menopause, 'suffering from disorders of the circulation, glandular disturbances and nervous illusions which made him feel that his stomach was swollen like a water-skin and that he had a suffocating stoppage in his gullet'. Hajj Ahmed confided that the serpent would not allow him to touch a woman. 'Perhaps he wants them for himself. When I lie with a woman the accursed thing breaks my back, cuts my nerves, and I am as limp as a eunuch.'

The doctor could not shake his patient's conviction, and finally agreed to open the man's stomach. 'O Hajj Ahmed, if there is no serpent, I will close the stomach again and will say to you: my brother, I was right. If, on the other hand, I find the serpent, I will drag him out and you shall crush his head so that he shall never again trouble the sons of Adam.' He chloroformed the sick man, made a cut with his lancet 'sufficient for the extraction of even a young crocodile', and then sewed up the wound. Hajj Ahmed was carried home, along with a cardboard box containing an unfortunate serpent, previously procured.

The following day the doctor found his patient in fine form, and overflowing with magnanimity. 'We may all make mistakes, *tebīb* – only God is all-wise. You see, there *was* a serpent; my father did not lie and I did not misunderstand his words.' Hajj Ahmed didn't wish to see the doctor mortified. He embraced him. 'But you have saved me, O wise one! It was you who had the idea of opening my stomach to liberate me from the accursed thing! . . . Praise be to God, Who has granted you knowledge and wisdom.'

Retold from *A Cure for Serpents*, 1955

Some men there are love not a gaping pig;
Some, that are mad if they behold a cat;
And others, when the bagpipe sings i' the nose,
Cannot contain their urine: for affection,
Mistress of passion, sways it to the mood
Of what it likes, or loathes.
. . . there is no firm reason to be render'd,
Why he cannot abide a gaping pig;
Why he, a harmless necessary cat;
Why he, a wauling bagpipe; but of force
Must yield to such inevitable shame
As to offend, himself being offended.

Shakespeare, *The Merchant of Venice*, 1596–7

The seeds of the aversion which persons often have to particular things are usually lodged so deep that it is in vain to search after them. Although but freaks of imagination, we see them so mixed up with the whole being of individuals as to form what is commonly called a second nature. A still more curious circumstance is that they extend to all sorts of objects, beautiful as well as ugly, delicious as well as disgusting. The rose is charming; and yet we read of two cardinals, Cardona and Caraffia; of a Venetian nobleman of the family of Barbaragi; and of a fair lady, who was maid of honour to Queen Elizabeth, Lady Heneage; all of whom were in the habit of swooning away at the sight of this queen of flowers. An apple, too, is delicious; and yet there was a whole family in Aquitaine, called the Faesii, who had such a hereditary dislike to this fruit that they could never see an apple without their noses falling a-bleeding. Olive oil is a nice ingredient in sauces; but such was the antipathy which a certain Count D'Armstadt had to it that, though introduced in the smallest proportion into any dish presented to him, he was immediately seized with fainting fits . . . The squirrel, though not a very engaging animal, has nothing particularly frightful about it. The celebrated Marquis de la Roche Jacquelin, however, who had courage enough to brave a world in arms, could never face this little harmless creature without trembling and turning pale. He would laugh at and ridicule his weakness in this respect; but all his efforts could never enable him to triumph over the physical effect which the presence of a squirrel involuntarily produced on his nerves . . .

Signs in the heavens impress most people with a degree of awe; but some to a degree melancholy to contemplate. Augustus Caesar was so afraid of thunder and lightning that, though he carried about with him the skin of a sea-calf, which was in those days accounted an excellent *paratonnerre*, whenever he saw a tempest coming he used to fly for refuge in some vaulted place under ground. Caius Caligula, who rivalled Augustus in his fears in this respect, took a more foolish way of consulting safety. Suetonius tells us that it was his custom, when it thundered, to wrap his head in some covering; or if in bed, to leap out of bed and hide himself under it.

Charles d'Escaro, Bishop of Langres, was wont to faint away at the commencement of a lunar eclipse, and to continue insensible till the eclipse ended. When he became very old and infirm the habit still remained with him; and fainting as usual, at an eclipse which happened to take place, he was unable to recover from it, and so expired.

The Percy Anecdotes

Chorus Sancti Viti, or S. *Vitus'* Dance; the lascivious dance, Paracelsus calls it, because they that are taken with it, can do nothing but dance till they be dead, or cured. It is so called, for that the parties so troubled were wont to go to S. *Vitus* for help, & after they had danced there a while, they were certainly cured. 'Tis strange to hear how long they will dance, & in what manner, over stools, forms, tables; even great-bellied women sometimes (and yet never hurt their children) will dance so long that they can stir neither hand nor foot, but seem to be quite dead. One in red clothes they cannot abide. Musick above all things they love, & therefore

Magistrates in *Germany* will hire Musicians to play to them, and some lusty sturdy companions to dance with them.

Burton, *The Anatomy of Melancholy*

Selwyn's nervous irritability and anxious curiosity to observe the effect of dissolution on men, exposed him to much ridicule, not unaccompanied with censure. He was accused of attending all executions; and sometimes, in order to elude notice, disguised in a female dress. I have been assured that, in 1757, he went over to Paris expressly for the purpose of witnessing the last moments of Damiens . . . Being among the crowd, and attempting to approach too near the scaffold, he was at first repulsed by one of the executioners; but having informed the person, that he had made the journey from London solely with a view to be present at the punishment and death of Damiens, the man immediately caused the people to make way, exclaiming at the same time: 'Faites place pour monsieur; c'est un Anglois, et un amateur.'

J. H. Jesse, *George Selwyn and his Contemporaries*, 1843

Hysteria may be fitly called *mimosa*, from its counterfeiting so many diseases, – even death itself.

Coleridge, *Table Talk*, 23 May 1830

As she laughed I was aware of becoming involved in her laughter and being part of it, until her teeth were only accidental stars with a talent for squad-drill. I was drawn in by short gasps, inhaled at each momentary recovery, lost finally in the dark caverns of her throat, bruised by the ripple of unseen muscles. An elderly waiter with trembling hands was hurriedly spreading a pink and white checked cloth over the rusty green iron table, saying: 'If the lady and gentleman wish to take their tea in the garden, if the lady and gentleman wish to take their tea in the garden . . .' I decided that if the shaking of her breasts could be stopped, some of the fragments of the afternoon might be collected, and I concentrated my attention with careful subtlety to this end.

T. S. Eliot, 'Hysteria', 1915

It might be maintained that a case of hysteria is a caricature of a work of art, that an obsessional neurosis is a caricature of a religion, and that a paranoiac delusion is a caricature of a philosophical system.

Sigmund Freud, *Totem and Taboo*, 1913; tr. James Strachey

At a cotton manufactory at Hodden Bridge, in Lancashire, a girl, on the fifteenth of February, 1787, put a mouse into the bosom of another girl, who had a great dread of mice. The girl was immediately thrown into a fit, and continued in it, with the most violent convulsions, for twenty-four hours. On the following day, three more girls were seized in the same manner; and on the 17th, six more. By this time the alarm was so great, that the whole work, in which 200 or 300 were employed, was totally stopped, and an idea prevailed that a particular disease had been introduced by a bag of cotton opened in the house. On Sunday the 18th, Dr St Clare was sent for from Preston; before he arrived three more were seized, and during that night and the morning of the 19th, eleven more, making in all twenty-four. Of these, twenty-one were young women, two were girls of about ten years of age, and one man, who had been much fatigued with holding the girls. Three of the number lived about two miles from the place where the disorder first broke out, and three at another factory at Clitheroe, about five miles distant, which last and two more were infected entirely from report, not having seen the other patients, but, like them and the rest of the country, strongly impressed with the idea of the plague being caught from the cotton. The symptoms were anxiety, strangulation, and very strong convulsions; and these were so violent as to last without any intermission from a quarter of an hour to twenty-four hours, and to require four or five persons to prevent the patients from tearing their hair and dashing their heads against the floor or walls. Dr St Clare had taken with him a portable electrical machine, and by electric shocks the patients were universally relieved without exception. As soon as the patients and the country were assured that the complaint was merely nervous, easily cured, and not introduced by the cotton, no fresh person was affected. To dissipate their apprehensions still further, the best effects were obtained by causing them to take a cheerful glass and join in a dance. On Tuesday the 20th, they danced, and the next day were all at work, except two or three, who were much weakened by their fits.

The Gentleman's Magazine, March 1787

As if the natural calamities of life were not sufficient for it, we turn the most indifferent circumstances into misfortunes, and suffer as much from trifling accidents as from real evils. I have known the shooting of a star spoil a night's rest; and have seen a man in love grow pale, and lose his appetite, upon the plucking of a merry-thought. A screech-owl at midnight has alarmed a family more than a band of robbers: nay, the voice of a cricket hath struck more terror than the roaring of a lion. There is nothing so inconsiderable, which may not appear dreadful to an imagination that is filled with omens and prognostics. A rusty nail, or a crooked pin, shoot up into prodigies.

I remember I was once in a mixt assembly, that was full of noise and mirth, when on a sudden an old woman unluckily observed there were thirteen of us in company. This remark struck a panic terror into several who were present, insomuch that one or two of the ladies were going to leave the room; but a friend of mine taking notice that one of our female companions was big with child, affirmed, there were fourteen in the room, and that, instead of portending one of the company should die, it plainly foretold one of them should be born. Had not my friend found this expedient to break the omen, I question not but half the women in the company would have fallen sick that very night.

Addison, 'Omens', *The Spectator*, 8 March 1711

My daughter was in bed, suffering badly; her mother had placed an armchair at the foot of her bed to pass the night near her. I had retired, restless. I prayed ardently, or at least as ardently as I was able. I commended the sister to the sister [the sick Adèle to the dead beloved Léopoldine], then I fell asleep. I occupy the look-out, right at the top of the house: a cell, opening on the sea, and separated only

by a partition from the room where the two chambermaids sleep. In
the dead of night I woke up, and mused sadly while praying. A few
minutes later, in the universal silence (calm weather, no wind, no
sound from the sea) I heard a singing very close to me; it seemed to
come from the neighbouring room. I listened; it was a human voice,
sweet, light, uncertain, faint, ethereal. I thought that one of the
maids had woken up and was singing; but the sweetness of the voice
had something wonderful, something infinite, about it, which made
me reject the idea. I had supposed it was in her sleep, or while
dreaming, that one of them was singing thus, but the melody,
inarticulate and without words, had a sustained rhythm, perfectly
observed and knit together, utterly incompatible with the incoher
ence of sleeping and dreaming. Thinking these things over, I ended
by believing I was dreaming myself; I sensed the melody floating
indistinctly close to my ear, and I fell asleep again.

Some time elapsed, it couldn't have been long, and I woke up. This
time it was the song that aroused me, still as if coming from behind
the partition; it was more distinct than the first time, clearly defined,
at once melancholy and captivating, and I regretted I wasn't a
musician and able to take it down. It was like the murmur-music of
Titania.

In the morning I asked the maids which of them had been singing.
They had slept through the night without a break, and my question
astonished them. I went down to hear about my daughter's night;
her condition had worsened; neither she nor my wife had slept. For
my part, I wasn't going to mention what I had heard, when
suddenly, in the midst of details about her daughter's fever, my wife
said: 'One thing worries me. Towards midnight I heard singing in
the fireplace; Adèle wasn't sleeping, and when I asked her whether
she heard anything, she said, yes, but she hadn't spoken of it for fear
I would think she was delirious.' Then I questioned my wife: 'What
did the singing remind you of?' She replied: 'It was very faint, very
sweet, exquisite, in part like a cricket, in part like a nightingale.' My
daughter, who was listening, broke in: 'No, it wasn't the cry of an
insect, nor the song of a bird. It resembled a tiny human voice.' Then
my wife said that Adèle had been rather frightened, and she had told
her not to be afraid, it was a cricket singing, the little nightingale of
the hearth.

The song had lasted more than four hours without interruption. It was too muted, they both said, to be heard anywhere outside their room. Equally, the sound that woke me up was too faint even to be heard on the floor below me. There are two floors, quite high, between the ladies' apartment and my own; theirs is at the front, mine at the back. Moreover the voice couldn't have reached me by way of the chimney, since there is no fireplace in my room, or even on my floor.

Victor Hugo, Hauteville House, Guernsey,

6/7 December 1856; notebooks

He was a nervous man, easily depressed; fond of everybody that he was used to, and hating to part with them; hating change of every kind. Matrimony, as the origin of change, was always disagreeable; and he was by no means yet reconciled to his own daughter's marrying, nor could ever speak of her but with compassion, though it had been entirely a match of affection, when he was now obliged to part with Miss Taylor too; and from his habits of gentle selfishness, and of being never able to suppose that other people could feel differently from himself, he was very much disposed to think that Miss Taylor had done as sad a thing for herself as for them, and would have been a great deal happier if she had spent all the rest of her life at Hartfield . . .

There was no recovering Miss Taylor, nor much likelihood of ceasing to pity her; but a few weeks brought some alleviation to Mr Woodhouse. The compliments of his neighbours were over; he was no longer teased by being wished joy of so sorrowful an event; and the wedding-cake, which had been a great distress to him, was all eaten up. His own stomach could bear nothing rich, and he could never believe other people to be different from himself. What was unwholesome to him, he regarded as unfit for anybody; and he had, therefore, earnestly tried to dissuade them from having any wedding-cake at all; and, when that proved vain, as earnestly tried to prevent anybody's eating it. He had been at the pains of consulting Mr Perry, the apothecary, on the subject. Mr Perry was an intelligent, gentleman-like man, whose frequent visits were one of the comforts of Mr Woodhouse's life; and upon being applied to, he could not but acknowledge (though it seemed rather against the bias of inclination) that wedding-cake might certainly disagree with many – perhaps with most people – unless taken moderately. With such an opinion, in confirmation of his own, Mr Woodhouse hoped to influence every visitor of the new-married pair; but still the cake was eaten, and there was no rest for his benevolent nerves till it was all gone.

There was a strange rumour in Highbury of all the little Perrys being seen with a slice of Mrs Weston's wedding-cake in their hands; but Mr Woodhouse would never believe it.

Jane Austen, Emma, 1816

'Mr Bennet, how can you abuse your own children in such a way! You take delight in vexing me. You have no compassion on my poor nerves.'

'You mistake me, my dear. I have a high respect for your nerves. They are my old friends. I have heard you mention them with consideration these twenty years at least.'

'Ah! you do not know what I suffer.'

'I told you in the library, you know, that I should never speak to you again, and you will find me as good as my word. I have no pleasure in talking to undutiful children. – Not that I have much pleasure, indeed, in talking to anybody. People who suffer as I do from nervous complaints can have no great inclination for talking. Nobody can tell what I suffer! – But it is always so. Those who do not complain are never pitied.'

Austen, Pride and Prejudice, 1813

When a late Duchess of Bedford was last at Buxton, and then in her eighty-fifth year, it was the medical farce of the day for the faculty to resolve every complaint of whim and caprice into 'a shock of the nervous system'. Her Grace, after enquiring of many of her friends in the rooms what brought them there, and being generally answered for a nervous complaint, was asked in her turn, what brought her to Buxton? 'I came only for pleasure,' answered the healthy duchess, 'for, thank God, I was born before nerves came into fashion.'

The Percy Anecdotes

As Chirac, a celebrated physician, was going to the house of a lady who had sent for him in a great hurry, he received intelligence that the stocks had fallen. Having a considerable property embarked in the Mississippi scheme, the news made so strong an impression on his mind that, while he was feeling his patient's pulse, he exclaimed, 'Mercy upon me, how they fall! lower, lower, lower!' The lady in alarm flew to the bell, crying out, 'I am dying. M. de Chirac says that my pulse gets lower and lower, so that it is impossible I should live!' 'You are dreaming, madam!' replied the physician, rousing himself from his reverie. 'Your pulse is very good, and nothing ails you. It was the stocks I was talking of.'

The Percy Anecdotes

When the university acquired its first indigenous vice-chancellor there was fear and trembling, especially among expatriate teachers, for the new man was a government nominee and known for his past zeal in replacing British civil servants with local citizens. The department of English was already in bad odour for pushing such pernicious foreign substances as Wordsworth and Chaucer.

Once installed, however, the vice-chancellor embraced the cause of university autonomy and academic freedom with an alarming fervency, a devotion never seen before in those parts. Trouble wasn't long in coming. The government ordered that certain candidates admitted to the university on the strength of their school examinations should now be silently struck off, they being considered security risks. Naturally the grounds for this would not be disclosed to the university.

It would surely be improper, said the vice-chancellor, to serve as a cat's-paw of the Special Branch! University Senate supported his views wellnigh unanimously, though with renewed fear and trembling. The government, famous for its chronic inexorability, threatened to cut off funds unless the vice-chancellor either toed the line or resigned within a week. Feelings ran high. Senate met, University Council met, the Students' Union met, the Cabinet met, cabals argued feverishly in every corner of the Staff Canteen. Virtuous sentiments alternated with prudent reservations. It was desirable to have principles; it was necessary to have a job.

What the professor of English had was an abscess on a tooth, which began to rage during an acrimonious session of the Staff Association. Stuffed with aspirin, and with antihistamine taken to relieve a mysterious allergy whose effect was to turn his face a bright, hot red, as if in irreversible embarrassment, he went to his dentist, a prominent Chinese citizen and chairman of Council.

'Dear me,' the dentist said. He probed. He sighed. 'Have to go, I'm afraid. Pity, but there's no choice.'

'Pa'on?' the professor mumbled, his mouth full of the dentist's fingers.

'Have to go.' The dentist straightened up and shook his head. 'No other way.'

'Carry on then,' the professor whimpered bravely. 'Take it out.'

'What?' said the dentist. 'The vice-chancellor, I mean.'

In the event the tooth was saved. Nothing could save the vice-chancellor.

MS found in a bottle

Breakdown and Madness

'When a man mistakes his thoughts for persons and things, he is mad.' Coleridge's definition has the virtues of brevity and neatness, as has Voltaire's, in his *Dictionnaire Philosophique*: madness means having incorrect perceptions and reasoning correctly from them. And likewise Johnson's account, in the opening passage here, of how madness often reveals itself.

The notion that madness is morally superior to sanity, and that, since the outside world is plainly lunatic, the inmates of the asylum ought to switch places with their warders, is a useful device in social and political polemic. 'Change places,' said Lear, an ex-king, 'and, handy-dandy, which is the justice, which is the thief?' Moreover, the theory enables us who are at liberty to feel a little more comfortable; especially since we know it is not going to be carried into practice.

Yet it seems unlikely that the mad are customarily so crazy that, could they express themselves lucidly, they would indicate a preference for madness. It was safe for Torrismond, in Dryden's play *The Spanish Friar*, to claim that 'There is a pleasure, sure,/ In being mad, which none but madmen know!' And since he was sane, the statement is meaningless as well.

In Musil's *The Man Without Qualities*, the fact that Clarisse, visiting an asylum, wasn't sure which of those around her were patients and which were nurses can be largely imputed to confusion and embarrassment. One old gentleman had the visage of a highly cultivated person, framed in thick white hair, and 'as insufferably noble-looking as are only faces described in fifth-rate novels'. A case of depressive dementia paralytica, the effect of long-standing syphilis, the doctor in charge explains, the noble expression being caused by slackening of the facial muscles.

Madness as a concomitant or indeed source of artistic genius is an opinion already mooted. It should be noted that the speaker in the excerpt from Mann's *Doctor Faustus* is the Devil, who doesn't invariably speak the whole truth; and Proust's du Boulbon, though a man of taste, doesn't impress us as a doctor of any great competence. Other witnesses have submitted that artistic genius is a concomitant or indeed source of madness. Baudelaire's mother said pathetically of her son that his mind had worked too much. And Mme Flaubert spoke of the mania for sentences that had dried up her son's heart. If a tinge of madness helps to make an artist, art helps to make its practitioners more than a little mad.

———

I have preserved the following short minute of what passed this day [24 May 1763]: –

'Madness frequently discovers itself merely by unnecessary deviation from the usual modes of the world. My poor friend Smart shewed the disturbance of his mind, by falling upon his knees, and saying his prayers in the street, or in any other unusual place. Now although, rationally speaking, it is greater madness not to pray at all, than to pray as Smart did, I am afraid there are so many who do not pray, that their understanding is not called in question.'

Concerning this unfortunate poet, Christopher Smart, who was confined in a madhouse, he had, at another time, the following conversation with Dr Burney. BURNEY: 'How does poor Smart do, Sir, is he likely to recover?' JOHNSON: 'It seems as if his mind had ceased to struggle with the disease; for he grows fat upon it.' BURNEY: 'Perhaps, Sir, that may be from want of exercise.' JOHNSON: 'No, Sir; he has partly as much exercise as he used to have, for he digs in the garden. Indeed, before his confinement, he used for exercise to walk to the alehouse; but he was *carried* back again. I did not think he ought to be shut up. His infirmities were not noxious to society. He insisted on people praying with him; and I'd as lief pray with Kit Smart as any one else. Another charge was, that he did not love clean linen; and I have no passion for it.'

Boswell, Life of Johnson

21 December 1870.   Sir Gilbert Lewis [a Canon of Worcester] said mad people are apt to come to Cathedrals. There was a mad woman who came to Worcester Cathedral and gave him a great deal of trouble by screeching out. There was a Mr Quarrell who used to make antics at the time of the Communion. At a certain point in the service this man would bow down till he got his head on the pavement and his movements were so extraordinary that all they could do was to look at him and watch him. The authorities did not know what to do with him. They could not say, 'You shall not be a Communicant', but they let him know indirectly that they thought his proceedings very ridiculous. 'Ah,' said Sir Gilbert, 'you don't know all the little games that go on in Cathedrals.'

Kilvert, Diary

Sisters and their husbands held a council.

'I did always think he was mad,' Chinta said.

Sushila, the childless widow, spoke with her sickroom authority. 'It isn't about Mohun I am worried, but the children.'

Padma, Seth's wife, asked, 'What do you think he is sick with?'

Sumati the flogger said, 'Message only said that he was very sick.'

'And that his house had been practically blown away,' Jai's mother added.

There were some smiles.

'I am sorry to correct you, Sumati sister,' Chinta said. 'But Message said that he wasn't right in his head.'

Seth said, 'I suppose we have to bring the paddler home.' . . .

When the men returned, dripping, with Anand sleepily and tearfully walking beside them and Govind carrying Mr Biswas in his arms, there was relief, and some disappointment. Mr Biswas was not wild or violent; he made no speeches; he did not pretend he was driving a motor car or picking cocoa – the two actions popularly associated with insanity. He only looked deeply exasperated and fatigued . . .

The doctor came, a Roman Catholic Indian, but much respected by the Tulsis for his manners and the extent of his property. He dismissed talk about having Mr Biswas certified and said that Mr Biswas was suffering from nerves and a certain vitamin deficiency. He prescribed a course of Sanatogen, a tonic called Ferrol with reputed iron-giving, body-building qualities, and Ovaltine. He also said that Mr Biswas was to have much rest, and should go to Port of Spain as soon as he was better to see a specialist.

Almost as soon as the doctor had gone the thaumaturge came, an unsuccessful man with a flashy turban and an anxious manner; his fees were low. He purified the Blue Room and erected invisible barriers against evil spirits. He recommended that strips of aloe should be hung in doorways and windows and said that the family ought to have known that they should always have a black doll in the doorway of the hall to divert evil spirits: prevention was better than cure. Then he inquired whether he couldn't prepare a little mixture as well.

The offer was rejected. 'Ovaltine, Ferrol, Sanatogen,' Seth said. 'Give Mohun your mixture and you turn him into a little capsule.'

But they hung the aloe; it was a natural purgative that cost nothing and large quantities were always in the house. And they hung the black doll, one of a small, ancient stock in the Tulsi Store, an English line which had not appealed to the people of Arwacas.

V. S. Naipaul, *A House for Mr Biswas*, 1961

Tossing about, Catherine increased her feverish bewilderment to madness, and tore the pillow with her teeth; then raising herself up all burning, desired that I would open the window. We were in the middle of winter, the wind blew strong from the north-east, and I objected. Both the expressions flitting over her face, and the changes of her moods, began to alarm me terribly; and brought to my recollection her former illness, and the doctor's injunction that she should not be crossed. A minute previously she was violent; now, supported on one arm, and not noticing my refusal to obey her, she seemed to find childish diversion in pulling the feathers from the rents she had just made, and ranging them on the sheet according to their different species: her mind had strayed to other associations.

'That's a turkey's,' she murmured to herself; 'and this is a wild duck's; and this is a pigeon's. Ah, they put pigeon's feathers in the pillows – no wonder I couldn't die! Let me take care to throw it on the floor when I lie down. And here is a moorcock's; and this – I should know it among a thousand – it's a lapwing's. Bonny bird; wheeling over our heads in the middle of the moor. It wanted to get to its nest, for the clouds had touched the swells, and it felt rain coming. This feather was picked up from the heath, the bird was not shot: we saw its nest in the winter, full of little skeletons. Heathcliff set a trap over it, and the old ones dare not come. I made him promise he'd never shoot a lapwing after that, and he didn't. Yes, here are more! Did he shoot my lapwings, Nelly? Are they red, any of them! Let me look.'

'Give over with that baby-work!' I interrupted, dragging the pillow away, and turning the holes towards the mattress, for she was removing its contents by handfuls. 'Lie down and shut your eyes: you're wandering. There's a mess! The down is flying about like snow.' , , ,

'Oh, I'm burning! I wish I were out of doors! I wish I were a girl again, half savage and hardy, and free; and laughing at injuries, not maddening under them! Why am I so changed? why does my blood rush into a hell of tumult at a few words? I'm sure I should be myself were I once among the heather on those hills. Open the window again wide: fasten it open! Quick, why don't you move?'

'Because I won't give you your death of cold,' I answered.

'You won't give me a chance of life, you mean,' she said sullenly. 'However, I'm not helpless, yet: I'll open it myself.'

And sliding from the bed before I could hinder her, she crossed the room, walking very uncertainly, threw it back, and bent out, careless of the frosty air that cut about her shoulders as keen as a knife. I entreated, and finally attempted to force her to retire. But I soon found her delirious strength much surpassed mine (she *was* delirious, I became convinced by her subsequent actions and ravings). There was no moon, and everything beneath lay in misty darkness: not a light gleamed from any house, far or near – all had been extinguished long ago; and those at Wuthering Heights were never visible – still she asserted she caught their shining.

'Look!' she cried eagerly, 'that's my room with the candle in it, and the trees swaying before it: and the other candle is in Joseph's garret. Joseph sits up late, doesn't he? He's waiting till I come home that he may lock the gate. Well, he'll wait a while yet. It's a rough journey, and a sad heart to travel it; and we must pass by Gimmerton Kirk, to go that journey! We've braved its ghosts often together, and dared each other to stand among the graves and ask them to come. But, Heathcliff, if I dare you now, will you venture? If you do, I'll keep you. I'll not lie there by myself: they may bury me twelve feet deep, and throw the church down over me, but I won't rest till you are with me. I never will!'

She paused, and resumed with a strange smile. 'He's considering – he'd rather I'd come to him! Find a way, then! not through that kirkyard. You are slow. Be content, you always followed me!'

Emily Brontë, Wuthering Heights, 1847

I felt a Cleaving in my Mind –
As if my Brain had split –
I tried to match it – Seam by Seam –
But could not make them fit.

The thought behind, I strove to join
Unto the thought before –
But Sequence ravelled out of Sound
Like Balls – upon a Floor.

Emily Dickinson, 'I felt a Cleaving in my Mind', c.1865

Long before they took him away things were going wrong.
Simple things. Badly wrong. Like birds
Talking to him, not exactly with words
But a kind of language that wasn't song.

The very old get like this but he wasn't so old,
Sixty-odd only, a kind age
For many men with work opening its cage
And their children's children crossing the threshold.

Perhaps that was partly it – failure in all he'd done,
Career botched, no wife, child or home,
A bare existence in a barely furnished room,
Loneliness breeding a lust to be alone.

Where lonelier, then, than the far shores of the mind?
Slowly we watched him pulling out

Over those moonstruck waters, a growing doubt
Startling his eyes as he saw us left behind.

What he found on that continent we shall never know.
If only he'd send a message back
In a bottle for the tide to throw up like wrack,
We could go. Would go. But still we cannot go.

So they took him away and left us with this heart-ache
Of helplessness that a brain
Should be so wronged. Guilt, too, that we should stay sane –
As we must somehow, if only for his sake.

J. C. Hall, 'Going Wrong', 1971

Odd how the seemingly maddest of men –
sheer loonies, the classically paranoid,
violently possessive about their secrets,
whispered after from corners, terrified
of poison in their coffee, driven frantic
(whether for or against him) by discussion of God,
peculiar, to say the least, about their mothers –
return to their gentle senses in bed.

Suddenly straightforward, they perform
with routine confidence, neither afraid
that their partner will turn and bite their balls off
nor groping under the pillow for a razor-blade;
eccentric only in their conversation,
which rambles on about the meaning of a word
they used in an argument in 1969,
they leave their women grateful, relieved, and bored.

Fleur Adcock, 'Madmen', 1983

Hölderlin's day is extremely simple. In the mornings, particularly
during the summer when he is in general much agitated and
tortured, he gets up with the sun, or before, and at once leaves the
house to walk in the grounds. This usually lasts between four and

five hours, so that he grows tired. He likes to amuse himself by taking a handkerchief and striking the fence posts with it or tearing out grass. Whatever he finds, though no more than a piece of iron or leather, he pockets and takes home. In the meanwhile he talks incessantly to himself, asking questions and answering them, now with 'yes', now with 'no', often with both, for he likes to use the negative.

Then he enters the house and paces about. His meals are brought to his room, and he eats with gusto; he is also fond of wine, which he would go on drinking as long as it was there . . . The rest of the day is passed in soliloquizing and walking up and down in his little room.

What can keep him occupied for days on end is his *Hyperion*. A hundred times, when I visited him, I could hear him declaiming loudly before I reached the house. His pathos is intense, and *Hyperion* almost always lies open; he has often read to me from it. When he has grasped a passage he will start to call out, with passionate gesticulations, 'O beautiful, beautiful, Your Majesty!', and then read on, suddenly interjecting, 'Look, gracious Sir, a comma!' . . .

I told him countless times that his *Hyperion* had been reprinted, and that Uhland and Schwab were collecting his poems. The only answer I ever received was a deep bow and the words, 'You are very gracious, Herr von Waiblinger! I am much obliged to you, Your Holiness.'

Music has not quite deserted him. He still plays the piano correctly, though in a highly singular fashion. Once he has started, he goes on for days. Throughout he pursues one childishly simple idea, playing it over hundreds and hundreds of times, to such an extent that no one can endure it. To this is added a rapid convulsive cramp, which often carries him up and down the keyboard with the speed of lightning – and also the disagreeable clicking of his overgrown finger-nails. For he hates to have these cut, and much cunning is required to prevail on him, as with obstinate and refractory children. When he has been playing for some time, and his soul has become tender, his eyes suddenly close, his head is lifted, he seems about to languish and fade away, and he begins to sing. In what language I could never discover, often as I have heard it; but he did so with extravagant pathos, and it made one shudder in every nerve to see and hear him. Melancholy and sorrow were the essence of his song; one could recognize what had once been a good tenor.

It gave him extraordinary joy when of late a small sofa was placed in his room at last. He announced this event to me with childlike delight when I went to see him, by kissing my hand and saying, 'Ah, look, gracious Sir, now I have a sofa.' I had to take my place on it at once, and for some time afterwards I used to find him sitting on it when I visited . . .

At times he gave answers which one could hardly forbear from laughing over, especially since his expression suggested genuine mockery. Thus, I once asked him how old he was, and he replied with a smile, 'Seventeen, Herr Baron.' This was no irony, however, but simply absence of mind . . .

Once I found a terrible and mysterious sentence among his papers. After many glorious sayings about the Greek heroes and the beauty of the ancient gods, he had written, 'Only now do I understand men, for I am living far from them and in solitude.'

Wilhelm Waiblinger, *Friedrich Hölderlins Leben,*
Dichtung und Wahnsinn, 1830

Dreams and Visions

June 10, 1876. dreamed a double dream, of carrying a hammer & pickaxe up a hill, to a rail station where I found a great packet sent to me, which I tore open and found valuable specimens of paper, MSS, &c – then left it open on the ground, walked dreamily down the hill without either hammer or pickaxe, and then told the whole, *as* a dream, to somebody, I forgot whom, – saying 'the dream was so vivid that just now, wide awake, I started, thinking I had really left that parcel open and its contents lying about, at the rly station.'

October 29, 1877. half sleepless night again – and entirely disgusting dream, about men using flesh and bones, *hands of children especially*, for fuel – being out of wood and coals. I found a piece to put on someone's fire, and found it the side of an animal's face, with the jaw and teeth in it.

February 4, 1878.   Late up getting room in order after two eggs at tea – and nothing worse at night than a dream of some head of a college dining with me, of my wearing a white surplice – which dropped under the table after dinner and got mixed up with my napkin, and of my just recollecting after the head of a college had departed that I hadn't given him any wine.

February 5.   Late down. I think the eggs came into play the second day, – but there was bad fish at dinner, peasoup and pheasant – any how I had a horrid dream of being on a slope of crumbling earth above a chasm a thousand feet deep, with no way of moving visible but to fall – and woke with taste in mouth, – and all wrong.

December 28, 1879.   The tiredness pronounces itself as definite cold: which is a relief – with stomach so far wrong as to give just a disagreeable tone to dreams, for instance last night I was at a pleasant musical entertainment, with nicely dressed ladies, which was interrupted by consternation of some managing person who pointed out that small drops of oil were falling from the ceiling. Woke hot and uncomfortable for a while. How strange – that I never dream of what's most in my waking mind. I had been working at serpents all the evening – if I had not, in all probability I should have dreamed of some in my old way – but, having my mind entirely occupied with them I never dreamed of so much as a tail end.

January 21, 1880.   I lying awake since five, thinking over the great dream, which I am ashamed to find is beginning to pass from me – and that too, in one of its most wonderful parts – the great contest between the Devil and – Georgie [Georgiana, Lady Burne-Jones]! (who represented throughout the adverse queenly or even archangelic power) for the Kingdom of the world. I dreamed that every seven thousand years it had to be run for in a chariot race – and that the Devil won always, because he knew some way of overlapping at the end of the last round, and counted the turns so that he always must win. This is the part that has got dim to me; but I thought that the secret had somehow become known to Georgie and that she raced him, and won.

January 9, 1881. Yesterday another lovely day of sun and calm, and I did much but had nasty and terrific nightmare of a puppet serpent, which suddenly came to life – grotesque, like a clown, but terrific and inevitable. – Also, of bathing in a deep pool, with some one holding me – and of rather pretty but saucy country women passing close above – pretending to be greatly astonished and shocked.

January 22, 1883. A frightful night of ugly nightmares – (not monstrous) but that I was getting bald, and that Miss Wakefield [Augusta Mary Wakefield, well-known amateur contralto] couldn't sing my music, &c., all of humiliation – caused I know not why, unless by drinking Aleatico [a sweet wine]. Now, mist – as dirty as nightmare over everything and I, 'blackened in heart' . . .

February 2. Candlemas. How often have I resolved to try for nobler life on this day, and always fallen back to the wretched one . . . And now – how am I even forgetting the lessons of my three illnesses, of contention between good and evil! I will try to fasten some, here – after noting for today's gift, the recurrence of the text to me as proper head of all to be taught or learned by me. 'If ye live after the flesh ye shall die, but if, &c.'

Well – the first thing to be noted of those three illnesses, that in the first there was the great definite Vision of the contention with the Devil, and all the terror and horror of Hell – & physical death. In the second, there was quite narrowed demoniacal vision, in my room, with the terrible fire-dream in the streets of London; in the third, the vision was mostly very sad & personal, all connected with my Father.

February 3. Going on from last page – observe that the sad part of the third vision, and the terrible, was all in its beginning and crisis, but, as soon as I began to get better, I had the delightful notion that Ruth [his favourite nurse] had been Rosie's nurse, and that she had hidden Rosie [Rose La Touche] away and was going to bring her

back to me, and I was expecting Rose every evening to come to tea –
and watched the different doors of the nursery – and then when
Ruth or Martha [housemaid] came in, instead – bore it as best I
could, waiting always for tomorrow.

In the second vision, here, the first part of it was my setting out to
walk to her grave – the second part, her coming with her mother,
and the interruption by the owl's cry.

Recollect the Madeleine part.

(The Madeleine part was, in the 1881 illness, I suppose, the period
of highest exaltation, showing the exact connection of pride with
insanity – I thought I had a kind of crucifixion to go through – and
to found a farther phase of Christianity and that Rose was as the
Magdalen to me. This part of the dream, I think, began – but all
beginnings and each are confused – with the hearing the seven guns
fired in heaven, as the end of this dispensation – a curious and
ludicrous confusion of them in my mind with the notion of guns
heard from Windsor.)

John Ruskin, *Brantwood Diary*

He had studied medicine diligently in all its branches; but had given
particular attention to the diseases of the imagination, which he
watched in himself with a solicitude destructive of his own peace,
and intolerable to those he trusted . . . When Mr Johnson felt his
fancy, or fancied he felt it, disordered, his constant recurrence was to
the study of arithmetic; and one day that he was totally confined to
his chamber, and I enquired what he had been doing to divert
himself, he shewed me a calculation which I could scarce be made to
understand, so vast was the plan of it, and so very intricate were the
figures: no other indeed than [that] the national debt, computing it
at one hundred and eighty millions sterling, would, if converted into
silver, serve to make a meridian of that metal, I forget how broad,
for the globe of the whole earth, the real *globe*.

Hester Lynch Piozzi, *Anecdotes of the late Samuel Johnson*, 1786

And I mean too that creative, genius-giving disease, disease that
rides on high horse over all hindrances, and springs with drunken

daring from peak to peak, is a thousand times dearer to life than plodding healthiness. I have never heard anything stupider than that from disease only disease can come. Life is not scrupulous — by morals it sets not a fart. It takes the reckless product of disease, feeds on and digests it, and as soon as it takes it to itself it is health. Before the fact of fitness for life, my good man, all distinction of disease and health falls away. A whole host and generation of youth, receptive, sound to the core, flings itself on the work of the morbid genius, made genius by disease: admires it, praises it, exalts it, carries it away, assimilates it unto itself and makes it over to culture, which lives not on home-made bread alone, but as well on provender and poison from the apothecary's shop at the sign of the Blessed Messengers. Thus saith to you the unbowdlerized Sammael.

Thomas Mann, *Doctor Faustus*, 1947; tr. H. T. Lowe-Porter

Yesterday I visited a home for neurasthenics. In the garden I saw a man standing on a seat, motionless as a fakir, his neck bent in a position which must have been highly uncomfortable. On my asking him what he was doing there, he replied, without turning his head, or moving a muscle: 'You see, Doctor, I am extremely rheumatic and catch cold very easily; I have just been taking a lot of exercise, and while I was getting hot, like a fool, my neck was touching my flannels. If I move it away from my flannels now before letting myself cool down, I am certain to get a stiff neck, and possibly bronchitis.' Which he would, in fact, have done. 'You're a fine specimen of neurasthenia, that's what you are,' I told him. And do you know what argument he advanced to prove that I was mistaken? It was this: that while all the other patients in the place had a mania for testing their weight, so much so that the weighing-machine had to be padlocked so that they should not spend the whole day on it, he had to be lifted on to it bodily, so little did he care to be weighed. He prided himself on not sharing the mania of the others without thinking that he had also one of his own, and that it was this which saved him from the other. You must not be offended by the comparison, Madame, for the man who dared not turn his neck for fear of catching a chill is the greatest poet of our day. That poor maniac is the most lofty intellect that I know. Submit to being called a neurotic. You belong to that splendid and pitiable family which is the salt of the earth. All the greatest things we know have come to us from neurotics. It is they and they only who have founded religions and created great works of art. Never will the world be conscious of how much it owes to them, nor above all of what they have suffered in order to bestow their gifts on it. We enjoy fine music, beautiful pictures, a thousand exquisite things, but we do not know what they cost those who wrought them in sleeplessness, tears, spasmodic laughter, rashes, asthma, epilepsy, a terror of death which is worse than any of these . . .

Proust, *The Guermantes Way I*, 1920; tr. Scott Moncrieff.
Dr du Boulbon speaking to the narrator's grandmother, who is actually suffering from uraemia

Madness and debauchery are two things I have plumbed so thoroughly, in which of my free will I have explored so well, that I shall never (I hope) be either a lunatic or a Sade. But then, I have smarted for it. My nervous illness has been the froth of those little intellectual pranks. Each attack was like a haemorrhage of the nervous system. It was seminal losses from the pictorial faculty of the brain, hundreds of thousands of images cavorting together, in a fireworks display. There was a tearing away of the soul from the body, atrocious (I am convinced I died a number of times). But what constitutes the personality, the rational being, saw it through to the end; otherwise there would have been no suffering, for I would have been wholly passive, whereas I was *conscious* all the time, even when I could no longer speak. Then, the soul was entirely folded in on itself, like a hedgehog wounding itself with its own quills.

Flaubert, letter to Louise Colet, 7/8 July 1853

I met Dumas yesterday, and he is writing to you today. He will tell you that I have recovered what by general agreement is called reason. But don't believe a word of it. I am still and always have been the same, and I am only surprised that people found me *changed* during those few days of last spring. Illusion, paradox, presumption – they are all of them enemies of common sense, which I have never lacked. Truly, I had a very amusing dream, and I miss it; I have even come to wonder whether it was not more *true* than what seems only explicable and natural to me nowadays; but as there are doctors and policemen here to make sure that no one extends the field of poetry at the expense of the public highway, I was allowed to go out and roam among reasonable people only when I admitted formally to having been *sick*, the which cost my pride a lot, and even my veracity. Confess! confess! they shouted at me, as they used to at witches and heretics in the old days, and to put an end to it I agreed to let them classify me under a *disease* defined by the doctors and called either Theomania or Demonomania in the medical dictionary. With the help of the clarifications given under those two headings, science has the right to conjure away or reduce to silence all the prophets and seers announced by the Book of Revelation, one of whom I flattered myself to be! But I am resigned to my plight, and if I miscarry in my predestination I shall accuse Doctor Blanche of having sneaked off with the divine spirit . . .

I feel confused and at a loss, falling out of the sky where I walked so familiarly a few months ago. What a pity that society as it is won't allow us, if not glory, at least the illusion of a perpetual dream.

Gérard de Nerval, letter to Mme Alexandre Dumas, 9 November 1841

I told Clare I had been much pleased with his lines on the daisy.

'Ugh! It is a tidy little thing,' replied he, without raising his eyes or appearing in the slightest degree gratified by my praise.

'I am glad you can amuse yourself by writing.'

'I can't do it,' replied he, gloomily; 'they pick my brains out.' I enquired his meaning.

'Why,' said he, 'they have cut off my head, and picked out all the letters of the alphabet — all the vowels and consonants — and brought them out through my ears; and then they want me to write poetry! I can't do it.'

'Tell me which you liked best, literature or your former avocation.'

'I liked hard work best,' he replied, with sudden vehemence; 'I was happy then. Literature has destroyed my head and brought me here.'

Agnes Strickland, in her 'Autograph-book', on visiting John Clare in the Northampton General Lunatic Asylum, 28 August 1860

The Progress of Madness

I cultivated my hysteria with enjoyment and terror. Now I have fits of giddiness all the time, and today, 23 January 1862, i received a strange warning, I felt the wing of imbecility brush against me.

Charles Baudelaire, *Journaux Intimes*

My health? you ask. How the devil do you want it to be good, with so many angers and cares? . . . What irritates me most of all, more than the misery, more than the stupidity that surrounds me, is a certain comatose state that makes me doubt my faculties. After three or four hours of work, I am no longer good for anything. A few years ago, I sometimes worked twelve hours, and with pleasure.

Baudelaire, letter to M. Ancelle, 26 November 1865

I have a feeling of emptiness in my head, of fogginess, of abstraction. It comes from that long series of attacks, and also from the use of opium, digitalis, belladonna and quinine. A doctor I called in didn't know that I had taken opium for a long time in the past. That's why he was sparing with it, and why I have had to double and quadruple the doses. I've succeeded in changing the occurrence of the attacks; that's something. But I'm very tired.

Baudelaire, letter to M. Ancelle, 26 December 1865

To give up beer, I'm delighted. Tea and coffee, that's more serious; but it's bearable. Wine? That's damned cruel. But here comes a tougher animal, who says that I must neither read nor study. Funny sort of medicine that stamps out one's principal function! Another one tells me, as the only consolation, that I am *hysterical*. Don't you admire, as I do, the elastic use of these big words so well chosen to veil our total ignorance?

Baudelaire, letter to Sainte-Beuve, 15 January 1866

The doctors have not hidden from me the gravity of his condition, not regarding his physical health, but regarding his mind: *that mind has worked too much*, he is exhausted *before his time*.

Although his tongue isn't paralysed, he has forgotten *the memory of sound. Non, quie, quie*, the sole words he articulates, he shouts them out at the top of his voice . . . Evidently there is softening of the brain. When he's not angry, he listens and understands every-thing one says to him. I tell him things about his youth, he understands me, he listens attentively. And then when he wants to reply, the impotent efforts he makes to express himself throw him into a rage . . . No extravagant behaviour, no hallucinations . . . He eats, he sleeps, he goes out in the carriage with Stevens and me, or on foot, with a cane, along the public promenade, in the sun. But, no words. I shan't leave him, I shall look after him like a little child . . .

I don't think he can read, he would always have a book in his hand; if he picks up a book, he can no longer make out the letters and he rejects it.

When he sees me, he is moved. Aimée [Mme Aupick's servant] says that *he seems to be holding back pleasure*. He isn't naughty. I have influence over him. He grows calm when I speak softly to him. Never any anger with me, not even sulking . . . He lost his temper with me this morning for the first time . . . He is very changeable. A fortnight ago he hated Aimée, now he gets on very well with her. Nerves play a great part. Sometimes, after he has lost his temper, he breaks into long bursts of laughter, which frighten me. He grows irritable when I take up my pen. He never gets angry without reason.

He points with disgust to something in a corner of the room. Everything is brought to him. He still points, in terrible anger. The dirty linen that was under a bed is brought to him. He quietens down. Such a care for cleanliness . . .

He is certainly not in a condition to be deprived of his freedom, that would be inhuman, that would be a crime. He has one fixed idea: *not to be dominated.*

Letter from Mme Aupick, Baudelaire's mother, to M. Ancelle, June 1866;
Baudelaire died at the end of August in the following year

Tact was his very nature. No one had ever been more delicately organized for the exercise of that faculty in which instinct and reason both play their part. And now he is losing that faculty, which was so highly developed in him; he can no longer gauge the degrees of politeness befitting the rank of the people he meets; he can no longer gauge the degrees of intelligence suited to the minds with which he comes in contact.

For some time now – and it grows more noticeable every day – there have been certain letters that he pronounces badly, r's that he elides, c's that become t's in his mouth. I remember, when he was a little boy, how sweet and charming it was to hear him stumbling over those two consonants. To hear the same childish pronunciation today, to hear his voice as I used to hear it in the distant and forgotten past, where my memories encounter nothing but things long dead, frightens me.

Over that beloved face, once so full of intelligence and irony, that shrewd and wonderfully malicious countenance of the mind, I can see the haggard mask of imbecility slipping minute by minute. Little by little he is stripping himself of his affectionate nature, *dehumanizing* himself; other people have begun to lose their reality for him, and he has started to return to the cruel egoism of childhood.

To witness, day by day, the destruction of everything that once went to mark out this young man – distinguished among all others – to see him emptying the salt-cellar over his fish, holding his fork in both hands, eating like a child, is too much for me to bear.

So it was not enough that this busy mind should stop producing, should cease creating, should be inhabited by nothingness. The human being had to be stricken in these qualities of grace and elegance which I imagined to be inaccessible to sickness, in these gifts of the man who is well born, well bred, well brought up. And finally, as in the old vengeance of the gods, all the aristocratic virtues in him, all the superior graces inherent so to speak in his skin, had to be degraded to the level of animality.

The Goncourt Journal, March–April 1870; Edmond on his brother
Jules's last illness

No worst, there is none. Pitched past pitch of grief,
More pangs will, schooled at forepangs, wilder wring.
Comforter, where, where is your comforting?
Mary, mother of us, where is your relief?
My cries heave, herds-long; huddle in a main, a chief-

woe, world-sorrow; on an age-old anvil wince and sing —
Then lull, then leave off. Fury had shrieked 'No lingering! Let me be fell: force I must be brief.'

O the mind, mind has mountains; cliffs of fall
Frightful, sheer, no-man-fathomed. Hold them cheap
May who ne'er hung there. Nor does long our small
Durance deal with that steep or deep. Here! creep,
Wretch, under a comfort serves in a whirlwind: all
Life death does end and each day dies with sleep.
    Gerard Manley Hopkins, 'No worst, there is none', 1885

Farewell, dear scenes, for ever closed to me,
Oh, for what sorrows must I now exchange ye!

                        *

Me miserable! how could I escape
Infinite wrath and infinite despair!
Whom Death, Earth, Heaven, and Hell consigned to ruin,
Whose friend was God, but God swore not to aid me!
    Cowper, 'Lines Written upon a Window-Shutter at Weston', 1795

Why have you made life so intolerable
And set me between four walls, where I am able
Not to escape meals without prayer, for that is possible
Only by annoying an attendant. And tonight a sensual
Hell has been put on me, so that all has deserted me
And I am merely crying and trembling in heart
For death, and cannot get it. And gone out is part
Of sanity. And there is dreadful hell within me.
And nothing helps. Forced meals there have been and electricity
And weakening of sanity by influence
That's dreadful to endure. And there is Orders
And I am praying for death, death, death,
And dreadful is the indrawing or out-breathing of breath
Because of the intolerable insults put on my whole soul,
Of the soul loathed, loathed, loathed of the soul.

Gone out every bright thing from my mind.
All lost that ever God himself designed.
Not half can be written of cruelty of man, on man,
Not often such evil guessed as between man and man.

Ivor Gurney, 'To God', Barnwood Mental Hospital, 1922

Old Bethlehem, or Bedlam – every trace of which has been swept away, and the hospital for lunatics removed to Saint George's Fields – was a vast and magnificent structure. Erected in Moorfields in 1675, upon the model of the Tuileries, it is said Louis the Fourteenth was so incensed at the insult offered to his palace, that he had a counterpart of St James's built for offices of the meanest description . . . But, the besetting evil of the place . . . was that this spot – which of all others should have been most free from such intrusion – was made a public exhibition. There all the loose characters thronged, assignations were openly made, and the spectators diverted themselves with the vagaries of its miserable inhabitants.

Entering the outer gate, and traversing the broad gravel walk, Jack ascended the steps, and was admitted, on feeing the porter, by another iron gate, into the hospital. Here he was almost stunned by the deafening clamour resounding on all sides. Some of the lunatics were rattling their chains; some shrieking; some singing; some beating with frantic violence against the doors. Altogether, it was the most dreadful noise he had ever heard. Amidst it all, however, there were several light-hearted and laughing groups walking from cell to cell, to whom all this misery appeared matter of amusement.

The doors of several of the wards were thrown open for these parties, and as Jack passed, he could not help glancing at the wretched inmates. Here was a poor half-naked creature with a straw crown on his head, and a wooden sceptre in his hand, seated on the ground with all the dignity of a monarch on his throne. There was a mad musician, seemingly rapt in admiration of the notes he was extracting from a child's violin. Here was a terrific figure gnashing his teeth, and howling like a wild beast – there a lover, with hands clasped together, and eyes turned passionately upward. In this cell was a huntsman, who had fractured his skull while hunting, and was perpetually hallooing after the hounds – in that, the most melan-

choly of all, the grinning, gibbering lunatic, the realization of
'moody madness, laughing wild'.

William Harrison Ainsworth, *Jack Sheppard*, 1839;
the date in the narrative is 1724

Those in the beds produced a continuous agitated flutter, screaming,
rolling their eyes, waving their arms. It was as if each of them were
shouting out into some space that existed only for him; and yet too
they all seemed to be engaged in one vast tumultuous discussion, like
exotic birds all shut up in one cage and each of them chattering in the
language of some other island. Some of them were free, others were
tied to the bed with bandages which prevented them from moving
their hands much.

'Safeguard against attempted suicide,' the doctor explained, and
went on to name the forms of insanity: paralysis, paranoia,
dementia praecox – names that might indeed have been those of
species of exotic birds.

Musil, *The Man Without Qualities*

Many of the inmates of the asylum were sufferers from GPI or
general paralysis of the insane, the final stage of syphilis. They
gawped, shambled and mumbled, though occasionally they cursed
the universe loudly. They were permitted to see films on Wednesday
afternoons so long as these were of a sedative nature. But it was hard
to know what a sedative film was. *Pride and Prejudice* caused a riot
and had to be stopped at the point where Darcy said: 'Miss Bennet, I
admire and love you.' Some of the patients had perverse talents
engendered by their disease. I was introduced to a human compt-
ometer who could, from a slobbering idiot mouth, announce
immediately and accurately the product of a hard long multiplica-
tion. Another could give the day of the week for any date in history. I
tried him on June 16, 1904, and he came out at once with 'A
Tursday'. There was a morose hulk of a man who had taught himself
to play violent rhapsodies on the piano. These were atonal but
coherent and embodied distorted memories of classical themes, as
though picked up by a starling. It was like listening to a summary of

human history ending with doomsday. There was a sort of poet who had written with a pencil stub a sort of Blakean prophetic book full of characters like Eveson and Grimsthorpe. He was temporarily lucid when I met him and was concentrating on epitaphs. He had just written one on the head of the asylum orchestra:

> To write your epitaph it is a pleasure.
> You were a liar in full measure.

One or two of the patients were voluble and plausible. I listened for an hour to an account of inventive achievement which included an alphabet without digraphs and a smokeless boiler. Then came: 'In 1931 I was made a sir but I said no to further honours.'

Anthony Burgess, *Little Wilson and Big God*, 1987

> Utrillo on the wall. A nun is climbing
> Steps in Montmartre. We patients sit below.
> It does not seem a time for lucid rhyming;
> Too much disturbs. It does not seem a time
> When anything could fertilize or grow.
>
> It is as if a scream were opened wide,
> A mouth demanding everyone to listen.
> Too many people cry, too many hide
> And stare into themselves. I am afraid.
> There are no life-belts here on which to fasten.
>
> The nun is climbing up those steps. The room
> Shifts till the dust flies in between our eyes.
> The only hope is visitors will come
> And talk of other things than our disease . . .
> So much is stagnant and yet nothing dies.

Elizabeth Jennings, 'A Mental Hospital Sitting-Room', 1966

> She looks from the window: still it pours down direly,
> And the avenue drips. She cannot go, she fears;

And the Regatta will be spoilt entirely;
    And she sheds half-crazed tears.

Regatta Day and rain come on together
Again, years after. Gutters trickle loud;
But Nancy cares not. She knows nought of weather,
    Or of the Henley crowd:

She's a Regatta quite her own. Inanely
She laughs in the asylum as she floats
Within a water-tub, which she calls 'Henley',
    Her little paper boats.
                Hardy, 'Henley Regatta', 1928

Young and Old

What is rather disconcerting when collecting material relating to the elderly is that the old people of the past turn out to have been quite young. Joanna Baillie's enfeebled grandfather was probably in his early fifties; and when he wrote in hoary and valedictory fashion, shortly before he died, that prolific author Trollope was no more than sixty-seven.

It stands to reason, then, that the young inclined to be less youthful, since they needed to mature faster. Marjory Fleming ('I hope I will be religious again but as for regaining my character I despare'), dead at eight years, sounds enormously grown up. But so – unless we grown-ups are flattering ourselves – does the ten-year-old, mentioned by R. D. Laing, who wanted to finish *The Pickwick Papers* before he died.

They are the mayflies of our species, in the sense in which Josef Skvorecky spoke, in *The Engineer of Human Souls*, of a Czech factory girl who died young of tuberculosis: '. . . how she was simple as a clarinet counterpoint in a village band and yet full of surprises . . . how she had displayed the wisdom of a beautiful mayfly who is crushed under foot before she can fulfil the one meaning her life has. But no. Nadia's life had a different meaning. It was more than mere biology.'

———

Thou who didst hang upon a barren tree,
My God, for me;
    Though I till now be barren, now at length,
    Lord, give me strength
To bring forth fruit to Thee.

Thou who didst bear for me the crown of thorn,
Spitting and scorn;

Though I till now have put forth thorns, yet now
    Strengthen me Thou
That better fruit be borne.

Thou Rose of Sharon, Cedar of broad roots,
Vine of sweet fruits,
    Thou Lily of the vale with fadeless leaf,
    Of thousands Chief,
Feed Thou my feeble shoots.
                    Christina Rossetti, 'Long Barren', 1865

You count the fingers first: it's traditional.
(You assume the doctor counted them too,
when he lifted up the slimy surprise
with its long dark pointed head and its father's nose
at 2.13 a.m. – 'Look at the clock!'
said Sister: 'Remember the time: 2.13.')

Next day the head's turned pink and round;
the nose is a blob. You fumble under the gown
your mother embroidered with a sprig of daisies,
as she embroidered your own Viyella gowns
when you were a baby. You fish out
curly triangular feet. You count the toes.

'There's just one little thing' says Sister:
'His ears – they don't quite match. One
has an extra whorl in it. No one will notice.'
You notice like mad. You keep on noticing.
Then you hear a rumour: a woman in the next ward
has had a stillbirth. Or was it something worse?

You lie there, bleeding gratefully.
You've won the Nobel Prize, and the VC,
and the State Lottery, and gone to heaven.
Feed-time comes. They bring your bundle –

the right one: it's him all right.
You count his eyelashes: the ideal number.

You take him home. He learns to walk.
From time to time you eye him,
nonchalantly, from each side.
He has an admirable nose.
No one ever notices his ears. No one
ever stands on both sides of him at once.

He grows up. He has beautiful children.

Fleur Adcock, 'Counting', 1988

My mother groan'd, my father wept;
Into the dangerous world I leapt,
Helpless, naked, piping loud,
Like a fiend hid in a cloud.

Struggling in my father's hands,
Striving against my swaddling bands,
Bound and weary, I thought best
To sulk upon my mother's breast.

Blake, 'Infant Sorrow', 1793

As a drenched, drowned bee
Hangs numb and heavy from a bending flower,
So clings to me
My baby, her brown hair brushed with wet tears
And laid against her cheek;
Her soft white legs hanging heavily over my arm
Swing to my walking movement, weak
With after-pain. My sleeping baby hangs upon my life,
Like a burden she hangs on me;
She who has always seemed so light,
Now wet with tears and pain hangs heavily,
Even her floating hair sinks heavily

Reaching downwards;
As the wings of a drenched, drowned bee
Are a heaviness, and a weariness.
                    Lawrence, 'A Baby Asleep after Pain', 1909

In watching the infancy of my own children, I made another
discovery – it is well known to mothers, to nurses, and also to
philosophers – that the tears and lamentations of infants during the
year or so when they have no *other* language of complaint run
through a gamut that is as inexhaustible as the Cremona of
Paganini. An ear but moderately learned in that language cannot be
deceived as to the rate and *modulus* of the suffering which it
indicates. A fretful or peevish cry cannot by any efforts make itself
impassioned. The cry of impatience, of hunger, of irritation, of
reproach, of alarm, are all different – different as a chorus of
Beethoven from a chorus of Mozart. But if ever you saw an infant
suffering for an hour, as sometimes the healthiest does, under some
attack of the stomach, which has the tiger-grasp of the Oriental
cholera, then you will hear moans that address to their mothers an
anguish of supplication for aid such as might storm the heart of
Moloch. Once hearing it, you will not forget it.
                    De Quincey, *Suspiria de Profundis*, 1845

Lit by the small night-light you lie
And look through swollen eyes at me:
Vulnerable, sleepless, try
To stare through a blank misery,
And now that boisterous creature I
Have known so often shrinks to this
Wan ghost unsweetened by a kiss.

Shaken with retching, bewildered by
The virus curdling milk and food,
You do not scream in fear, or cry.
Tears are another thing, a mood
Given an image, infancy

Making permitted show of force,
Boredom, or sudden pain. The source

Of this still vacancy's elsewhere.
Like my sick dog, ten years ago,
Who skulked away to some far lair
With poison in her blood: you know
Her gentleness, her clouded stare,
Pluck blankets as she scratched the ground.
She made, and you now make, no sound.

The rank smell shrouds you like a sheet.
Tomorrow we must let crisp air
Blow through the room and make it sweet,
Making all new. I touch your hair,
Damp where the forehead sweats, and meet –
Here by the door, as I leave you –
A cold, quiet wind, chilling me through.
                            Anthony Thwaite, 'Sick Child', 1963

Careless for an instant I closed my child's finger in the jamb. She
Held her breath, contorted the whole of her being, foetus-wise,
    against the
Burning fact of the pain. And for a moment
I wished myself dispersed in a hundred thousand pieces
Among the dead bright stars. The child's cry broke,
She clung to me, and it crowded in to me how she and I were
Light-years from any mutual help or comfort. For her I cast seed
Into her mother's womb; cells grew and launched itself as a being:
Nothing restores her to my being, or ours, even to the mother who
    within her
Carried and quickened, bore, and sobbed at her separation, despite
    all my envy,
Nothing can restore. She, I, mother, sister, dwell dispersed among
    dead bright stars:
We are there in our hundred thousand pieces!
                            David Holbrook, 'Fingers in the Door', 1960

My dear little Mama, — I was truly happy to hear you were all well. We are surrounded with measles at present on every side, for the Herons got it, and Isabella Heron was near Death's Door, and one night her father lifted her out of bed, and she fell down as they thought lifeless. Mr Heron said, — 'That lassie's deed noo' — 'I'm no deed yet.' She then threw up a big worm nine inches and a half long.

Marjory Fleming, September 1811

When I was sick and lay a-bed,
I had two pillows at my head,
And all my toys beside me lay
To keep me happy all the day.

And sometimes for an hour or so
I watched my leaden soldiers go,
With different uniforms and drills,
Among the bedclothes, through the hills;

And sometimes sent my ships in fleets
All up and down among the sheets;
Or brought my trees and houses out,
And planted cities all about.

I was the giant great and still
That sits upon the pillow-hill,
And sees before him, dale and plain,
The pleasant land of counterpane.

Robert Louis Stevenson, 'The Land of Counterpane', 1885

Pain and weariness, aching eyes and head,
    Pain and weariness all the day and night:
Yet the pillow's soft on my smooth soft bed,
    And fresh air blows in, and mother shades the light.

Thou, O Lord, in pain hadst no pillow soft,
    In Thy weary pain, in Thine agony:
But a cross of shame held Thee up aloft
    Where Thy very mother could do nought for Thee.

I would gaze on Thee, on Thy patient face;
   Make me like Thyself, patient, sweet, at peace;
Make my days all love, and my nights all praise,
   Till all days and nights and patient sufferings cease.
        Christina Rossetti, 'A Sick Child's Meditation', 1855

I love my little son, and yet when he was ill
I could not confine myself to his bedside.
I was impatient of his squalid little needs,
His laboured breathing and the fretful way he cried
And longed for my wide range of interests again,
Whereas his mother sank without another care
To that dread level of nothing but life itself
And stayed day and night, till he was better, there.

Women may pretend, yet they always dismiss
Everything but mere being just like this.
        Hugh MacDiarmid, 'The Two Parents', 1935

Because Vietnamese names are very repetitive, we gave most of the younger children a nursery name that would fix them indelibly in our memory. We named them after artists and musicians, after poets and prose writers; philosophers and theologians; after saints and sinners. There were children named from the Bible and children from ancient mythology; there were others named after the great lovers of history and literature. There were children celebrating virtues, nature, the seasons, the cities of our birth, our personal friends and favourites; fairy-tale characters, and the mood of the moment. We had a Van Gogh, a Michelangelo and a Mozart; a Will Shakespeare, Dante and a C. S. Lewis; Socrates, Jean-Paul Sartre and Thomas Aquinas; Juliana of Norwich, Joan of Arc and Mary Magdalene. We had an Abraham, Moses and Solomon as well as a Zeus, Ulysses and Agamemnon. There was a Tristan and an Isolde; an Eloïse and an Abelard; a Julius Caesar, Marc Antony and a Cleopatra. There was Courage, Fidelity and Patience; Rainbow, Petunia, Mopoke, Epiphany and Autumn; Berlin, Melbourne and

Adelaide. There was a Daniel Berrigan, Thomas Merton, and a Cinderella; also Wonder, Surprise and Desperation.

Some children came to us beaten and bruised and a few, like Helen of Troy and Tom, with fractured bones; others were physically unscarred but retarded in all aspects of their development. One child was cranky and miserable and vomited up a tapeworm; another child was inexplicably merry all the time and we delayed his placement for a while, trying to detect the cause for his unwarranted good humour. Some children came to us in a severely malnourished condition and had to be built up; a rare few, like Blancmange, seemed too fat and we suspected some other kind of maladjustment. There was Michelle, who may have been abandoned because she was inauspiciously born with a tooth already visible; then there was a five-year-old, Bach Mai, whose dental X-rays showed her second teeth just weren't there. There were a host of others with a mouthful of rotting stubs.

Pami was about three years old and a picture of misery when she came to Newhaven nursery [in Saigon] in April 1975. She was given the nursery name of 'Joy' as an incentive and an expression of optimism; it seemed the least we could do for her in the time that remained. She was evacuated to the USA on 26 April and her parents [adoptive] came from Finland to fetch her:

> We found her sitting glassy-eyed in the corner of her crib in a Denver hospital, and rattling the bars. She had a big belly and a skin rash. Her legs were too weak to support her. In the beginning communication was difficult and Pami just wanted to sit and cry. But she had a good appetite and dark rye bread and pea soup were her favourites. If we tried to stop her from overeating, she responded vigorously by spitting on us and whistling like a street boy.
>
> After a few months' steady progress, Pami had to be hospitalized for tuberculosis. Unwilling to adapt to her new surroundings, she simply climbed out of the window and was later found chasing birds in a nearby park.
>
> As Pami learnt to express herself in Finnish, her story came out: her father was killed. Long-haired soldiers came down from the

sky and shot everyone. 'I hid under the house. Why do they always come down when it is cloudy?' she asked. 'I fled with my sister to the river where the boats go. A crocodile attacked one of the children but was shot by the soldiers. There were also bananas in the trees but we didn't tell anybody.'

Rosemary Taylor, *Orphans of War: Work with the abandoned children of Vietnam 1967–1975*, 1988

'My son has gone under the hill.
We called him after a clockmaker
but God meets all such whimsy
with his early-striking hands.

That night of his high fever
I held a stream against me,
his heart panicky as a netted bird,
globes of solder on his brow.

Then he was lost in sea-fret,
the other side of silence,
his eyes milky as snowberries
and his fifteen months unlearned.

They have taken him away
who was just coming to me,
his spine like the curve
of an avocet's bill.'

Blake Morrison, 'Meningococcus', 1984

He was ten years of age and had hydrocephalus due to an inoperable tumour the size of a very small pea, just at the right place to stop his cerebrospinal fluid from getting out of his head: which is to say that he had water on the brain and it was bursting his head, so that the brain was becoming stretched out into a thinning rim, and his skull bones likewise. He was in excruciating and unremitting pain.

One of my jobs was to put a long needle into this ever-increasing fluid to let it out. I had to do this twice a day and the so-clear fluid that was killing him would leap out at me from his massive ten-year-old head, rising in a brief column to several feet, sometimes hitting my face . . . But this little boy unmistakably endured agony. He would quietly cry in pain. If he could only have shrieked or complained . . . And he knew he was going to die.

He had started reading *The Pickwick Papers*. The one thing he asked God for, he told me, was that he be allowed to finish this book before he died.

He died before it was half finished.

R. D. Laing, *The Bird of Paradise*, 1967

Address to dear Isabella on the Authors recovery

O Isa pain did visit me
I was at the last extremity
How often did I think of you
I wished your graceful form to view
To clasp you in my weak embrace
Indeed I thought Id run my race.
Good Care Im sure was of me taken
But indeed I was much shaken
At last I daily strength did gain
And O at last away went pain
At length the docter thought I might
Stay in the Parlour till the night
I now continue so to do
Farewell to Nancy and to you.
Wrote by M.F.

Marjory Fleming's last poem, written on 15 December 1811,
four days before her death, at the age of eight, of complications,
possibly meningitis, following measles

Nature abhors the old, and old age seems the only disease; all others run into this one.

Ralph Waldo Emerson, 'Circles', *Essays: First Series*, 1841

Old people are fond of giving good advice, to console themselves for
no longer being in a position to give bad examples.

> François, Duc de La Rochefoucauld, *Maxims*, 1665

Now king David was old and stricken in years; and they covered him
with clothes, but he gat no heat.

Wherefore his servants said unto him, Let there be sought for my
lord the king a young virgin: and let her stand before the king, and
let her cherish him, and let her lie in thy bosom, that my lord the king
may get heat.

So they sought for a fair damsel throughout all the coasts of Israel,
and found Abishag a Shunammite, and brought her to the king.

And the damsel was very fair, and cherished the king, and
ministered to him: but the king knew her not.

> I Kings, 1

What is it to grow old?
Is it to lose the glory of the form,
The lustre of the eye?
Is it for beauty to forego her wreath?
— Yes, but not this alone.

Is it to feel our strength —
Not our bloom only, but our strength — decay?
Is it to feel each limb
Grow stiffer, every function less exact,
Each nerve more loosely strung?

Yes, this, and more; but not
Ah, 'tis not what in youth we dream'd 'twould be!
'Tis not to have our life
Mellow'd and soften'd as with sunset-glow,
A golden day's decline.

'Tis not to see the world
As from a height, with rapt prophetic eyes,

And heart profoundly stirr'd;
And weep, and feel the fullness of the past,
The years that are no more.

It is to spend long days
And not once feel that we were ever young;
It is to add, immured
In the hot prison of the present, month
To month with weary pain.

It is to suffer this,
And feel but half, and feebly, what we feel.
Deep in our hidden heart
Festers the dull remembrance of a change,
But no emotion – none.

It is – last stage of all –
When we are frozen up within, and quite
The phantom of ourselves,
To hear the world applaud the hollow ghost
Which blamed the living man.

Matthew Arnold, 'Growing Old', 1867

He observed, 'There is a wicked inclination in most people to suppose an old man decayed in his intellects. If a young or middle-aged man, when leaving a company, does not recollect where he laid his hat, it is nothing; but if the same inattention is discovered in an old man, people will shrug their shoulders, and say, "His memory is going." '

Boswell, *Life of Johnson*, 30 March 1783

'Why, highty tighty, sir!' cried Mrs Gamp, 'is these your manners? You want a pitcher of cold water throw'd over you to bring you round; that's my belief; and if you was under Betsey Prig you'd have it, too, I do assure you, Mr Chuffey. Spanish Flies is the only thing to draw this nonsense out of you, and if anybody wanted to do you a kindness, they'd clap a blister of 'em on your head, and put a mustard poultige on your back. Who's dead, indeed! It wouldn't be no grievous loss if some one was, I think!'

'He's quiet now, Mrs Gamp,' said Merry. 'Don't disturb him.'

'Oh, bother the old wictim, Mrs Chuzzlewit,' replied that zealous lady. 'I ain't no patience with him. You give him his own way too much by half. A worritin' wexagious creetur!'

No doubt with the view of carrying out the precepts she enforced, and 'bothering the old wictim' in practice as well as in theory, Mrs Gamp took him by the collar of his coat, and gave him some dozen or two of hearty shakes backward and forward in his chair; that exercise being considered by the disciples of the Prig school of nursing (who are very numerous among professional ladies) as exceedingly conducive to repose, and highly beneficial to the performance of the nervous functions. Its effect in this instance was to render the patient so giddy and addle-headed, that he could say nothing more; which Mrs Gamp regarded as the triumph of her art.

'There!' she said, loosening the old man's cravat, in consequence of his being rather black in the face, after this scientific treatment. 'Now, I hope, you're easy in your mind. If you should turn at all faint we can soon revive you, sir, I promige you. Bite a person's thumbs, or turn their fingers the wrong way,' said Mrs Gamp, smiling with the consciousness of at once imparting pleasure and instruction to her auditors, 'and they comes to, wonderful, Lord bless you!'

Dickens, Martin Chuzzlewit, 1844

— Crouched in her crib, diapered, dark as a nut, with three tufts of hair like dandelion floss sprouting from her head, an old woman was making loud shaky noises.

'Hello Aunty,' the nurse said. 'You're spelling today. It's lovely weather outside.' She bent to the old woman's ear. 'Can you spell weather?'

This nurse showed her gums when she smiled, which was all the time; she had an air of nearly demented hilarity.

'Weather,' said the old woman. She strained forward, grunting, to get the word. Rose thought she might be going to have a bowel movement. 'W-E-A-T-H-E-R.'

That reminded her.

'Whether. W-H-E-T-H-E-R.'

So far so good.

'Now you say something to her,' the nurse said to Rose.

The words in Rose's mind were for a moment all obscene or despairing.

But without prompting came another.

'Forest. F-O-R-E-S-T.'

'Celebrate,' said Rose suddenly.

'C-E-L-E-B-R-A-T-E.'

You had to listen very hard to make out what the old woman was saying, because she had lost much of the power to shape sounds. What she said seemed to come not from her mouth or her throat, but from deep in her lungs and belly.

'Isn't she a wonder,' the nurse said. 'She can't see and that's the only way we can tell she can hear. Like if you say, "Here's your dinner", she won't pay any attention to it, but she might start spelling *dinner*.'

'Dinner,' she said, to illustrate, and the old woman picked it up. 'D-I-N-N . . .' Sometimes a long wait, a long wait between letters. It seemed she had only the thinnest thread to follow, meandering through that emptiness or confusion that nobody on this side can do more than guess at. But she didn't lose it, she followed it through to the end, however tricky the word might be, or cumbersome. Finished. Then she was sitting waiting; waiting, in the middle of her sightless eventless day, till up from somewhere popped another word. She would encompass it, bend all her energy to master it.

Alice Munro, from 'Spelling', 1980

'We fell in love with it ten years ago – for the view. And I must say we've never regretted it, not even in the winter. It's so peaceful. Do you know last spring when I was walking along the path from the village I saw something standing at the front gate. I could see it as I turned the corner by the wood. It looked like a dog but it didn't, if you know what I mean. And do you know what it was? It was a badger . . .'

When she phones it is usually about him rather than herself.

'I'm worried about him, doctor, he's got a pain in his back and I think it might be a slipped disc. It all came on in that wet spell last week when he insisted upon digging the vegetable garden, the first chance for two months, he said, and now he can't straighten up.'

Sometimes it sounds more serious.

'He's been in bed for three days and he has great difficulty in breathing. When he breathes at night – and I simply can't get to sleep listening to him – I keep on thinking he's talking, his breathing sounds like words, doctor.'

She is there at the door waiting.

'I'm so glad you've come. His whole body is collapsing. I better let you talk to him yourself, because he won't tell me what he's complaining of, he won't come out with it, he's funny like that you know, he just says all his organs are going. Which? I say. What do you mean? But he won't tell me, he just says all his organs.'

The husband, aged seventy-three, explains that he can't hold his water and that he has some pain in the lower part of the abdomen. The doctor checks his chest and stomach. He does a rectal examination to feel the prostate and to discover whether any growth is pressing on the bladder. He tests the urine for sugar and albumen. The sugar is just problematic. He diagnoses a mild urinary infection.

Thirty-six hours later she phones.

'He just can't take any liquid at all now. He can't drink. He hasn't taken a drop since yesterday breakfast. And he keeps on falling asleep. Right in the middle of my talking to him he just falls off – I don't know what to do. He just can't keep awake, not even when I'm talking to him, he just falls asleep and then he's sleepy and he falls asleep again even when I'm talking to him.'

The doctor smiles into the phone. Yet, just conceivably, if almost impossibly, the sleeping might be the beginning of a diabetic coma: the diabetes made manifest by the urinary infection. To be certain he must do another blood test for sugar.

At that gate where the badger stood, he pauses and looks down at the view with which they fell in love, and then he remembers her saying in a more intense, more sibilant voice than her ordinary one:

'All we've got is each other. So we have to be very strict. We watch over each other very carefully when we are ill, we do.'

John Berger, *A Fortunate Man: The Story of a Country Doctor*, 1967

Grand-dad, they say you're old and frail,
Your stockèd legs begin to fail:
Your knobbèd stick (that was my horse)
Can scarce support your bended corse;
While back to wall you lean so sad,
   I'm vexed to see you, dad.

You used to smile and stroke my head,
And tell me how good children did;
But now, I wot not how it be,
You take me seldom on your knee;
Yet ne'ertheless I am right glad
   To sit beside you, dad.

How lank and thin your beard hangs down!
Scant are the white hairs on your crown;
How wan and hollow are your cheeks!
Your brow is rough with crossing breaks;
But yet, for all his strength is fled,
   I love my own old dad.

The housewives round their potions brew,
And gossips come to ask for you:
And for your weal each neighbour cares,
And good men kneel, and say their pray'rs:
And ev'rybody looks so sad,
   When you are ailing, dad.

You will not die, and leave us then?
Rouse up and be our dad again.
When you are quiet and laid in bed,
We'll doff our shoes and softly tread:
And when you wake we'll aye be near,
   To fill old dad his cheer.

When through the house you shift your stand,
I'll lead you kindly by the hand;
When dinner's set, I'll with you bide,

And aye be serving by your side;
And when the weary fire burns blue,
　I'll sit and talk with you.

I have a tale both long and good,
About a partlet and her brood;
And cunning greedy fox that stole,
By dead of midnight, through a hole,
Which slyly to the hen-roost led –
　You love a story, dad?

And then I have a wond'rous tale
Of men all clad in coats of mail,
With glitt'ring swords – you nod, I think?
Your fixèd eyes begin to wink;
Down on your bosom sinks your head;
　You do not hear me, dad.
Joanna Baillie, 'A Child to his Sick Grandfather', 1790

　　　　　　　Pray, do not mock me:
I am a very foolish fond old man,
Fourscore and upward, not an hour more or less;
And, to deal plainly,
I fear I am not in my perfect mind.
Methinks I should know you and know this man;
Yet I am doubtful: for I am mainly ignorant
What place this is, and all the skill I have
Remembers not these garments; nor I know not
Where I did lodge last night. Do not laugh at me;
For, as I am a man, I think this lady
To be my child Cordelia.
　　　　　　Shakespeare, *King Lear*, c.1605

What happened? Winter. Went out for a drink, late.
On the way home it hit me – from inside. I fell.
Lay there. How long? Two coppers arrived. Thought I was drunk.
Dragged me back to the flat. Dumped me. Lay on the floor.

How long? Couldn't get to the bed. Couldn't eat. Nobody called.
I was going down. Then came to again. It was day
Or night. I was cold. Somebody banged on the door. When?
Couldn't shout, couldn't move. The banging stopped.
Another night. Or day? All the time it was getting darker,
Inside me. And now they broke in. Ambulance men.
Took me to hospital. Dumped me again, to wait
For a doctor, a ward. Said I'd have to be moved
To another building. A stroke, they said, and pneumonia.
But their voices were fading. Knew I was for it, the dark.
Name, address of my next of kin. Didn't want her, my daughter
I hadn't seen in years. Let her come when I'm gone
And clear up. Get rid of the bits and pieces
She told me off for collecting – ornaments, books,
All that's left of my life. And grab the indifferent
Useful things. Only don't let her bother me now.
Stick in those tubes, if you like. They'll feed my going.
But no more questions. Enough of words now. Enough of me.

                    Michael Hamburger, from 'Old Londoner,' 1975

They're waiting to be murdered,
Or evicted. Soon
They expect to have nothing to eat.
As far as I know, they never go out.

A vicious pain's coming, they think.
It will start in the head
And spread down to the bowels.
They'll be carried off on stretchers, howling.

In the meantime, they watch the street
From their fifth-floor window.
It has rained, and now it looks
Like it's going to snow a little.

I see him get up to lower the shades.
If their window stays dark,
I know that his hand has reached hers

Just as she was about to turn on the lights.
Charles Simic, 'Old Couple', 1983

My briefcase falls open in the street. Displayed:
Aspirins for migraine, chocolates for my wife.
Despite my 'Oh, bugger', strangers come to aid
The old boy picking up his bits of life.
Roy Fuller, 'Accident' from 'Quatrains of
an Elderly Man', 1980

I am getting to an age when I can only enjoy the last sport left. It is
called hunting for your spectacles.
Lord Grey of Fallodon, *The Observer*, 1927

I look into my glass,
And view my wasting skin,
And say, 'Would God it came to pass
My heart had shrunk as thin!'

For then, I, undistrest
By hearts grown cold to me,
Could lonely wait my endless rest
With equanimity.

But Time, to make me grieve,
Part steals, lets part abide;
And shakes this fragile frame at eve
With throbbings of noontide.
Hardy, 'I Look Into My Glass', 1898

I can, with due time, walk up anything, – only I cant sleep, walking
or not walking. I cant write, as you see, because my hand is
paralysed. I cant sit easily because of a huge truss I wear, and now
has come this damnable asthma! But still I am very good to look at;
and as I am not afraid to die, I am as happy as other people.
Trollope, letter to E. A. Freeman, October 1882

Animals

In Ted Hughes's poem 'The Rat's Dance' the trapped rat cannot reason 'This has no face, it must be God', but

> The rat understands suddenly. It bows and is still,
> With a little beseeching of blood on its nose-end.

Elias Canetti's question, in his *Aufzeichnungen* for 1949, whether animals know less fear because they live without words, may expect an answer in the negative, and certainly implies no disdain for animals, since he would like to see them, sheep and cows in particular, rising up against us humans. Rather like children, sick animals (we suppose) do not understand what is happening to them. And yet – and not only in the more fanciful stretches of Pliny – they can show what strikes us as a sort of dumb, stoical wisdom.

Possibly their lack of words serves to arouse less apprehension in us, or less solicitude. Equally, it may encourage more, as does the wordlessness of children.

Where pain is concerned, aside from the pains of foreboding and surmise, there cannot be much difference between the species, or the ages. In corporal suffering, Shakespeare wrote, the poor beetle we tread on 'finds a pang as great as when a giant dies'.

————

Elephants are particularly sensitive to cold, and that, indeed, is their greatest enemy. They are subject also to flatulency, and to looseness of the bowels, but to no other kind of disease. I find it stated, that on making them drink oil, any weapon which may happen to stick in their body will fall out; while, on the contrary, perspiration makes them the more readily adhere. If they eat earth it is poison to them, unless indeed they have gradually become accustomed by repeatedly doing so . . . They have the greatest aversion to the mouse of all animals, and quite loathe their food, as it lies in the manger, if they perceive that it has been touched by one of those animals. They experience the greatest torture if they happen to swallow, while drinking, a horseleech. The leech fastens upon the windpipe, and produces intolerable pain.

When an elephant has happened to devour a chameleon, which is of the same colour with the herbage, it counteracts this poison by means of the wild olive. Bears, when they have eaten of the fruit of the mandrake, lick up numbers of ants. The stag counteracts the effect of poisonous plants by eating the artichoke. Wood-pigeons, jackdaws, blackbirds, and partridges, purge themselves once a year by eating bay-leaves.

Canine madness is fatal to man during the heat of Sirius, and it proves so in consequence of those who are bitten having a deadly horror of water. For this reason, during the thirty days that this star exerts its influence, we try to prevent the disease by mixing dung from the poultry-yard with the dog's food; or else, if they are already attacked by the disease, by giving them hellebore . . . Columella informs us, that if, on the fortieth day after the birth of the pup, the last bone of the tail is bitten off, the sinew will follow with it; after which, the tail will not grow, and the dog will never become rabid.

Horses have very nearly the same diseases as men; besides which, they are subject to an irregular action of the bladder, as, indeed, is the case with all beasts of burden.

Bees are by nature liable to certain diseases of their own. The sign that they are diseased, is a kind of torpid, moping sadness: on such occasions, they are to be seen bringing out those that are sick before the hives, and placing them in the warm sun, while others, again, are providing them with food. Those that are dead they carry away from the hive, and attend the bodies, paying their last duties, as it were, in funeral procession. If the king should happen to be carried off by the pestilence, the swarm remains plunged in grief and listless inactivity; it collects no more food, and ceases to issue forth from its abode; the only thing that it does is to gather around the body, and to emit a melancholy humming noise. Upon such occasions, the usual plan is to disperse the swarm and take away the body; for otherwise they would continue listlessly gazing upon it, and so prolong their grief. Indeed, if due care is not taken to come to their aid, they will die of hunger. It is from their cheerfulness, in fact, and their bright and sleek appearance that we usually form an estimate as to their health.

> Pliny the Elder, *Natural History*, AD 77;
> tr. John Bostock and H. T. Riley

These animals [foxes], constantly accustomed to scenes of blood, cannot hear without pain the cries of their little ones in suffering. Doubtless, poultry have small reason to consider foxes as compassionate; but their females, their little ones, and even all the members of their species, have no cause to complain of them.

We are positive that animals never fail to distinguish between the cry of terror and that which expresses love. Their different agitations have different intonations which characterize them . . . Can we assert that the expressions of a male and female during the period of their intercourse are not very various, when we can clearly perceive in them a thousand movements, all differing one from another – eagerness, more or less pronounced, on the part of the male; reserve, mingled with allurement, on that of the female; pretended denials, rage, jealousy, quarrels, and reconciliations?

> Charles Georges Leroy (1723–89), *The Intelligence and*
> *Perfectibility of Animals*; tr. anon.

It is not, however, so much on account of the rarity of the creature, that I have introduced it here, as for the purpose of relating a wonderful operation that was performed on it by Miss Sabrina, the schoolmistress.

There happened to be a sack of beans in our stable, and Lady Macadam's hens and fowls, which were not overly fed at home, through the inattention of her servants, being great stravaggers for their meat, in passing the door, went in to pick, and the Muscovy seeing a hole in the bean-sack, dabbled out a crap full before she was disturbed. The beans swelled on the poor bird's stomach, and her crap bellied out like the kyte of a Glasgow magistrate, until it was just a sight to be seen with its head back on its shoulders. The bairns of the clachan followed it up and down, crying, the lady's muckle jock's ay growing bigger, till every heart was wae for the creature. Some thought it was afflicted with a tympathy, and others, that it was the natural way for suchlike ducks to cleck their young. In short, we were all concerned, and my lady having a great opinion of Miss Sabrina's skill, had a consultation with her on the case, at which Miss Sabrina advised, that what she called the Caesarian operation should be tried, which she herself performed accordingly, by opening the creature's crap, and taking out as many beans as filled a mutchkin stoup, after which she sewed it up, and the Muscovy went its way to the water-side, and began to swim, and it was as jocund as ever; insomuch, that in three days after it was quite cured of all the consequences of its surfeit.

John Galt, *Annals of the Parish*, 1813

When I wrote to you last year on reptiles, I wish I had not forgot to mention the faculty that snakes have of stinking in self-defence. I knew a gentleman who kept a tame snake, which was in its person as sweet as any animal while in good humour and unalarmed; but, as soon as a stranger, or a dog or cat, came in, it fell to hissing, and filled the room with such nauseous effluvia as rendered it hardly supportable. Thus the squnck, or stonck, of Ray's *Synop. Quadr.*, is an innocuous and sweet animal; but when pressed hard by dogs and men, it can eject such a most pestilent and fetid smell and excrement, that nothing can be more horrible.

Gilbert White, *The Natural History of Selborne*, 30 August 1769

Fido's paw is bleeding.
Fido's master finds the cut,
puts a nice clean bandage on,
gives his pet a slice of meat.

Fido's paw is hurting.
Fido cannot offer proof.
Fido's master tries to ease it
when his dog begins to whimper
how could he withhold belief?

Master's heart is broken.
Master's mistress left his roof.
Did she find his house oppressive?
Who can tell – she would not speak,
simply packed her gear and left.
Polly screeches, 'Shut your beak!'
Polly isn't talking sense.

Fido's paw is better,
but he whimpers round the house.
Who could teach him this pretence?
Polly goes on screeching.
Master writes a lyric poem
so his pain is manifest.
Polly scatters seed and swears.
Master's mistress taught the bird
language hardly fit for use.

Fido in his kennel
makes no claims about the world.
Master gets a blanket,
throws it over Polly's cage.
Out of doors the rising moon
flames above earth's darkening rim
lifts a yellow eye aloft.
Master in his lonely room
counts the wing-beats of his pain
pours another glass of wine
on the dryness of his song.
Wonders where it all went wrong.
Gwen Harwood, 'Fido's Paw Is Bleeding', 1975

They've gone. Did I receive my worth
For strife of feeding, care and birth?
Am I inhuman? Am I numb
And cold, to curse the day they'd come?
No, – it is but a mother's pain
To watch them come – then go again.
I cannot think of how they'd tease –
Banished are memories like these.
Just happy recollections stay
And even these shall fade away
As I lose yet another litter –
My life – a tear – so ever bitter!
Say tears may dance with laughter too –
Such tears are short and rare and few.

                     Lucy Howard, aged nine,
'Separation: A Mother of Piglets Speaks', 1988

Poring on Caesar's death with earnest eye,
I heard a fretful buzzing in the pane:
'Poor bee!' I cried, 'I'll help thee by-and-by';
Then dropp'd mine eyes upon the page again.
Alas! I did not rise; I help'd him not:
In the great voice of Roman history
I lost the pleading of the window-bee,
And all his woes and troubles were forgot.
In pity for the mighty chief, who bled
Beside his rival's statue, I delay'd
To serve the little insect's present need;
And so he died for lack of human aid.
I could not change the Roman's destiny;
I might have set the honey-maker free.

             Charles Tennyson Turner, 'Julius Caesar
                     and the Honey-Bee', 1880

But how, they seriously say, can you ever compare
the death of your mother to the death of your cat?
I answer: easily. After she had the pin in her hip-joint,
as she haltingly pushed her walking-frame towards the loo
she simply foreshadowed his slow limping progress,
with the bone-cancer distorting his harmed right shoulder,
towards the cat-pan, the cat-tray (whatever you call it).
Both of these, to see, were equally pathetic.

And as she lay in the hospital, with noisy breathing,
hardly eating, seldom conscious; and as *he* lay,
in unhappy lethargy, not touching his food,
drinking a little, liquid intake only – surely he deserved
equally the drug that pushed him into unconsciousness
and it was good that both were separated from pain?
            Gavin Ewart, 'Sonnet: Cat Death', 1982

So zestfully canst thou sing?
And all this indignity,
With God's consent, on thee!
Blinded ere yet a-wing
By the red-hot needle thou,
I stand and wonder how
So zestfully thou canst sing!

Resenting not such wrong,
Thy grievous pain forgot,
Eternal dark thy lot,
Groping thy whole life long,
After that stab of fire;
Enjailed in pitiless wire;
Resenting not such wrong!

Who hath charity? This bird.
Who suffereth long and is kind,
Is not provoked, though blind
And alive ensepulchred?

Who hopeth, endureth all things?
Who thinketh no evil, but sings?
Who is divine? This bird.
    Hardy, 'The Blinded Bird', 1917

His gaze, going past those bars, has got so misted
with tiredness, it can take in nothing more.
He feels as though a thousand bars existed,
and no more world beyond them than before.

Those supply-powerful paddings, turning there
in tiniest of circles, well might be
the dance of forces round a centre where
some mighty will stands paralytically.

Just now and then the pupils' noiseless shutter
is lifted. – Then an image will indart,
down through the limbs' intensive stillness flutter,
and end its being in the heart.
Rainer Maria Rilke, 'The Panther: Jardin des Plantes, Paris',
                    1903; tr. J. B. Leishman

A Robin Redbreast in a Cage
Puts all Heaven in a Rage.
A Dove house fill'd with Doves and Pigeons
Shudders Hell thro' all its regions.
A Dog starv'd at his Master's Gate
Predicts the ruin of the State.
A Horse misus'd upon the Road
Calls to Heaven for Human blood.
Each outcry of the hunted Hare
A fibre from the Brain does tear.
A Skylark wounded in the wing,
A Cherubim does cease to sing.
The Game Cock clip'd and arm'd for fight
Does the Rising Sun affright.

Every Wolf's & Lion's howl
Raises from Hell a Human Soul.
The wild Deer wand'ring here & there
Keeps the Human Soul from Care.
The Lamb misus'd breeds Public strife
And yet forgives the Butcher's Knife . . .
He who shall hurt the little Wren
Shall never be belov'd by Men.
He who the Ox to wrath has mov'd
Shall never be by Woman lov'd.
The wanton Boy that kills the Fly
Shall feel the Spider's enmity.
He who torments the Chafer's sprite
Weaves a Bower in endless Night.
The Catterpiller on the Leaf
Repeats to thee thy Mother's grief.
Kill not the Moth nor Butterfly
For the Last Judgement draweth nigh.

   Blake, from 'Auguries of Innocence', *c.*1801

Invalids and Convalescents

A Dutch proverb has it that 'Sickness comes on horseback and departs on foot.' Aldous Huxley said that for D. H. Lawrence existence was one continuous convalescence, and 'it was as though he were newly reborn from a mortal illness every day of his life', sickness and health alternating at rapid intervals. A full life, you could say.

Oliver Wendell Holmes, a doctor of medicine and professor of anatomy, is cheery on the subject of aches and pains: they are signs of continuing life. And Robert Louis Stevenson sees in invalidism a gentle, merciful preparation for the long sleep, as one by one our desires quietly leave us. Ripeness – if that is what we can persuade ourselves it is – is all.

Although necrology is no part of this book's brief, perhaps it should be mentioned, to satisfy what Keats called the 'irritable reaching after fact and reason', that Barbellion (Bruce Frederick Cummings), liveliest of long-term invalids, died seven months after his *Journal* appeared, a victim of multiple sclerosis; the last entry in his *Last Diary* reads, 'Tomorrow I go to another nursing home.' William Soutar's trouble was spondylitis or inflammation of the vertebrae, and pneumonia left his lungs badly affected. And Denton Welch suffered from tuberculosis of the spine, the result of a cycling accident thirteen years before his death, and kidney failure.

These deserve to be numbered among Emerson's heroes of illness, though scarcely as vindications of it, considering their years.

=====

Invalidism is the normal state of many organizations. It can be changed to disease, but never to absolute health by medicinal appliances. There are many ladies, ancient and recent, who are perpetually taking remedies for irremediable pains and aches. They *ought* to have headaches and backaches and stomach-aches; they are not well if they do not have them. To expect them to live without frequent twinges is like expecting a doctor's old chaise to go without creaking; if it did, we might be sure the springs were broken.

> Holmes, 'Currents and Counter-Currents in Medical Science'

I have been told that when Aunt Etty was thirteen the doctor recommended, after she had a 'low fever', that she should have breakfast in bed for a time. *She never got up to breakfast again in all her life . . .*

Unfortunately Aunt Etty, being a lady, had no real work to do; she had not even any children to bring up. This was a terrible pity, for she had nothing on which to spend her unbounded affection and energy, except the management of her house and husband; and she could have ruled a kingdom with success. As it was, ill health became her profession and absorbing interest. But her interest was never tinged by self-pity, it was an abstract, almost scientific, interest; and our sympathy was not demanded. She kept her professional life in a separate compartment from her social life.

She was always going away to rest, in case she might be tired later on in the day, or even next day. She would send down to the cook to ask her to count the prune-stones left on her plate, as it was very important to know whether she had eaten three or four prunes for luncheon. She would make Janet put a silk handkerchief over her left foot as she lay in bed, because it was that amount colder than her right foot. And when there were colds about she often wore a kind of gas-mask of her own invention. It was an ordinary wire kitchen-strainer, stuffed with antiseptic cotton-wool, and tied on like a snout, with elastic over her ears. In this she would receive her visitors and discuss politics in a hollow voice out of her eucalyptus-scented seclusion, oblivious of the fact that they might be struggling with fits of laughter. She characteristically wrote to a proposed visitor: *'Don't come by the ten o'clock train, but by the 3.30, so as to give me time to put you off, if I am not well.'*

> Gwen Raverat, *Period Piece*, 1952; Aunt Etty (1843–1929)
> was a daughter of Charles Darwin

In the next room I could hear my aunt talking quietly to herself. She never spoke save in low tones, because she believed that there was something broken in her head and floating loose there, which she might displace by talking too loud; but she never remained for long, even when alone, without saying something, because she believed that it was good for her throat, and that by keeping the blood there in circulation it would make less frequent the chokings and other pains to which she was liable; besides, in the life of complete inertia which she led, she attached to the least of her sensations an extraordinary importance, endowed them with a Protean ubiquity which made it difficult for her to keep them secret, and, failing a confidant to whom she might communicate them, she used to promulgate them to herself in an unceasing monologue which was her sole form of activity. Unfortunately, having formed the habit of thinking aloud, she did not always take care to see that there was no one in the adjoining room, and I would often hear her saying to herself: 'I must not forget that I never slept a wink' – for 'never sleeping a wink' was her great claim to distinction, and one admitted and respected in our household vocabulary.

Suddenly my aunt turned pale. 'What, three o'clock!' she exclaimed. 'But vespers will have begun already, and I've forgotten my pepsin! Now I know why that Vichy water has been lying on my stomach.' And falling precipitately upon a prayer-book bound in purple velvet, with gilt clasps, out of which in her haste she let fall a shower of the little pictures, each in a lace fringe of yellowish paper, which she used to mark the places of the greater feasts of the Church, my aunt, while she swallowed her drops, began at full speed to mutter the words of the sacred text, its meaning being slightly clouded in her brain by the uncertainty whether the pepsin, when taken so long after the Vichy, would still be able to overtake it and to 'send it down'. 'Three o'clock! It's unbelievable how time flies.'

Proust, *Swann's Way*, 1913; tr. Scott Moncrieff

I can say, like Romeo, 'I am fortune's fool!' I stand in front of the great soup-bowl, but I lack a spoon . . . What use is it to me, that enraptured youths and maidens adorn my marble bust with laurels, when the withered hands of an aged nurse are pressing Spanish fly behind my real ears? What use to me, that all the roses of Shiraz glow and exhale fragrance so tenderly for me? Ah, Shiraz is two thousand miles from the rue d'Amsterdam, where, in the irksome loneliness of my sick-room, I get nothing to smell except perhaps the perfumes of warmed napkins. Alas, God's mockery weighs heavily on me. The great Author of the Universe, the Aristophanes of Heaven, wanted well and truly to show me, the little, earthly, so-called German Aristophanes, how my wittiest sarcasms were paltry raillery in comparison with his, and how wretchedly inferior I am to him in humour, in colossal jesting.

Heine, Confessions, 1854

Still visit Dr —'s surgery each week. I have two dull spots at the bottom of each lung. What a fine expressive word is *gloom*. Let me write it: GLOOM . . . One evening coming home in the train from L— County Sessions I noticed a horrible, wheezy sound whenever I breathed deep. I was scared out of my life, and at once thought of consumption. Went to the Doctor's next day, and he sounded me and reassured me. I was afraid to tell him of the little wheezy sound at the apex of each lung, and I believed he overlooked it. So next day, very harassed, I went back to him again and told him. He *hadn't* noticed it and looked glum. Have to keep out of doors as much as possible.

6 February 1910

Walked in the country. Coming home, terrified by a really violent attack of palpitation. Almost every one I met I thought would be the unfortunate person who would have to pick me up. As each one in the street approached me, I weighed him in the balance and considered if he had presence of mind and how he would render first aid. After my friend, P.C. —, had passed, I felt sorry that the tragedy had not already happened, for he knows me and where I live.

11 February 1911

Who will rid me of the body of this death? My body is chained to me – a dead weight. It is my warder. I can do nothing without first

consulting it and seeking its permission. I jeer at its grotesqueness. I
chafe at the thongs it binds on me. On this bully I am dependent for
everything the world can give me. How can I preserve my *amour
propre* when I must needs be forever wheedling and cajoling a
despot with delicate meats and soft couches? – I who am proud,
ambitious, and full of energy! In the end, too, I know it intends to
carry me off . . . I should like though to have the last kick and,
copying De Quincey, arrange to hand it over for dissection to the
medical men – out of revenge.

22 April 1911

Bad heart attack all day. Intermittency is very refined torture to one
who wants to live very badly. Your pump goes a 'dot and carry one',
or say 'misses a stitch', what time you breathe deep, begin to shake
your friend's hand and make a farewell speech. Then it goes on again
and you order another pint of beer.

It is a fractious animal within the cage of my thorax, and I never
know when it is going to escape and make off with my precious life
between its teeth. I humour and coax and soothe it, but, God wot, I
haven't much confidence in the little beast. My thorax it appears is
an intolerable kennel.

3 May 1914

On a 'bus the other day a woman with a baby sat opposite, the baby
bawled, and the woman at once began to unlace herself, exposing a
large, red udder, which she swung into the baby's face. The infant,
however, continued to cry and the woman said, –

'Come on, there's a good boy – if you don't, I shall give it to the
gentleman opposite.'

Do I look ill-nourished?

7 August 1915

Suffering from indigestion. The symptoms include:
Excessive pandiculation,
Excessive oscitation,
Excessive eructation,
Dyspnoea,

Sphygmic flutters,
Abnormal porrigo,
A desiccated epidermis.

12 August 1915

I am over 6 feet high and as thin as a skeleton; every bone in my body, even the neck vertebrae, creak at odd intervals when I move. So that I am not only a skeleton but a badly articulated one to boot. If to this is coupled the fact of the creeping paralysis, you have the complete horror. Even as I sit and write, millions of bacteria are gnawing away my precious spinal cord, and if you put your ear to my back the sound of the gnawing I dare say could be heard.

20 January 1917

I lie on my back and rest awhile. Then I force myself on to the left side by putting my right arm over the left side of the bed beneath the woodwork and pulling (my right arm is stronger than any of the other limbs). Tonight, Nurse had not placed me in the middle of the bed (I was too much over on the right side), so even my long arm could not reach down beneath the woodwork on the left. I cursed Nanny for a scabby old bean, struggled, and at last got over on my left side. The next thing was to get my legs bent up – now out as stiff and straight as ferrules. When lying on the left side I long ago found out that it is useless to get my right leg up first, as it only shoots out again when I come to grapple with the left. So I put my right arm down, seized the left leg just above the knee and pulled! The first result is always a violent spasm in the legs and back. But I hang on and presently it dies away, and the leg begins to move upward a little . . .

And thus, any time, any week, these last eighteen months. But I have faith and hope and love in spite of all. I forgive even Nanny!

13 January 1919

I often laugh aloud at the struggles of Nurse with my perfectly ludicrous, impotent body. If you saw us, you would certainly believe in a personal devil; but when you saw what a devil he is, you would also see in him a most fantastic clown. My right leg is almost completely anaesthetized – curious experience this. You could poke the fire with it, and I shouldn't feel anything out of the way. I could easily emulate Cranmer's stoical behaviour. It is so dead that if you put my body out in the sun, the flies in error would come and lay their eggs on me. Yes, Satan was the first and chiefest of Pantaloons.

20 May 1919

W. N. P. Barbellion (1889–1919): from *The Journal of a Disappointed Man*, 1919, and *A Last Diary*, 1920

6 July 1943. For a month or two I have assumed in a casual way that I hadn't very long to live; and already I have some knowledge of one's reactions to a fatal certainty. I thought, 'Now that a major fact has confronted you, the minor happenings of everyday will take on their true proportions: you will cease to react with violent outbursts of irritated speech or gesture when little frustrations annoy; the presence of the major fact will remind you how small and transient are these vexations.' But as yet I have grown towards this serene status only a very little way; though I seem to sense a gradual awareness of a still centre within myself.

There is an increase in day-dream, in which I find I am often making elaborate preparation for the disposal of my cadaver and my manuscripts. Probably it is a compensation – but, since I have begun to accept that death is not so far away, I have also accepted as surety that I shall be remembered as a poet. How strange the fancies of semi-wakefulness; the other morning I thought: 'My right nostril is Scottish but my left is English.'

6 September. The coughing has become more of a nuisance since last I wrote, and about every hour I have to perform a clearing out process which in accumulation wastes a lot of time. The actual coughing isn't, so far, much of a strain, but my muscles inserted into the groin region have become strained and any sudden cough produces a most painful reaction; this makes me swear involuntarily. Fortunately, as yet, my sleep is little disturbed; and I am wakened but once or twice by the need to get rid of phlegm. One accepts the coughing as a nuisance, but breathlessness is an aggravation. The feeling of helplessness and frustration during a spell of breathlessness hurts one's pride and one grows angry. In our temporary weakness we tend to become childish; and not a few times my face has automatically puckered up as if I were about to cry: in the humiliation of extreme weakness one might actually cry like a child.

The curse of a cough is not that it curtails one's speech only but also one's laughter; the involuntary expression of mirth becomes guarded, and full enjoyment is modified. This condition would seem to react upon the feelings, and one begins to note fewer occasions for laughter: it is in one's sense of humour as a gradual diminution of memory.

6 *October.*   How snail-like the tempo at which I seem to be living now – and yet my days are hurrying out of the world. I do not think any of my friends suspect as yet that I am under the sentence of death; and it will be fine if they continue for a good while yet to imagine that I have a touch of bronchitis, or something like that: when at last they know, an undefinable restraint will come between the free interchange of friendship.

Desire, if one may use so strong a word, has been completely transferred from the thought of women to considerations of 'what we shall eat, and what we shall drink'. The other evening it came to me almost as a relief that for many months the attractiveness of women no longer disturbed me; that neither in dream or day-dream was I fretted by images of passion. Everything in my life is being quieted; and the great orbit of life is moving in from the bounds of the universe like the gradually diminishing circle of light from a wasting flame. Whether the mood adapts itself to the environment, or whether I have somehow achieved a sense of proportion which adapts itself readily to the inevitable, I am scarcely touched by regret or anxiety, but derive even an element of satisfaction from being able to stand back and watch myself busied or idling under the shadow of a doom which is but rarely remembered. So much can wither away from the human spirit, and yet the great gift of the ordinary day remains; the stability of the small things of life, which yet in their constancy are the greatest. All the daily kindness; the little obligations, the signs of remembrance in the homely gifts: these do not pass, but still hearten the body and spirit to the verge of the grave.

William Soutar (1898–1943), *Diaries of a Dying Man*, ed.
Alexander Scott, 1954

4 December 1946

Lying here, able to do nothing, I have realized that all the year has been a sinking into bed and a painful rising out of it, only to be dragged down again before I could breathe or spread my arms. I have realized how half-afraid I have been to do anything because of what comes after. How many hours, days have I had to let swim over my head? And I, who could be busy all day long. The feeling has come over me that I must let everything melt away, that I am no longer in command at all. And in my idleness all I can think of are rich strange dishes wonderfully cooked, amazing little houses in fine gardens, rare and lovely objects for these tiny palaces, and then wills and bequests both fantastic and more down to earth . . .

I see now that day-dreams like these, very material – always of things, wealth, security – crowd in as the chance to finish work recedes. Agitation, fear of all the things that may never be done, is suppressed. One can no longer plan happily to begin or to complete, so only wealth is left to dream about.

28 January 1947

I wonder all the time I am ill if I shall be able to earn enough money, since so much time is wasted. I am strangely worried and unworried about it, as if it were only a problem I had set myself. I suppose I feel I shall have the money somehow, that I shall recover in time, that my books will bring me in some more. Then, as I said before, my mind in illness runs to the idea of inheriting; it turns over all the chances and possibilities, and is now hopeful, now despondent. It is all a game to keep one warm and secure-feeling.

In all the illness, I have had the horrible sensation that the tables, chairs, lamps and confusion of books near me were writhing into life and becoming extensions of myself, like new limbs, utterly unwanted, but insisting on living and doing my bidding. All the time I would wish nothing to be done, and yet would give all these things their horrible senseless life. And I even myself grew to a wretched largeness and was invaded too with the activity of nothingness. It was an endless toiling and posturing and living for nothing, so heart-breaking and deadening that I longed and longed to be still, to stop churning and to sleep for a little.

Sight, sound, touch were all distorted. I was living in a twisted stretched world, where I invaded everything and was the horror that

I could not escape. There was no self-love left, only an exhausted disgust.
Denton Welch (1915–48), *The Journals*, ed. Michael De-la-Noy, 1984

It is not in such numbness of spirit only that the life of the invalid resembles a premature old age. Those excursions that he had promised himself to finish, prove too long or too arduous for his feeble body; and the barrier-hills are as impassable as ever. Many a white town that sits far out on the promontory, many a comely fold of wood on the mountainside, beckons and allures his imagination day after day, and is yet as inaccessible to his feet as the clefts and gorges of the clouds. The sense of distance grows upon him wonderfully; and after some feverish efforts and the fretful uneasiness of the first few days, he falls contentedly in with the restrictions of his weakness. His narrow round becomes pleasant and familiar to him as the cell to a contented prisoner. Just as he has fallen already out of the mid race of active life, he now falls out of the little eddy that circulates in the shallow waters of the sanatorium. He see the country people come and go about their everyday affairs, the foreigners stream out in goodly pleasure parties; the stir of man's activity is all about him, as he suns himself inertly in some sheltered corner; and he looks on with a patriarchal impersonality of interest, such as a man may feel when he pictures to himself the fortunes of his remote descendants, or the robust old age of the oak he has planted over-night.

In this falling aside, in this quietude and desertion of other men, there is no inharmonious prelude to the last quietude and desertion of the grave; in this dullness of the senses there is a gentle preparation for the final insensibility of death. And to him the idea of mortality comes in a shape less violent and harsh than is its wont, less as an abrupt catastrophe than as a thing of infinitesimal gradation, and the last step on a long decline of way. As we turn to and fro in bed, and every moment the movements grow feebler and smaller and the attitude more restful and easy, until sleep overtakes us at a stride and we move no more, so desire after desire leaves him; day by day his strength decreases, and the circle of his activity grows ever narrower; and he feels, if he is to be thus tenderly weaned from the passion of life, thus gradually inducted into the slumber of death, that when at last the end comes, it will come quietly and fitly. If anything is to reconcile poor spirits to the coming of the last enemy, surely it should be such a mild approach as this; not to hale us forth with violence, but to persuade us from a place we have no further pleasure in. It is not so much, indeed, death that approaches as life that withdraws and withers up from round about him. He has outlived his own usefulness, and almost his own enjoyment; and if there is to be no recovery; if never again will he be young and strong and passionate, if the actual present shall be to him always like a thing read in a book or remembered out of the far-away past; if, in fact, this be veritably nightfall, he will not wish greatly for the continuance of a twilight that only strains and disappoints the eyes, but steadfastly await the perfect darkness. He will pray for Medea: when she comes, let her either rejuvenate or slay.

Stevenson, 'Ordered South', 1881

If there be a regal solitude, it is a sick-bed. How the patient lords it there; what caprices he acts without control! how king-like he sways his pillow — tumbling, and tossing, and shifting, and lowering, and thumping, and flatting, and moulding it, to the ever-varying requisitions of his throbbing temples.

He changes *sides* oftener than a politician. Now he lies full length, then half length, obliquely, transversely, head and feet quite across the bed; and none accuses him of tergiversation. Within the four curtains he is absolute. They are his Mare Clausum.

How sickness enlarges the dimensions of a man's self to himself! he is his own exclusive object. Supreme selfishness is inculcated upon him as his only duty. 'Tis the Two Tables of the Law to him. He has nothing to think of but how to get well. What passes out of doors, or within them, so he hear not the jarring of them, affects him not . . .

He has put on the strong armour of sickness, he is wrapped in the callous hide of suffering; he keeps his sympathy, like some curious vintage, under trusty lock and key, for his own use only.

He lies pitying himself, honing and moaning to himself; he yearneth over himself; his bowels are even melted within him, to think what he suffers; he is not ashamed to weep over himself.

He is forever plotting how to do some good to himself; studying little stratagems and artificial alleviations.

He makes the most of himself; dividing himself, by an allowable fiction, into as many distinct individuals as he hath sore and sorrowing members. Sometimes he meditates – as of a thing apart from him – upon his poor aching head, and that dull pain which, dozing or waking, lay in it all the past night like a log, or palpable substance of pain, not to be removed without opening the very skull, as it seemed, to take it thence. Or he pities his long, clammy, attenuated fingers. He compassionates himself all over; and his bed is a very discipline of humanity, and tender heart . . .

To be sick is to enjoy monarchal prerogatives. Compare the silent tread and quiet ministry, almost by the eye only, with which he is served – with the careless demeanour, the unceremonious goings in and out (slapping of doors, or leaving them open) of the very same attendants, when he is getting a little better – and you will confess, that from the bed of sickness (throne let me rather call it) to the elbow-chair of convalescence, is a fall from dignity, amounting to a deposition.

How convalescence shrinks a man back to his pristine stature! Where is now the space, which he occupied so lately, in his own, in the family's eye?

Charles Lamb, 'The Convalescent', *The Last Essays of Elia*, 1833

For my part I reckon being ill as one of the great pleasures of life, provided one is not too ill and is not obliged to work till one is better. I remember being ill once in a foreign hotel myself and how much I enjoyed it . . . not only to be a lotus-eater but to know that it was one's duty to be a lotus-eater.

Samuel Butler, *The Way of All Flesh*, 1873–5

Sickness also has its hero and brilliant vindication. Fontenelle, born feeble, a puny delicate creature, by care and nursing was preserved for a hundred years to be the delight of France and of Europe – laid up, they said, like a vase of porcelain in a cabinet and railed up and guarded to hold the softest and most volatile of perfumes. Mr Pope also was born sick and a cripple, yet by care and study of these facts, and engaging, wherever he went, nursing and rubbing from the domestics, he lived long and enjoyed much and gave others much to enjoy.

    Emerson, *Journals*, 30 October 1841. Bernard Le Bouvier de Fontenelle, versatile thinker and man of letters, lived from 1657 to 1757; Alexander Pope died just after his fifty-sixth birthday

Short and Sharp

In *The Rule and Exercises of Holy Dying* (1651) Jeremy Taylor argued that since our life is very short, it is very miserable, and since it is miserable, it is as well that it should be short. And Sir Walter Ralegh, testing the edge of the axe that was to remove his head, remarked, ''Tis a sharp remedy, but a sure one for all ills.'

The heroine of *Diana of the Crossways* asserted, not very originally, that there was no suffering of the body that the soul might not profit by. The human race is adept in locating consolations, those flowering islands, in Shelley's words, which lie in the waters of wide Agony, even though they may be as tiny or tenuous as Hopkins's comfort such as 'serves in a whirlwind', or Edgar's reflection in *King Lear* that the worst hasn't happened so long as we can say 'This is the worst.'

The present anthology, which has set out to entertain, to instruct perhaps, and conceivably to solace, concludes with a selection of short, sharp sayings. Not all of them are emollient, or tonic, but what can't be cured must be endured.

Life is a sexually transmitted disease
Graffito

Life is an incurable disease
Cowley, from 'To Dr Scarborough', 1656

. . . this long Disease, my Life
Pope, from 'Epistle to Dr Arbuthnot', 1734

Duncan is in his grave;
After life's fretful fever he sleeps well
Shakespeare, *Macbeth*, 1606

      . . . this strange disease of modern life,
      With its sick hurry, its divided aims,
      Its heads o'ertaxed, its palsied hearts
      Arnold, from 'The Scholar-Gipsy', 1853

Life is a disease; and the only difference between one man and another is the stage of the disease at which he lives

      Shaw, *Back to Methuselah*, 1921

Life is a fatal complaint, and an eminently contagious one

      Holmes, *The Poet at the Breakfast Table*, 1872

Be long sick, that you may be soon hale

      Collection of Scottish Proverbs, 1721

The chamber of sickness is the chapel of devotion

      Treasury of Ancient Adagies and Sententious Proverbs, 1616

The sickness of the body may prove the health of the soul

      Handbook of Proverbs, 1855

He who never was sick dies the first fit

      Gnomologia, 1732

Sickness tells us what we are

      Gnomologia

Mrs Home (Home it seems was the name) had been a very pretty, but a giddy, careless woman, who had neglected her child, and disappointed and disheartened her husband. So far from congenial had the union proved, that separation at last ensued – separation by mutual consent, not after any legal process. Soon after this event, the lady having over-exerted herself at a ball, caught cold, took a fever, and died after a very brief illness.

      Charlotte Brontë, *Villette*, 1853

. . . the famous Dr Edwards who was talked about a lot in 1822. It was said he killed a thousand frogs a month and was going to discover both how we breathe and a cure for the chest ailments of pretty women. You know that each year in Paris eleven hundred young women die from the cold they catch coming out of balls. I've seen the official figure.

Stendhal, *Memoirs of an Egotist*

Medical writers inform us, that spasms and convulsions are usually produced by debility; and we have generally observed, that the more feeble a writer's genius is, the more violent and terrific are the distortions into which he throws himself.

Francis Jeffrey, *The Edinburgh Review*, January 1807

Sir, Of the 1,207 men and women whose obituaries were printed in your paper in 1987, 134 were stated to have had their education and/or their employment at Oxford, as against 163 from Cambridge.

We can only suppose that the fevers and agues emanating from the surrounding fens continue to constitute a hazard here.
Yours faithfully,
E. S. Leedham-Green
University Archives
University of Cambridge.

Sir, As a graduate of Cambridge University I would interpret the statistics submitted by Dr Leedham-Green as showing that those receiving a Cambridge education subsequently prove more worthy of an obituary notice than those from the other place.
Yours faithfully,
Nicholas Coral
London, NW1.

Letters to *The Times*, January 1988

I suppose I shall subscribe to hospitals. That's how people seem to give to the poor. I suppose the poor are always sick. They would be, if you think.

Ivy Compton-Burnett, *A Family and a Fortune*, 1939

The two old women Hannah Jones and Sarah Probert were both
lying in bed and groaning horribly. I gave them some money and
their cries and groans suddenly ceased.

Kilvert, *Diary*, 13 April 1872

Life is a hospital in which each patient is possessed by the desire to
change his bed. This one wants to suffer in front of the stove, and
that one thinks he will be cured near the window.

Baudelaire, 'Any where out of the world', *Le Spleen de Paris*, 1867

> Take heed, sickness, what you do:
> I shall fear you'll surfeit too.
> Live not we as all thy stalls,
> Spitals, pest-house, hospitals,
> Scarce will take our present store?
> And this age will build no more.
>
> Jonson, from 'To Sickness', 1616

In athletes a perfect condition that is at its highest pitch is
treacherous. Such conditions cannot stay the same or remain at rest,
and, change for the better being impossible, the only possible change
is for the worse.

Hippocrates, *Aphorisms*

A more entertaining aberration was that of a very buxom and
powerful young woman who, as the climax of her first labour came
on, insisted on getting out of bed and sitting on a chamber-pot. The
combined efforts of her mother, the qualified midwife (or 'gamp'),
and myself failed to get her back into bed, and when she finally stood
up, there was a pink and healthy infant squalling in the pot. She had
managed the delivery in her own way quite successfully.

Geoffrey Keynes, *The Gates of Memory*, 1981; of *c.*1910

Baby, who is weaned, requires to be fed often, regularly, and not too
much at a time.

I know a mother whose baby was in great danger one day from convulsions. It was about a year old. She said she had wished to go to church; and so, before going, had given it its three meals in one. Was it any wonder that the poor little thing had convulsions?

> Florence Nightingale, 'Minding Baby',
> *Notes on Nursing for the Labouring Classes*, 1861

The case is recorded of a nurse who, having failed to remove a button from a child's ear, actually *tried to push it out the other side*. We need hardly say that not only would such a thing be impossible but such treatment is highly dangerous.

> *The Cyclopaedia of Practical Medicine*, ed. John Forbes,
> Alexander Tweedie, John Conolly, 1833

Adam and Eve had many advantages, but the principal one was that they escaped teething.

> Mark Twain, *Pudd'nhead Wilson*, 1894

A problem is easier to countenance if it has been aired and put into words. I felt rather small recently when a father, thanking me for giving some psychological treatment to his son, said: 'I think it's done him a lot of good being able to tell all his troubles to someone. When I was his age I used to tell all my troubles to a large rubber duck, and it seemed a great help. I suppose you're much the same sort of thing.'

> Richard Asher (1912–69)

It might be said of psychoanalysis that if anyone holds out a little finger to it, it quickly grasps his whole hand.

> Freud, *Introductory Lectures on Psychoanalysis*, 1916;
> tr. James Strachey

Psychoanalysis is that mental illness of which it deems itself the cure.

> Karl Kraus, *Die Fackel*, 30 May 1913

Speaking at a conference on alcohol abuse held in Liverpool in April 1987, Mrs Edwina Currie, the junior health minister, advised doctors to amend their own drinking habits before telling patients to drink less. The number of people in the medical profession suffering from cirrhosis of the liver, she said, was three times the national average.

Press report

Preserving one's health by too rigorous a regimen is a tiresome disease.

La Rochefoucauld, Maxims

One of the most widespread illnesses is diagnosis.

Kraus, Pro Domo et Mundo, 1912

Honour a physician according to thy need of him with the honours due unto him: For verily the Lord hath created him.

   He that sinneth before his Maker, Let him fall into the hands of the physician.

Ecclesiasticus, 38

Here where illnesses are so cheap and medicine so expensive.

Lichtenberg, Sudelbuch

Medicine: Your money and your life!

Kraus, Sprüche und Widersprüche, 1909

I remember my father's senior partner saying, 'Never send in big bills. Send in small bills frequently. Cut and come again.'

Jonathan Gathorne-Hardy, Doctors

My faithful general Phenobarbus, treacherous to the last?

Malcolm Lowry, 'Through the Panama', 1956

For, medicine being a compendium of the successive and contradictory mistakes of medical practitioners, when we summon the wisest
of them to our aid, the chances are that we may be relying on a
scientific truth the error of which will be recognized in a few years'
time. So that to believe in medicine would be the height of folly, if
not to believe in it were not greater folly still, for from this mass of
errors there have emerged in the course of time many truths.

Proust, *The Guermantes Way I*

They bring us crushed fingers,
mend it, doctor.
They bring burnt-out eyes,
hounded owls of hearts,
they bring a hundred white bodies,
a hundred red bodies,
a hundred black bodies,
mend it, doctor.
on the dishes of ambulances they bring
the madness of blood,
the scream of flesh,
the silence of charring,
mend it, doctor.

And while we are suturing
inch after inch,
night after night,
nerve to nerve,
muscle to muscle,
eyes to sight,
they bring in
even longer daggers,
even more thunderous bombs,
even more glorious victories,

idiots.
Miroslav Holub, 'Casualty', 1962; tr. Ewald Osers

'Tis not onely the mischief of diseases, and the villany of poysons, that make an end of us; we vainly accuse the fury of Guns, and the new inventions of death; it is in the power of every hand to destroy us, and we are beholding unto every one we meet, he doth not kill us.

> Browne, *Religio Medici*

> Man must either fall in love
> with Someone or Something,
> or else fall ill.
> Auden, from 'Shorts', 1972–3

> 'What would you do
> if I suddenly died?'
>
> 'Write a poem to you.'
>
> 'Would you mourn for me?'
>
> 'Certainly,' I sighed.
>
> 'For a long time?'
>
> 'That depends.'
>
> 'On what?'
>
> 'The poem's excellence,' I replied.
> Irving Layton, 'The Well-Wrought Urn', 1965

Although the swallowing of food is ordinarily preceded by a feeling of desire on the part of the stomach, there is in the case of vomiting no corresponding desire from the mouth-parts for the experience.

> Galen (c.129–?199), *On the Natural Faculties*; tr. A. J. Brock

> Here sleeps at length poor Col, & without Screaming,
> Who died, as he had always liv'd, a dreaming:

Shot dead, while sleeping, by the Gout within,
Alone, and all unknown, at E'nbro' in an Inn.
Coleridge, 'an Epitaph, which I composed in my Sleep, for myself,
while dreaming that I was dying', letter to Thomas Wedgwood,
16 September 1803

I am still sick and now and then I suspect that I am on the great
railway leading to the other side of the grave. At times this thought is
very painful, at other times I find in it the solace one experiences on a
train: the absence of responsibility in the face of a superior and
irresistible force.

Prosper Mérimée, *Lettres à une inconnue*, 1874

I mentioned to him a friend of mine who was formerly gloomy from
low spirits, and much distressed by the fear of death, but was now
uniformly placid, and contemplated his dissolution without any
perturbation. 'Sir,' said Johnson, 'this is only a disordered imagination taking a different turn.'

Boswell, *Life of Johnson*, 18 September 1777

A French cobbler had resolved to commit suicide, and, to make his
exit the more heroic, prepared the following memorial in writing: 'I
follow the lesson of a great master, and as Molière says, "When all is
lost, and even hope is fled." ' He had just written thus far, and
applied the fatal instrument to the carotid artery, when suddenly
recollecting, he stopped, and cried to himself, 'Eh! but is it Molière
who says so? I must make sure — I shall be laughed at.' He now got
Molière, read a few comedies, and returned to his usual occupation
of mending shoes.

The Percy Anecdotes

Far happier are the dead, methinks, than they
Who look for death, and fear it ev'ry day.
Anon.; tr. from the Greek by William Cowper

I'm sick of gruel, and the dietetics,
I'm sick of pills, and sicker of emetics,
I'm sick of pulses' tardiness or quickness,
I'm sick of blood, its thinness or its thickness, –
In short, within a word, I'm sick of sickness!

Thomas Hood, 'Fragment', c.1844

Acknowledgements

For permission to reprint copyright material the publishers gratefully acknowledge
the following:

Dannie Abse and Anthony Sheil Associates Ltd for lines from 'A Smile Was',
Copyright © Dannie Abse 1968, first published by Hutchinson in A Small
Desperation, and for 'The Silence of Tudor Evans', Copyright © Dannie Abse 1977,
first published by Hutchinson in Collected Poems 1948–1976 (Hutchinson/Univer-
sity of Pittsburgh Press, 1977); Fleur Adcock for 'Counting'; Oxford University Press
for 'Madmen' from Selected Poems by Fleur Adcock (OUP, 1983); Mrs Margaret
Asher and the British Medical Association for extracts from A Sense of Asher by
Richard Asher, edited by Ruth Holland (The Keynes Press, BMA, 1984); Faber and
Faber Ltd and Random House, Inc. for lines from 'Marginalia' 1965–1968 Part XII,
and lines from 'Shorts' 1972–1973 Part XIII from W. H. Auden: Collected Poems
edited by Edward Mendelson (Faber, 1976) copyright © 1976 by Edward Mendel-
son, William Meredith and Monroe K. Spears, Executors of the Estate of W. H.
Auden; David Higham Associates Ltd for extract from Augustus Carp, Esq., by
Himself by Sir Henry Howarth Bashford (Heinemann, 1924); Macmillan, London
and Basingstoke for extract from 'The Heiligenstadt Testament' from The Letters of
Beethoven, Vol. III, as translated by Emily Anderson (Macmillan, 1961 reprinted
1985); Connie Bensley for 'Entrails'; John Berger for extract from A Fortunate Man:
The Story of a Country Doctor (Allen Lane, 1967); Faber and Faber Ltd and Farrar,
Straus & Giroux Inc. for 'The Alcoholic in the 3rd Week of the 3rd Treatment' from
Henry's Fate and Other Poems 1967–1972 by John Berryman (Faber, 1978),
copyright © 1969 by John Berryman; John Murray (Publishers) Ltd for 'Five
O'Clock Shadow' from Collected Poems by John Betjeman (John Murray, 1970);
The Yale Editions of The Private Papers of James Boswell, William Heinemann Ltd
and McGraw-Hill Publishing Co. for extracts from Boswell: The English Experiment
1785–1789 edited by Irma S. Lustig and Frederick A. Pottle (Heinemann/McGraw-
Hill, 1986); Times Newspapers Ltd for 'Warning: Art can damage your health' by
Roger Boyes (The Times, 2 May 1987) © Times Newspapers Ltd, 1987; Methuen &
Co. for 'On His Mortality', translated by H. B. Mallalieu, from Bertolt Brecht: Poems
1913–1956 edited by John Willett and Ralph Manheim (Methuen, 1976); Anita
Brookner, A. M. Heath and Pantheon Books, a Division of Random House, Inc. for
extract from Look at Me by Anita Brookner (Jonathan Cape, 1983) Copyright ©
Anita Brookner 1983; Hamish Hamilton Ltd for extracts from 'A Case-Historical
Fragment of Autobiography' from Baroque-'n'-Roll by Brigid Brophy (Hamish
Hamilton, 1987); William Heinemann Ltd and Weidenfeld and Nicolson Inc. for
extract from Little Wilson and Big God by Anthony Burgess (Heinemann/Weiden-
feld, N.Y., 1987) Copyright Anthony Burgess 1987; Michael Burn for 'In the London
Library'; Oxford University Press for extract from The Journals and Letters of Fanny

Burney Vol. VI edited by Joyce Hemlow (OUP, 1975); John Murray (Publishers) Ltd and Harvard University Press for extracts from *Byron's Letters and Journals*, Vols 2 and 11 edited by Leslie A. Marchand (John Murray, 1973–82); Duke University Press, Durham, N. Carolina, for extracts from *The Collected Letters of Thomas and Jane Welsh Carlyle*, Vol. I edited by Charles Richard Sanders and Kenneth J. Fielding (Duke University Press, 1970); Oxford University Press for extracts from *The Collected Letters of Samuel Taylor Coleridge* Vol II edited by Earl Leslie Griggs (OUP, 1956); Curtis Brown Ltd for extract from *A Family and a Fortune* by Ivy Compton-Burnett (Victor Gollancz, 1939) Copyright © The Estate of Ivy Compton-Burnett 1939; Nicholas Coral for letter to *The Times* (23 January 1988); Carcanet Press Limited for 'Deaf Man's Rhapsody' by Tristan Corbière from *The Centenary Corbière*, translated by Val Warner (Carcanet Press, 1975); Victor Gollancz Ltd and Vincent Cronin, Literary Executor, for extract from *Adventures in Two Worlds* by A. J. Cronin (Gollancz, 1952); The University of Oklahoma Press for extract from *Medical Biographies: The Ailments of Thirty-Three Famous Persons* by Philip Marshall Dale (University of Oklahoma Press, 1952) Copyright © 1952, 1987 by the University of Oklahoma Press; André Deutsch Ltd and Mrs K. N. Naylor for extracts from *A Cure for Serpents* by Alberto Denti di Pirajno, translated by Kathleen Naylor (Deutsch, 1955); The Proctors and the Trustees of Amherst College for 'I felt a Cleaving in my Mind' from *The Poems of Emily Dickinson* edited by Thomas H. Johnson (Cambridge, Mass: The Belknap Press, of Harvard University Press) Copyright 1951, © 1955, 1979, 1983 by the Trustees and Fellows of Harvard College; Little, Brown and Company for 'After great pain a formal feeling comes' from *The Complete Poems of Emily Dickinson* edited by Thomas H. Johnson (Cambridge, Mass: The Belknap Press, of Harvard University Press) Copyright 1914, 1929, 1935, 1942 by Martha Dickinson Bianchi, Copyright © renewed 1951, 1963 by Mary L. Hampson; Penguin Books Ltd for extract from *The Idiot* by Fyodor Dostoevsky, translated by David Magarshack (Penguin Classics, 1955) copyright © David Magarshack, 1955; The General Collection, The Beinecke Rare Book and Manuscript Library, Yale University for extracts from *The George Eliot Letters* Vol II edited by Gordon S. Haight (OUP, Geoffrey Cumberlege and Yale UP, 1954) Copyright 1954, by Yale University; Faber and Faber Ltd and Harcourt Brace Jovanovich Inc. for 'Hysteria' from *Collected Poems 1909–1962* by T. S. Eliot (Faber, 1963); Century Hutchinson Limited for 'Sonnet: Cat Death' from *The New Ewart: Poems 1980–1982* by Gavin Ewart (Century Hutchinson, 1982); Oxford University Press for 'Night of the Scorpion' from *Latter-Day Psalms* by Nissim Ezekiel (OUP, 1982); Curtis Brown Ltd for extract from *The Doctors* by Paul Ferris (Gollancz, 1965) © Paul Ferris, 1965; Princeton University Press for extract from *The Letters of Edward Fitzgerald Vol I: 1830–1850* edited by Alfred McKinley and Annabelle Burdick Terhune (Princeton UP, 1980) Copyright © 1980 by Princeton University Press; Sigmund Freud Copyrights Ltd, The Institute of Psycho-Analysis and The Hogarth Press, and W. W. Norton & Company, Inc. for extracts from *The Standard Edition of the Complete Psychological Works of Sigmund Freud* Vols XIII, XV and XVI, translated and edited by James Strachey (The Hogarth Press, 1955); Martin Secker & Warburg Limited for 'Accident' from 'Quatrains of an Elderly Man' from *New and Collected Poems 1934–84* by Roy Fuller (Secker & Warburg in association with London Magazine Editions, 1985) Copyright © Roy Fuller 1985; Weidenfeld & Nicolson Ltd for extracts from *Doctors: The Lives and Work of GPs* by Jonathan Gathorne-Hardy (Weidenfeld, 1984); Martin Secker & Warburg

Limited and Random House, Inc. for extract from *If It Die . . .* by André Gide, translated by Dorothy Bussy (Secker & Warburg, 1951) Copyright © 1935 and renewed 1963 by Random House, Inc.; Libris for 'Roman Elegy XVII' by Goethe from *Roman Elegies and The Diary* translated by David Luke (Libris, 1988); Oliver D. Gogarty for 'To his Friends when his Prostate shall have become Enlarged' (1943) by Oliver St John Gogarty; Flammarion & Cie for extracts from *Pages from the Goncourt Journals* translated by Robert Baldick (OUP, 1962) English translation © Robert Baldick 1962; Martin Secker & Warburg Limited and Harcourt Brace Jovanovich, Inc. for extracts from *Local Anaesthetic* by Günter Grass, translated by Ralph Manheim (Secker & Warburg, 1970) Copyright 1969 © by Hermann Luchterhand Verlag GmbH, Neuwiedland Berlin, English translation copyright © 1970 by Harcourt Brace Jovanovich, Inc. and Martin Secker & Warburg Ltd; Oxford University Press for 'To God' from *Collected Poems of Ivor Gurney*, edited by P. J. Kavanagh (OUP, 1982); Naomi Mitchison and David Higham Associates Ltd for 'Cancer's a Funny Thing' (1964) by J. B. S. Haldane; The author for 'Going Wrong' from *A House of Voices* by J. C. Hall (Chatto & Windus, 1973); The author for 'Old Londoner' Pt II from *Collected Poems 1941–1983* by Michael Hamburger (Carcanet Press, corrected edition 1985); Angus & Robertson (UK) for 'Hospital Evening' and 'Fido's Paw is Bleeding' from *Selected Poems* by Gwen Harwood (Angus & Robertson, 1981); David Higham Associates Ltd for 'A Charm Against the Toothache' from *Collected Poems 1943–1987* by John Heath-Stubbs (Carcanet Press, 1988); Suhrkamp/Insel Publishers Boston Inc. for lines from 'Abroad' by Heinrich Heine from *The Complete Poems of Heinrich Heine* translated by Hal Draper (OUP, 1982) Copyright © 1982 by Hal Draper; Harvard University Press and The Loeb Classical Library, for extracts from *Hippocrates* Vol II *The Sacred Disease*, and Vol. IV *Aphorisms*, both translated by W. H. S. Jones (Heinemann/Harvard University Press 1923 and 1931); Anvil Press Poetry Ltd for 'Fingers in the Door' from *Selected Poems 1961–1978* by David Holbrook (Anvil Press, 1980) Copyright © David Holbrook 1980; Carcanet Press Limited for 'Hospital' from *Selected Poems* by Molly Holden (Carcanet Press, 1987); Bloodaxe Books Ltd for 'Casualty' from *The Fly* by Miroslav Holub, translated by Ewald Osers (Bloodaxe Books, 1987); Lucy Howard for 'Separation: A Mother of Piglets Speaks'; Faber and Faber Ltd for lines from 'The Rat's Dance' from *Wodwo* by Ted Hughes (Faber, 1967); Hodder & Stoughton Ltd and Curtis Brown Ltd for extract from *The Diseases of Civilisation* by Brian Inglis (Hodder & Stoughton, 1981) © Brian Inglis; Curtis Brown Ltd for extract from *Fringe Medicine* by Brian Inglis (Faber, 1964) © Brian Inglis; Dodd, Mead & Co. Inc./The William Morris Agency, Inc. for extracts from *The Diary of Alice James* edited by Leon Edel (Rupert Hart-Davis, 1965) Copyright 1934 by Dodd, Mead & Co. Inc. Copyright © 1964 by Leon Edee; Eric J. Trimmer for extract from *The Natural History of Quackery* by Eric Jameson (Michael Joseph, 1961); David Higham Associates Ltd for 'A Mental Hospital Sitting-Room' from *Collected Poems 1953–1985* by Elizabeth Jennings, (Carcanet Press, 1986); Martin Secker & Warburg Limited and Schocken Books, Inc., published by Pantheon Books, a Division of Random House, Inc., for extract from *Franz Kafka: Letters to Felice*, translated by James Stern and Elisabeth Duckworth, edited by Erich Heller and Jürgen Born (Secker & Warburg and Schocken Books, 1967 Copyright © 1967, 1973 by Schocken Books Inc.; Hodder & Stoughton Ltd and Doubleday, a Division of Bantam, Doubleday, Dell Publishing Group, Inc. for extract from *The Story of My Life* by Helen Keller (Hodder & Stoughton, 1903); Oxford University Press for extracts from *The Book of Margery Kempe* modernized by W. Butler-Bowdon (OUP, 1954); Oxford University Press for extract from *The Gates of Memory* by Geoffrey Keynes (OUP, 1981); Francis King for extracts from 'Questions of life, death and hospital visitors' (*Independent*, November 1988); J. C. A. Literary Agency, Inc. for an extract from 'The Miracle of the Roses' by Jules Laforgue from *Moral Tales*, translated by William Jay Smith (New Directions, 1985) Translation copyright © 1985 by William Jay Smith; Penguin Books Ltd for extract from 'The Bird of Paradise' from *The Politics of Experience and the Bird of Paradise* by R. D. Laing (Penguin Books, 1967) copyright © R. D. Laing, 1967; Macmillan, London and Basingstoke, for extracts from *Wisdom, Madness & Folly* by R. D. Laing (Macmillan, 1985); Faber and Faber Ltd for 'Ambulances' from *The Whitsun Weddings* by Philip Larkin (Faber, 1964); David Laurence and Ms Jocelyn Laurence for extract from *The Stone Angel* by Margaret Laurence (Macmillan, 1964) Copyright © Margaret Laurence, 1964; the Canadian publishers, McClelland & Stewart, Toronto, for 'The Well-Wrought Urn' from *Collected Poems* by Irving Layton (McClelland & Stewart, Toronto, 1965); Miss E. S. Leedham-Green for letter to *The Times* (19 January 1988); Harcourt Brace Jovanovich, Inc. for extract from *The Fifty-Minute Hour* by Robert Lindner (Rinehart & Winston, 1954); The author for extract from 'Wearing Two Hats' from *The Night Watchman* by Edward Lowbury (Chatto & Windus, 1974); The Executors of the Malcom Lowry Estate, Jonathan Cape Ltd and Sterling Lord Literistic Inc. for an extract from 'Through the Panama' from *Hear Us O Lord from Heaven Thy Dwelling Place* and for extract from *Lunar Caustic* both by Malcolm Lowry (Cape, 1962 and 1968); Penguin Books Ltd and Pantheon Books, a Division of Random House, Inc., for extracts from *George III and the Mad Business* by Ida Macalpine and Richard Hunter (Allen Lane, The Penguin Press, 1969) copyright © Ida Macalpine and Richard Hunter, 1969; Macmillan Publishing Co. for 'A Cold in Venice' from *Stars Principal* by J. D. McClatchy (Macmillan Publishing Co. Inc., 1986) Copyright © 1986 by J. D. McClatchy; Grafton Books Ltd for 'The Two Parents' from *Collected Poems* by Hugh MacDiarmid (MacGibbon & Kee, 1962); Methuen & Co. for 'I've got dyspepsia from love' by Macedonius the Consul from *Two Hundred Poems from the Greek Anthology*, translated by Robin Skelton (Methuen, 1971); Martin Secker & Warburg Ltd and Alfred A. Knopf, Inc. for extracts from the following by Thomas Mann, translated by H. T. Lowe-Porter: *Buddenbrooks* (1902) (Martin Secker, 1924). *The Magic Mountain* (1924) (Martin Secker, 1927) Copyright 1927 by Martin Secker Ltd, London. Copyright 1927 and renewed 1955 by Alfred A. Knopf, Inc. Copyright 1952 by Thomas Mann. *Dr Faustus* (1947) (Secker & Warburg, 1949) Copyright by Martin Secker & Warburg Ltd. Copyright 1947 by Thomas Mann. Copyright 1948 by Alfred A. Knopf, Inc.; The Observer Ltd for extract from 'Hypochondria: A Sick Joke?' by Tessa Miller (*The Observer*, 18 January 1987); Chatto & Windus for 'Meningococcus' from *Dark Glasses* by Blake Morrison (Chatto & Windus, 1984); Penguin Books Ltd and Virginia Barber Literary Agency, Inc. for an extract from 'Spelling' from *The Beggar Maid: Stories of Flo and Rose* by Alice Munro (Allen Lane, 1980) Copyright © Alice Munro, 1977, 1978, 1979; Martin Secker & Warburg Limited and Alfred A. Knopf, Inc. for extracts from *The Man Without Qualities* Vol. III by Robert Musil translated by Eithne Wilkins and Ernst Kaiser (Secker & Warburg, 1960) (Knopf edition translated by Sophie Wilkins) Copyright © 1960 by Robert Musil; Aitken & Stone Limited for an extract from *A House for Mr Biswas* by V. S. Naipaul (André Deutsch, 1961); A. P. Watt Ltd and Victor Gollancz Ltd for extract from

Doctor! Doctor! by Michael O'Donnell (Gollancz, 1986); The authors for an extract from *Claude Bernard and the Experimental Method of Medicine* by J. M. D. Olmsted and E. Harris Olmsted (Abelard Schuman, 1952); Olwyn Hughes and Harper & Row, Publishers, Inc. for 'Paralytic' from *Collected Poems* by Sylvia Plath (Faber and Faber, 1981) Copyright © 1963 by Sylvia Plath. Copyright Ted Hughes, 1965 and 1981; Oxford University Press for extracts from *The Correspondence of Alexander Pope*, Vol. IV edited by George Sherburn (OUP, 1956); Oxford University Press for lines from ' "Talking Shop" Tanka' from *Collected Poems* by Peter Porter (OUP, 1983); Faber and Faber Ltd for extract from 'A Silver Plate' from *Rich* by Craig Raine (Faber, 1984); Faber and Faber Ltd for extract from *Period Piece* by Gwen Raverat (Faber, 1952); Martin Secker & Warburg Ltd for extract from C by Peter Reading (Secker & Warburg, 1984) Copyright © Peter Reading 1984; The Estate of Rainer Maria Rilke, St John's College, Oxford, Chatto & Windus and New Directions Publishing Corporation for 'The Panther: Jardin des Plantes, Paris' from *New Poems* by Rainer Maria Rilke, translated by J. B. Leishman (The Hogarth Press, 1964) Copyright © 1964 by The Hogarth Press Ltd; Faber and Faber Ltd and Doubleday, a Division of Bantam, Doubleday, Dell Publishing Group, Inc., for 'Meditation in Hydrotherapy' from *The Collected Poems of Theodore Roethke* (Faber, 1968) Copyright 1937 by Beatrice Roethke as administratrix for the Estate of Theodore Roethke; Yale University Press for extracts from *The Brantwood Diary of John Ruskin* edited by Helen Gill Viljoen (Yale UP, 1971) Copyright © 1971 by Yale University; Gerald Duckworth & Co. Ltd for extracts from *Awakenings* and *The Man Who Mistook His Wife For a Hat* by Oliver Sacks (Duckworth, 1973 and 1985); Michel Petheram for translated extract from *Mémoires* by Saint-Simon; Constable Publishers for extract from *The Life of Reason* by George Santayana (Constable/MIT Press, 1905–6); Oxford University Press for extracts from *The Journal of Sir Walter Scott* edited by W. E. K. Anderson (OUP, 1972); Oxford University Press for an extract from *The Pillow Book of Sei Shōnagon* translated by Ivan Morris (OUP, 1967); Chatto & Windus and Simon & Schuster for extract from *Mortal Lessons* by Richard Selzer (Chatto & Windus, 1981); The Society of Authors on behalf of the Bernard Shaw Estate for extracts from *The Doctor's Dilemma* (1906) and *Back to Methuselah* (1921) by George Bernard Shaw; Station Hill Press Inc. for 'Old Couple' by Charles Simic, © 1983 by Charles Simic. Originally published by Station Hill Press, Barrytown, New York, 12507 in *Weather Forecast For Utopia & Vicinity: Poems 1967–1982*; Chatto & Windus, Lester & Orpen Dennys Publishers Ltd, Canada, and Alfred A. Knopf, Inc. for extract from *The Engineer of Human Souls* by Josef Skvorecky, © 1977, translated by Paul Wilson © 1984 (Chatto & Windus, 1985); Oxford University Press for extracts from *The Letters of Sydney Smith* edited by Nowell C. Smith (OUP, 1953); The Executor, James MacGibbon and New Directions Publishing Corporation for 'The Deserter' from *The Collected Poems of Stevie Smith* (Penguin Modern Classics, 1983) Copyright © 1950 by Stevie Smith; Piotr Sommer for 'Papers' (1982); Penguin Books Ltd and Deborah Rogers Ltd for extract from *Illness as Metaphor* by Susan Sontag (Allen Lane, 1979; Farrar Straus & Giroux, 1978) Copyright © Susan Sontag, 1977, 1978; Bloodaxe Books Ltd for 'Cure', translated by Joanna Gebbett-Russell from *The Biggest Egg in the World* by Marin Sorescu (Bloodaxe Books, 1987); The National Library of Scotland for extracts from *Diaries of a Dying Man* by William Soutar, edited by Alexander Scott (Chambers, 1954, reissued 1988); Chatto & Windus Ltd for extracts from *Stendhal: Memoirs of an Egotist*, translated by David Ellis (Chatto & Windus, 1975); Times

Newspapers Ltd for extracts from 'Medical Briefing' by Dr Thomas Stuttaford (*The Times*, 10 March and 14 April, 1988) © Times Newspapers Ltd, 1988; Agenzia Litteraria Internazionale SRL, Milan for extracts from *Confessions of Zeno* by Italo Svevo, translated by Beryl de Zoete (Secker & Warburg, 1930) © Knopf; Thomas Szasz and A. M. Heath & Co. Ltd for extract from *The Theology of Medicine* by Thomas Szasz (OUP, 1979); Princeton University Press for 'Report from the Hospital' from *Sounds, Feelings, Thoughts: Seventy Poems* by Wislawa Szymborska, translated by Magnus J. Krynski and Robert A. Maguire (Princeton UP, 1981) Copyright © 1981 by Princeton University Press; Professor Donald E. Stanford for 'With Healing in His Wings' from *The Poems of Edward Taylor* edited by Donald E. Stanford (Yale UP, 1960); Collins, Publishers, for extracts from *Orphans of War* by Rosemary Taylor (Collins, 1988); Oxford University Press for extracts from *The Letters of Alfred Lord Tennyson*, Vols I and II edited by Cecil Y. Lang and Edgar F. Shannon, Jr. (OUP, 1982); Harvard University Press for extracts from *The Letters and Private Papers of William Makepeace Thackeray, Vol. IV 1857–1863* edited by Gordon N. Ray (Harvard UP, 1946) Copyright 1946 by Hester Thackeray Ritchie Fuller and the President and Fellows of Harvard College, renewed 1974 by Belinda Norman-Butler; Harvard University Press for extracts from *Family Book* by Hester Lynch Thrale from *The Thrales of Streatham Park* by Mary Hyde (Harvard UP, 1977) Copyright © 1976, 1977 by Mary Hyde; Curtis Brown Ltd for 'The Sick Child' from *Poems 1953–1983* by Anthony Thwaite (Secker & Warburg, 1984) © Anthony Thwaite, 1963; Ivor C Treby for 'a descent of man' (1981); Lloyds Bank Financial Services Limited, Bristol as Trustee of the Estate of Muriel R. Trollope for extract from *The Letters of Anthony Trollope* Vol. II edited by N. John Hall (Stanford UP, 1983); The Gracious Permission of Her Majesty The Queen to publish material which is subject to copyright from *Darling Child. Private Correspondence of Queen Victoria and the Crown Princess of Prussia, 1871–1878* edited by Roger Fulford (Evans Bros. Ltd, 1976); Unwin Hyman Ltd for 'Illness' and 'On His Baldness' by Po Chü-I from *Chinese Poems* translated by Arthur Waley (Allen & Unwin, 1946); Collins, Publishers and Liz Darhansoff Literary Agency, NY for extracts from *A Loss for Words* by Lou Ann Walker (Collins, 1987); David Higham Associates Ltd for extracts from *The Journals of Denton Welch* edited by Michael De-la-Noy (Allison & Busby, 1984) © University of Texas; Harper & Row, Publishers, Inc. for an extract from *Letters of E. B. White* by E. B. White (Harper & Row, 1976) Copyright © 1976 by E. B. White; Cambridge University Press for extract from *Physics, Psychology and Medicine* by J. H. Woodger (CUP, 1956); The Executors of the Virginia Woolf Estate and Chatto & Windus for extract from 'On Being Ill' from *The Complete Essays of Virginia Woolf*, Vol. 4 (The Hogarth Press, 1967); Carcanet Press Limited for 'By the Effigy of St Cecilia' from *To the Gods the Shades: Collected Poems* by David Wright (Carcanet Press, 1976).

Faber and Faber Ltd apologize for any errors or omissions in the above list and would be grateful to be notified of any corrections that should be incorporated in the next edition or reprint of this volume.

Index of Authors and References

Index of Unascribed Passages